THE COST OF FREEDOM WAS
THE HIGHEST PRICE HE'D EVER PAY

Philip Kent, warrior, patriot and rebel, inspired by men of vision, driven by human desires—he etched his destiny against the sweeping drama of the American rebellion.

Sharing his dream of a nation with the woman he loved, Kent was one of the many who fought so bravely, sacrificed beyond bearing, for a cause that would change the course of the world.

THE REBELS
THE KENT FAMILY CHRONICLES,
VOLUME TWO

The Kent Family Chronicles

With all the color and sweep of American history itself, THE SEEKERS continues The Kent Family Chronicles—a mighty saga of heroism and dedication, patriotism and valor, shining spirit and abiding faith.

Here is the story of our nation—and an amazing family living in the turbulent times that began the American Experience.

This magnificent series of novels is more than absorbing, entertaining reading—it is a resounding affirmation of the greatness of America.

NOVELS IN THE SERIES
THE BASTARD #1
THE REBELS #2
THE SEEKERS #3
THE FURIES #4
THE TITANS #5
THE WARRIORS #6
THE LAWLESS #7
THE AMERICANS #8

The Rebels

JOHN JAKES

A JOVE BOOK

Thirty previous printings

First Jove edition published August 1978

40 39

Library of Congress Catalog Card Number: 74-29354

Printed in the United States of America

Jove books are published by Jove Publications, Inc.,
200 Madison Avenue, New York, NY 10016

For my daughter Andrea.

"You will think me transported with enthusiasm, but I am not. I am well aware of the toil, and blood, and treasure, that it will cost us to maintain this declaration, and support and defend these States. Yet, through all the gloom, I can see the rays of ravishing light and glory. I can see that the end is more than worth all the means, and that prosperity will triumph in that day's transaction, even although we should rue it, which I trust in God we shall not."

John Adams,
writing to his wife Abigail
from Philadelphia.

July 2, 1776:

Contents

Book One

Our Lives, Our Fortunes and Our Sacred Honor

Book Two

The Times That Try Men's Souls

Book Three

Death and Resurrection

The Rebels

Book One

Our Lives, Our Fortunes and Our Sacred Honor

CHAPTER I

A Taste of Steel

A BRITISH DRUM STARTED a slow march cadence. Others joined in. The thudding spread across a broad front at the southeast end of the Charlestown peninsula.

For a moment the drums sounded abnormally loud in the hot summer air. There was a temporary lull in the crashing of the cannon from the Copp's Hill battery in Boston across the Charles, and from the ships that had ringed the peninsula in order to rake it from all sides.

On Philip Kent's left, a skinny black man with a squirrel gun grinned uneasily.

"Guess Tommy finished his dinner, all right."

"Guess he did," Philip said. Speaking was difficult. His throat was so parched he could barely whisper.

He twisted the ramrod twice more to seat the paper wad on top of the powder and the ball in the muzzle of his precious British-issue Brown Bess musket. He wished to God he could find a drink of water.

His stomach growled. Actually hurt from lack of food. All the rations he'd packed when they mustered in Cambridge at sunset last night were gone.

Besides that, he ached. My God, how he ached. All night long he'd labored with the other colonial soldiers on top of Breed's Hill, digging a redoubt after the officers settled their argument about the exact wording of the orders. Were the men to fortify Breed's Hill, or Bunker's, which lay northwest toward the isthmus connecting the Charlestown peninsula with land more easily defensible?

Finally, an engineering officer named Gridley settled it. Breed's. Concealed by darkness, the Americans dug their square fortification, almost a hundred and forty feet on a side, with an arrow-shaped redan jutting from its south side to overlook the sloping meadow that ran down to the Charles River.

The black man next to Philip in the redoubt had said his name was Salem Prince. Philip had no idea where he'd come from. But then, he didn't know a fraction of the several hundred soldiers jammed down inside the dusty pit in the earth, where the temperature this blazing June afternoon had to be well above a hundred.

It was doubtful that the black man belonged to the Massachusetts regiments. Or the Connecticut forces under the old Indian fighter, Putnam, who were digging in behind them on a knoll on farmer Bunker's property. The black man had simply appeared one moment when Philip was crouched down, head covered, as a cannon ball screamed over. The ball had blasted a crater into the hillside leading down to the Mystic River on the left of the redoubt. When Philip looked up, the black man stood at his left, running his hand up and down the muzzle of his antique squirrel gun and smiling shyly. Though the American army was a ragged one, the black was even more ragged. Probably he was a free man of color who had slipped out to the peninsula on his own accord. The army, such as it was, didn't mind volunteers one bit.

Now Philip and Prince exchanged anxious glances. Both heard the drums. Both tried to shrug and grin cynically as if the sound didn't matter. Both knew otherwise.

Philip was nearly as dark as Salem Prince by now. Dirt stained his skin, his knee breeches and patched hose and loose, sweat-sodden shirt. In the confusion of men running in and out of the redoubt, there was no way of telling to which unit a man belonged. Few wore uniforms.

But the ebb and flow was constant. New volunteers arrived. Other men sneaked away, using the moment when a cannon ball exploded and heads were covered to escape the hot, filthy fortification that somehow reminded Philip of a large, freshly dug grave.

The man on Philip's right craned up on tiptoes, peered over the earthwork. Another cannon ball struck, and another. Closer. Clods of dirt showered down on Philip, who had shut his eyes.

But he couldn't shut his ears. He heard the drum cadence growing louder.

A terrifying image swam in his thoughts. Bodies lying unidentified in this dirty, foul-odored pit. Christ, what if one of them should be his—?

Philip Kent, born near the village of Chavaniac, France, 1753. Died on a beautiful Saturday, the seventeenth of June, in the year 1775—

Anne—! he thought, anguished. Somehow, he would come through.

The drums thudded. Another cannon-crash shook the ground. At least they were getting accustomed to the roar of those iron monsters.

The American fortification had been dug by stealth, during the dark hours early on the seventeenth. The activity had been discovered by some sharp-eyed fellow aboard His Majesty's Ship *Lively*. The first round thundered from the ship at about four in the morning.

Some of the green troops screamed in outright terror. Not long after, another ball blew off the head of a man named Pollard working outside the redoubt. The corpse tumbled into the damp grass in the first faint light of morning.

Pollard's blood-gouting stump of a neck was a vivid warning—if one were really needed—prophesing what the day might bring to every man on Breed's Hill.

17

As the hot morning wore on, the realization dawned that the British guns in the river and over in Boston weren't angled properly to do much damage. Yet their incessant thunder had a power to rip the nerves and clutch the bowels with a universal message that could be seen on most every sweaty face:

Today I may die for daring to take up arms against His Majesty, King George III.

Now the cannonading increased again. Philip wanted to peek over the earthwork, see what he and his fellow soldiers would be confronting. For a moment he lacked the nerve. A shout brought him pivoting around:

"Oh, goddamn them shitting British—they've fired Charlestown."

Even before Philip raised up to risk a look, he saw the smoke and flames. Under an intensified bombardment of red-hot ball mixed with carcasses that shattered on impact, releasing their oiled combustibles, fires were already burning on rooftops in the little waterside town of two or three hundred houses. The town's frightened residents had already fled.

"The reinforcements have beached," someone said.

"Royal Marines," someone else added.

Another voice, shaky, put in, "The regulars have started up. Look—"

"Keep quiet so you can hear the command to fire!"

That hard, cracking voice belonged to the field commander, tall and graying Colonel Prescott of Pepperell. Through the tangle of men in the redoubt, Philip saw Prescott collapse a spyglass and head for the fortification's single rear entrance. Just one means of escape for all these hundreds. What if the redoubt were overcome? He felt more and more like a man already interred.

Suddenly, he caught an excited murmur:

"Warren—it's Dr. Warren—"

An exceedingly handsome and fair-haired man with musket and sword had just stalked into the redoubt. Dr.

18

Joseph Warren, a Boston physician, was one of the prime movers of the patriot cause in Massachusetts. Philip had come to know Warren while working at the Edes and Gill printing house.

"Your servant, sir," the unsmiling Warren said to Prescott.

Prescott seemed taken aback for a moment. Recovering, he spoke over the drumming and the cannon-fire:

"General Warren." He saluted. "You're entitled to take command."

"No, Colonel, I'm here as a volunteer. My commission still exists only on paper, waiting to be signed. I'll take my place with the others."

Men nearby raised a brief cheer as the physician, a figure of supreme if sweaty elegance in his gold-fringed coat, walked through the dust to a position at the dug-out earth wall. Prescott vanished at the redoubt's narrow opening, to take charge at the breastwork which ran down the side of the hill on the left.

The drumming grew louder. *I should look at the enemy,* Philip thought.

Just then, Warren spotted him. The physician hurried over, managing a smile:

"Kent?" He extended his hand.

"Yes, Dr. Warren, good afternoon."

"I hardly recognized you."

"The work in here has been a mite dirty."

"But well done, that's plain. So you're serving—"

"We all must, I guess."

"I hear you've a new wife. Lawyer Ware's daughter."

"Yes, sir, we were married a month ago. Anne's living in rented rooms in Watertown. Her father, too."

"Well," said Warren, "if we give Tommy a sharp fight, you'll get back to see her soon."

With a wave, the doctor returned to his place at the wall. His presence still produced gapes and admiring stares. Warren was one of the most important leaders of

19

the rebel cause. In concert with John Hancock, the Adams cousins, Samuel and John, the silversmith Paul Revere and others, he had been instrumental in pushing the Americans of Massachusetts to armed confrontation with the British. That a man of such prestige and position would come to this potential death trap to fight like an ordinary soldier seemed to have a heartening effect on those in the redoubt. It certainly did on Philip Kent.

What time was it? About three o'clock, he guessed from the angle of the sun. Despite the almost incessant pounding of the cannon, he stood up on tiptoe to look out toward Morton's Hill and see the challenge facing them this afternoon.

He gasped when he saw the red lines advancing across virtually the entire peninsula. His hand closed around the muzzle of his Brown Bess. His palm sweated, cold.

Scarlet. Everywhere, scarlet. A thousand or two thousand British soldiers at least. And the American forces must have shrunk to half that number by now.

The British advanced in orderly fashion, climbing stone walls, slipping past trees, maintaining perfect marching order. Their flags snapped in the sultry summer wind.

It was a parade march. Slow; steady. A march to the drumbeats that thudded between cannon bursts. The soldiers formed long scarlet lines stretching to the Mystic River. Company flanking company, they were marching against the redoubt; against the breastwork; and, further down, against the hastily erected rail fence where straw had been piled to stop musket balls. Still further down, more companies were advancing against the stone wall erected hastily between the fence and the river's edge. Behind the various fortifications, shabbily dressed colonials waited.

Philip turned in another direction, surveying the entire scene. Across the Charles River in Boston town, thousands of people watched from windows and rooftops as white blooms puffed from the muzzles of the Copp's Hill battery.

Almost hypnotically, Philip's eye was drawn back to the lines advancing up the hillside. Someone had said the troops were personally commanded by Major General Sir William Howe, one of the three officers of like rank who'd arrived in mid-May to bolster the command of General Thomas Gage.

"No firing," an officer shouted from the redoubt's far side. "Hold fire until you hear the signal. Let the bastards get close enough so your muskets can reach 'em."

It would take forever, Philip thought.

He counted ten companies across the broad British front. And ten more immediately behind. Hundreds and hundreds of red-coated men laboring in slow step. A scarlet wall. *Coming on—*

Sweat rivered down his chest under his soggy shirt, so he knew what the British must be feeling, stifled in their red wool and burdened with packs containing full rations, blankets—a staggering weight. Yet they continued to march steadily, breaking cadence only to climb over or go around obstacles. Philip began to discern features. A large scar on a man's chin. Bushy, copper-colored brows. Sweat-bright cheeks.

"Hold fire," came the order again. "Prescott will give the word."

Swallowing, Philip rested his Brown Bess on the lip of the earthwork. The black man, Salem Prince, and the others took up similar positions. Down on the left, Philip glimpsed Prescott in the blowing cannon smoke. The colonel was striding back and forth behind the breastwork, ducking only when a ball whizzed over and crashed.

The drums throbbed. Philip recognized the uniforms of the crack troops marching up to crush the Americans who had been unwise enough to fortify one of the two chief areas overlooking Boston. In addition to regular infantry, the British barges had brought over the pride of their fighting forces—the light infantry and grenadier companies of various regiments. From behind the marching assault troops, small fieldpieces banged occasionally.

What terrified Philip Kent most was the determined, ceaseless forward flow of the soldiers. And, on the ends of their muskets, glittering steel—

The steel of bayonets.

Hardly an American on Breed's or Bunker's Hill had that kind of deadly instrument affixed to the end of his weapon. The colonials held the bayonet in contempt. Philip wondered now whether that attitude wasn't foolish—

After the first outbreak of fighting at Lexington and Concord in April, Philip had been among the hundreds of militiamen who had harried the shattered, astonished British expeditionary force all the way back to Boston, pinking at the lobsterbacks from behind stone walls, watching them drop one by one, the ranks decimated by a disorganized but deadly attack to which the British were not accustomed. Afterward, the Americans had been jubilant; supremely confident. Who needed precise formations and steel when a colonial's sharp eye aimed a musket?

Today it might be different. Up the hill came the world's finest military organization. Orderly. Fully armed and moving steadily, steadily higher toward the redoubt, and across swampy lower ground toward the rail fence, the stone wall—

If we have to go against those bayonets, Philip thought, *we're done.*

ii

"Godamighty, when they gonna let us shoot?" raged

22

Salem Prince. Philip wondered the same thing. But again the order was passed by the officers:

"Colonel Prescott says no firing until you can look them in the eye and see the white."

Slowly, inexorably, the grenadiers and light infantry climbed through the long grass. Philip wiped his forehead. For a moment he felt faint.

He hadn't slept all the long night. He was exhausted; starved. This whole confrontation seemed futile. That the colonies he'd adopted as his homeland would dare to challenge the armed might of the greatest empire the world had known since Rome was—madness. No other word would fit.

He looked out again. Faces took on even greater detail. Fat and thin; sallow or ruddy; young men and old. Clearly now, he could see the whites of nervous eyes—

Down behind the breastwork on the left, muskets erupted in a sheet of oily smoke and fire. All along the British front, men began to fall.

"Fire!" someone yelled in the redoubt. Philip pointed his Brown Bess—the musket was too inaccurate for precise aiming—and pulled the trigger. A moment later, he watched a light infantryman in his twenties—no older than Philip himself—drop in the grass, writhing.

Like some great leaden scythe, the American fire cut down the lines of the attacking British. But they kept marching. Kept climbing—

Now entire ranks were down, men thrashing and screaming while their comrades from behind marched past them, stepping over them—*on* them when necessary. The men still on their feet fired their muskets and re-loaded as they marched.

Philip heard the British musket balls go hissing through the air over his head and smack the rear earth wall. In the redoubt too, men cried out—but very few compared to the numbers of red-clad grenadiers and light infantrymen dropping all across the peninsula.

23

The Americans re-loaded as fast as possible, with speed, great speed, and continued firing. Philip had no time to think of anything save the repetitive routine of powder and ball and paper. *Load faster*, the officers kept urging. *Fire, goddamn it! Quickly, quickly—!*

"Look at that, mister! Looky!" Salem Prince shouted. Philip glanced up.

The British companies had halted their climb. Front lines turned on command, broke, retreated. Went streaming back toward Morton's Hill where they had eaten a leisurely lunch and smoked their pipes before beginning the assault.

In the redoubt, men started cheering. Philip didn't join in. He licked his palm, scorched by the hot metal of his musket, then leaned on the inner wall, panting for air.

Again he wished for a drink of water. There was none. Overhead, visible through the smoke that had thickened considerably, the sun broiled. With numbed fingers Philip checked his powder horn.

He'd loaded and fired so often, it was half empty. Others around him were grumbling over a similar lack.

"Hold your places," came the command. "They won't give up so easily."

Philip closed his eyes, tried to rest. He didn't want to die any more than the others did.

Near him, a Rhode Islander groveled in the dirt, gut-shot by a chance ball. A Massachusetts man was methodically relieving the wounded man of his musket, powder horn and crude wooden cartouche containing the precious wadding and ball.

The drumming had receded. But for how long?

The British would certainly try a new strategy next time, he felt. Advancing in perfect order, with perfect discipline, had given them command of the world's battlefields. Today, that method of fighting had proved disastrous.

24

But whatever their strategy, if they ever reached the American lines with those bayonets—

Philip tried not to think about it.

iii

After Concord, Philip Kent had experienced an almost euphoric joy that lasted several weeks.

The British had run—*run*—back to Boston. And an American army—ragtag, poorly organized, but still an army—had encircled the city where hostile attitudes between Crown and colony had built to the breaking point over a period of some ten years.

Once the siege lines were in place, the small local militia companies of the kind in which Philip had served in Concord were re-organized into larger state regiments. Similar home or state guard units from other colonies arrived, the whole being commanded somewhat haphazardly by old General Artemas Ward. Ward was lying abed in Cambridge this June afternoon, trying to manage the military force while the agony of a stone burned in his flabby body. The Massachusetts men on Breed's Hill had volunteered to serve in the new regiments until the end of the year. The eight-month army, the officers called it. Not exactly with humor.

Other colonies sent reinforcements to Boston. Rhode Island and New Hampshire and Connecticut—Old Put, the Indian fighter, had brought in three thousand Connecticut men plus a herd of sheep for food. Meantime, matters political were directed from the temporary provincial capitol, Watertown. Cambridge served as army headquarters.

But control resided in Watertown. From there came the orders that sent Colonel Benedict Arnold of Connecticut westward in late April, to raise a new levy of Massachusetts men and join forces in early May with Ethan Allen, a rough-hewn fighting man from the

25

Hampshire Grants. Allen led a contingent whose members styled themselves the Green Mountain Boys.

Continually wrangling over who had command of the expedition, Allen and Arnold still managed to surprise and force the surrender of the small garrison at Fort Ticonderoga on Lake Champlain. Not much of a victory in military terms, the officers around Boston admitted. Hardly more than forty Britishers captured. The value of Ticonderoga lay in its supply of military stores, the most important being cannon.

No one knew for sure how many cannon. But the prospect of even a few pieces in patriot hands was considered a blessing.

To the accomplishment of routing royal troops at Lexington and Concord—or the crime, depending on a man's political position—the colonials could now add the seizure of a royal fort and a quantity of royal artillery "in the name of Jehovah and the Continental Congress," as Allen put it when presenting the surrender demand. It was doubtful that the second Continental Congress, commencing to sit in Philadelphia in May, was aware that Ticonderoga's capture had been made in its name until one of the express riders pounding between the north and the Quaker City bore the surprising news. A rider making the return trip reported that the Congress intended to appoint a supreme commander to take charge of the Massachusetts siege.

But something far more important than military developments had contributed to Philip's happiness that spring. Philip and the girl he'd courted, Anne Ware of Boston, had been married in late April, in a small Congregational church in Watertown. Anne's father, a pop-eyed little lawyer who had written numerous essays supporting the patriot cause, gave the couple his grudging blessing. After all, Anne was already five months pregnant with Philip's child.

Like so many young husbands and wives, Philip and

Anne faced a cloudy future. Philip's dream of establishing himself in the printing trade would have to wait until the armed struggle was resolved. It might end soon, in a truce; reconciliation along with redress of colonial grievances. Overtures in that direction were being considered by the Congress, Philip had heard.

But if firebrands like Samuel Adams had their way, the war could go on and on—a titanic struggle whose goal would be Adams' own: complete independency for the thirteen colonies.

Re-loading his Brown Bess now, Philip could hardly believe that this corpse-littered battleground was the same pastoral peninsula where, back in September of '73, he had clumsily tried to seduce Anne. It seemed unreal, all that long past with its beginnings in the French province of Auvergne, the trouble in England with the high-born Amberly family, Philip's emigration to America and his work for the patriot printer, Ben Edes. Philip had come a long way in the rebel cause, from indifference to confusion to firm belief.

Still, a cause was one thing, reality another. He glanced up at the scorching sun behind the smoke, wiped his sticky forehead. He wanted to live. He wanted to see Anne again; see their child born whole and sound—

But he and Anne had agreed that he had to serve. In truth, Philip had been the first to raise the issue—at the same time he announced his decision. He was committed to the cause. Anne had fired him with her own zeal. So when he told her he would henceforth be living in the military barracks hastily converted from buildings at Harvard College, she had nodded and kissed him gently, holding back her tears—

Last night, around six, Reverend Langdon, the president of the college, had prayed for the men who mustered in Harvard Yard, bound for the Charlestown peninsula. The move was designed to counteract a

27

British attempt to fortify the Dorchester Heights, rumored to have been scheduled for Sunday, June eighteenth.

With blankets, one day's provisions and entrenching tools, the Americans—no more than a thousand, Philip guessed—had marched into the darkness, leaving General Ward groaning in bed, and Reverend Langdon seeing to the loading of wagons that would carry the precious volumes of the Harvard library to safety in Andover. If the British ever stopped hesitating and moved out of Boston in massive numbers, those books could be burned—destroyed—just like Charlestown this afternoon—

On Breed's Hill, Philip felt none of the exuberant confidence he'd enjoyed in the days following the skirmish at Concord.

Wounded men moaned in the redoubt. Philip looked around as Salem Prince said quietly, "They coming again."

Philip closed his eyes and drew a deep breath of the fetid air. Prince was right.

He heard the drums.

iv

The second attack was much like the first. Stupid on the part of the British, Philip thought. He and the others fired and fired and fired again. The withering flame that leaped outward from the American muskets devastated the steadily advancing soldiers a second time. Sent the survivors into retreat a second time. Now the colonials had real cause for cheering—

But it was short-lived:

"I've only powder for two or three more shots," Philip said to the black man after the second charge had fallen back. The smoke in the redoubt was thicker than ever.

28

"You better off 'n I am," the black said, up-ending his empty powder horn. "Ball almost gone, too."

A passing officer spun on them. "If you have powder, fire anything you can find. Rocks—or this." He snatched up a bent nail left over from the erection of the redoubt's timberwork. He disappeared in the smoke, leaving Philip to stare in dismay at the nail.

How late was it? Four-thirty? Five? Philip peered over the earthwork, saw hundreds of fallen grenadiers and light infantrymen, flowers of scarlet wool and blood strewing the hillside. He squinted through the acrid, choking clouds, hastily grabbed the black's arm, pointed.

"General Howe, he finally got some brains," the black observed. But his eyes were fearful.

The re-forming British ranks looked different. The soldiers were stripping themselves of their cumbersome packs and field gear. They tossed aside their mitre-like hats or bearskin caps. Threw off their white crossbelts, red uniform jackets—

Down the line, Dr. Warren was likewise discarding his fine coat. "I think they mean to break through this time," he said. "Howe has all the powder he needs. He must know we're running short."

"Why the hell doesn't someone send for more?" a man complained.

"Someone did," Warren told him.

"Then where the hell is it?"

Warren shook his head. "I don't know. Perhaps the message was intercepted." His mouth twisted. "Or the messenger ran away. I've noticed that's not unusual this afternoon—"

The drumbeats resumed. Philip swallowed, reloading.

The British marched up the hillside and across the swampy patches in front of the rail fence and stone wall. This time, they looked much grimmer. They stepped

29

over their fallen comrades without glancing down, but the rage on their faces was obvious.

The soldiers kept coming, gaiters splashed with blood from the previous engagements. Up and down the line, the Americans began firing. For a few moments, it seemed as if the pattern of the first two assaults would be repeated. The front ranks faltered. Men stumbled, pitched over, shrieking—

The smoke in the redoubt was suffocating. It settled over Philip and the others like a pall. He was frightened out of his wits when he used his last powder to shoot the bent nail. The Brown Bess might explode—

It didn't. But he couldn't see whether he'd hit anyone.

Bayonets shining dully in the smoke, the British were halfway up the side of Breed's Hill. Suddenly Philip heard a change in the level of sound—

Fewer and fewer American muskets were shooting.

"Fire!" Colonel Prescott screamed, somewhere out of sight down on the left. Hoarse voices answered:

"Powder's gone!"

Then Philip's heart nearly stopped. The loud gulp of Salem Prince was audible too. They and the others still on their feet in the redoubt heard a dreadful new sound, almost like a mass chant on the other side of the earthwork. The British soldiers were calling encouragement to one another:

"Push on. Push on. Push on—"

Philip peered over the lip and knew what was coming: a direct breach of the redoubt. There was no longer enough firepower to repel the advance.

All at once a few British soldiers began to run toward the hill's summit. Then more. Soon the whole front rank was charging, bayonets thrust out ahead. Salem Prince leaned his elbows on the little ledge to steady them, fired his last ball with powder he had borrowed from Philip. The ball drilled a round red hole in a portly sergeant's forehead.

But they kept coming, on the run:

"Push on. Push on. Push on—"

In the last terrible seconds of waiting, Philip raised his Brown Bess like a club, grimly aware of its limitations as a weapon against bayonets. British discipline, instilled as a tradition not to be violated, had paid off after all. In the wake of two disastrous charges, they intended to make the third succeed:

"PUSH ON! PUSH ON!"

A bayonet flashed above Philip's head. Musket clutched in both hands, he fended the downward thrust of the British light infantryman towering at the edge of the redoubt. Philip smashed the musket against the soldier's left leg. The man pitched forward into the redoubt. His bayonet gored Salem Prince through the chest.

The black fell screaming. The British soldier floundered on top of him, struggling to rise. A bayonet raked Philip's left shoulder from behind. He dodged away, raised his musket by the muzzle, struck the fallen soldier's head once, twice, three times, panting as he hit. The soldier's skull caved in. He collapsed across the dead black man.

But there were hundreds more of the soldiers jumping into the redoubt now, those murderous bayonets slashing and stabbing. In the smoke it was almost impossible to tell friend from foe. Philip heard an officer's cry:

"Retreat! Retreat to Bunker's! Abandon the redoubt—!"

Hysteria then. Pandemonium.

Royal Marines who had reinforced the infantry regiments leaped into the redoubt, firing at close range. Philip kicked and clubbed his way toward the narrow entrance packed with frantic men. His chest hurt from breathing smoke. He coughed. His eyes streamed tears.

Another bayonet wielded by some phantom came tearing at his cheek. Philip kicked the unseen soldier, hit

31

his calf, heard him curse. The bayonet slid by Philip's shoulder and into the eye of a Rhode Islander behind him in the stampede. Blood gushed over Philip's filthy neck, hot, ripe-smelling. He wanted to scream but he didn't.

He saw Dr. Warren in the crush, brandishing a musket. Random sunlight made Warren's face gleam like a medal for a moment. A bayonet speared Warren's ribs. Then the doctor went rigid, as if a musket ball had hit him. Horrified, Philip watched the patriot leader disappear in the smoky carnage.

He fought ahead. Saw sunlight gleaming—the outer end of the entrance passage. He raised his Brown Bess horizontally, ducked and battered through, his only goal that patch of brilliant light beyond the earth walls.

His chest on fire from the smoke he'd inhaled, he broke out and began to run down through the orchard on the northwest slope of Breed's Hill. From the redoubt he still heard screaming, muskets exploding, and the howls of the redcoats taking vengeance.

V

The sun was dropping behind the smoke. It had to be almost six o'clock, Philip thought as he scrambled toward the top of Bunker's Hill. There, Old Put's men had dug another fortification—

Empty now.

Everywhere, the colonials were fleeing. Rushing toward the all-too-narrow strip of land that was the only escape route from the peninsula jutting into Boston harbor. Philip headed that way, running for his life because that was the order he heard yelled from all sides:

"Retreat, *retreat!*"

The Charlestown Neck proved almost impassable. Men shoulder to shoulder beat and clawed one another to gain a yard's forward passage. Off in the Mystic River, the guns of *Glasgow* erupted. Cannon balls tore the Neck to pieces, shot up huge gouts of earth, blasted men to the ground. Philip felt something sticky strike him in the face. He glanced down, gagged. A hand blown from a body—

He wiped some of the blood away and struggled ahead, trying not to be sick.

Near him, a weary Rhode Islander shouted with false jubilation:

"I hear Tommy lost a thousand 'r more, and us but a hundred!"

It might be so, Philip thought, gouging and shoving his way over the perilously narrow piece of land. It might be so, but it was no American victory. Even if the British had paid with fifty times the number of dead, how could anyone call it a victory? Though the king's troops had died by the score in the first two charges, they had broken through on the third—with those invincible bayonets that still blazed in Philip's imagination—

All at once he felt totally discouraged, disheartened. Even more disheartened than he'd been during what was perhaps the lowest point in his life: the grim sea voyage on which his mother, Marie Charboneau, had died, and he had taken a new name before stepping foot on the shore of his adopted land. Years from now, Breed's Hill might or might not be deemed a victory of sorts. But he saw it as a clear defeat.

As he ran on in the smoky sunset, glimpsing safe ground ahead at last, he knew that he and his wife and their unborn baby confronted a future that had become utterly bleak in a single afternoon's two-hour engagement.

The thirteen colonies faced exactly the same future. At last, the might of Great Britain had asserted itself.

Very likely the king would spare nothing to bring the Americans to their knees with fire and steel; that terrible steel—

The struggle of the patriots could be very long. And doomed.

CHAPTER II

Shermon Hill

"JUD DARLIN'?"

He reached across her naked hip for the jug of rum they'd shared. The cabin was warm this June evening, accentuating the woman's smell: a faintly gamy combination of sweat and farm dirt that never failed to excite him. When he'd consumed sufficient rum.

"Jud?" she said again.

"What?"

"That all for tonight?"

"Not by a damn sight, my girl."

He drank; emptied the jug. Dropped it and heard it thud on the dirt floor. He rolled toward her, stroking a moon-dappled patch of thigh. She guided his hand up her hard belly to one of her breasts. She laughed; a coarse, harlot's laugh:

"Good. The old fool, he won't be back till the cock crows, I bet. Means to show the gentry he's doin' his duty, ridin' patrol with the best. If he only knowed he could meet some of the gentry right in his own bed—!" She giggled.

"Lottie, stop talking so goddamned much." He gave her a fierce kiss that was half passion, half punishment.

She complained that it hurt, shoved his exploring fingers away. The straw crunched as she shifted out of his grasp:

"You're not treatin' me proper this evening, Jud Fletcher. Like to took my head off with that kiss."

"Sorry."

He reached for the rum, remembered it was gone, swore softly. A ravening thirst still burned in him. But then, when didn't it?

"That all you can say? *Sorry?*"

"What else should I say, Lottie? Conversation's not one of your better skills, so let's get down to the one in which you excel, shall we?"

Once more he reached out to touch her nakedness. His hand was moonlit for a moment. It was a strong young man's hand with fine golden hairs downing the tanned back.

But he'd angered her:

"No, sir, I want to know where your head's at tonight, Mr. Judson Fletcher."

His laugh aped the crude guffaws heard at taverns, or around the gamecock ring. Like downing rum, that sort of laugh somehow came easy. He said:

"I'll show you where it ought to be, honeylove—"

He bent his bare back, his mouth seeking. Again she struggled away. She was beginning to irritate him considerably.

Pettish, she said, "Listen, you yelled out somebody's name last time."

"Oh hell no I didn't."

"Yes you did, I heard it, right there at the end."

"All right, I got plumb excited and yelled your name."

"No, sir, Judson Fletcher, it wasn't Mrs. Lottie Shaw you was yellin' about—" Another laugh; vicious. "You were givin' somebody else a hard ridin' and I don't take kindly to it."

Furious, he wrenched away. He stood up, naked in the moonlight falling through the curtainless, glassless window of the crude little farm cabin. "For Christ's sake, woman, you got what you want from me. What that old wreck your papa married you off to can't deliver—"

"I want a little respect too," the young woman whined. "A little feelin'—I don't want somebody pokin' around in me and callin' out 'Peggy, Peggy!' "

He seized her bare shoulder. "Shut your mouth, Lottie."

"Leggo!" She writhed. "I heard it clear. *'Peggy!'* Think I don't know which Peggy that is?" She was growing shrill, matching his anger. "Think the whole damn county don't know whose head you wisht you could put horns on—?"

He found the rum jug and hurled it at her half-seen form. She yelped, dodged away. Outside, her husband's yellow hound began to bark.

Judson grabbed up his clothes, practically yanked them on. By then, Lottie Shaw had realized her error. She leaped naked through the patch of moon, doubled over in exaggerated penitence, pressed her cheek against his ribs as she clasped his waist. While stuffing his fine lace-fronted shirt into his pants, Judson gave her an elbow in the nose, not entirely by accident.

Lottie hung on. Judson's blue eyes and fair, clubbed hair looked all afire in the light from the window. Lottie began to cry in earnest:

"Don't get mad, darlin'. I spoke too sharp. Come on back and love me again—"

Judson leaned down toward her in the patch of moonlight, a tall, elegantly handsome young man with a long, sharp nose and just a slight softness at the edges of his mouth. His fingers closed on her muscled forearm. He looked like some avenging angel of scripture as he said quietly:

"You ever speak her name again in my presence—or if I ever hear of you speaking it to anyone, Lottie, I'll come here and kill you. Now think about that."

Pulling loose, he yanked on his boots of costly Russian leather, picked up his rich coat of dark green velvet and stalked out of the cabin.

37

He shied a stone at the yellow hound to drive him away, then pulled himself up on the beautiful roan he'd tethered to a low branch of a scrawny apple tree the farmer was trying to grow in his dooryard. Still shaking with anger, he galloped out the lane and turned into the road leading toward the Rappahannock, and home.

It was a fine, balmy evening in late June. He reached behind him, pried up the flap of his saddlebag, wiggled his fingers down inside, let out an oath. He was half drunk and wanted to be completely so. And he was out of rum.

Lottie Shaw was another kind of medicine he took on the sly. Tonight, by catching him when he'd accidentally cried *her* name, Lottie had gone dry on him too.

He cropped the roan without mercy, thundering down the dirt road in the sweet-smelling night because fleeing from the pain of having uttered Peggy's name without thinking had plunged him into this star-hung dark and pain of a different sort, equally hurtful.

ii

Riding the roads of Caroline County, Virginia, always reminded him of his one best friend of boyhood. George Clark, the second of farmer John Clark's six sons.

The bond between George and Judson had been a powerful one in the years when they were growing up together, even though George's father was relatively poor, while Judson Fletcher's was rich. Maybe the reason was simply that any human being of any age liked to find another who would act as pupil—and George Clark, though two years younger than his friend, had discovered early that Judson was something besides a typical tobacco planter's son. In fact, Judson loathed Sermon Hill. He much preferred studying what George, a boy who had roamed the Virginia woodlands since he could toddle, taught so eagerly.

The geography of the heavens, for instance. Even swaying in the saddle, Judson could pick out the pole star, and the Cross.

In their days and nights of wandering the fields and forests together, George Clark had taught him many things. How to discover a fly-up-the-creek, the little green heron that hid for protection on river banks. How to find hives full of wild honey, and to tell which plants and berries were edible. How to look to the horizon and identify objects and details of terrain at twenty miles—or spot a nighthawk at dusk just on the other side of a meadow. Far sight, was George's name for it. He developed it with practice. He would need it where he was going, he always said.

They'd traveled to fairs in Richmond, too. Spoken with rough, buckskin-clad men who carried long squirrel guns and claimed to have tramped the wild country west of the shimmering barrier of the Blue Ridge Mountains—the Blue Wall, Virginians called it. Out there, the long hunters remarked while spitting tobacco in a delightfully ill-mannared way, was a sea of forest and grass, sky and cloud. Enough animals to last a man a lifetime, whether he trapped and sold their pelts, or ate their flesh to survive, or both.

Three years ago, in 1772, Judson's friend and mentor had disappeared out that way; crossed the Blue Wall. He seemed to have a courage Judson lacked.

Also, George Clark was not in love with a woman he couldn't possibly win.

Twice in the intervening time, George had reappeared for brief visits at his parents' home. On those occasions, Judson had been invited to share an evening meal—and George's wondrous tales.

He described how he'd reached a raw frontier settlement that had grown up near Fort Pitt at the fork where two rivers flowed into one much larger one—the beautiful water, the red Indians called it. *O-hi-o. La Belle Riviere,* according to the French fur trappers.

George Clark had gone down this immense river. Taken to the poplar, as the companions with whom he traveled termed it. He'd journeyed a long way down the Ohio, through a vast, hushed wilderness, paddling in that sixty-foot hollowed poplar log marked with bloodstains and the grease of pelts.

On his second trip he'd traveled the river again. And wintered with a tribe of Indians called Mingos. He'd learned their tongue. He spoke glowingly of the gentle wisdom and forest skills of their old tribal leader, Logan.

It was difficult for Judson to absorb all the amazing detail of these narratives. But it wasn't hard at all to be entranced; to have his imagination lifted, until his mind's eye built an immense wooded kingdom where dark-skinned savages slipped silently along the game trails. A kingdom where a man could claim land if he wished it. Or simply find room to do as he pleased. To be what he was, not what someone else expected him to be.

The western forest was the only part of the continent for him, George Clark averred on those all-too-brief evenings before he vanished again, sterner-looking than he'd been in youth. Toughened now. Lean. He came and went across the Blue Wall like some red-haired ghost, and each short visit somehow freed Judson of the confinements of his own life—if only for a few hours.

The visits saddened him, too. Perhaps he belonged in the western forest. A great many bold, enterprising fellows were drifting that way, George said. Some families as well. More and more land companies were being formed to explore—and exploit—the vast wilderness. On occasion Judson thought that maybe he was a fool not to pack and follow his friend—

There was just one problem. Judson had inadvertently brought it up tonight, when he should have been murmuring Lottie Shaw's name instead.

Judson saw George Clark's face in his mind as he thundered the Virginia roads under soughing trees. The eyes of his friend never seemed at rest. They always seemed to be searching past a man's shoulder—

For what? he wondered. Freedom? The constantly retreating horizon—?

"It's that goddamned red hair," Judson exclaimed thickly, just before a branch nearly took his head off. He straightened up again, reflecting that red hair was one painless way he rationalized George's boldness. In the Clark family, it was said that red hair marked a man. Set him apart. Destined him for remarkable deeds. Of John Clark's six sons, two had red hair. George Rogers, gone now three years, and the tad, William, still at the farm, only five.

Why in hell wasn't I born with red hair? he thought fuzzily as he rode. It was certainly a convenient excuse to relieve misery of the sort he'd encountered in Lottie Shaw's cabin. And the different kind of misery he found along the dark, earth-smelling roads. Roads alive with memories of the friend who possessed some intangible quality of which he, Judson Fletcher of Caroline County, Virginia, had been unjustly deprived.

iii

Judson had ridden the roan so hard, the animal's flanks were lathering. A measure of sobriety returned when he noticed it. He reined in, dismounted at the roadside. He wandered aimlessly while the roan blew and stamped.

Judson belched, scratched his crotch under his fine gray trousers. Be just his luck to catch the pox from Lottie.

Suddenly he stumbled across something propped against the rail fence. He crouched, uttered a surprised

41

oath, fingered a crude dummy of white rags and straw stuffing. A fragment of slate lay in the dummy's lap.

He carried the slate out from under the tree branches. Turned it this way and that. He finally made out the word scrawled on the slate. His spine grew cold.

"Buckra," he said. And again: *"Buckra."*

The West African word for white man.

He dragged the dummy into the road. By the light of the moon and a thousand summer stars, he saw what he'd missed before. A wooden stake driven into the dummy's chest. The hole was smeared with something dark.

Judson knelt, fingered the smeared cloth and whittled stake. Little sweaty places formed on his neck and behind his ears. He tried to still his alarm by talking aloud:

"Has to be chicken's blood. Or pig's—where'n hell you suppose it came from?"

Abruptly, he heard hoofbeats down the road. He whipped his hand to his right boot, where a discreet scabbard in the Russian leather accepted a slim dagger. A gentleman's protection. He retreated to the shoulder, unpleasantly sober—and cautious.

He saw lanterns bobbing around a bend. Half a dozen riders. He stepped into the road, hailed them: "It's Judson Fletcher—"

The horses reined in. It was the patrol that kept constant watch on the roads for runaway slaves, rotating its personnel nightly. Mounted on a fine sorrel at the head of the patrol was slender, gentle-looking Seth McLean. Behind him, shabbily dressed, a gray failure, Tom Shaw slumped on a sore-ridden nag.

Tom Shaw spoke first, pathetically polite:

"Evenin', Mr. Fletcher."

Judson's profile, lantern-limned, was sculptured arrogance. "Evening, Shaw." The reply was so brusque, Shaw looked visibly hurt. Judson accented the social difference by greeting the others more cordially: "Mr. Wells—Mr. Squire—Seth."

"Taking the air again, Judson?" Seth asked, his smile innocent.

"That's right." Ah, this was rich! The man he cuckolded regularly, and the one he wanted to cuckold above all, and never would. "I found something down here you gentlemen should see."

He led them to the stabbed dummy and the slate. Concern was instantaneous.

"I knew them niggers was up to somethin'," Tom Shaw exclaimed. "My Lottie, she sweared she heard a drum two, three nights ago. That way. From the river—"

"Impossible," Seth McLean said. "You know there's not a planter in the district who allows his nigras ownership of a drum. Too easy to signal with them. My hands get nothing but dried beef bones—those, they can rattle all they please." He addressed the others: "Gentlemen, would you continue the patrol without me? I'd like to speak privately with my friend Judson. He may be able to assist us."

In what way, Judson couldn't imagine. But the others seemed to understand, and readily agreed. Judson fetched his roan, mounted up, and was soon jogging beside Seth back along the road by which the horsemen had arrived. The patrol's lanterns vanished in the other direction.

"I didn't want to admit it to Tom Shaw," Seth remarked finally, "but there may be nothing wrong with his wife's hearing."

"I can't say. I never listen for drums at night."

Seth laughed. "I know. Only for the rustle of the skirts of married women."

Judson went rigid in the saddle. Seth slapped him on the shoulder and Judson relaxed. Apparently there was nothing personal in the joke. His friends in the district

43

had treated him to variations of it on more occasions than he could remember.

"There have been rumblings about possible trouble," Seth said, serious now.

"You mean with the nigras?"

Seth nodded gravely.

"At your place?"

"Possibly."

Judson was surprised. Seth McLean was reasonably humane in his treatment of his three-hundred-odd field bucks and wenches.

"I don't see what it has to do with me," Judson shrugged.

"I'll explain over a glass of port, if you don't mind." Seth spurred ahead toward the lights of his elegant house near the shore of the Rappahannock. Judson studied the illuminated windows on the second floor. One was Peggy's room. He knew the location by heart.

He followed Seth McLean down a lane between dark, rustling tobacco fields. The green leaves were ripening toward the end-of-summer harvest. Seth's lean silhouette stood out momentarily against the lamps at his front door. Reining in a second later, Judson felt criminal. Seth was decent.

At the same time, Judson was amused in a perverse way. It's sort of like the fly inviting the spider home with him, he thought.

iv

A huge London-made clock ticked in the library; a quarter past midnight. The library doors were open to the candlelight in a cool, airy foyer two floors high.

Seth poured wine for himself. Judson begged off, helped himself to Rhode Island rum instead. Then he settled his long frame in a chair, trying not to appear nervous or reveal his guilt—he was getting pretty good at that by now. He'd crawled into bed with his first married woman when he was fifteen.

Judson heard footsteps. His heartbeat picked up until he realized the steps were too heavy for a woman's. A grizzled black man in livery glanced in the doorway.

Seth McLean looked at the black, his piece of property, said:

"Nothing further tonight, Andrew. I'll serve our guest."

With a polite murmur that might have been Judson's name—a servile acknowledgement of his presence—the slave withdrew. Seth McLean rolled his wine glass between his palms.

"Have you heard nothing about discontent among the nigras, Judson?"

"You know me, my friend. The skirts swish too temptingly. The dice clack, the horses run, the cocks scream—and my father, the old bastard, swears a good bit, too. At me." Judson's mouth wrenched. "There's altogether too much noise for me to hear anything significant. It's different with you, I gather."

"Well, as I said, there have been signs. Insolence out of the ordinary. My overseer has been forced to the whip three times this week."

"Ours is never forced," Judson said, the sour smile remaining in place. "He looks for opportunities."

"Shaw," McLean reflected. "Old Tom's younger brother."

Judson nodded. "Cruel, illiterate bastard. Not like your Williams."

"But even Williams is being pushed hard. These things go in cycles, Judson. I'm uneasy—I just fear the wheel's almost around again. I've questioned Andrew and his wife—they're very loyal. They don't know much about what's happening. But they do admit there's wide

45

unrest. It has—spread."

Judson knocked back the rum, felt it scald his belly. Not with relief this time, but with an upsetting fire. The clock ticked loudly. The room's shadows became ominous somehow. Clotting in the corners; blurring the gold stampings on the couple of hundred books on the high shelves.

"Spread from here?"

"From Sermon Hill. Andrew has heard that a nigra named Larned is at the center of it."

"Larned—" Judson's mind saw a slab-muscled figure with blue-black skin. "Big buck nigger. Damn near gigantic. Just two years off the Richmond block. Came from the West Africas in a Boston ship. My father says he never made a better investment."

"Breeding stock?"

"Yes. And Larned's smart with the natural kind of smartness some of 'em have. That may be his trouble."

Seth McLean cocked a dark eyebrow that contrasted with his pale, almost ascetic face. "Or ours."

"You mean Larned may be fomenting rebellion?" Judson ambled to the sideboard for a refill of rum. "Possible. He took a mighty handsome wife. Young yellow girl named—let me see—Dicey. Up till three days ago, she was this big—" One hand sketched pregnancy in the air. "She produced twin boys for Larned. I heard Shaw brag last Christmas time that he was fucking her, too."

"Well, that's certainly cause enough for trouble."

"I don't suppose Larned found out. Those wenches are always too scared to tell their men."

"But Larned could have heard it round about. Anything else?"

Judson pondered. "Shaw laid eight strokes on Dicey two weeks before her term was up. Some trivial excuse."

"But not trivial to a particularly intelligent and resentful nigra."

46

Judson nodded. "I'll wager the excuse was just that. Shaw probably wanted to exercise overseer's rights and take Dicey with a full belly. If she refused, he'd find reason to whip her."

"Another grievance for Larned."

Judson had no comment.

Seth McLean sighed. "Regardless of causes, the figure you found *is* pretty definite proof something's in the wind—"

Judson nodded again, uneasily. "And you think it's centered at Sermon Hill."

"I do. If it should break out as a full-fledged revolt—"

Seth's unfinished sentence conjured chaos. Judson glanced at the curtains blowing; the darkness outside. He didn't care for the responsibility being pushed onto him:

"Seth, I understand all you're saying. But Lord, man, what can I do?"

"I've spoken to your father several times in hopes of getting him to moderate his treatment of his nigras. I've had no luck."

Judson guffawed. "You think mine will be any better? Christ, Seth, you know he hates me."

"No," Seth returned quietly, "I don't believe that's true."

"Bullshit. I'm the second son. Automatically second best."

"But you and Donald are both his flesh."

"And we're both traitors because Donald went to the Raleigh Tavern last year, and I went along. Spiritually, anyway," Judson added with a wry smile.

He was referring to the gathering of members of the House of Burgesses who had assembled in the Williamsburg tavern at the urging of Patrick Henry, gentleman lawyer of Hanover County.

47

Henry, a natural leader, was the chief spokesman in the Burgesses for the back-country people. Over the last ten years, that segment of Virginia's population had found itself almost constantly opposed to the more conservative tidewater planters.

Henry had stirred Virginia with his hot oratory against Crown infringements of colonial rights. And when the royal governor, Lord Dunmore, had temporarily dissolved the legislature in May of the preceding year, Henry immediately led most of the Burgesses to a rump session at the Raleigh. There they appointed a delegation to the first Continental Congress. Along with Judson's older brother and several other Virginians, Henry was presently away at the second Congress, where his stock stood high because of an inflammatory speech given in March of this year. In the speech, Henry had taken an inflexible stand against Great Britain. The alternatives for him, he'd declared, were liberty or death—no middle ground. Governor Dunmore promptly issued a proclamation branding Henry an outlaw, which only enhanced his status further among Virginia's patriot faction.

Judson continued to Seth, "I think my father would have horsewhipped Donald if Donald would have allowed it. At the moment there are a great many people on my father's list of political enemies. Donald, myself, Henry—even Colonel Washington of Fairfax County, because he went up to Philadelphia too. On top of that—"

Judson sloshed another slug of rum into his glass. He was growing tipsy again:

"The lord of Sermon Hill happens to consider me a drunken wastrel. A prodigal on whom he squandered a deal of money for an education at William and Mary. He's commented that the sterling notes would have served a better purpose if they'd been used for wiping asses in the outhouse." Judson toasted an unseen presence. "So saith Angus Fletcher, in one of his less biblical moods."

"Still, can't you talk to him?"

"Well," Judson said, drawling out the word, "we do speak every month or so."

"Suggest he say something to Shaw, then. Try to get the man to moderate his behavior until we isolate the cause of the problem, or it calms down."

Glum, Judson shook his head. "Seth, I repeat—I exert no influence whatsoever at Sermon Hill. I sometimes wonder why I'm even allowed to live there."

"Because you're Angus Fletcher's son! Judson—for friendship's sake—and the tranquility of this district—*try*."

Judson poured more rum. "All right. I'll say something. A remark or two. I'd be rash to promise more."

"It's a start." Seth pumped his hand. "Thank you—"

"I must go." Judson finished his drink quickly, asking himself why he had given in to Seth. He knew the answer. It was a cheap way to purchase temporary absolution of guilt—

The shadow across the floor at the library entrance made him glance up sharply.

She stood there; slender, dark-haired, fair-skinned and lovely in a peach-colored night robe whose high collar and decorous lines still set off her figure to advantage. She was all grace and gentility; a perfect lady he had loved since he was seventeen.

But she had been Peggy Ashford, respectable, while he had been—still was—Judson Fletcher; something less.

Their two-year relationship before her marriage had scarred them both. In those tempestuous times, Judson had never touched her other than to kiss her, though it had been obvious they both desired much more than that. Perhaps that restraint was what compounded the agony now.

49

Seth knew very well that the two had courted. Meeting at cross-country hunts. Attending balls together at wealthy houses up and down the river. All with the growing disapproval of the Ashfords, as Judson's nature asserted itself in frequent public drunkenness and brawling.

Finally, the Ashfords forced Peggy to stop seeing him. It was heartbreaking for her. But she was a dutiful daughter. Presently Seth stepped in. When the marriage was arranged and solemnized, Seth expected his friend Judson to behave like a gentleman. Which Judson did, in atypical fashion, because, above all, he did not want to bring Peggy any further hurt or scandal.

Now Seth simply assumed that while Judson, being a man, might harbor certain lingering impulses that could lead to adultery, he would never permit those impulses to become deeds. Seth also considered Peggy above reproach—

And those stories about Judson's affairs with other men's wives—well, it was doubtful whether Seth fully believed them. Judson knew his friend failed to understand how deeply his feelings ran—or how close he'd come to making advances to Peggy on several occasions. In business affairs, Seth was reasonably worldly. In human ones, no—

Still, Judson managed to keep his distance. To him, Peggy Ashford McLean was something of a shrine. Unsullied, as few things in his life were any longer. He had never been able to explain why he loved her. She was sweet, intelligent, attractive; but many women along the tidewaters were that. What was it in her special combination of dark-eyed glances, smiles and small feminine gestures that had continued to torment him after he lost her? Perhaps part of his passion sprang from a realization even during their courting that she would probably never be allowed to marry him. For a man like Judson

Fletcher, permanent frustration had its twisted charms—

"Melissa told me we had a guest," Peggy said. "Good evening, Judson."

"Good evening." He managed a bow. "I'm just on my way—"

He hardly dared glance at her for fear he'd reveal his feelings. He had seen her often since the marriage, of course. At holiday fetes, or the Richmond fair. On such occasions, he could never read her expression. He suspected that whatever she'd felt once was completely gone. Speaking marriage vows would have begun to destroy it automatically. Her code of behavior said that was only decent and proper—

Peggy turned to her husband. "You're home early, Seth."

"To speak with Judson. I'm seeking his help in regard to the unrest."

"I warned him he might as well ask for help from a woodpecker," Judson said with a merry laugh, walking quickly past the woman, still unwilling to face those well-remembered eyes. He went straight to the imposing main doors and out, with a hail:

"I'll be in touch if I've any results to brag about, Seth. Which I doubt."

Into the saddle, he tore down to the Rappahannock rippling silver under the stars. He never once glanced over his shoulder at Seth McLean's large, colonnaded white house with its rows of slave cabins at the rear, near the curing barns. But all the way to Sermon Hill, Peggy rode with him. The starlight that put highlights on the river glimmered on the tracks of angry tears on his cheeks.

v

Sermon Hill, five thousand acres of prime tobacco land worked by five hundred male and female slaves,

51

fronted the river as McLean's did. But Sermon Hill boasted its own wharf, where the huge tobacco canoes tied up in the autumn to load the casks that carried eight hundred pounds of cured brown leaf.

That is, the canoes had anchored there every autumn for as far back as Judson Fletcher could remember, then floated downriver with the casks lashed across their gunwales. Trading ships anchored in the navigable waters of the estuary took the casks to market overseas. Whether they would so do this year in view of the worsening trouble with England was a question no one could answer. News of exchanges of fire between royal troops and colonial militia in April, someplace up in the Massachusetts Bay area, had cast doubt on all commercial ventures involving overseas trade—and on the placid quality of life itself.

But Judson wasn't thinking of that two mornings later. By way of fulfilling Seth's request, he rose earlier than usual—at sunrise, for God's sake!—to take a stroll around to the slave quarters.

The slaves lived in two long rows of whitewashed cottages that faced each other across an expanse of dirt. At the head of the avenue sat the small house belonging to the overseer. Outside this house, Judson spied a crowd of field bucks and wenches gathered in the orange light of early morning.

Moving closer, he heard the cracking of a whip. Because of the crowd, he couldn't see the victim.

He ran. Past the windowless cottages where barefoot black children wandered in the tiny okra patches, or squatted, dropping excrement from their bottoms, or simply sat in the doorways, picking at their hair and examining the creatures they discovered. In terms of sanitation and living standards for slaves, Sermon Hill was no different—no better and no worse—than most major tobacco plantations along the river—

Except in the matter of Reuven Shaw, general overseer.

Judson dashed up to the slaves at the rear of the crowd. They recognized him, quickly stepped aside. He spoke to one strong-looking buck:

"Who's being punished?"

"Dicey. Shaw, he say she fit to work. Dicey, she say no."

"Jesus—!" Judson exploded. "Where's her husband?"

"Field already," was the reply.

For a moment Judson stared into brown eyes that seemed to add silently, *Good thing for Mist' Shaw*. Or was that only his imagination?

He shoved through the crowd, saw the skinny, ill-clad Shaw, younger brother of Lottie's husband, raise his long blacksnake to make another mark on Dicey's yellow-brown back.

Shaw looked up, threat in his eyes. It simmered less hotly when he recognized the man in boots, hose, trousers, shirt—one of the owner's sons.

Judson gestured at the wench, who had been forced to discard her ragged dress—Shaw liked to punish the wenches naked—and kneel in the dirt with her head bowed over her knees. Dicey's back bore three bleeding stripes.

"Want to lay on a few, Mr. Judson?" Shaw asked. It was said with thinly concealed contempt. Judson and the overseer had long disliked each other.

"You ignorant son of a bitch, I'll take the whip to you instead. That wench birthed twin boys only five days ago." Judson held up one hand, fingers spread. "Five!"

"Three's the most I 'low 'fore they go back to work," Shaw grumbled.

"Dicey, put your dress on and go back to your cabin," Judson ordered. " 'Till next Monday morning."

"Listen here! I'm in charge of—" Shaw began. Judson leaped forward, seized the whip and looped it around Shaw's neck. He yanked both ends:

"What'd you say?"

"N—nothing, Mr. Judson," Shaw gasped, pop-eyed. God, how he stank. Judson shoved him. "Get their black asses to work and quit causing unnecessary trouble." With that, Judson let go of the whip and turned to walk away.

"The snake is all that's keepin' us from havin' trouble—!"

Again Judson whirled, staring into the warped, resentful face of the sunburned white man.

"Did you have another comment, Shaw?" he inquired, almost whispering.

Shaw swallowed, watched Dicey gather her dress and flee barefoot. "No," he mumbled. "No, I dint." But Judson didn't miss the hate in Shaw's eyes—

Nor, for that matter, in the eyes of the bucks and wenches who stood aside to let him pass back toward the rambling, two-story, twenty-three-room house where he intended to have his breakfast.

Strange, he thought as he walked, his fair hair shining in the morning sun, very strange indeed. Striding by all those silent blacks, he'd had the uncanny feeling that their hatred was directed as much at him as at Reuven Shaw. Perhaps just being white did it, he thought wearily. Just as being black got you bought, whipped or fucked at the pleasure of your owners. Somehow, moving up the cabin avenue and hearing the chatter of the group breaking into field gangs, he didn't care to look back.

At Shaw *or* the slaves.

vi

The silver service gleamed, then suddenly distorted, reflecting a wizened face, white hair, enraged eyes.

Lounging on the veranda, Judson glanced from the reflection in the bulge of the pot to the creator of the image: his father, a tiny-boned man with a pointed chin and skin like old leather.

Angus Fletcher never tried to look prosperous, not even on social occasions. This morning his hose drooped, there was a rip in the knee of his breeches, and his shirt was wet with sweat. He came into the veranda's shade, shot his head forward like a turkey, confronting his son:

"I just had a report from Mr. Shaw. Apparently you interfered with him while I was down seeing to the repairs on the dock."

"And I just had a letter from Donald." Judson used a smile to conceal his uneasiness as he lifted the document in question. "A hired courier brought it from Richmond not ten minutes ago."

"Wondered who that trespasser was," Angus Fletcher garrumphed. He sat down in one of the large basket chairs. "You may keep the letter to yourself. I've no interest in tidings from that nest of traitors up north. That my own son should allow himself to be influenced by those perfidious wise men of the East—"

Judson laughed at his father's use of the term that Tories, and even some rebels, applied to the influential patriot leaders of Massachusetts. "Father, you'll have to put Colonel Washington even more firmly among the traitors now. Donald says that he and the other Congressional delegates appointed the colonel to lead the Continental armies. It happened just the middle of this month. Washington will have the rank of general and will go to Boston to take command."

He consulted the letter quickly, enjoying his father's fuming.

"And there's been more fighting. Some place called Breed's Hill. The British won the day, but our side acquitted itself well—"

"Your side, not mine!" Angus Fletcher leaped for the letter, flung it away. "Those fools will bring down ruin on all of us. We should be suing for peace before matters get worse." Again he shot his head forward. " 'Blessed are the peacemakers, for they shall be called—' "

" '—the children of God,' " Judson finished wearily. Of all his father's annoying personal characteristics, the old man's fondness for scripture offended Judson the most. Angus was especially partial to St. Matthew. So taken was he with the message and language of the Sermon on the Mount, he had re-named his own father's plantation on its low hill above the Rappahannock in honor of it.

"Shall we move to another text?" Judson asked. " 'Blessed are the merciful—' "

"I want to hear what in damnation angered Shaw!"

Judson stared at his father. Despite his age—he was nearly sixty—Angus Fletcher's slight frame suggested great strength. He worked diligently at the business affairs of Sermon Hill every day of the week except Sunday, when he attended church in the morning, prayed in the privacy of his bedchamber all afternoon, and forbade anything that smacked of light amusement on his property throughout the entire Sabbath. The old man did have a certain biblical majesty, Judson reflected as he studied the seated figure outlined against the river and the rolling, heat-hazed hills beyond.

But he could never remember a time when there had been tenderness or even kindness between father and son. Even in Judson's earliest recollections, it seemed that his father had treated him sternly; as a full-grown man. Wanting—demanding—more than a boy could give. Judson had resigned in defeat by the time he was ten. He could never be as clever, as strong, as pious as Angus expected him to be. Perhaps that was part of the trouble.

Of course, being the second son was another part. He

56

could not inherit, hence was less important than Donald. Even so, the same kind of relationship existed between the old man and Donald, ten years Judson's senior.

Donald was gout-ridden at thirty-five. He downed great quantities of port and claret when Angus wasn't watching. Further, he never shrank from proclaiming how proud he was to be a member of the Burgesses chosen to represent Virginia at the Congress.

Of their mother Judson could remember next to nothing. She had died when he was four. Donald recalled her as a kindly, religious woman who slipped silently through the house attending to her duties, totally in awe of her husband.

Resentful of Angus' outburst about Shaw, Judson said, "The text I had in mind will bring us to that subject. Remember, Father—the merciful 'shall obtain mercy.' Shaw's doing his best to see you get just the opposite."

Angus made a face, rang a handbell. In a moment, one of the liveried house blacks—they were a caste above the field hands—glided to the old man's elbow with a goblet of cold spring water. Angus Fletcher extended his hand. The goblet was placed into it. He did not look around. He expected the drink to be where it was supposed to be, and it was.

He sipped, then said, "Be more explicit, I have work to do."

"Shaw was whipping Dicey. I stopped him."

"You *stopped* him? You don't run Sermon Hill! And unless you change your whoring ways and your politics to boot, you won't even receive so much as one shilling when I pass on."

"I've heard that threat before," Judson returned. He was cool, but it took effort. "I think you're facing a more immediate one—"

Briefly, he described his conversation with Seth McLean, as well as the stabbed figure and slate he'd

57

found by the roadside. The description seemed to unnerve Angus Fletcher slightly. At least, the wrinkled hand and the water goblet shook for a moment.

Solely to antagonize the old man, Judson crossed his boots, stretched and yawned. It worked:

"Go on, go on!" Angus exclaimed.

Judson still took his time before resuming:

"Seth heard a rumor that our buck Larned may be responsible for stirring up some of the discontent. Since Dicey is Larned's woman, I stopped Shaw in the hope of preventing real trouble. I also stopped him because what he was doing was wrong."

"Spare me your false piety, please!"

"Why, Father, I thought you thrived on piety."

Angus colored.

"All right," Judson shrugged, "we needn't debate on moral grounds. I thought I was doing you a good service. Isn't a little restraint preferable to an outbreak? To seeing Sermon Hill set afire, for instance? Rebellions have happened before."

"Never here. And they won't. I'll chain up every one of those unwashed sons of Ham before—" He blinked twice as Judson raised a languid hand. "What, what?" he roared.

"Your biblical scholarship is faulty, I'm afraid," Judson informed him. "The name Ham means swarthy, not black. If Noah's son had any real descendants—other than fairy-story ones, that is—" Again Angus' cheeks darkened. "—they were doubtless the Egyptians, or those people called Berbers, not the poor bastards the blackbirders bring from the West Africas to do your hard work."

"When did you become a biblical expert, may I ask?" Angus sneered.

Judson smiled with great charm. "Why, at college. You paid for the lessons."

"You're not only disloyal to His Majesty, you're a

58

disgrace to the very flesh that bore you! To think I wasted hard money so your head could be filled with godless rot—"

"Any rot, as you call it, was probably acquired at Sermon Hill."

Angus Fletcher flung the cold water in his son's face.

Judson jumped up. He almost went for the old man's throat. But he checked, big veins standing out in his strong hands as he sat down again and gripped the arms of his chair.

Angus Fletcher set the glass on a wicker stand, rose and walked toward his son. Despite his small stature he looked commanding, looming there in the shadows of the veranda. His voice shook:

"Month after month, I've prayed to God to make you realize what you have been born to, Judson Fletcher. On my knees I have begged God to help you understand how much struggle and toil has gone into building this estate—"

"Black struggle and black toil, you mean. And black blood."

"Your grandfather labored and died to—"

"Oh, for Christ's sake, stop it."

"Blasphemer! You take the Lord's name in—"

"Yes! Because I've heard that whitewashing till I'm sick of it!" Judson thundered. "I've known the real story for a long time—others in this district are more accurate reporters. Your father was a catchpenny redemptioner from Glasgow—a criminal, most likely, since he never signed his real name to his indenture papers—and didn't even honor his contract. Two days after they landed him in Philadelphia, he ran away from the soul-driver trying to unload him for transportation plus profit! Years later, he bragged about it! He turned up here in Virginia and got a farmer's girl pregnant and had to marry her, and then the farmer died suddenly of a fall from a horse while just he and my grandfather were riding in the woods. Believe me, I know all about how the first land for this whited sepulcher was acquired! It's going to come down unless you stop thinking you're the anointed of God, ruling the impious. Those black bucks and wenches are human beings! Dumb, dirty—but people nonetheless. Seth McLean understands that."

"Seth McLean is a weakling and a fool. He owns a tenth of the land I do because he's a tenth as canny."

"A tenth as brutal!" Judson shouted. "A tenth as immoral!"

Angus Fletcher tried to strike his son. Judson caught the thin wrist, easily pushed it down. The old man was breathing heavily. For a moment Judson was worried. But he quickly recognized the raspy breathing as a sign of rage, not seizure:

"I've raised a liar, a drunkard, a lecher—"

"Who wishes to Christ—"

"You will not blaspheme in my presence!"

"—he'd never set eyes on this place."

"Twenty-five years old and look at you! Dissolute—idle—your head full of sin and poisonous idolatries! Well, go chase after your painted whores in Richmond. Go follow your crazy friend George Clark who's probably dead in the wilderness by now. *Or go join your damned brother and the traitors in Philadelphia!*"

Judson Fletcher was so full of fury, he was afraid he might hit his father and injure him. And the father would not be able to stay the son's hand. To protect himself from launching an attack which he knew he'd ultimately regret, Judson fought for control, tried the Bible again, with a forced smile:

" 'Agree with thine adversary quickly, while thou art in the way with him, lest at any time the adversary deliver thee to the judge—' "

"Hold your filthy tongue! You have no right to quote our Savior!"

"If you understood your Savior, old man, you'd do something about Reuven Shaw."

"I will. I'll order him to enforce even stricter discipline. To search the cabins for a drum—and to give a hundred strokes to any nigger hiding one."

Red-faced, Judson started away. "I'll inform Seth McLean of your decision."

"I'm sure you will," the old man jeered. "So as to get another opportunity for lewd concourse with his wife."

Judson stopped as if he'd been bludgeoned. For the first time, Angus Fletcher looked amused; master of the situation. He actually laughed as he resumed his seat:

"If I have secrets which are public, so do you. Do you think I don't remember how you felt about the McLean woman? How you still ride by her house night after night? One more reason I brand your friend McLean a fool. If you came on my property feeling about my wife as you feel about his. I'd put a ball in your head."

With grudging admiration, Judson said, "You old bastard. Sometimes I forget how foxy you are. Figured me out, have you?"

"Aye, long ago. But I constantly find new examples of your sinfulness—to my everlasting disgust. It came as no surprise to me when the Ashfords finally refused to permit their daughter to see you."

"Your faith in me is constantly overwhelming—!"

Angus ignored that; pointed a wrathful finger:

"What decent folk would want you as a son-in-law? For any woman you'd marry, there'd be naught to look forward to save anguish over your debauchery. And if she bore you a child, she'd go to her grave in despair because of the taint you'd lay on the babe—"

Thunderstruck, Judson gaped at the old man. "What taint? *Your* taint—if any!"

Angus Fletcher shook his head in dogmatic denial. "Something in yourself has ruined you, Judson. Better to shoot any child you'd father than let him live his life with your devil's blood poisoning him and all his generations after hi—"

"Be damned to you, you sanctimonious hypocrite!" Judson fairly screamed. "If I've devil's blood, you've only to look in a glass to see who's the source!"

If the words affected Angus, he concealed it. His features hardened into that expression of smug piety Judson hated with such passion.

"You're carrying on like a raving fool," Angus declared, "because you know this for a fact—Peggy McLean should thank heaven she was prevented from marrying you."

"It—" Judson could barely speak. "—it must give you great pride and satisfaction to say that about your own flesh."

"It gives me great sadness."

"You vile, lying old—"

Unable to continue, he wheeled and rushed away down the veranda. Angus shouted after him:

"At least you can have the decency to keep yourself from her presence. She knows your wicked purpose for calling at McLean's! 'Ye have heard that it was said by them of old time, Thou shalt not commit adultery—' "

Scarlet again, Judson stalked straight ahead, fearful that if he turned back, there would be blows struck—or worse. It required an act of total will for him to continue toward the main door of the house as Angus' voice grew more and more shrill:

" 'But I say unto you, That whosoever looketh on a woman to lust after her hath committed adultery with her already in his heart—' "

Judson slammed the door, stormed past the startled house blacks who saw his thunderous look and glanced away.

He raced up to his room, tore off his sweated shirt in exchange for a new one. He hated his father. Yet surely some of the guilt for these dreadful confrontations was his. He took pleasure in tormenting the old man, in revenge for the old man tormenting him. *What in the name of God was wrong with him?*

Even Donald's faults were mild in comparison. In their father's eyes, Donald's chief sin was his conviction that the oppressive taxes and restrictive policies of Britain could no longer be borne. To that iniquity Judson added a score more, from adulterer to defender of slaves—

Ten minutes later, he was galloping one of the dirt lanes that crisscrossed the plantation. His saddlebags bulged with two unopened jugs of rum.

Judson saw black heads turn in the fields. One slate-blue face burned bright: the buck Larned, bare-shouldered, risen like some demonic figure from his weeding among the ear-shaped leaves of the tobacco plants.

Larned watched him ride on, and it seemed to Judson that his back was afire from the slave's venomous glare. Judson was a white man, and Angus Fletcher's son. No matter what he'd done for the wench Dicey, Larned would surely twist it so that it acquired a practical—a despicable—motivation: to preserve the wench for further work, perhaps. Or sex with Judson himself. What the hell was the use of trying to intervene if it generated so much hate from all of them?

That Judson understood how the whole slave problem had gotten so thoroughly out of hand in a hundred and fifty years didn't mitigate his sense of outrage—or his sad conviction that the system would produce continuing friction and violence unless it was abolished.

The agricultural economy in which he'd grown up was based on grueling physical labor. So he really couldn't fault the people of the southern colonies for buying black workers in preference to white ones when the latter were far less desirable.

Men such as his grandfather, for example, could be counted on to work for their buyers only until the expiration of their indenture contracts. Of course his grandfather hadn't been willing to wait even that long!

The problem of finding a stable work force had grown still more difficult early in the century, when some combination of geniuses in the mother country had conceived the idea of clearing Britain of many of its undesirables—thieves, pickpockets, whores—whose crimes weren't quite serious enough to earn them hangropes. The answer was to transport them across the ocean at three to five pounds a head, to be purchased on arrival for negotiated periods of servitude. But just exactly like the man who voluntarily indentured himself, transportees eventually were eligible for freedom —earned legally or, sooner, by flight.

What planter who prided himself on efficiency—and ledgers that showed a profit—wouldn't prefer to purchase a cowed, completely unlettered black from Africa? A black whose legal status, from the beginning, was vague? And whose fatally distinctive coloration made him easier to detect if he fled his bondage? Even the meanest petty criminal from the London stews at least had a white skin to keep him relatively invisible if he succeeded in escaping.

But what had begun as a natural tendency to seek the most stable and permanent kind of agricultural labor force had degenerated into outright ownership of one human being by another.

It was a source of sardonic amusement for Judson to recall that the very first blacks on the continent—twenty—were put ashore and sold at the Jamestown colony by the largely British crew of a Dutch privateer. The date was 1619—one year before the arrival of the *Mayflower* at Plymouth, carrying forty-one stiff-necked Puritan families whose children and grandchildren prided themselves on being descended from

64

"founding fathers." What a pity there were no genealogical tables to permit the offspring of the Jamestown twenty to dispute that claim!

In the early years of the colonial blackbird trade, the word *slave* had seldom if ever been spoken. Gradually, though, it came into common use as the more unscrupulous members of the landed class realized that New England shipowners were quite willing to supply a constant stream of African bucks and wenches, and that a combination of evolving custom and clever writing of new statutes could transform purchased black workers into permanent chattels with no hope of ever earning freedom—a condition the redemptioners and transported prison inmates never faced.

Now the institution had grown so entrenched —producing fear and repression on one side, submission and hatred on the other—that Judson could only foresee an eventual confrontation between those who listened to their consciences and those who heard nothing but the jingling voice of the pound.

By mid-morning, his reflections had put him in thoroughly miserable spirits. He lay in a grove at the edge of the plantation, glooming over the explosive potential of the situation with the local blacks, then experiencing even deeper depression over his own behavior.

Why in God's name was he driven to such excesses of word and deed, both in his father's presence and elsewhere? Gazing out across the tobacco fields where heat-devils rippled the air, he saw the white walls of Sermon Hill rising on the crest of the low rise above the Rappahannock and wished he were anywhere but here.

He wished he were out beyond the Blue Wall with his friend, for instance. In empty country. No laws, no Bible-spouting hypocrites, no incipient rebellions, no pea-headed overseers, no—

No Peggy to haunt him.

His father's words came back to him with tormenting clarity.

Taint.

Poisoned.

Devil's blood—

Try as he might, he couldn't scoff away the uneasy suspicion that Angus had struck a vein of truth. One from which Judson turned in terror and loathing. The only way to blunt the fear was with rum. Slowly drinking himself insensible, he was able to convince himself that he only needed to escape Virginia to escape his demons.

He fell into a stupor that brought bizarre dreams.

He saw flame-haired George Rogers Clark stalking through the wilderness, standing as tall as the trees themselves. He saw Peggy naked, beckoning him with lewd gestures, a slut's teasing smile. He saw his father, fierce as Moses, hand raised to deliver a blow while lightning flashed in a sky of churning storm—

He awoke suddenly. Lying on his back in the grass, he felt chilly. Nearby, his roan stood head down, a statue against the first faint stars. In the west, red stained the horizon.

Judson licked the inside of his furred mouth. He heard a sound so faint that the slightest change in the direction of the breeze silenced it for a moment. But he recognized the sound.

The hollow boom of a hand drum.

The moment he identified the sound, it stopped completely. But he could have sworn the eerie thudding had drifted from the direction of Sermon Hill.

CHAPTER III

Birth

RAGGED AND louse-ridden, Philip Kent
trudged through the mud of what passed for a street in
the camp of the American army.

He was physically exhausted. Not from working at
digging and fortifying new earthworks; not from
trenching out new vaults when the old ones overflowed
with human waste. From boredom. The endless, uncertain waiting—

Constant worry about his wife Anne only added to
the strain. He got to see her once or twice a week if he
was lucky. Regulations were haphazard in the American
siege lines surrounding Boston. Sometimes he could obtain permission to slip away to Watertown of an evening, sometimes not. He seldom knew in advance.
Tonight he'd been fortunate, and gotten leave to go.

A drizzling mid-September rain fell, worsening conditions in the already wretched camp that had sprung up
and spread as various volunteer regiments from all over
the colonies arrived during the summer and settled in
beside one another, helter-skelter. Since taking charge in
early July, the new commanding general of the Continental Army, George Washington of Virginia, had
been trying to bring some organization to the chaos. He
hadn't made much progress, even though new orders
relating to camp discipline or procedures came streaming out of Wadsworth House in Cambridge almost every
day.

Philip Kent, a short, wide-shouldered young man with dark eyes and hair tied up in a queue, scarcely looked like a soldier as he slogged along in boots worn perilously thin on the bottoms. But then, few of the volunteers resembled soldiers.

There were some exceptions, of course. The Rhode Islanders with their neat tents, each equipped with its own front awning. Their encampment looked almost British. The same held true for the Twenty-first Massachusetts, men from Marblehead who had given up their occupations as shipwrights and fishermen but not their seafaring heritage. The Marbleheaders were outfitted in trim blue seacloth jackets and loose white sailor's trousers. But apart from a handful of such regiments, the Americans dressed and often acted like rabble. Their living places matched.

Most of the men, Philip included, lived in shelters made of whatever materials they had purchased, brought from home, or stolen. Philip's Twenty-ninth Massachusetts infantry regiment, camped between Cambridge and the earthworks at the center of the American line overlooking the Charles River, made do in shanties knocked together from warped boards. But as he walked, Philip saw many other types of structures, from sailcloth tents sagging under the drizzle to crude shelters of fieldstone chinked up with turf. Some units simply lived on the ground between constantly soggy blankets.

To add to the confusion, it was often impossible to tell officers from enlisted men. General Washington had tried to outfit the volunteer soldiers in some semblance of a uniform. Amid the flurry of organizational orders and new commissions issuing from the house formerly occupied by Harvard's president, he'd sent off a request to the Continental Congress for ten thousand smock-like hunting shirts. No action had been taken on the request before the assembly adjourned early in August. Washington had meantime authorized officers to adopt scarves, cockades, second-hand epaulets—whatever they could find to identify themselves.

Not that it made much difference to the men who served under them.

The army encamped at Boston consisted mostly of farmers and artisans, all waiting to see whether a full-scale war would break out, or would be defused by moves toward reconciliation already taken by the Congress that represented every colony except Georgia. The men who made up the army didn't understand military discipline and in fact resented it. Philip recalled hearing a prediction that this attitude might prevail, and prove disastrous. The prediction had been made by his friend Henry Knox, the fat Boston bookseller who was somewhere in the lines acting as a sort of supervising engineer in charge of artillery. Philip had not seen Knox all summer, though.

No one knew how many volunteers had arrived in Massachusetts since the outbreak of hostilities. Philip had heard figures ranging from twelve to twenty thousand. The reaction of these summer soldiers to the commander-in-chief's various orders forbidding such activities as gambling and "profane cursing," and demanding attendance at "divine services" twice daily, ranged from indifference to outright defiance.

A few shrewd commanders recognized the problem and tried to deal with it. One such was Iz Putnam of Connecticut, the old Indian fighter who had defended the king's interests during the American phase of the Seven Years' War. Putnam invented schemes to sharpen his men for combat and keep them diverted at the same time.

Since the terrifying shelling of Breed's and Bunker's Hills in June, most of the Continentals had learned they had little to fear from the barrages of the British batteries in Boston. But the artillery fire was almost constant in clear weather. So Putnam sent his men darting out of their earthworks to recover spent cannon shot, in short supply on the American side. The prize for each round was a tot of rum. An explosive shell earned two tots—provided it didn't blow up the man who went after it. Philip wished that the Twenty-ninth Massachusetts had that kind of imaginative commander.

Now, as he slogged along in the mud, his mind began to veer from camp life to the other world he lived in whenever he could. The world of Watertown—and Anne. He paid less and less attention to the men idly attempting to wipe their muskets dry inside lantern-lit hovels. He dodged the bones of an evening fish ration flung into his path. Unseeing, he passed two volunteers urinating in the open—the accepted custom. He went by tents and lean-tos noisy with quarreling, drinking and forbidden dicing. In some of the temporary dwellings, feminine giggling could be heard, indicating that "immoral practices"—likewise prohibited—were in full swing. Head down, hands in the pockets of his sodden coat, he thought only about his wife.

She was near her term; immense of belly. She'd been extremely weak the past month or so, abed most of the time in the rented rooms Lawyer Ware had taken in Watertown.

But even more disturbing, the Connecticut surgeon whom Philip had located with such difficulty in mid-summer, and hired to take over Anne's care on a once-weekly basis, had been shot and killed the preceding week after an argument about cards.

Philip had paid the cheerfully greedy doctor with money saved from his earnings at the Edes and Gill print shop. He'd gotten the money from Ben Edes personally. Edes, who had set up his patriot press in Watertown, had been keeping the funds for Philip. Now the money was of no use. The doctor was permanently unavailable.

In the past few days Philip had searched frantically

for someone to replace the doctor. The quest so far had been fruitless.

Wiping rain from his cheeks, he turned a corner past another hovel. He glanced up suddenly at the sound of a brawl in progress between a double row of tents a few steps further down. Damnation! He should have watched his route more carefully. Avoided this most contentious section of the American center. Now he was caught.

He walked rapidly, determined to pass the twelve or fifteen men punching, kicking and yelling in the middle of the muddy street. He kept close to the line of the tents, eyed the combatants. Virginians to a man.

The Virginians had become the marvel of the camps when the first contingent reached Boston in July, boasting a march of six or seven hundred miles in three weeks, with no one ill, no deserters. They were tall, peculiar, violent men with skins the color of browned autumn leaves. Their clothing—especially their voluminous white hunting shirts and their headgear: round, broad-brimmed hats or caps with dangling fur tails—excited comment wherever they walked.

The Virginians automatically pushed aside all men smaller than themselves, and many who weren't smaller. Their height and tough bearing gave them the authority. So did their strange weapons: guns much longer and narrower through the barrel than the familiar smoothbore muskets.

The backwoodsmen from Virginia called their weapons Kentucky rifles, though they claimed the pieces were manufactured in Pennsylvania. Using the rifles, they challenged all comers to shooting contests—and always won—shattering bottle targets at impossible ranges of two or three hundred yards. Philip's Brown Bess could barely fire half that distance before spending its ball.

Though the rifles took longer to load than muskets,

71

and could not be fitted with bayonets, they were deadly accurate. So were the eyes that aimed them. Eyes that had supposedly gazed on distant country where blue mountains climbed toward a sea of cloud, and tribes of the red-skinned, savage Indians roamed.

This evening, the Virginians were having at each other again. That too was a familiar occurrence. Men gleefully booted the groins of their opponents, stepped on faces, bit ankles or wrists. Half the fighters were on their knees or backs or bellies, covered with gummy mud. But they kept slugging and thrashing and getting up again. And—to Philip's astonishment—for the most part, they were laughing.

He moved faster, determined to get clear of the brawl post haste.

He skirted the churning mass of men while other Virginians lounging near the tents eyed him with arrogant curiosity. Further down the camp street, a phaeton turned the corner, heading away from the brawlers. Suddenly one of the phaeton's three cloaked occupants lurched to his feet. He grabbed his driver's shoulder. In a moment, the team was charging back toward the fight, which continued without letup.

One side of the battle abruptly grew like a living organism, rolling outward until Philip was virtually on the edge. He had to jump aside to avoid a whizzing fist. Someone shoved the small of his back:

"Hey, Zech, if you need somebody to punch, here's one of them wise men!"

Philip had been pushed by a spectator. Off balance, he cursed and fisted his hands. He got angry when men from other colonies taunted the Massachusetts soldiers with the epithet applied to the Boston radicals. But before he could swing on the man who'd shoved him, he inadvertently stumbled into the melee. A huge, hard hand blasted into his stomach, doubled him over—

He dropped to his knees, madder than ever. But the

72

burly Virginian who'd punched him had already turned his attention to one of his own—a tall, skinny, mud-slimed man with a mouthful of crooked teeth and one eye that pointed off at the oblique. Positively the ugliest specimen Philip had ever seen.

Philip's attacker kicked the tall fellow in the groin. The man grimaced as he lost his footing, toppled into the mud. He floundered on hands and knees. His burly opponent bellowed a laugh, laced his fingers together, intending to chop them down in a murderous blow to the other man's exposed neck.

Philip could have avoided further involvement by sneaking away. But he was tired, and thus not hard to provoke. Finding steady footing at last, he grabbed the burly man's shoulder, pulled hard.

The man wheeled, aborting his vicious blow at the tall fellow's neck. The burly man took one look at Philip, smiled an oafish, infuriating smile and resorted to his favorite tactic—a lightning kick between the legs. Philip clenched his teeth to keep from screaming in pain.

"Dunno who the hell you are, little boy," the burly man growled. Philip realized the man was ugly drunk. "But this here's Virginny territory. You go play someplace else 'fore I spank you good."

Shaking, Philip said, "Come on and try."

The tall, ugly fellow darted up from behind and bashed his opponent in one ear. The burly man didn't appear to feel it. Only his eyes showed a reaction. He stabbed his hand down past a tangle of thrashing, mud-covered arms and legs. Instantly, Philip saw what he was after—

A spade someone had used as a weapon.

The man seized the spade's handle—but Philip wasn't the target. The burly man swung the spade toward the tall fellow, howling:

"I'll take yer head off, Eph Tait!"

Philip made another two-handed lunge at the burly

73

man's forearm. The Virginian with the cocked eye ducked and the spade hissed on through the air. Except for Philip's restraining grip, it would have completed its arc—

To smash into the face of the officer who had climbed from the phaeton.

The spirit seemed to drain from the burly man in a second. His mud-daubed face lost color. All he could breathe out was a raspy, "Oh, heavenly Christ—"

Philip was equally alarmed, to put it mildly. No man in the American lines could fail to recognize the towering officer. His thrown-back cloak revealed a dark blue coat with buff facings, a buff waistcoat and, above the white breeches, his purple sash of rank.

He had somehow lost his hat. Rain glistened in his clubbed reddish-brown hair. He was in his early forties, with huge hands, equally large feet whose size was emphasized by his big boots. In fact the man looked almost ponderous. But he moved with startling speed as he seized the spade and hurled it to the ground. Philip noticed a light pitting of pox scars on pale cheeks that bore traces of sunburn—or the flush of anger. The man's gray-blue eyes raked the brawlers:

"I expect better than this from Virginians! Where is the commanding officer?"

The fighting had all but stopped. One of the mud-covered men shouted:

"Dead drunk—as usual."

"To your quarters, every damn one of you. And think about this while you wait for the orders for punishment I intend to issue before this night's over. I have made a pretty good slam since I came to this camp. I broke one colonel and two captains for cowardice at Bunker's Hill. I've caused to be placed under arrest for trial one colonel, one major, one captain and six subalterns—in short, I spare no one, particularly men of my own colony, and you will find that reflected in the redress of this

74

disgrace. *Dismissed!*" he shouted, suddenly pointing at Philip. "All except you."

Philip stood frozen, swallowing hard. The officer's temper had moderated. His speech took on a softer quality; the genteel, almost drawling quality of his native Fairfax County:

"You don't belong to this regiment, do you, soldier?"

"No, sir."

"What's your name?"

"Philip Kent, General."

"Your unit?"

"Twenty-ninth Massachusetts."

"Why aren't you with your unit?"

"I have my commander's permission to visit Watertown, sir. My wife's there—she's expecting a baby and not doing well—"

"I can vouch for this man's identity, General Washington."

The new arrival stumping up on fat legs brought Philip momentary relief from the absolute terror he felt under the blue-gray stare of the chief of the American forces. The new arrival was a pie-faced young man with a white silk scarf wrapped around his crippled left hand. He weighed close to three hundred pounds and wore civilian clothes.

Shooting a quick glance at Philip—a warning for him to stand fast—he continued:

"He served with me in the Boston Grenadier Company before the trouble broke out. If he says his wife's in Watertown, and that he's been given leave to see her, it's undoubtedly the truth."

"I'll take your word, Knox," Washington said. He smiled faintly. "Especially since this soldier's hand on that fool's arm—" He pointed at the burly drunk being lugged away by two companions. "—saved me from a broken skull. My thanks, Kent."

Washington whirled on the goggling laggards:

"Inside, the rest of you. Smartly—*smartly!*"

The Virginians ran, including the toothy, cock-eyed fellow who seemed to be trying to grin some sort of appreciation at Philip. Washington pulled his rain-drenched cloak down across his blue-and-buff uniform and turned to stride back to his phaeton. Henry Knox lingered, his round young face beaming:

"I'd heard you were out here, Philip."

"But not in officer's territory."

"Oh, I'm not there myself. Only on the border. Neither fish nor fowl, it seems. Still, I'm happy to serve where I can be useful."

"Your name's been widely circulated, Henry. I understand General Washington's impressed with your knowledge of artillery."

"I trust he will increase his reliance on what little I've learned," Knox said, no longer smiling. "Only cannon can defeat the British garrison in Boston."

"I've also heard you may be commissioned a colonel."

Knox made no comment. But he couldn't hide a prideful look. Before he'd shuttered his Boston bookshop to join the American army, Henry Knox had deliberately turned the shop into a haven for British officers of the occupying force. He had a purpose: to draw out the enemy's best thinking on the subject that fascinated him—the proper use of artillery. "Lucky you had a good reason for your presence," Knox observed finally. "The general's determined to birth an army out of this dismaying collection of ruffians. He was correct when he said he spares no one—least of all himself."

"Well, that may be true, but—" Philip hesitated.

"Go on with what you were about to say."

"Maybe I'd better not. It concerned the general."

"You can be candid. God knows everyone else in this camp is!"

Still Philip held back. Knox smiled wearily:

"Did you intend to tell me that most of your compatriots have doubts about the general's ability?"

Embarrassed, Philip nodded. Knox waved:

"Don't worry, I've heard that ten times over—from high and low. I've heard it all. That he was nothing more than a militia colonel before. And that while fighting the French and Indians, he lost several engagements. But I tell you this, Philip. Judge him by what he does now, not by his past."

"I suppose that's the fair way," Philip agreed. It was pointless to go into all the widely expressed reasons many soldiers considered Washington a poor choice for his high post.

Aware of the general watching impatiently from the phaeton, Knox himself changed the subject:

"So you're on your way to see your wife, are you?"

"That's right."

"I do believe I heard you'd married Mistress Ware—"

"Back in April."

"And she's with child. You're to be congratulated."

Philip didn't smile. "As I said, she's been sickly—"

"*Knox!*" Washington's shout from the phaeton hurried the fat young man's departure:

"I hope that condition reverses itself promptly. Give Anne and her father my compliments. I'm glad to find you again," he added as he waddled off. "I might have need for a couple of quick-witted men for a scheme I'm hatching—"

With a wave of the silk-wrapped hand, he was into the phaeton, a cloaked mountain hulking beside the general and the other officer as the carriage vanished in the murk.

Philip turned and hurried away from the Virginia encampment. He had only a few hours—and he was already late.

"Anne?"

Kneeling beside the bed, Philip kept his voice to a whisper:

"Annie? It's me—"

Slowly, Anne Kent's eyes opened. Her head moved slightly on the sweat-dampened bolster. The brown eyes reflected the flame of a candle by the bedside. Rain pattered the roof of the cramped upstairs bedroom in the house on a shabby side street in Watertown.

His mouth dry, Philip closed his hand around his wife's, felt its heat. Her chestnut hair glistened with sweat just above the forehead. The light dusting of freckles on either side of her nose—prominent when her skin was wholesomely tanned by sunshine—had almost faded into invisibility.

Suddenly Anne rolled onto her side, gasping while her hand sought and touched the great mound of her stomach beneath the comforter.

Fearful, Philip bent closer. He smelled the staleness of her breath. "I'll find you a doctor, Annie. I'm trying hard as I can—"

Her glazed eyes showed no sign that she heard. The hand on the comforter knotted convulsively.

Gradually the pain passed. She relaxed again. Philip's voice sounded hoarser than ever:

"Annie, look at me. Don't you know me?"

The brown eyes closed. Her breathing became more regular.

Despairing, Philip stumbled to his feet. In the shadows behind him, a sneeze exploded.

"I've caught a plagued disease myself! Guess I shouldn't be in here—"

Sneezing into a kerchief a second time, Abraham Ware stumped back into the lamplit parlor crowded with large and small trunks: the belongings of a prosperous Boston lawyer who had been forced to flee his home, and his livelihood, because of his patriot convictions. Philip heard his father-in-law walk into the other bedroom.

Gently, he stroked Anne's forehead. He wished she could speak to him. Wished she could listen to a pledge that he would desert the damned army, if necessary, to locate a physician. But she neither saw nor heard.

Just looking at her pale, drawn face was agony for him. Despite her youth, she bore little resemblance to the pretty, quick-witted and independent girl he'd first encountered in Henry Knox's London Book-Store. She seemed frail and altogether vulnerable as she muttered in her sleep.

Close to tears, Philip remembered the joyous moments of their courting. And the times when he had questioned his own feelings for her, tempted as he was by the daughter of the Earl of Parkhurst, who had almost lured him away from Anne in Philadelphia—

Then the past receded. Only the present counted. He loved his wife with every fiber of his soul. That love made his helplessness all the worse.

He uttered a frustrated curse, blew out the candle, tiptoed out leaving the door ajar. Abraham Ware, disheveled in an expensive suit that showed hard use, had returned from the bedroom with a fresh kerchief and was helping himself to what amounted to little more than a thimbleful of precious claret. With overseas trade at a standstill because of the hostilities, everything was in short supply—including money to buy life's necessities. Ware was spending his savings to shelter himself, his daughter and her near-penniless husband during these days when no man could accurately predict what would happen next.

Philip sat down wearily on the battered travel trunk in which Anne had carefully stored the sum of his worldly possessions—three items. The first was a small, worn leather casket with brass corners. It contained letters from James Amberly, Duke of Kentland, to the French actress from Auvergne whom he'd loved and reluctantly left in Paris. The Duke, still alive in England, was Philip's father.

Just the preceding spring, after fruitless and near-fatal attempts to claim the portion of Amberly's fortune which he'd been promised, Philip had finally burned one particular document from the casket. That document was a letter declaring Amberly's intention to share his riches with his illegitimate son. Philip had decided he wanted no part of Amberly's world, in which the rich and the powerful exploited others. Destroying the letter, he'd become an American in spirit as well as in fact.

Also in the trunk was a memento of his boyhood in the French provinces: a splendid sword. The grenadier's briquet had been presented to him by a young nobleman he'd helped out of a difficult situation. The nobleman's title was the Marquis de Lafayette. But Philip would always think of him by one of his given names—Gil. One day, he'd hang Gil's sword in a place of honor above the mantel in his house. Provided he lived long enough to build a house!

The last of the three items was a small bottle of green glass filled with flakes of dried English tea. He'd found the tea in his shoes on the December night in 1773 when he'd joined Samuel Adams' band of bogus Indians and helped destroy three shiploads of tea chests in Boston harbor, as a protest against one of the king's repressive taxes. The souvenir of that evening had another, much more memorable meaning as well. That same night, in his cheap cellar room at the Edes and Gill printing house in Dassett Alley, he had first made love to the young woman he'd married—

The young woman whose condition now tormented him with anxiety.

"How long has she been feverish?" Philip asked his father-in-law.

"Since last evening." Ware's protuberant eyes were doleful. The man had lost weight. Appeared bent; shriveled. He extended the decanter. "You'd better down some of this yourself, lad. You look like you bathed in mud, and your teeth are knocking like a bride's knees."

Philip didn't move. From the hem of his soaked coat, a drop of water plopped to the shabby carpet. The rain beat on the roof.

"Damn it, there's got to be a doctor someplace!" he exclaimed suddenly.

"Not one. I've asked everywhere."

"But we've got to do something! I don't know how to tend a pregnant woman. Annie's liable to die from plain neglect!"

Ware drank, and shivered. "Do you think the possibility hasn't occurred to me? I am as worried as you."

"You're sure there are no doctors here in Watertown?"

"None. They've all gone off to the lines."

"A midwife, then."

"I located one. But she's taken to her bed, out of her wits with grief. Her son was bayoneted to death in the Breed's Hill redoubt. There's no telling whether she'll recover in time for Annie's delivery—and I'd hate to trust my daughter to a woman in such a precarious mental state anyway."

"God, I wish the whole abominable mess were over, so we could go back to living like human beings!"

Ware tried to smile. "Annie would scold you if she heard that, Philip. No, more than scold. Tongue-lash you—and make you like it, as only she knows how—"

His son-in-law didn't answer. Ware's forced smile faded.

Philip jumped up, began pacing. To take his mind off the seemingly insoluble problem of Anne, he asked,

"Has there been any more word on the petition?" He referred to the so-called Olive Branch resolution drafted in Philadelphia before the Congress adjourned. A direct appeal to George III, the petition pleaded for the king to effect a reconciliation before further conflict developed.

Ware shook his head: " 'Twas only dispatched in July. With six to ten weeks of sea travel involved each way, we won't have the answer for a long while, I expect. Besides, you know what that answer will be. It's the king as much as his puppet ministers pushing this break to the limit. Too many fail to understand that fact."

What the lawyer said was true, Philip knew. He'd heard similar views expressed by everyone from Samuel Adams to Dr. Benjamin Franklin, the eminent scientist and diplomat whom he'd known in London and met again in Philadelphia just this past April. No, there wasn't any realistic basis for hoping the fighting would end before his enlistment ran out—

A moment ago, he'd decided not to drink any claret. Now he changed his mind, and poured half a glass. The wine warmed his belly but not his mood.

Ware stifled another sneeze. "I don't doubt that when and if His Majesty replies to the petition, it will be with a 'damned to you, sirs!' I encountered Hancock the other morning. Before the Congress closed its session, there were already rumors afloat that His Majesty has dispatched confidential agents into Europe. To Brunswick, Anspach, Hesse-Hanau—"

Philip shook his head, not understanding.

"Those are principalities in Germany. There, the house of Hanover would find receptive ears."

"Receptive to what?"

"A plea for troops, perhaps. Troops to crush the rebellion."

"Would the Germans ally themselves with Britain?"

"For money they might. If that should ever happen,

82

there would be no turning back."

"Well, all I care about is Anne. I've got to find *someone*—"

"I will continue my inquiries. I don't hold out great hope. I—" Abruptly, Ware was seized with a long, wheezing cough that drained every last bit of color from his sunken cheeks.

"Perhaps you ought to be in bed too, sir," Philip said.

Ware rejected the suggestion emphatically: "I know you must return to the lines soon. I'll watch Annie after you've gone. Don't think you need stay here and chatter with me, Philip. Go where you want to be—in there with her."

Philip thanked him and left the room.

He sat at the bedside for almost an hour, holding his wife's hand and listening to her stertorous breathing. She cried out whenever pains in her belly twisted her from side to side. Philip's own hands were chill and stiff by the time he heard the small parlor clock chime eleven. He'd be almost an hour late returning to the encampment—

"Annie. *Annie.*" He felt so helpless, no other words would come.

She didn't answer. He crept out.

Lawyer Ware had fallen into a drowse, his mouth hanging open. Philip bundled himself into his damp coat and let himself out, sick with fright as he half walked, half ran through the rainy September darkness.

iii

Two days later, the sky cleared and the British batteries started rumbling again.

In the mellow twilight, Philip sat on the ground outside his quarters, trying to bite through the petrified leather that passed for the day's ration of corned beef. Even washing the stuff down with the locally brewed spruce beer that was regular issue failed to make it more palatable. At least the royal troops in Boston were faring no better. The American soldiers had guffawed over a story about a prominent officer, the Earl of Percy. The Earl had given an elaborate dinner at which, by necessity, the main dish was roast colt.

On the ground next to Philip lay a scrawled note from Abraham Ware. The note had arrived earlier in the day. It reported that Anne's fever had broken but she remained weak, and was asking for him. It would be two more nights before Philip could get leave to return to Watertown—

An elongated shadow fell across his legs. He glanced up and started, spilling his mug of beer. An immense, gangly figure silhouetted against the sinking sun warned him of danger—

Until he recognized the face, and saw it bore no signs of malice.

A vast display of crooked teeth partially masked a certain shyness as the Virginian with the cocked·eye and unmercifully ugly countenance scratched at his scrotum and shifted from foot to foot. In one hand the man carried his Kentucky rifle. At last he said:

"Hello."

Philip's nod was cautious. "Hello."

A long silence. Then:

"Got sent to Cambridge with a dispatch. Got lost on the way back. Seen you sittin' there. Figured I should stop and say thanks for keepin' me from gettin' kilt the other night."

Philip waved. "I doubt that drunk would have done much damage."

"Listen, he could of busted my neck, coming at me like he did. I'm obliged to you."

"Did you boys get punished pretty severely?"

"Damn if we didn't," said the other, in slow, soft speech that contrasted with Philip's somewhat more nasal New England tone. "We're down to half rations and confined to quarters 'cept while we're on duty or 'ficial business. Next time any of us bust out, Squire Washington says he's gonna put the cat on our backs. And when that man promises, he don't forget." The tall frontiersman spat once, eloquent emphasis.

"Gather you think he's a pretty good soldier."

"They don't make 'em no damn better. The difference 'tween the colonel—I mean the general—and some o' them peacocks on his staff like that Charlie Lee is this. When Washington takes the wrong fork once, he don't ever do it again. He ain't perfect, but he's got balls, and he knows woods fightin', too. That may count for more than all the fancy-dancy soldierin' that's been done by Lee and his crowd. By the way—" The ugly man extended a callused hand. "Been jawing and jawing and ain't even said hello proper. I'm Experience Tait of Albemarle County. Most call me Eph."

They shook. "Kent's my name. Philip Kent."

"Well, you're a little rooster, but you fight pretty good—" Tait grinned. "For a wise man."

"Thanks. From a Virginian, that's a real compliment."

"Well—" Tait spat again. "Guess I better haul shanks. 'Ficial business, y'know. And soon's I get back, I'm 'sposed to sew up a lieutenant's hand. Fuckin' fool can't handle his own sword proper—be seein' you, mebbe—"

Philip ran after the backwoodsman. "Wait a minute, Mr. Tait."

"Eph, I said it's Eph."

"You also said something about sewing up a hand. You—you're not any kind of doctor?"

"Only the back country kind," Tait shrugged. "I do smithing, barbering, mix up tonics to cure boils and minor complaints of the bowels, minister to expectant heifers an' women, includin' my wife—little of everything, guess you could say. In the Blue Ridge, a man's

85

got to know a smatter of this and a smatter of that just to stay alive."

A lump had formed in Philip's throat. He was almost afraid to speak for fear he'd be refused. But the hesitation didn't last:

"Eph, would you have a minute to share a drink of spruce beer?"

Tait reflected. "Well—no more'n a minute. But I drink fast," he grinned. "Fast as I shoot with this thing—"

He lifted the long, beautiful muzzle loader with its grooved barrel: the rifling that imparted such speed, distance and accuracy to the balls it discharged.

Philip gestured. "Come on, then—"

Experience Tait cocked his one good eye at the entrance to Philip's shanty. "There's some of your friends inside, ain't they? Will we have a set-to? Much as I wouldn't mind one, I cain't afford 'nother fight."

"I'll fetch the beer and we'll drink it out here. I've a favor to ask, Eph—if you're really serious about thanking me."

"Shit, I ain't goin' to pay or nothin', if that's what you mean," Eph Tait returned with a grin abruptly tempered by suspicion.

"No, it's something else. And you're the man to do it."

"Don't sound good," Tait commented as Philip ducked inside. "They warned us to stay away from twisty wise men. Trick the buttons right off a man's pants, you Massachusetts fellas. Least that's what we got told—"

But he leaned on his Kentucky rifle in the sunset light, and waited for the beer anyway.

iv

Philip walked up and down, up and down—just as he'd been doing for half an hour.

At first, between sneezes and swallows of the dwindling claret, Lawyer Ware had expressed annoyance. But when Philip showed no signs of calming down, the little man drained the rest of the decanter and went to sleep after a final tense glance at the closed door.

Philip had been alternately walking and sitting for about three hours. His eyes itched. His clothing stank. His stomach hurt. He hadn't eaten since early morning. The clock ticked loud as the strokes of judgment sounding—

Quit thinking such morbid thoughts! Philip chastised himself. But he couldn't help it. All he loved or cared about in the world lay hidden from his sight behind the bedroom door. Occasionally he heard a small sound. Water sloshing. A stifled cry from Anne. The murmur of another voice. His mind built monstrous imaginings—

Death.

Deformity.

An outcome so devastating, she would never want to have another—

A squall rooted Philip to the carpet. His scalp crawled. White-faced, he stared at the closed door.

The squalling gurgled away to silence.

Philip wiped his stubbled cheek, crossed the room to where his father-in-law was on the point of sliding out of his chair. Philip shook him.

Ware grumbled, smacked his lips. Philip shook him again, still staring in hypnotic fascination at that door. *Why was there no more sound?*

Suddenly Lawyer Ware bolted up. "My God, what's happened? Is Annie—?"

Before he could finish, the door was open. Experience Tait said:

"What's happened is, everybody done a good job—me and your wife and the Almighty and the youngster too. He come out kickin' and I'm thirsty as hell. If you ain't got any likker in this place, somebody go fetch some because I figure I deserve some kind o' reward for my first-class work." As he spoke, the tall Virginian wiped his hands and forearms on the large piece of rag tied around his waist. The lean hands and big-boned arms left bright blood on the rag. The long hilt of a skinning knife stuck up from his belt.

"Well, go on, go on!" Eph Tait waved to Philip, exasperated. "Don't you want to see your own child? An' you, you runt," he added to Ware, "go find me that drink!"

Ware licked his lips, bulging eyes on the doorway. "Is—is she—?"

"Fine, fine! But she wants to see *him*, not you. God!" he sighed to a still-stunned Philip. "You're some husband—get a move on!"

Philip looked swiftly at the clock. A quarter past twelve. At a quarter past twelve on the morning of September 29, 1775, in Watertown, Massachusetts, his son had been born—yes, Experience Tait had distinctly said *he*—

Philip pushed past the bloodied, craze-eyed woodsman lounging against the jamb. From the bedroom's dimness he heard the miraculous sound of an infant making moist sucking sounds.

"*Annie?*" he bellowed.

"Jesus blue lightning, don't jump all over her!" Tait shouted behind him. Philip paid no attention. For the second time in his adult life, loudly and without shame, he was crying.

v

Anne Ware Kent was awake, propped up on the bolster and several rolled blankets. Philip knelt beside two basins of pink-tinged water. In one of them floated something that resembled a short piece of bloody rope.

Anne looked sleepy and pale. Yet there was a ra-

88

diance to her face. In the crook of one arm she cradled a small, rag-wrapped bundle from which protruded a reddish gnome's head almost as sinfully ugly as Eph Tait.

Philip couldn't find words. He reached one trembling hand toward a miniature fist whose longest finger was shorter than his thumb from knuckle to nail.

"You can touch him," Anne said softly, smiling. "He's yours, after all."

Marveling, Philip stroked the clutching little fist. The child whose head was capped with dark fuzz promptly screwed up its face and shrieked.

Comforting the baby with wordless murmurs, Anne gazed lovingly at her husband. "We must name him, Philip. Have you thought—?"

"Some. I'd like him to be called Abraham, if that's all right."

"Papa would be pleased."

"Did—did you hurt a lot?"

"Oh, enough." Again the drowsy smile. "But Mr. Tait is a gentle man. His hands look so big but his fingers are as supple as a woman's. Where ever did you find him?"

"In the mud."

"What?"

"I'll tell you another time. He's a Virginian, just like General Washington."

"So he told me—I think. I don't remember everything."

"What's this?" Philip said, picking up a length of fresh-whittled wood from the floor. The wood bore teeth marks.

Anne focused on the wood with difficulty. "I had to bite on that when the pains were strongest. Mr. Tait doesn't believe in giving wine or beer during deliveries. But he must have quite a thirst himself. All he could speak of was hurrying matters along so he could swallow his pay. Philip—" Anne began to rock the infant gently. The fuzzed head all but disappeared under folds of rag. "How is it with you?"

"Bearable. Lonesome without you. The days just drag and drag—"

"No action on either side?"

"Shelling from the British, that's all. Washington sent an expedition against Canada earlier this month. I'm not sure whether it'll accomplish anything—or is supposed to. But all the men in camp—fifteen, twenty thousand by now—they're getting restive. Either the British will break out of Boston, or we'll overwhelm them and drive them out. It has to be one or the other, unless there's a settlement."

"A few days ago Papa said he thought any such hope was foolish."

"I think so too. But my eight months will be up at the end of the year, and it won't matter after that. I'll be with you all the time."

Her voice surprisingly clear, Anne said quietly, "What do you mean?"

"I mean when my enlistment's finished, so am I. The colonies can't win a war against Great Britain."

"I agree—not with men who go home." Her brown eyes sparked; the Anne he remembered.

"Annie, for God's sake—!" he protested. "I'm a father now. With responsibilities—"

"I doubt you're the only father in the colonial army."

"But we've the future to think about!"

"Exactly what do you propose to do, Philip? Turn Tory?"

"Annie—!"

"I mean it. What are your plans?" She was challenging him, and he knew what it must be costing her in terms of discomfort. Her body shifted frequently beneath the covers Eph Tait had tucked neatly back into place. "Do you want to creep back to Boston and set up a press to print pamphlets supporting the king? I'd hate to tell our son that, wouldn't you?"

"Annie, you know as well as I do—this rebellion has no support at all! Everyone says less than a third of the people in the colonies are in favor of it—"

"Does that make it wrong?"

"Of course not, but—"

"Does that give you leave to quit?"

"Dear God, you're stubborn!"

"Yes, because when you came back from Philadelphia this spring, you made a decision. You chose your side. Will you forget that so quickly when things grow difficult? The man I thought I married wouldn't forget it."

Stung, he colored. There was a moment of strained silence. Then Philip let out a long sigh, and nodded:

"I guess you're right. I'm sorry."

With one of those tart yet loving smiles he knew so well, she said, "You're forgiven. I don't blame you for wavering. Papa's told me about the wretched conditions and poor discipline in the army—"

"The *army* doesn't even deserve the name. It seems all you can think about in camp is the next minute, then the next one after that. You eat, sleep, dig, dodge cannon shot—you lose track of what it's all about."

Still smiling, she touched his face. "That's why you need a wife, my darling."

He laughed, the tension broken. Just as during their sometimes-stormy courtship, it was Anne who put his frequently muddled and imperfect thinking into proper order and focus. That was just one of the many reasons he loved her so much.

She saw he was still troubled, though:

"Don't worry, we won't lose track of what we've planned for Abraham. A good house for our family—your own printing establishment—Kent and Son. How does that sound?"

"Grander than anything in this world." He hugged her. The baby began to squall again.

Humming a little, Anne soothed the newborn infant back to sleep. Awestruck, Philip stared at the lumpy bundle that represented his flesh and hers. He knew he was only one man among multitudes who had experienced the same supreme moment of joy and wonder down through the centuries. Yet he couldn't help feeling moved, as if he were biblical Adam gazing on creation's first-born son—

"By God," he breathed at last, "he is a big boy, isn't he?"

"Seven or eight pounds, Mr. Tait said. But I wish you wouldn't look at him quite so much."

Philip's eyebrows shot up. "Why not?"

Warm and loving, she caressed his face again.

"Because I'd like for you to kiss me."

vi

When Philip and Experience Tait walked back toward the American lines at dawn, Philip told his new friend that he'd changed his mind. If the war should last beyond December, he would re-enlist.

Tait's crazed eye seemed to glow like a small moon in the first flush of eastern light. "Damn fool," was his reply. "That's how fine young girls like your wife turn into widders. Guess I'll do the same thing, though."

"You said you had a wife didn't you, Eph?"

"Yep. And fourteen youngsters back in Albemarle County."

"Fourteen! My Lord, you don't look that old."

"Started when I was fourteen years old. Besides, it ain't how old, it's how stiff." He gave Philip a lewd nudge in the ribs, and belched. Presently, noticing Philip's dour look, he asked:

"What the hell's got you down now?"

"Oh, just that I really thought about quitting—until Annie helped me see things straight again."

"Heck, don't feel bad. I'd sooner be back home huntin', far as that goes. The Blue Ridge is mighty pretty this time of year. And it's too dang cold up in these parts. But I guess I'd rather have my kin remember me as a fella who died free an' sassy, instead of kissin' that old Dutchman's royal ass just to stay alive."

"That's about how Anne put it," Philip told him.

"Oh hell no she didn't!" Eph said. "She's a lady. Ladies don't cuss half as colorful as us Virginians."

"You're right about that," Philip said with a tired smile. Far away, he heard the ominous thump of the Boston batteries beginning the day's bombardment. The sound erased the smile as if it had never existed.

CHAPTER IV

The Uprising

DONALD FLETCHER'S hired coach brought the weary delegate back to Sermon Hill in mid-August. The father's greeting of his elder son was brief and perfunctory. What few meals the three family members took together in the long, airy dining room of the main house were strained and virtually devoid of conversation.

Donald, a steady-minded but phlegmatic man, took to spending most of his holiday in his younger brother's company. Whenever possible, the two snatched meals in the great kitchen, away from Angus. The company of the black housewomen who tended the huge iron stove and brick hearth was far more relaxing.

In Judson's opinion Donald didn't look well. He'd gained weight. His normally soft face was puffier than ever. His eyes were perpetually reddened with fatigue, and he could neither mount nor dismount without the assistance of a slave at the stirrup. From mid-calf downward, his left leg was swathed in heavy bandages. Yet he persisted in drinking the wine the physicians claimed only worsened his gout.

Donald had married late, at age thirty. His wife, the daughter of a prosperous tobacco factor with headquarters in Richmond, had gone to her childbed thirteen months later—and both she and her infant daughter had died there. After that, Donald's only pleasure or release seemed to lie in his involvement in the political affairs of the colony. This in itself guaranteed continual strain at Sermon Hill.

Angus Fletcher refused to discuss either politics or the management of the property with his older son, even though Sermon Hill, at least, should have been a subject of frequent conversation. Theoretically Donald would inherit when the old man died. In private, Donald told Judson that he suspected Angus had already entertained thoughts about altering his will. In fact, he believed Angus might well have Sermon Hill sold off after his death, the proceeds to be distributed among an assortment of distant relatives still living in Scotland. Their names and whereabouts were carefully recorded in the family Bible Angus kept at his bedside, Donald said. Angus had shown him the list of relatives several times. Perhaps as a threat.

Donald seemed resigned to whatever happened. Besides, he was interested in more significant matters. These came up for discussion one muggy day in early September.

The brothers were taking a turn around the countryside on their horses. Near noon, they ended the ride at the wharf beside the river. Three plantation wagons were being unloaded by blacks under the supervision of Reuven Shaw's drivers—specially appointed slaves who served as his assistants. As the brothers rode down the pier, Judson noticed many a black face turned in their direction. He also saw not a few resentful stares.

"Lord, you can almost smell the anger," Donald said, his voice heavy with the wheeze he'd developed in Philadelphia.

"Yes, but the old man won't stay Shaw's hand one iota."

"I understand they caught the nigger with the drum."

Judson nodded, his blue eyes ranging along the hazed river. By this time of year, the hand-hewn tobacco canoes should have appeared—forty feet long, five wide

95

and lashed together in threes and fives to carry big loads. Because of the trouble, no one as yet knew whether the canoes would come to load the casks. The agents of the factors—most of whom were Tory sympathizers—hadn't shown up at the plantations in the neighborhood to begin finalizing purchases.

"Who had it?" Donald asked.

"The drum? One of Seth McLean's field hands. Built it on the sly, out of woodshed scraps and a goatskin. Seth burned it, then had fifty laid on the culprit. The punishment damn near crippled the man. It wasn't much easier on Seth. But he said it had to be done."

Donald scratched his veined nose as Judson walked around and helped him dismount. In the process, Donald nearly fell.

Leaning on his younger brother, he hobbled toward the end of the wharf where the Rappahannock lapped softly. The sky was graying in the northwest, promising storm before the afternoon was over.

Donald tried his best to stand upright, bracing himself on the cane he always carried. Without looking at Judson, he said:

"You don't sound convinced that Seth did the right thing."

"Living around this place, how can you be certain of anything? Except the old man's dislike for both of us."

Donald chose to let that go for the moment. "Is Seth of the opinion the slave problem's quieted, then?"

"Gone under the surface, would be more like it." Judson slapped a gnat on his sweaty neck, turned to stare into the west, a blur of hills beneath the blackening clouds. His expression conveyed his disgust over the entire situation.

Donald shifted his weight to favor his bandaged foot. "If you find Sermon Hill so opprobrious, why do you stay on?"

The younger brother shrugged. "Where would I go

instead?"

"That's what I wish to discuss with you."

Judson's head snapped up, his blue eyes hooding with suspicion; Donald had sounded almost schoolmasterish. He, in turn, saw Judson's temper flaring. He held up a hand to reassure him:

"Surely you've expected it. The old man's been quite pointed in the few talks I've had with him. You're drinking too much. And he says you're worthless—wait, that's his word, not mine—when it comes to running the place."

"I wouldn't deny that," Judson replied coldly.

"Then what does keep you here?" Donald's face showed sympathy. "McLean's wife?"

"Goddamn it, Donald, you know that's over!"

"On a practical basis, of course I do. But a man doesn't heal a wound in his heart all that easily. I speak from some experience," he added after a moment. "However, I won't press you if you prefer not to speak about it."

That was good, Judson thought sourly, because he'd only have been forced to tell more lies. And it was hard to lie to the one member of the family with whom he could discuss things on a halfway intimate basis. Hard, but not impossible. Very few actions frowned on by so-called respectable people were impossible for him any more.

"Jud," Donald resumed, leaning on his cane and staring at the river turning glassy under the fast-moving clouds, "this siege between you and Father will only come to a bad end. You need to leave Sermon Hill for a while."

"I repeat—to go where?"

"I've a suggestion about that. Nothing definite as yet, but I feel compelled to mention the idea for your sake as well as mine."

Judson sat down on the end of the Wharf, lolling one

of his expensive Russian leather boots in and out of the water. Behind him, he heard the grunting of the blacks unloading the huge casks of cured leaves. One of the drivers shouted angrily. A whip popped twice. The offender yelped. Judson preferred not to turn and look. He waited for Donald to continue:

"As you know, I must return to Philadelphia in a week or two. The long hours of the Congress, the rich food, the drinking—they haven't served me well. I lay abed three weeks during the last session. I got about the rest of the time only with great difficulty. There's important work to be done when the delegates reconvene—particularly if the king rejects the petition on reconciliation. I'd like to go north confident that if my strength fails, someone trustworthy could be appointed to fill my seat."

Realizing at last what his brother was getting at, Judson almost burst out laughing. Donald's intense, pain-wracked expression checked the impulse. Judson said instead:

"You mean I'd be your replacement?"

"If a replacement became necessary, yes."

Stunned by the idea, Judson sat in silence. Finally he shook his head:

"I'm flattered you'd even consider me, Donald. But I doubt very much that the members of your delegation would welcome someone like me." A mocking smile. "A gentleman who's seldom sober, and hence surely doesn't deserve the name."

"But you are my brother. More important, your politics are proper."

"If not my morals?"

"See here, do you suppose the morals of the delegates are all that spotless? I've sat at table with Dr. Franklin and watched him turn to stone consuming Madeira. I'm not attending a conclave of angels, you know—only of men. So long as you create no public scandal—stay

98

within the bounds of decency—"

Amused, Judson said, "For years I've been trying to find out where those are located. Every man places 'em differently, it seems." He pondered a bit longer. "You know, I wouldn't want to wish you ill—but I will admit the possibility's intriguing."

"Good."

"In fact I'd be more than happy to get away from this damned place for such a purpose. Still, can you just— just wave your hand and appoint me to attend in your stead?"

"Naturally not. You'd have to be duly elected to the delegation. But there's precedent. Richard Henry Lee saw to the election of his brother, Francis Lightfoot, when old Bland had to come home because of his infirmities. With words in the proper ears, I could swing it. I'm on good terms with Tom Jefferson of Albemarle County, for instance. He's highly respected despite his youth—yes, I could definitely swing it. Mind you, I'm not saying it *will* become necessary. But I'd rest easier up there knowing that if this blasted gout does lay me low again, my place would be occupied by a man who's as determined as I am to stand fast against the king and his ministers."

For a moment Judson was tempted; exceedingly tempted. To his private shame, he nearly wished that his older brother would be incapacitated. Then reality took over. He shook his head again:

"Oh, I don't think it would work, Donald. I have no experience in politics."

"I realize that. Some of the other delegates are pretty short on it themselves. I want to say something else, Jud. I say it as a brother who feels affection for you. Eventually, you're going to have to decide what you are—and where you belong. The kind of life you're leading now—surely it brings you no real pleasure—"

"I hate it, for Christ's sake," Judson said savagely.

99

"But as to what I am—that's been settled up at the big house."

"Then at least don't shut out a possibility that might relieve the situation. All I want today is your pledge that I can depend on you if I need you."

Westward, fast-flying clouds showed flickering white light. Judson watched the bleached wood of the pier dot with the first raindrops.

"All right," he said with a wry shrug that concealed a feeling of futility. Donald had probed the painful riddle that Judson struggled with for hours on end. He knew he didn't belong here at Sermon Hill, where his father's disapproval and the nearness of Peggy Ashford McLean were constant torments. But just as certainly, he didn't belong in the learned councils of the patriots in Philadelphia.

Where, then?

Where?

He stared morosely at the lightning-ridden clouds on the western horizon, confronting again the damning truth:

He was a misfit. His father hadn't been entirely wrong when he claimed that devil's blood ran in his son's veins. And to make matters worse, not only did Judson not know where he belonged in the world, he didn't know how to find out.

The closing of Donald's fingers on his shoulder took him by surprise. The compassionate look in Donald's tired, reddened eyes startled him, then filled him with a warmth he hadn't experienced in—Lord, it must be years.

"Thank you," Donald said.

"You've made a wretched mistake, you know," Judson laughed with a false heartiness, helping Donald hobble back to the horses.

"Who can be sure? You might discover you have a flair for oratory and backstairs finagling. Besides, while the winters in Philadelphia are miserable, I understand the ladies are quite flirtatious."

"You understand? Haven't you persuaded even one to tumble into bed with you?"

Donald responded to the teasing with a grimace. "I fear these damned bandages would prove—hampering, shall we say? You, though—that's another story. See what you have to look forward to?"

"You haven't mentioned this to the old man, have you, Donald?"

"What would be the purpose? It's merely a contingency."

"Contingency or no, please do me a favor and keep it private. Otherwise I'll be rousted to camp in the fields."

Donald laughed. "I suspect you're right. I'll keep quiet."

The first of the empty wagons was pulling away as they mounted in the pattering rain. The huge casks were somber reminders of the canoes that might never come.

One buck in the second wagon glared at them when they rode by. Wincing with pain, Donald didn't see. Judson pretended he didn't either.

ii

In the second week of September, Donald Fletcher left in a coach, heartened by a letter from his friend Tom Jefferson. The letter said that, for the first time, the Congress might soon represent all thirteen separate political entities up and down the eastern seaboard. Reluctant Georgia was apparently planning to dispatch a delegation at last.

After Donald departed, Judson was also the recipient of an unexpected communication: four closely written foolscap pages dated almost eight months earlier, and wrapped inside a pouch one of the Clark boys brought to Sermon Hill. The letter was one of a packet that had been sent east by Judson's friend George. The packet had been posted at Pittsburgh.

The Clark boy said George had informed his family that he was well and in good spirits. As a member of the Virginia frontier militia, he had scouted for the royal governor, the Earl of Dunmore, in sharp action against the "savages" late the preceding year.

Dunmore had personally gone across the mountains at the head of an expeditionary force numbering a thousand men. His purpose was to put down raiding by the Indian tribes. The raiding had been provoked by Dunmore's own seizure of land in western Pennsylvania, and by the arrival of settlers in the country below the river with the Indian name—Ohio.

In the letter directed to Judson, George Clark wrote of a successful military engagement at a place called Point Pleasant. There, a Shawnee war chief named Cornstalk and his followers had been decisively defeated. Most of the rest of the letter concerned itself with the breathtaking beauty of the wilderness south of the Ohio.

On earlier expeditions, George Clark had looked at its dark, lush shores from a poplar canoe. But now, at last, he had set foot in Kentucky, and explored it.

The letter described strange, eerie marsh hollows where animals stole down to lick at frosty-white deposits of salt, and woodsmen marveled at bones thrusting up from the ooze. George wrote that he had personally seen time-bleached ribs as long as the roof pole of a cabin, and thigh bones thick as tree trunks:

I believe we gazed upon the remains of phenomenal Beasts which may have roamed our earth before the coming of the human kind. At least I have never heard of skeletons so immense, save in fanciful tales.

Judson's mind couldn't quite comprehend such a

bizarre curiosity. But he knew George Clark would never invent a story merely to impress him. He actually felt a thrill of awe down his spine as he read the passage.

Kentucky, already divided into three large counties which nominally belonged to Virginia, now boasted several white settlements. In 1769, a man from the back country of North Carolina had crossed the barrier mountains to explore the territory. Subsequently, he'd led members of his family to the rich new land. The Boone clan had journeyed through the notch in the mountains called Cumberland Gap, and established a few isolated stockades.

Inhabitants of the frontier outposts lived with constant danger. The reason was simple: Kentucky had long been a hunting ground for the Creek and Cherokee tribes who ranged up from the south—and also for the more ferocious Miamis, Shawnee and Wyandots who claimed the forests north of the Ohio. In spite of the threat of Indian attacks from two directions, Clark saw the Kentucky wilderness as a promised land for men of free spirit:

Such spacious domains, my friend, have doubtless never before been viewed by Human eyes. Here is land where a man can breathe sweet, untainted air. Stroll all day through forests with branches that arch overhead like the vaults of Cathedrals. The limestone soil is fertile, and game astonishing in its abundance. Fat Turkeys of gold and purple—Buffalo grazing the canebrake which rises taller than a rider on horseback—Elk and Deer beyond counting—Paradise, notwithstanding its perils. In Kentucky a man relies solely upon Himself and a few trusted Comrades of like mind. It is here, I may say with conviction, that I have found both Beauty to entrance the Soul, and vast spaces whose exploration and defense give purpose to my Life at last.

The letter closed with a brief but sincere wish that Judson was in good health, and that George Rogers Clark might again share his experiences in person, if ever the mounting conflict with England gave him reason to return to the Virginia colony which had taken so much of the western forest in its own name.

The letter fired Judson's imagination just as George's two visits had done. It also filled him with a heightened loneliness, and a sense of deepening confusion. At a river-front inn, he withdrew to a corner and read the foolscap pages again and again. Rum helped paint vivid pictures of his lanky, red-haired friend striding along under those immense green arches, smoothbore over his shoulder, listening to the wild bird calls and sharing the friendship of a night campfire. The names rolled sonorously in Judson's inner ear—

Pittsburgh.

Kentucky.

Ohio.

Shawnee.

By their very sketchiness in his own mind, the lands beyond the Blue Wall became richer and more colorful moment by moment; then day by day.

More painful to think about, too.

He took a trip to Richmond. The trip had no purpose other than to allow him to spend the better part of two days in bed with a cheerful whore who didn't constantly whine for demonstrations of affection, the way Lottie Shaw did. On the trip he heard that George Clark had indeed acquitted himself well in the battle at Point Pleasant. His name was mentioned in the taverns along with those of other well-known frontiersmen—Kenton, Girty, Boone. Thanks to men like George, Lord Dunmore's western war had been a success. God alone knew when Judson Fletcher would be able to say the same about his own existence.

In early November, Donald sent Judson a letter saying that grim news had arrived on a transatlantic schooner recently docked at Philadelphia. In August, George III had refused to receive the petition for reconciliation, and formally proclaimed the American colonies in open rebellion. Said Donald:

Such as John Adams of Mass. Bay are jubilant. It is plain that we shall soon be past the point of possible compromise, if we are not already. I was advised of the unhappy turn of events while at rest in my quarters. The d——d gout has once again confined me, together with what one of the local croakers diagnoses as a congestion in the breathing passages, brought on by exposure to a prolonged spell of wet, foul weather.

"The vile, perfidious spawn of Satan!" Angust Fletcher cried, much too exercised to touch the hog cutlet and greens on his plate. "The wretched, deceiving miscreant!" The old man bunched his fingers and hit the polished dining table so hard the candle-glasses rattled. A spoon fell to the pegged floor.

Into his fourth or fifth glass of claret, Judson Fletcher lounged in his chair at the opposite end of the long dinner table. A nervous house black stepped forward to retrieve the spoon. He retreated when Angus glared.

Muttering private curses, the old man covered his eyes with both hands. The tall windows of the dimly lit room were open on the November dark. The evening was unusually warm; Judson's neck cloth was undone.

"And all along I thought you and His Excellency were kindred souls," he said.

Angus Fletcher whipped his hands down. "I need no clack from you, you damned young traitor."

Judson smiled. "Strikes me it's Lord Dunmore who's the traitor to those who thought him a friend. That he'd try to recruit a loyalist army is to be expected. But promising freedom to any nigra who deserts his master to join—that's a delightful fillip, to say the least. After Seth heard the news, he was talking like the hottest rebel."

Livid, Angus opened his mouth to reply. He was so upset, he couldn't say a word. Judson glanced away, momentarily ashamed of himself.

Yet he hadn't held back, had he?

The opportunity was just too rich. In one stroke, the Tory governor had undercut the very planters who were his strongest adherents. Men like Seth McLean could switch sides quickly when their economic position was threatened. But Angus, believing both in the slave system and the authority of the king, was not so flexible. He'd been suffering ever since the surprising announcement had been circulated in the neighborhood the preceding day.

"I'd expect you to relish my discomfort," Angus snarled at his son. "To gloat—because you've no brains in your head! No notion of the turmoil Dunmore may have unleashed. We put the lid on the kettle that was stewing all summer. Now the damn fool's pulled it off again. Only Jehovah in His wisdom knows what will—"

Boots rapped on the pegged floor. Judson swung around.

Looking apologetic, Reuven Shaw stood just inside one of the tall windows. His long blacksnake whip was draped over his left shoulder and under his right armpit.

"Blast you, Shaw," Angus said, "you're never to interrupt my dinner and you know it."

Shaw seemed unnaturally pale. "Yessir, I realize, but—" The overseer swallowed. "Number two curing

106

barn's afire."

The room was absolutely still. Angus turned as white as Shaw:

"Afire?"

"Yessir. I been smellin' something comin' all day. The niggers been jumpy as hell. I got a gang working to control the fire, but—"

Angus leaped up. "The niggers set it?"

"Who else, Mr. Fletcher? Half the bucks ain't in their cabins. Sneaked out after sunset, I reckon—"

Judson felt no further impulse to laugh. Outside, behind the overseer, a dull red glare was rising. He heard strident voices through the November darkness.

"Sneaked out!" Angus thundered. "Don't you have anyone watching to prevent that? Who's your driver tonight? Why didn't he sound the alarm?"

Reuven Shaw wiped a hand across his mouth. "My driver tonight was Beau. You know Beau—a good nigger. I just found him by the pond. His body was lyin' on the bank, an' his head—his head was floatin' in—"

Shaw stopped, looking nauseated.

Well he might, Judson thought, chilled despite the mildness of the evening. There had been occasional slave rebellions throughout the southern colonies in the past. Not many. But each one was usually disastrous, at least at first, because the white owners and overseers were numerically inferior.

"You mean to tell me niggers are loose with field knives?" Angus whispered.

Again Shaw nodded, sick-faced. "Guess that's how they butchered Beau. Larned, he's gone for sure. I checked."

Judson saluted Shaw with his goblet. "Congratulations. I was told you hided him twice this afternoon."

"Sassy bastard kept braggin' he was gonna enlist in Dunmore's nigger army. I shoulda castrated him last

107

summer, 'fore this got out of hand."

"Well, it obviously *is* out of hand," Angus seethed. "Why haven't I heard the bell?"

"I come to report first. There ain't much we can do to save number two barn—"

"Go ring the goddamned bell!" Angus screamed. "We've got to turn out every white man on the river before this spreads!"

The old man's profanity indicated the depth of his fear. The house black who had been waiting on table had disappeared, Judson noticed. Angus dashed from the dining room, headed for his office. His passage made the flames of the candles jump and cast distorted shadows of Judson rising from his chair.

On his way out, the overseer gave the younger man a questioning look.

"If you're counting on me to help slaughter the nigras—" Judson realized he was more than slightly drunk. He had trouble articulating the last word:

"Don't."

Shaw scowled. "Like Mr. Fletcher said, we need every man—"

Judson waved. "Shit. I didn't bring this on. I won't help finish it."

Reuven Shaw trembled, but not from fear. He gathered spit in his mouth and blew a gob onto the pegged floor. Then he spun and ran into the red-glaring dark.

Judson tossed off the last of his wine. He was setting the fine crystal goblet on the polished table when he heard a hideous shriek from out on the grounds.

He bolted for the window, raced down the lawn toward the rear corner of the big house. Beyond it he saw flames leaping from the curing barn, and terrified bucks and wenches running to and fro, adding their hysteria to the din. Other male slaves were trying to round up the frightened ones with profane shouts or,

108

in some cases, drivers' whips.

Before Judson reached the corner of the house, his boots struck something in the neatly scythed grass. He halted, crouched down, tasted vomit in his throat—

Reuven Shaw, lying crooked as a doll. The overseer was dead. An immense gash had been cut in his throat. The distant firelight lit the still-wet blood drenching his right sleeve and the front of his coarse shirt.

Out back, the alarm bell on its great iron Y began to toll—but not before Judson heard a stirring up on his left, in the dark near the unlighted windows of the conservatory.

"Jesus God—!" he breathed, lurching to his feet as an ebony figure shot toward him from the shadowy concealment. Firelight glittered on one of the knives used to chop off the leaves at harvest.

The black man was red to the elbows. Judson's sotted mind screamed the danger. Somehow he managed to duck as the frenzied face loomed, white teeth and eyes glaring. The long knife slashed in an arc where Judson's head had been a moment before.

He dropped to his knees, grappled for the slave's ragged trousers. A work-toughened hand clasped his throat, cutting off his air. He heard the guttural breathing of his attacker, then the *whissh* of the knife hacking at his throat—

Wildly, Judson wrenched free and rolled. The slave jumped after him, hacked again. The blade struck Judson's left boot, cut through the leather but didn't break the skin. The renegade slave's downward stroke had thrown him off balance. Judson sprang up, used his head to butt the black in the stomach. In seconds, fright had torn the cobwebs out of his mind.

The slave pitched over backwards. He cursed Judson in West African dialect. The cursing ended in a yelp as Judson stamped on the slave's wrist. The gory right hand opened. The field knife was loose. Judson snatched it up, leaped back, panting—

A shadow fell across the lawn from the dining room. Judson whipped his head around, saw his father with his sword buckled on and a British-made horse pistol in each hand.

"Kill him," Angus ordered as the terrified slave struggled to rise.

Judson hesitated. Angus made a sound deep in his throat; a wordless condemnation. In two steps he reached the floundering slave, who blocked his face with his scarlet forearms, shrieking, "Mist' Fletcher —*don'*—"

Angus shoved the horse pistol against the slave's chest and fired.

Clang and *clang*, the Sermon Hill bell spread its message of terror through the still November night. Angus treated his son to one final glare of utter loathing, then disappeared around the corner of the house, on the run.

Judson turned his back on the grisly corpse with the huge, dripping cavity in the chest. The curing barn collapsed in a crash of burning timbers and sky-spraying sparks. The slaves were being whipped into submission by the black drivers; being formed up into bucket lines that stretched from the springhouse. He heard two more shots, new screaming—and then, off across the fields, a series of ululating yells that sent worms of horror gnawing through his mind.

The renegade slaves were loose not just at Sermon Hill, but out in the countryside—

That made him run like a man demented.

Upstairs first, for his own horse pistol and the knife for the sheath in his boot. Then through the red confusion to the stable, where he flung a saddle on his roan, trying not to hear the pitiless crack of the whips beating the less able-bodied slaves back to their cabins.

The fire seemed under control now. It had spread to the roofs of the other curing barns, but slaves on ladders were dousing the flames with buckets of water. Judson mounted, jerked the roan's head savagely, galloped past the cabins and down to the main road.

At a crossroads he encountered a dozen men from neighboring estates, all summoned by the bell. They reined in, shouting questions at him.

"Stand aside!"

When they didn't, he booted the roan, jumped the roadside ditch and thundered by along the shoulder, tortured by what he saw through the trees in the distance.

Seth McLean's house. Ablaze.

He booted the roan still harder, the wind carrying those piercing howls to him twice more before he turned into the lane leading to Seth's property.

Riding fast toward the curving front drive, he saw that his original estimate of the situation had been wrong. Slave cabins, not the main residence, were afire. But the front door of the great house stood open. He heard terrified wails from within.

He jumped from the saddle and sped across the veranda between the tall white pillars. He heard mounted men back along the lane. He paused in the doorway, saw another eight or ten galloping toward the house, swords swinging from their hips, muskets and pistols in their hands. In the distance, the bell still clanged.

Judson wiped his sweat-blurred eyes, entered the foyer and gagged.

Hacked by a field knife, Seth McLean lay on the parquet. An ear was missing. An arm. One foot. The sickening stench of blood filled the air.

Judson heard something stir in the darkened parlor. He aimed the horse pistol at the arch—

And watched two black girls in long dresses and kerchiefs come forward out of the gloom. Both were

111

young—and weeping. House help.

"Upstairs," one pleaded in a feeble voice. "Love o' God, Mist' Fletcher—*upstairs*."

In the drive, the plantation men were dismounting. Judson swayed a moment, drunk again. But not from wine. From the slaughter; from the unavoidable truth:

This is what happens when one man chains another. God damn my father for not understanding—

Somewhere on the upper floor, a woman screamed.

Judson climbed the stairs three at a time, maddened almost beyond sense. His heart hammered so violently his chest hurt. The memory of Seth lying butchered brought bile back to his throat. But he kept running, toward the source of that scream keening down the long corridor where two chimneyed candles flickered, islands of yellow in the darkness—

At the hall's end, a door on the left stood open. The screaming came from that room; mindless; mortally afraid. He shouted Peggy's name as he plunged toward the rectangle of light on the carpet, skidded to a stop outside, hate welling when he looked in.

She lay on the floor. Half of her nightgown was in shreds, the rest completely gone. A young black bent over her, his trousers around his ankles. A field knife shone in one hand.

The slave turned at the sound of Judson's footsteps. His other hand held scraps of pastel fabric. Behind him, Peggy thrashed and wailed, her legs spread. A moment's distorted glance showed Judson the secret place he'd thought about so often; the curling dark hair against the pale skin. He saw her small, firm breasts as well. But there was no excitement in it; only horror. Seth's wife shielded her face with her forearms as she screamed—

Desperately, the slave lunged with the field knife. His pants at his ankles made him stumble. Judson hammered the barrel of the horse pistol on the slave's wrist. The knife clacked to the floor.

112

The black swayed forward, afraid now. Judson used his free hand to catch the sweaty chin, prop the slave up. The weight put great strain on his arm and shoulder. His right knee buckled. But he needed only a moment more—

The young slave saw what was coming. His mouth opened like some ivory-lined chasm. Judson shoved the muzzle of the horse pistol between the black's teeth and pulled the trigger.

The black's body seemed to leap upward, then landed half on top of Peggy McLean. She recoiled from the weight she couldn't identify, tore at it with maniacal hands and kept on screaming. Judson tried not to look at the reddened gobbets of brain matter and bone the pistol ball had deposited on the rumpled bed and the wall behind.

He kicked the dead slave's body aside, laid the still-smoking pistol on the carpet, bent over the flailing woman. He started to speak, noticed something else: a few glistening drops of milky fluid in the black tangle between her legs. And drying stains inside her thighs.

He closed his eyes, bent his head, jammed one palm over his face until he was able to control himself.

Then, as gently as possible, he touched her hair.

"Peggy?" he whispered. "Peggy, look here. It's Judson."

The backs of his fingers accidentally brushed her cheek. She shrieked again, trying to hitch her bare body away from whoever was touching her.

"Peggy, you're all right. For God's sake look at me," Judson pleaded, unaware of the tears on his cheeks. He repeated it:

"*Look at me!*"

She opened her eyes; those beautiful, luminous dark eyes he'd coveted for so long. Her gaze was unfocused; opaque.

She lifted one hand, as if on the threshold of recognition. Then something quenched it. She recoiled, hand whipping over to shield her face as the screaming started again, louder and shriller than before. She bent her knees, hitched her hips away from the terror in her own mind—

Dry-eyed now, Judson ran downstairs and found the two shivering house girls. From behind the main building came the familiar crack of whips and discharging pistols.

"Go up to her," Judson ordered. "Lock yourselves in with her and take care of her. Don't open the door unless it's someone you know personally. A white man. If anything happens to her, I'll come back and kill you both."

They obeyed without hesitation as Judson ran out into the darkness.

V

Some forty men answered the summons of Sermon Hill's alarm bell that night. Mounted, they stormed through the tobacco fields, youths with torches in the van. They shot, sabered or whipped any black they found running loose. Judson traveled with one group and did his part, short of actually firing his pistol. He rode like a man half dead, only marginally conscious of details of what was going on.

Though not completely like the vividly remembered outbreaks of past years, the one that had ignited at Sermon Hill, McLean's and one other plantation further downriver resembled earlier uprisings in at least one way. It was fueled and given momentum by rage more than reason. Poorly organized and planned, it began to weaken as soon as the planters took to the saddle with their superior weapons and jangling shackles. It crumbled further as whites rode in leading chained slaves in twos and threes. It dissolved completely about midnight, when another group arrived at Sermon Hill

114

with the corpse of big, blue-muscled Larned dragging on the ground, pulled by a rope around one ankle.

Larned had been shot in the back with a musket ball while attempting to swim the Rappahannock. His noisy thrashing attracted a passing party of whites. Down on the river bank, they killed him.

"Poor dumb nigger," remarked one of the party, without any real pity. "He was trying to swim across to the other side. Didn't have one damn idea of the way to Williamsburg."

Angus Fletcher ordered Larned's head cut off and exhibited on a pole in front of the cottage belonging to the dead overseer.

More and more slaves were rounded up in the hours after midnight. Most wailed for mercy, claiming that they had only done what they thought was right: "S'posed to go fight with Gummer Dunmo." To start the outbreak, Larned and a few co-conspirators had circulated word of Dunmore's outrageous offer.

Judson listened to the fearful, unlettered pleas and shook his head sadly. At minimum, each runaway would receive a murderous lashing that might cripple him for life.

One pocket of resistance remained. Half a dozen slaves, male and female, hadn't surrendered, yet hadn't been quick enough to escape from Sermon Hill after the diversionary fire was discovered. The slaves had thoughtlessly holed up in the smokehouse. Angus Fletcher issued orders for brushwood to be piled around the building. He had been informed that Larned's woman, Dicey, was one of those inside.

While Judson watched from horseback a few yards away, Angus lighted a torch. The old Scot turned his back on his son's obvious disapproval and applied the torch to the brush. Within minutes, there was a stench of scorching flesh. Cries of human pain mingled with the fire's crackling.

A charred door fell outward. Dicey appeared, soot-covered, pleading for mercy. Angus Fletcher ordered her shot. A planter with a freshly loaded musket put it to his shoulder and obliged.

Judson wheeled his roan away from the carnage, wanting the solace of alcohol. As much alcohol as he could consume, as quickly as he could consume it.

First, though, he made inquiries of the loyal house blacks. Yes, the situation at McLean's was under control. Peggy's mother and father had been summoned from the Ashford plantation.

Perhaps thirty blacks in all had been slain outright. Scores more would be maimed by their punishment. Still, that represented a smaller economic loss than if the rebellion had gone unchecked even for another few hours. Judson heard men laughing and congratulating each other as he headed upstairs.

He locked himself in his room and started to drink himself insensible. For some reason it proved difficult. Long after he should have fallen into a daze, he heard the last dreadful cries from the smokehouse.

Or were they only in his mind?

Judson's chin sagged onto his chest. He speculated in a thick-witted way that the burning alive of six prime bucks and wenches would no doubt be considered a good investment by old Angus. An example to insure tranquility for months, even years to come—

Presently the rum did put him in a stupor. Yet even then, he heard the slaves' screaming.

And Peggy's.

vi

Seth McLean's funeral was held at an immaculate white Presbyterian church six miles from Sermon Hill. The whole district attended—except for Seth's widow. Three days earlier, her father had taken her away from the McLean house in a closed coach, so that she might recuperate—if that were possible—among her closest kin. In the interim, McLean's overseer Williams was to operate the plantation.

Judson rode to the church ten minutes after Angus left Sermon Hill. He didn't care to share the old man's company.

When the pastor finished eulogizing Seth McLean and turned to speculating on Jehovah's mysterious and unfathomable reasons for taking human life in its prime, Judson rose up in a back pew. He had been drinking since dawn. In fact he had taken his last pull at the doorway of the little country church. He created a disturbance by shouting at the pastor:

"Jehovah didn't kill Seth. Or the nigras either. We did."

Several of the church elders converged on Judson and hustled him from the sanctuary. He laughed in a crazy, embittered way as they hoisted him onto his horse and sent him away up the road. Then the elders went back inside, shaking their heads.

There, Judson supposed as he groped for another jug in his saddlebag, Angus Fletcher would be seated in the very front pew, his head bowed in abject prayer for the forgiveness of sins—

Particularly those committed by his satanically inspired second son.

vii

A gray December morning, with rain tapping the glass. Judson let the curtain fall on the misted view of the wharf beside the Rappahannock.

The wharf was empty. A factor had been found, and the canoes had come at last. This year's crop had brought a modest profit. Trade with the ports of England hadn't ceased completely. But most of the

117

planters considered that inevitable—just as they now regarded war as inevitable.

Judson rummaged through the odds and ends of clothing remaining to be packed. He discovered he'd miscounted the pairs of linen underdrawers. He added two more to the pile.

He just wasn't thinking clearly. Images of Peggy McLean kept intruding. First the Peggy he'd courted, warm-eyed and laughing. Then the harrowing face of the screaming girl he'd discovered in the McLean bedroom—

Finishing his counting, he saw the second picture again. He began to shudder. Only one remedy for that. He relied on it almost constantly these days. Since he had to face his father shortly, that justified a second drink.

He set the jug aside and picked up the folded sheets of parchment. Carrying these, he lurched down the graceful curving staircase to his father's cramped corner office behind the conservatory.

Judson rolled back the sliding door and walked in. Then he rolled the door shut with a loud bang.

Framed against a window overlooking the slave cabins and the raw lumber already nailed up for the framework of a new smokehouse and curing barn, Angus Fletcher took his old clay pipe out of his mouth and scowled. The room reeked of Sermon Hill's own fragrant leaf.

"You know I don't care to be disturbed when I'm working on the accounts, Judson." The old man waved the pipe's long stem at several open ledgers.

"Appears to me you're smoking, not doing figures, Father."

Angus sighed. "May God forgive you for your never-ending disrespect."

"Oh, I think He's too busy with more worthy folk to bother with the likes of me," Judson grinned. He held up

118

the parchment sheets. "I thought you'd want to know the contents of Donald's letter. It came two days ago and you haven't asked—"

Angus cut him off: "The activities in that nest of vipers are of no interest to me."

"Well," Judson announced with another muzzy smirk, "you needn't count Donald among the vipers any longer."

That caught the old man's attention. With bitterness, Judson recognized concern breaking through the flint facade. *There'll never be such concern for me,* he thought.

Angus asked, "What does Donald say, then?"

"That the gout is afflicting him severely. And the pleurisy. As soon as he can arrange transportation, he'll be returning home."

One veined hand darted out. "Let me see—"

"Sorry, there are parts of the letter that are personal." Judson folded it and shoved it in his belt.

Angus Fletcher sucked on his pipe. "You delight in baiting me."

"I guess I do," Judson admitted in a moment of candor.

"It's your pleasure, your sport. Along with drunkenness—"

"For Christ's sake don't start that."

"How often must I tell you to refrain from blasphemy in my presence, Judson?"

"All right." A weary shrug hid his sudden hurt.

Despite their differences—and the serious imperfections of each—Judson knew he should love this old man. And be loved in return. Sometimes the fact that both seemed incapable of it produced pain that was damn near unbearable.

Judson quickly regained control. His customary mask of smiling arrogance back in place, he continued:

"Truth is, you won't have to suffer my blasphemies at

119

all from now on."

"What do you mean?"

"I'm packing to go to Philadephia. I'm to serve as Donald's alternate in the Congress until he recovers."

Angus Fletcher sat down in his hand-hewn pine chair, dumbfounded. But not for long:

"Apparently there is no limit to your waywardness."

Weaving on his feet, Judson replied, "Why, I'd say I've been an exemplar of virtue since that unfortunate business at the chapel—"

"An example of debauchery," the old man snorted. "Besotted every waking minute—"

"I told you, don't start—"

" off at that slut Lottie Shaw's most nights oh, yes, I know about that, too." Reaching out as if he wanted to conceal something private of his own, the old man closed the ledgers one by one, then stacked them. "It's time we had an accounting."

"No accounting necessary, Father. I'm leaving, that's all."

"How will you travel?"

"On horseback." The purpose of the question eluded him.

Angus rectified that: "I can't spare a single nigger to accompany you. Not one, is that clear?"

"Oh, I see. Surely. I'll hire some piece of white trash, then. Send him for the trunk—"

"You are an abomination in the eyes of the Lord," Angus Fletcher declared. "A disgrace to your heritage, to your upbringing—"

"Dammit, I've had enough of your prating!" Judson exploded. "My politics are no different than Donald's!"

"Donald is a misguided innocent compared to you," his father told him. "You shame me in front of the church congregation, you scandalize the Fletcher name with your concern for widow McLean's welfare—no, don't argue! I know how you've had someone from the

120

house bustling over there almost daily to inquire about her! If she hadn't been hurt the night of the rebellion, you'd never have ridden the fields to capture the niggers."

"You've certainly outlined the charges well," Judson said. If only the old man would speak to him kindly just once. *Once!* But that was a forlorn hope. And he recognized that effort was sorely lacking on his side as well. He went on:

"There's not much I can add to your expert presentation of the evidence. I stand accused. Proudly, sir. Proudly—"

"*When will you stop your insolence?*" the old man fairly screamed.

Judson smiled his most charming smile. "The day you're rotting in hell, which I sincerely hope is your destination."

Paling, Angus Fletcher blinked several times. Water appeared at the corners of his eyes. In a peculiar, strangled voice he asked:

"What is it that you have against me, Judson? Why is it that you hate me so?"

"I've often wondered the same about you, Father. Goodbye—"

As he started to leave, Angus' voice regained its old harshness:

"One moment more."

Judson turned back; recognized the familiar sternness of the lined face. That moment of hesitation and hurt in which they might have reached out symbolically to touch one another was gone. He felt overpoweringly thirsty.

In a level tone, Angus said, "You do not approve of my loyalties to the government which has made it possible for the Fletcher family to prosper. You do not approve of the system of labor that keeps this plantation operating profitably. You certainly never respond to my

121

suggestions for improving your lax morals. It seems to me there is nothing more for you at Sermon Hill—"

He leaned over the desk, pressing his knuckles on the closed ledger on top of the stack:

"Am I plain enough? Nothing—not a farthing."

"I take it this is your way of informing me I'll have no consideration in your will?" It was an upsetting thought, though not entirely unexpected.

"That's correct. You have already tried me beyond all reasonable limits. Go to Philadelphia—step off this property for that purpose—and I will never permit you to set foot on it again."

"Oh—" Judson tried to muster another grin, couldn't. "A little bait dangled? If I repent, everything will be well?"

"What's the harm in that? I'd redeem your soul if I could, since you won't do it yourself." All at once the old man sounded tired. "You seem bent on destroying yourself."

"Thoughts like that are too deep for me," Judson said with a loose shrug. Inside, something broke with tearing pain. He shut his eyes a moment. Then he reopened them, managing at last the kind of totally cavalier smile that could light his face. He reached for the door. "Goodbye, sir."

"You do understand what I intend, Judson?"

"Of course. 'And if thy right hand offend thee, cut it off and cast it from thee, for it is profitable for thee—' "

"Stop."

" '—that one of thy members should perish—' "

"Stop, goddamn you!"

But Judson kept on, loudly: " '— and not that thy whole body should be cast into hell.' All right, I'll do the service in hell in your place. For the moment! That way, you can keep fancying yourself spotless and sanctified. Until you arrive to join me." He walked out, rolling the door shut with a bang.

122

Rain rattled on the windows as he hurried through the conservatory. Suddenly he thought he heard a muffled outcry from the office. A cry of grief. His heart leaped—

He hesitated. Thought about going back—

But he didn't.

It was much too late.

viii

Half an hour later, Judson Fletcher left Sermon Hill. His cloak belling behind him, his tricorn cocked low over his forehead to keep off the worst of the rain, he galloped down to the river and turned southeast in the direction of the ferry that would take him across to the road leading north. At a front window of the great house, one curtain was held aside by an unseen hand until Judson's flying cloak vanished in the December mist. Then the curtain was slowly put back in place.

CHAPTER V

The Guns of Winter

A BITTER GALE off the Atlantic flung sleet through the November twilight. Philip turned in at the front gate of the Vassall house on Brattle Street, Cambridge. He was chilled clear through, and nervous. Only an hour before, one of his occasional visits with his wife and son had been concluded in unexpected fashion.

Philip had arrived in Watertown to find Anne feeding their stocky infant at her breast. Her color was good, her strength increasing daily. Apart from a continuing concern about the likelihood of full-scale war, what troubled Anne Kent at the moment was her father's poor health.

The lawyer had lain abed for more than three weeks. Wracked by chills and constant coughing, he lacked appetite and was steadily losing weight. During the hour Philip spent with his family, the raspy cough from Ware's bedroom was a worrisome counterpoint to conversation.

On his way back to his regiment, Philip stopped at the tiny shop near the Charles River where his former employer, Ben Edes, had reassembled his press after smuggling the pieces out of Boston in a rowboat. With a few fonts of type, Edes was struggling to publish his patriot newspaper, the *Gazette*, on a more or less regular basis.

But when Philip arrived, he found Edes setting up the

press to print paper currency; special currency authorized by the Massachusetts provincial legislature.

There had already been talk in Philip's regiment that such money might be used to pay the soldiers. The possibility caused grumbling and resentment. Money made legal only by the legislative act of a colony in rebellion might not be worth much. Certainly it wouldn't be as readily spendable as the sterling pound. The new currency was being printed in desperation, to purchase needed supplies and materiel for the army. Edes, who looked tired, emphasized the point by showing Philip several plates for various denominations. When Edes turned the plates over, Philip recognized Revere engravings, prints of which had been sold at the old shop in Dassett Alley. Revere had worked one new design on the back of his popular depiction of the Boston Massacre.

"Even new copper for etching the worthless stuff can't be had," Edes complained, just as the front door banged open.

"Are you Philip Kent of the Twenty-ninth Massachusetts?"

Philip whirled to confront the gruff-voiced arrival: an officer of the Marblehead Twenty-first. The unit's trimly outfitted men had been chosen as personal guards for the commanding general's headquarters.

"I'm Kent, yes, sir."

"Christ, you roam around a lot. First I rode to your regiment, then your wife's rooms—come along smartly, if you please. I've a horse for you outside."

"Come along where?" Philip asked. "I'm due back in camp—"

The ruddy-cheeked man seemed skeptical of his own reply:

"No, you're to come with me. To General Washington."

Even Ben Edes looked flabbergasted.

During the uncomfortable ride to Cambridge, Philip's uneasiness increased. The officer said he had no information about the reason for the summons.

Presently they arrived at the large, imposing residence on what was coming to be called Tory Row. Like many of his neighbors, Mr. Vassall, owner of the property taken over by Washington, had fled to sanctuary with the British in Boston. A few other loyalists who hadn't as yet departed had painted black rings around their chimneys, to signify continuing allegiance to the king.

As he tethered his horse, Philip decided that his involvement in the brawl in the Virginia encampment had somehow caught up with him, and he was due for punishment.

He slipped and slid up the sleet-covered walk. Three officers emerged from the brightly lighted house, arguing. Philip stepped aside, remembering to offer a salute. The officers returned it in perfunctory fashion, giving him over-the-shoulder stares as they hurried on to their horses. Their expressions showed their astonishment at the sight of a common soldier of the line approaching headquarters; a soaked, bedraggled soldier at that.

More apprehensive than ever, Philip moved on. Near the front of the house, wind tore at a swaying pole. At the top, a flag cracked and fluttered. A flag Philip hadn't seen before. Britain's Union Jack in the upper left corner was familiar, but not the red and white horizontal stripes. He counted thirteen, just before the armed Marblehead men flanking the doorway demanded identification.

Philip gave his name and unit. He was astonished when he was admitted instantly, with instructions to turn left and knock at the drawing-room door. He did.

"Come in, come in!"

Teeth chattering from more than the cold of the night, he obeyed.

126

Behind a littered writing desk, General George Washington faced a wall map representing the Boston area. A few candles lent a soft glow to the room. Philip was startled to see a familiar figure all but hiding most of a chair.

Henry Knox.

Knox lifted his silk-wrapped hand to acknowledge Philip's presence while the third—feminine—occupant of the room set a tray on a corner of the desk. On the tray were glasses, a decanter of madeira and several oranges.

The plump-cheeked, diminutive woman was dressed in an elegant gown of pale blue. She glanced at Philip and smiled in a friendly way. The same couldn't be said of Washington or Knox. Both looked weary; under strain.

Philip said, "Kent of the Twenty-ninth Massachusetts reporting as ord—"

The tall, big-boned general in dark blue and buff cut him off with a gesture:

"We may eliminate the formalities. Time presses." His gray-blue eyes shifted to the woman, softening a little. "Our thanks for the refreshments, my dear. Now if you'll be so kind as to allow us privacy—"

"Of course," the woman murmured, withdrawing quickly and closing the door behind her. Philip assumed the woman must be the general's wife, only recently arrived from the family plantation on the Potomac River in Virginia.

Camp gossip about Martha Custis Washington was uniformly favorable; she was reputed to be a kind, gracious person who preferred to be at her husband's side instead of at faraway Mount Vernon. Everyone knew the general loved his estate, and the refined squire's life it afforded. Everyone also knew that if a

British force ever penetrated up the Potomac, Mount Vernon would surely be burned.

Yet Washington's wife had placed her husband above her opulent home, and traveled north in bad weather over difficult roads to be with him. Unexpectedly, Mrs. Washington's arrival in Cambridge strengthened the general's own standing among the troops. Plainly delighted by his wife's presence, Washington seemed less austere; became something more of a human being in the eyes of the men who served him.

The general indicated the fruit and wine:

"Take your ease and help yourself to refreshments, Kent. Mr. Knox requested your presence."

"And your assistance, Philip."

"Certainly, Henr—sir. What can I do?"

"Find me at least one more good man to go with us on a mission of considerable urgency."

Philip picked up an orange, began to peel it clumsily. Breaking the skin with his thumbnail, he squirted juice onto his coat, further compounding his nervousness. *Us*, Knox had said. Then he recalled some reference to a scheme Knox was hatching; Knox had mentioned it back in September.

To cover his awkwardness, Philip slipped into a chair Knox indicated and dispensed with trying to eat the messy orange. Washington's shadow lay black and immense over the wall map. He put one finger on the outline of the coast:

"We face a perilous situation here at Boston, Kent. A situation which Mr. Knox with his special knowledge and abilities may help us remedy. I had hoped to be able to commission him colonel for this duty. That's temporarily delayed—the damn paperwork required to gain Congressional approval of an appointment is beyond belief. But Henry will still serve as commander of the expedition in question."

Washington knocked knuckles against the map.

128

"Prolonged hostilities now appear certain. Especially since His Majesty has declared us in rebellion. At any hour we can look for Billy Howe to break his ministerial troops out of Boston to attack our positions—"

General Howe, Philip knew, had already replaced the well-intentioned but ineffective Thomas Gage as commander of the Crown forces locked up on the Boston peninsula.

"—and here—" Again Washington knocked the map, in its southeast quadrant. The heights of Dorchester, overlooking the Neck and the city. "—we are vulnerable."

Knox put in, "For that reason I intend to procure a train of artillery. The guns we need to fortify our defenses and insure that Howe does not break out. I must have one or two dependable men with me, Philip."

"Knox recommends you," Washington said with a keen look, while Philip thought of his wife, his son, his ailing father-in-law. "You are of course not compelled to undertake the duty—"

Two pairs of eyes fixed on him, waiting. Washington's remark wasn't entirely truthful. Those steady gazes left him no choice.

"If I can be of use, General, then of course—"

Washington's smile was wry. "A refreshing attitude, eh, Henry?" He swung back to Philip. "Mr. Knox learned that you plan to re-enlist, Kent."

"Yes, sir, that's my intention."

"Well, you are in a minority," the general grumbled. "It seems that most of our men have no desire except to retire to their chimney corners. In fact, such a dearth of public spirit and want of virtue—such stock-jobbing and versatility in all the low arts to obtain personal advantage—such grubby self-seeking pervades this ill-formed army that I shouldn't be at all surprised at *any* disaster which—"

The rising voice cut off abruptly. Somehow it heartened Philip to see the general momentarily embarrassed by an excess of temper.

"However—" Washington cleared his throat. "You heard Mr. Knox say he needs a pair of aides he can count on—"

"Can you suggest someone from your own unit?" Knox asked.

Philip thought, chose words with care: "I know a great many men. But I'm not sure whether—"

"Whether they're trustworthy?" Washington broke in.

Philip's nod acknowledged the truth he'd been unwilling to speak. Then, an inspiration:

"There is one man I met—he seems very courageous and forthright. He's from your own colony, General."

That pleased Washington: "What's his name?"

"Experience Tait. I don't know anything about his military ability. But as a friend, I can't speak of him too highly. When I couldn't find a physician, he went to Watertown to deliver my wife of our son."

"For money?" Washington asked.

Philip smiled. "No, all he wanted was a drink afterward."

"A Virginian, all right," Washington said. To Knox: "Get him."

Knox nodded, said to Philip, "I'll arrange matters with your commandant so we can leave as soon as possible."

"If I may ask—"

The silence of both men gave Philip leave to continue.

"—where will we be going? To one of the outlying towns?" Before the outbreak of hostilities at Lexington and Concord, various patriot groups had hidden a few small artillery pieces to protect them from possible British seizure.

Knox stared at his bandaged left hand while Washington unrolled a map lying on the desk. Philip craned forward, bone-cold again. What Washington was spreading was not a map of the Massachusetts colony but the whole eastern seaboard of the continent. Philip began to understand why Henry Knox looked grim.

"We need many more cannon than we can find in the barns and cellars of Massachusetts Bay," Washington said. "There is only one place they may be had—difficult to reach, doubly difficult to return from this time of year. But Mr. Knox has volunteered to bring the cannon back regardless. You will be going after the artillery pieces captured some months ago at the British fort here—"

The Virginian's big-boned hand dropped down to thwack a blue patch on the map, far away from the Boston shore:

"Ticonderoga."

The drawing-room windows whined under the onslaught of the November wind. The orange fell from Philip's suddenly slack hand, thumped the floor and rolled to Knox's feet.

The fat young man picked it up and tossed it back to Philip with an empty smile:

"I'm not surprised at your reaction. The roads are poor where they exist at all—the distance is formidable—and there's winter to contend with. But we *will* bring back the guns, because our cause is in extreme danger until they're in place. I suppose we should again offer you the option of withdrawal—"

Philip shook his head. "No, I agreed to go. I will."

Washington and Knox exchanged brief smiles. But that didn't relieve Philip's awareness of the staggering problems of the venture to which he'd just committed himself. Sleet struck the windows like a rattle of small-arms fire, and the panes once again gave off a forlorn, whining sound.

iii

On the eve of the new year, 1776, Philip Kent half

131

believed that he'd been submerged in a nightmare from which he would never awaken.

How long he'd been working, he didn't know. Since eternity, it seemed. The axe felt twenty times as heavy as it should. He swung it up again, brought it down, chopped through the slushy surface of the ice—

And heard a terrifying crack just to his right.

"Better stand back!" Eph Tait yelled from a couple of yards away. "She sounds ready to go—"

No sooner was the last word out than Philip felt the ice of the Mohawk River give way. A large section dropped out from under one foot. He teetered wildly, off balance.

His right boot plunged into icy water. Eph Tait threw down his axe and leaped, pulling Philip back to safety with a yank. Tait let go and Philip sat down hard on his rump. The ice crackled again, but held. Philip climbed to his feet and rubbed his rear, grimacing.

"Better 'n a river bath, ain't it?" Tait wanted to know.

"Not much."

"Some thanks I get," Tait said, grinning.

From one shore of the Mohawk to the other, shadow-figures—hired teamsters plus volunteers dragooned locally by the persuasive, determined Knox—continued to chop openings in the ice. The holes permitted water to flood up and freeze a new layer over the perilously thin crust on which the men worked. A high winter moon lit the landscape and the workmen with eerie touches of white. Behind Philip and Tait, the lights of the settlement called Half Moon gleamed on a point of land where the Mohawk and Hudson met. In Half Moon right now, Knox was undoubtedly engaged in his interminable haggling for more sledges, more horses and oxen, more drivers to push the bizarre caravan southward—

"All this work's a waste!" Philip exploded, his breath a cloud in the moonlight. He was still butt-sore; dull pain tormented every muscle. His rag-wrapped hands were stiff as sticks. "We'll never get them across such thin ice."

"We will with a good sharp freeze." Eph Tait slapped his friend's shoulder. "Come on, let's mosey back. I'd say we could draw our whiskey ration 'bout now, wouldn't you? Half an hour's rest'll do our bones some good."

"A half hour standing still and I'll be frozen to death."

"Listen, I'm the one oughta be complainin'!" Tait retorted as they crossed the slippery, moon-bright ice. On their right, the black line of trees on the Hudson's east bank showed an edge of silver. "You volunteered me for this damn duty! A real honor! 'Bout the only honor I'll get is if I get killed an' they bury me. Say, you 'spose Washington'd come to our funerals personal, Philip?"

"If he could, I think he would," Philip said absently.

"Least he could do for a pair o' fine gentleman volunteers, I'd say—"

As always, Tait's chatter helped relieve Philip's gloom, and the immediate prospect of a warming drink took his mind off his yearning to be back in Massachusetts with Anne and their son. He slogged on toward the bank where oxen lowed and men huddled around a log fire built near the sledges with their precious cargo lashed down by a webbing of ropes.

At first the journey with Knox had been a delight. Philip reveled in unexpected vistas of mountainous country; the vast, silent forests of York State blanketed with fluffy, fast-melting snow. They had reached Fort George in early December, then pushed north to star-shaped Fort Ticonderoga where the "noble train of artillery," as Knox termed it, waited for them.

Fifty-eight pieces. Four-pounders to twenty-four-pounders. Howitzers and some small coehorns and a few mortars including one giant that had been

133

nicknamed The Old Sow. In size, the captured cannon ranged from a foot long to eleven feet; in weight, from a hundred pounds to over five thousand. A hundred and twenty thousand pounds in all, Knox calculated. To be transported through wilderness, south and then eastward, three hundred miles in the depth of winter.

Initially, the artillery—along with one invaluable barrel of fine-quality British flints and twenty-three crates of shot—had to be freighted down Lake George in a collection of pirogues and batteaux. A single big scow took the largest pieces. At Sabbath Day Point, the scow foundered and sank. But in shallow water. Bailing operations set her afloat again.

With the help of the wealthy York State patrician Philip Schuyler, already appointed a major general in the Continental forces, Knox secured eighty specially built sledges and eighty yoke of oxen. But thawed, mushy ground prevented the caravan from getting underway immediately. Finally, late in December, snow pelted down—and the drivers began to lash their beasts forward, the sledges slipping and sliding on runners. New Year's brought the train of wrangling men, laboring animals and precious guns to the river junction—where capricious weather once again betrayed them. In hopes of strengthening a route to the Mohawk's southern shore, the hired men and local volunteers had been set to work making holes in the ice.

"Be damned if I ain't goin' home, and my team too," Philip heard a man complain as he and Tait approached the welcome warmth of the bonfire. "Twenty-four shillings a day ain't half enough when the animals won't be fit to work after this here trip's over. Hell, they'll probably be drowned 'fore it's done." Philip recognized a yellow-bearded farmer named Crenkle. The man had hired on with his oxen at Glens Falls.

"Twenty-four shillings is what you agreed to, neighbor," Tait said in an unfriendly tone as he picked up a dirty earthenware cup. He popped the bung of a whiskey cask resting on a trestle. "You should of bitched to Colonel Knox then."

"Don't give me that colonel shit," Crenkle said. "He ain't nothin' but a civilian. A lazy one to boot! Sittin' on his ass in the village—eatin' dinner while we work ourselves half to death on that blasted river—"

"No, sir. Not dining."

The voice whirled Crenkle around. In the firelight his breath plumed as he exhaled.

Cloaked, Henry Knox came waddling out of the darkness leading his fretful horse. Despite his girth and his pudding face, there was a severity in his eyes that made Crenkle step backward.

"I have been hunting men to serve in the stead of cowards and malingerers like you." Knox snatched a cup from Crenkle's hand and flung it away.

The cup shattered against the muzzle of a howitzer. Filthy, half-frozen men around the fire exchanged furtive looks. Some of the men were amused; others far from it. Their guilt showed.

"Drag home like a cur if you wish, Crenkle," Knox said. "But if you do, you've broken your contract. I will feel free to confiscate your oxen as a penalty."

"Confiscate—!" Crenkle screamed. "You ain't got any right whatsoever—"

"Why sure he does, brother. Here 'tis."

Philip spun, startled. He hadn't been aware of Eph Tait slipping off into the dark. Tait had returned as silently as he'd gone—bringing with him his Kentucky rifle that traveled carefully lashed in place on the sledge carrying The Old Sow. The long muzzle glittered with highlights from the fire.

"She's primed and ready to jine the argument," Tait advised the furious Crenkle. "What was you sayin' about the colonel's rights?"

"Damned high-handed bunch of army bastards—!"

135

Crenkle began, wiping his beard with a wind-raw hand. But he sounded less than sure of himself.

Knox glared. "Get back to the river or go home. Now."

Muttering, Crenkle crept away from the campfire.

Toward the river.

Knox sighed in a disgusted way, tramped to Tait and Philip. "Tonight I sent a letter to General Washington, advising him of our delay. I assured him we'll cross the Mohawk the moment it's reasonably safe to do so. Can we hope that'll be soon?"

"Ice is still pretty weak, Henry," Philip said through stiff lips.

"We must risk it. We've another crossing down at Albany—and after we turn east, the hardest terrain of all. The longer we wait, the worse the danger of a blizzard."

Neither Philip nor Tait required convincing. Having ridden west with Knox and pored over his maps, they were well aware of the mountains separating the Hudson valley and Boston. There were no conventional roads or easy passes through the range. To be caught there in a full-scale winter storm might mean days or weeks of delay.

Eph Tait sighed. "We was goin' to lay off half an hour like the rest of 'em. But I guess we better not. Come on, Philip, let's go chop us some more ice."

"And watch that man Crenkle," Knox advised. "I'd count on him to sacrifice one of the guns—or any one of us—to save his scurvy hide."

iv

The Mohawk was crossed a day later, with the temporary loss of only one eighteen-pounder. Several hours' labor with pulleys and chains retrieved the sunken cannon.

By the end of the first week in January the straggling

136

caravan reached Albany, a substantial town where a spirit somewhat more patriotic than Crenkle's prevailed. The ruddy-faced burghers turned out to cheer the arrival of the first sledges and half-frozen men.

General Schuyler was a resident of the district. His influence produced a good-sized party of new volunteers who helped speed the guns across the Hudson, reasonably solid now thanks to a spell of much colder weather. On the crossing another large cannon drowned, but next morning it was raised back up through a four-teen-foot hole in the ice. In return for the help of the citizens who manned the salvage equipment, Knox christened the piece The Albany.

The caravan was far behind schedule. In November, Knox had told Washington that the entire overland journey of three hundred miles could be accomplished in fifteen days. On the tenth of January, the first teams were just starting their climb toward the snow-powdered spruces and pines in the foothills of the mountain bar-rier that still lay between the guns and the general who needed them so desperately.

v

At a night camp, fresh snow ankle-deep on the ground, Eph Tait asked Philip how he'd come to be in-volved in the military struggle:

"I mean, once or twice I heard kind of a funny turn of phrase out o' you. Like you was foreign, maybe."

Philip held stiff palms toward the fire, ignoring a sullen stare from Crenkle across the way.

"I am, Eph. I was born in France. I learned English early, but sometimes I don't say a word quite the proper way."

"Be damned," Tait declared. "How'd you get to Boston?"

Philip shared the entire story with his friend.

137

Described how his father's wife and son, the Amberlys in England, had tried to dispute his claim to his inheritance, then had cruelly hoaxed Philip and his mother into believing James Amberly had died. Because he had incurred the wrath of Amberly's one lawful son, Roger, Philip and his mother had been forced to flee the Kentish countryside. They sought sanctuary in London, hoping to hide in its crowds and teeming streets.

For a time, the plan worked. Philip learned the printing trade at a shop operated by a family named Sholto, Met Dr. Franklin, the American, who encouraged him to emigrate to the colonies.

But in Kent, Philip had done more than make his half-brother angry; he'd crippled Roger Amberly's hand in a fight. The vengeful young man hired a professional assassin to track Philip and his mother. Again they were forced to flee.

This time, Philip followed Franklin's advice and chose new opportunity in a new land, instead of a return to their life of poverty in France. Broken-hearted because her dream of wealth and position for her son had been destroyed, Philip's mother died on the sea voyage.

In Boston Philip again took up the printing trade, with Mr. Ben Edes. As a result, he was slowly drawn into the patriot movement. He met Samuel Adams. The rich, dandified merchant, John Hancock. Paul Revere—

Philip exhibited a front tooth for Eph. A tooth carved out of hippo tusk and wired in place by Revere, who practiced dentistry to help support his family—when he wasn't grinding out engravings on popular subjects, working in silver, or riding express for the patriot committees.

Philip told Eph about the unexpected arrival of his half-brother Roger as an officer in the British forces garrisoning the city. He even described how he'd helped an infantryman, a redcoat named George Lumden, to desert—and how he'd run Roger through with a British bayonet to save Anne Ware.

"I suppose secrets like those don't matter much any more."

"Wouldn't think so," Eph said. The gazes of both men were drawn almost unconsciously toward the steep, dark slopes where great evergreens soughed in the night wind. Tomorrow they would begin the ascent of those slopes.

Eph got tickled then, huddling closer to the fire and wrapping his hands around his body as he laughed:

"My Lord, I didn't realize I fell in with such fancy company. A duke for a papa—!"

"And his son's blood on my hands," Philip said somberly.

He had omitted only one major part of the story: his violently emotional affair with the young woman who was Roger's fiancee in England and, later, his wife. Alicia Amberly, daughter of the Earl of Parkhurst, had undertaken the difficult Atlantic crossing to be with her mortally wounded husband, who was being cared for by Alicia's relatives, wealthy Philadelphia Tories. In answer to a letter from Alicia, Philip had ridden to the Quaker city to see her, and for a time, he thought of resuming their liaison. Even thought of marrying the beautiful, passionate young girl.

Then, in a chance encounter with Franklin who had just returned from England, Philip discovered the hoax perpetrated by Roger and Lady Jane Amberly. Philip's father was still alive. And Alicia knew it. She'd only reestablished contact because Philip stood to inherit everything now that Roger was dead.

Though Alicia professed love for him, the revelation of her deceit was a turning point for Philip, bringing him at last to a sorting-out of his own thoughts and emotions. He returned to Boston to marry the girl he knew he really loved; and to fight in the army.

"To date, a not particularly distinguished career," he

said at the end. "I'm not proud of some of the things I've done to survive. I've killed more than just my half-brother—"

"Figgered that," Tait said. "It shows in a man's eyes. Philip—you 'spose this crazy-quilt army's got any chance atall? I heard the lobsterbacks might even bring over hired Germans."

"So did I. To answer your question—I don't know, Eph."

"But you think all this is worth it, whatever happens?"

"I guess I do. Most of the time any more, I don't go that deep. I just go day to day."

"Smart, I reckon," Tait said, looking again to the star-silvered foothills above them. "Tomorrow ain't gonna be one of the better ones, I bet."

vi

"Another checkrope! You up there—*tie her fast!*"

Philip's shouted order started the teamster moving. The man was behind him, near the top of the forty-degree slope. The hillside was layered with fresh snow; patterned in blazing white and deep shadow by the January sun falling between the huge trees. The sun was melting the snow's crust just enough to worsen the already treacherous surface.

On its third day in the roadless mountains, the artillery train was stretched out for several miles. Each descent of the rolling terrain had to be negotiated with special care, and proper distance maintained between the sledges in case of accident. Philip was about halfway to the bottom of the hill, tramping beside the sledge bearing The Old Sow.

Below, on level ground, another sledge carrying two coehorns was about to start upward again. Eph Tait ran alongside while the drivers lashed their balky horses.

Over his arm Tait carried a number of heavy drag chains which he'd unhooked from the runners as soon as the coehorn sledge reached the bottom of the steep hill.

Now The Old Sow was being freighted down that same hillside, and four checkropes fastened to trees higher up were proving insufficient. One had already frayed and popped, causing Philip to yell at the man near the summit. The teamster was starting to string another rope around a thick bole. But slowly. Too damn slowly—

The drag chains under the Sow's sledge seemed to be having little effect. The sledge kept sliding faster. Foundering in the snow, the yoked oxen felt the push. Crenkle, their driver, didn't help matters by screaming obscenities and whipping them frantically with a supple stick.

The sledge lurched sideways, to the left. Philip jumped back to keep his feet from being crushed by the runners. Despite the chill air, he was awash with sweat under his filthy clothing.

"Crenkle, ease up with the stick, they're panicky enough," Philip bawled at the farmer. Crenkle threw him a defiant look and kept flailing.

The back end of the sledge lurched again, further left—toward a natural drop-off of about twenty feet. If even part of the sledge slipped over, oxen and all would go. The mortar might be cracked beyond repair—

"Hurry up with the rope!" Philip screamed, hand cupped around his beard-stubbled mouth. The man higher up still seemed to be moving with maddening slowness. He was just starting to secure the end of the rope that led all the way back down to the vehicle bearing the Sow. Six ropes in all were lashed to staples on the bed of the sledge. One had broken; only one more was available, trailing loose on the hillside, tracing a snake pattern in the snow.

Tense, Philip watched the sledge slide again. Only a

couple of feet this time—

He whipped his glance back up to the man struggling with the rope. *Why couldn't he get it tied faster?*

One of the oxen bellowed, a terrifying sound that echoed through the mountain stillness. Philip spun, saw Crenkle flogging the left-hand ox, down on both forelegs. The rear of the sledge started another slide, straight toward the drop-off—

Just as the man fastening the checkrope around the tree finished his last knot, the sledge's back end swung all the way left, pointing toward the drop. The newly tied knots failed to hold. The rope snapped, uncoiled from around the trunk, end whipping free—

Another rope broke, leaving two in place. At that precise instant, Crenkle's maniacal beating of the oxen achieved results—disastrous ones:

The left-hand ox lurched up and lunged ahead. The other beast felt the pull and responded in tandem. The sledge was jerked forward too precipitously—no longer in danger of slipping over the drop, but given a sudden giant yank that started it sliding straight down the melted, slippery track—

The sledge picked up speed, spuming snow from the runners despite the drag chains. Crenkle saw the sledge gathering momentum. His reason deserted him. Before Philip could react, Crenkle dropped his stick, jerked a hatchet from his hide belt, started chopping the traces.

"Don't release them, Crenkle!" Philip yelled. But the frightened farmer paid no attention. He hacked the last of the traces, stretched out his free hand and jerked the pin connecting the yoketree to the front of the sledge.

The freed oxen lunged to the right, off the dangerously melted path. An instant later, the sledge left Philip and Crenkle behind, then hurtled by the oxen, still gathering speed.

Philip reached Crenkle and knocked him down with

one mauling fist. "You stinking yellow animal—!"

Crenkle snuffled, on his knees and trying to stop blood leaking from his nose. The sledge was a good way down the hill now, thundering toward the bottom where Eph Tait was just releasing the last drag chain from the coehorn carrier.

Tait heard the rumbling, turned his head. For a moment, sunlight made his bad eye glow like a star—

Time seemed to suspend. Philip was only marginally conscious of his legs pumping through the deep snow. He shouted incoherent warnings.

He saw Eph Tait frozen with surprise in the patch of sunlit snow; Eph's jaw dropping at the sight of the juggernaut hurtling toward him. The Virginian started to run.

The drag chains draped over his arm fell to the ground. Somehow he tangled his feet in one of them. Thrashing, he sprawled in the snow—

The mortar sledge hit the bottom of the slope and careened ahead. Tait threw an arm up in front of his face—

He disappeared as the sledge ran over him and slid on past the coehorns, losing momentum on the flat. The sledge's front end rose at the bottom of the next slope, the hillside soon braking its forward progress completely. In the snow behind, something grotesque and loose-limbed flopped.

Philip kept running toward his friend. Then the Virginian screamed.

Philip's beard-matted face distorted. Other teamsters were rushing to Tait's side. Squinting in the sunlight, Philip whirled and ran back up the hill in a shambling gait.

Above him, Crenkle crouched defensively, hatchet upraised. The defensive posture crumpled the moment Philip came close enough for the yellow-bearded farmer to see his almost bestial face. Crenkle threw his hatchet

143

away, turned and jumped from the edge of the drop-off.

At the bottom, he struggled to his feet, flung himself on down the slope, vanishing into a thick stand of pines. Philip retrieved the hatchet, raced for the drop. A voice got through to him then; one of the men from the coehorn sledge:

"Leave him go, Kent! Help us with Tait. He's still alive."

Philip hesitated. The numbed hand holding the hatchet shook. In the distance, the pathetic Crenkle put more ground between himself and the caravan, a scurrying figure appearing and disappearing in sun and shadow.

The teamster at the bottom of the hill shouted Philip's name again. Making a guttural sound, he flung the hatchet down. With a last look at the tiny figure fleeing into the snowy fastness, he went to answer the summons. He never saw Crenkle again.

vii

Forward progress of the artillery train stopped. The sledge carrying The Old Sow had survived the runaway descent with no damage. Nearby, Philip and some of the teamsters erected a crude tent from fresh-cut branches and blankets.

Ten minutes after the tent was put up, Philip crawled out of it backwards and let the end blanket fall. He blinked as his eyes adjusted to the blaze of the snow. The blinking didn't clear his vision.

A horseman was struggling down the slope where the Sow's sledge had come to rest. Philip watched the horse slip sideways, falter, then gallop forward, the mountainous figure of Henry Knox bouncing in the saddle.

Inside the improvised tent there was a tormented moan. Philip tried to hide his face by pretending to wipe his nose. But the other teamsters weren't looking at him. They studied the treetops, or gazed at the churned snow marked by Eph Tait's blood, or they simply stared at their rag-wrapped boots. Not a man said a word. The silence was broken only by the occasional whisper of the wind, the frozen creak of a bough, the soft thudding of the hoofs in the snow as Knox swung out of the saddle.

"I got your message and sent ahead for a doctor from Westfield," he said to Philip. He started toward the tent entrance.

Philip grabbed his arm:

"I wouldn't, Henry."

"I must see what attention he needs—"

"From here down—" Philip swallowed, touched his own waist. "No amount of attention is going to help."

Knox turned white as the snowfields. "My God. Is he awake?"

Forcing back tears, Philip nodded. "We dosed him with some whiskey. That stopped the worst of his raving. I even talked to him a minute or so. He—he knows how badly he's been hurt. He wants his rifle with him." Philip's stiff hand lifted in a sad, ironic gesture at the mortar sledge. Fastened to the bed by ropes tied to pins, Eph Tait's Kentucky rifle gleamed blue through a patchy dusting of snow.

"Well, fetch it if it'll be any comfort to him!" Knox said. "It'll take the doctor a while to trek here, so anything that—"

He stopped as Philip shook his head.

"Eph asked me to write his family later, Henry. He wants his rifle loaded."

Knox swayed. Philip had never seen him look so drained. He glanced around the little circle of York State drivers, face after weatherbeaten face, as if hoping one of the men would speak. Philip said to him:

"I'd say the decision's yours, Henry."

"No. No, it's his. Still—" Knox swiped at his face. "There is a moral question—"

"Then you tell him that, Henry. You look at what's left of him and tell him that. I won't."

Silence. The wind mourned through the pines. A branch broke loudly and fell.

"Get the rifle, would you please, Philip? I'll take it in to him. Unless you—?"

"We did our talking. You'll probably have to use more whiskey to wake him."

He turned, trudged to the mortar sledge, dimly aware of shouted curses and snapping whips beyond the crest of the slope down which The Old Sow had plunged. A new sledge struggling for the summit. Maybe the messengers sent in both directions from the scene of the accident had missed one of the vehicles laboring through the woods. The noise almost seemed a blasphemy as Philip laboriously untied the frozen ropes, opened the ammunition box lashed down beside the rifle, loaded the piece and carried it back to Henry Knox.

Another groan sounded from inside the tent. Then Eph Tait cried someone's name. A woman's, Philip thought. Knox bent to enter, carrying the rifle. Philip walked away.

About five minutes later, leaning his forearm on the cold iron of the giant mortar, Philip heard the shot. Hideously loud; echoing and reechoing through the tree-clad ridges and valleys. He stared at the mortar's maw as if he could destroy it with a single glance. He started when someone touched him—

Knox.

The drivers were shuffling away from the tent. The end blanket flapped in the wind.

Drifting clouds started to obscure the sun. Whorls of white powder danced on the hillsides. At the western summit, the sledge coming up had stopped. The teamsters peered at the peculiar scene below. The wind sang again, a low, pained sound.

"I think we should bury him here, Philip."

"I think so."

"The rifle's to be yours. He told me. We'll dig a proper place and I'll say a few words and—" His voice broke. "—and then we'll get these goddamned guns going again."

"Yes. All right," Philip said, staring at nothing. Knox left him standing in a cloud of wind-driven snow.

viii

The arrival of the artillery in the village of Westfield produced almost a carnival atmosphere.

Townsfolk followed the sledges on both sides, and small boys couldn't be kept from jumping aboard to touch the marvelous cold solidity of the great weapons.

The Westfield citizens offered the weary drivers huge quantities of food and drink. The men accepted eagerly, nearly starved after their passage across the worst of the mountains.

In return for the hospitality, the people of Westfield begged Henry Knox to show off the artillery by firing the most spectacular piece of all, The Old Sow. The exhausted Knox obliged. Philip made himself scarce during the demonstration, taking refuge in the local taproom. But he still heard the boom of the mortar, and the subsequent cheers, applause and shouted insults to King George. Philip immediately helped himself to another ale. Like everyone else, the landlord was outside enjoying the celebration.

ix

"Anne? Annie—I'm back!"

Yelling at the top of his voice, Philip climbed the stairs of the house in Watertown on the night of January twenty-sixth. The preceding day, the artillery train had arrived in Framingham, its journey complete for all practical purposes. Philip had ridden ahead with Knox, who gave him leave to go see his family. Knox galloped on to the Vassall House to report to General Washington.

Filthy and almost drained of strength, Philip shouted his wife's name again as he reached the landing. He shifted Eph Tait's Kentucky rifle to his left hand, raised his other hand to knock—

And stopped, paralyzed by what he saw hanging on the door.

A poorly made wreath of black crepe.

Fears for Anne and little Abraham flashed through his mind. He stood motionless, aware of doors opening on the lower floor, heads popping out—the whole house had been turned into a honeycomb of emergency apartments. He was certain his wife or his child had died in his absence—

The door opened. Philip almost wept at the sight of Anne's fatigued face.

Her chestnut hair was disordered, her dress stained and wrinkled. Philip couldn't speak. He was afraid to ask the obvious question.

"The baby's well," Anne said quietly. "He's sleeping now."

"Then it's your father. Oh, Annie—"

Suddenly she was tight against him, unable to hold back her sobs. He let the valuable rifle fall where it would. Heedless of how he was dirtying her with his filthy coat, he hugged her; buried his bearded, unwashed face in the warmth of her hair. She cried loudly for a minute or so, then fought to get herself under control.

Philip retrieved his rifle, guided her gently into the dim-lit parlor, shut out the curious faces at the bottom of the stairs.

"When, Annie?" he whispered.

"The fourth of January. All during December, the illness grew worse. And you know how it's all but impossible to find a doctor. Mr. Revere finally located a retired, half senile old fellow and practically kidnapped him from Roxbury. He diagnosed pleurisy—just as I'd done myself, weeks before—and of course he couldn't prescribe anything except the usual emetics and laxatives and—well, when he hauled out this positively filthy bleeding basin and a fleam with every last blade caked with rust, I paid him and thanked him and told him to leave. I knew it was hopeless."

Anne's face was white; Philip understood why. Pleurisy was the name of a dreaded disease of the lungs and chest; more common in bad weather, it took a high toll of those who contracted it.

Anne looked around in a strange fashion, almost as if seeking her father in the gloomy corners. Then:

"Papa was fortunate in one way. He went peacefully—in his sleep. But dear God, Philip!—at the same time, there was no word from you. Nothing except rumors from Cambridge that Henry Knox was still on the road. Having difficulties—accidents—" Her agony poured forth in one strident cry: "*I was afraid you were going to die too—*"

Again he held her close, touched her, stroked her shoulders, trying to soothe away the remembered horror. All at once he heard the impatient gurgling of his son waking in the bedroom. Even as he listened, the gurgling turned to a yell. He felt a shameful, completely inappropriate urge to whoop.

This time Anne broke the embrace, dabbing at her cheeks. "I'm sorry I took on so. Really, the worst has passed. I just broke down."

"You had to bury him yourself?"

"Yes, I arranged it here in the local cemetery. Ben Edes helped. There was no telling when we could get back to Boston. Philip—at Christmas, Papa asked me to

149

say goodbye to you. I'm sure he already knew what was going to happen—"

She started away, bothered by the baby's cry: "I must feed him—and you too. Why, you must have lost twenty pounds—"

She fought to hold a wan smile in place. That was so like her, he thought, filled with a wordless tenderness that somehow eradicated his exhaustion, his hunger, the unpleasantly cold, smoky stench of his clothing.

"There is one happy circumstance in all the grief," Anne added. "Papa left what money he has to both of us. And—oh wait, Abraham, wait, I'm coming!" she exclaimed as the squalling grew louder. "Papa said that if we could keep from spending all the money to live, we should use it to start your printing business one day. He thought well of you, Philip, he really did. He wanted you to know."

It should have been heartening news; something to bank away for the future. But he was again struck with grave doubts about that future.

He thought of Dr. Warren perishing in the redoubt.

Of Eph Tait buried in the wintry wastes of western Massachusetts, so far from the southern mountains from which he'd marched.

And he thought of Abraham Ware, who perhaps would never have contracted his fatal illness if he'd been warm and comfortable in his home on Launder Street, Boston—

Who would be the next to be scythed down?

When Philip speculated about the prospects for his infant son, the very act seemed macabre futility. Conceived in the joy of passion—born under a mantle of hope and love from his parents—what did the child have to look forward to save growing up in a country shattered by rebellion?

The struggle could conceivably drag on for years; wars often did in Europe. That America could win her fight seemed to him chancy at best. That she could win quickly was virtually unthinkable. There was no purpose in dwelling on the boy's future, or the inheritance either. Dead men had no use for handbills and calling cards. What printing equipment could you buy in a grave?

Possessed by pessimism, Philip felt a sudden, unexpected need to seize the small pleasures of the moment. The feel of his wife's warm shoulder beneath his arm. And something else:

"I want to see my son."

An hour later, Anne served a supper of cold lamb, fresh cheese, stale bread and hot tea. Though the fare was less than luxurious, there was plenty of it. Yet despite the poor rations he'd endured on the three-hundred-mile journey, he didn't feel like eating.

All at once, out of his need, fear, uncertainty, he reached for Anne's hand.

She looked at him and understood. At long last, a soft smile eased a little of the fatigue in her eyes. She was as uncertain and hungry as he.

Rising, she blew out the lamp in the corner of the parlor where they had sat down for their meal. Gently, lovingly, she took his other hand in hers.

"I should use a razor first," he said with an awkward little laugh. "Scrape off this bristle. It could do damage to a lady's cheek—"

"Don't worry," she said. "Just come—" She led him to the door.

In their large, high bed, their son sleeping nearby and cooing occasionally, she was warm and eager. Arms tight around his neck, she wept when he first kissed her. The touching, the caressing, and then the rhythm of their bodies seemed to drive back some of the world's lowering darkness.

But afterward, he couldn't sleep.

He stole out to the parlor, lit a lamp and spent more

151

than two hours composing one short letter to Experience Tait's wife in Albemarle County, Virginia. Even if it had cost every last shilling of Abraham Ware's money to have it posted and delivered, he would have paid.

CHAPTER VI

"The Seedtime of Continental Union"

"GENTLEMEN," said Dr. Benjamin Franklin, the tankard in his pudgy hand shimmering in the light from the hearth, "I give you our honored guest. By birth, an Englishman. By choice, an American. By disposition and God-given talent, a journalist of the first rank. In the manner of most authors who delve into politics in these treacherous times, he has chosen to see his pamphlet brought into the world anonymously. But to judge from the reception accorded it since publication one short week ago, I predict its distinguished creator will not long be able to conceal his identity. Certainly he may be named and honored by those gathered here. To a man, I believe we hold his inspired prose and irrefutable logic in the utmost regard."

Franklin turned toward the rather seedy-looking guest: a man with a large nose, a rough complexion, luminous sad eyes and the general air of one who, near age forty, recognized his own failure in life. Tonight, the guest smiled.

Dr. Franklin saluted him with the tankard:

"I give you Mr. Paine."

Stick ferrules hammered the floor of the private dining room of Philadelphia's City Tavern. "*Hear! Hear! Hear!*" Those among the twenty selected guests who lacked canes made noise with their boots.

Gradually, the hammering and stomping faded, replaced by a hubbub of conversation. In the fireplace,

153

two halves of a heavy log fell, scattering sparks. Franklin sat down beside the guest of honor. While serving as commercial agent for various colonies in England, Franklin had apparently met Mr. Paine, and induced him to come to America after Paine suffered assorted disasters in customs collecting, corset manufacturing and marriage.

There were calls for a speech. Applause greeted the suggestion. Thomas Paine rose, flushing:

"Gentlemen, thank you most sincerely. But I've prepared no remarks. I only wished to enjoy dinner and fellowship with the men I consider the most enlightened of all those holding sessions at the State House."

More applause, cane-thumping, boot-stamping, mingled with jokes and laughter. At his table near the fire, Judson Fletcher was hellishly warm. He was starting to sweat out all the dark brown ale he'd swilled down. But he joined enthusiastically in the uproar.

Certainly it was a select group from the Congress gathered at the City Tavern this rainy evening in late January. A select group of patriots—or a select group of the insane, depending on your side of the political fence.

Judson had gravitated to the group because Donald had been part of it. Around him sat politicians whose names were known in every one of the colonies. Franklin. The portly, high-voiced little Braintree lawyer, John Adams, seated at Paine's left. From Virginia, the Lee brothers, and gangling, red-haired Tom Jefferson, who occupied a chair just across the table from Judson. Once in a while, Judson was troubled by the realization that these refined, well-educated men were determined to push the colonies straight down one and only one perilous road.

John Adams jumped to his feet. "Then I will speak for you, Mr. Paine."

The Massachusetts lawyer always struck Judson as self-important. The guest looked relieved, though.

Adams went on:

"To paraphrase Mr. Jefferson there, we as a Congress and as a people want neither inducement nor power to declare and assert a separation from Great Britain. It is the will alone which is wanting—"

"Oh, we have the will to gallop the other way, Wilson style," said Francis Lightfoot Lee, referring to the Pennsylvania sponsor of a Congressional resolution of January ninth passed by a coalition of conscientious conservatives and the frankly faint-hearted. According to Judson's somewhat bleary recollection, the resolution declared that the colonies had "no design" to set themselves up as an independent nation. Consequently the mention of Wilson's name produced a few hisses, including a loud one from Judson.

Tom Jefferson, relaxed and pensive with his long legs stretched out toward the flames, gave Judson a speculative look, then glanced away. Judson belched. *Wonder what that was all about?*

Adams was continuing:

"—but with the publication of Mr. Paine's pamphlet, a great step forward has been taken toward solidifying public thought. We owe him a debt beyond our collective power to repay."

Once more the diners noisily expressed their approval as the Braintree lawyer sat down, pleased.

Judson had to admit that Adams, who was perhaps the most determined exponent of independence in the Congress, hadn't exaggerated. In the days since the release of Paine's tract of some fifty pages and fourteen thousand words, it had become a publishing phenomenon. People literally fought their way into Robert Bell's small shop in Third Street to purchase copies; either the version in a deluxe binding, or the one in less expensive paper covers.

Judson had finally gotten hold of one of the latter just this afternoon. So far he hadn't done more than examine

155

the title page. But he knew a little about the book's history.

Aitken, the local printer for whom Thomas Paine did menial shop work, had deemed his employee's material too inflammatory to print. But help and advice from Franklin and the ultra-radical Samuel Adams of Boston—not present tonight; even radicals like his own cousin John considered him a mite *too* radical—had led to the connection with Bell.

But Bell, who took the risk of bringing out the first edition, wasn't enjoying exclusive benefits—or profits—from his venture. All over Philadelphia, and in other cities as well, other presses were churning out copies. The eager public didn't care whether an edition was pirated or not. They just wanted to read it.

So did Judson. He was anxious to get away from this stultifying if augustly populated room, return to his rented quarters in Windmill Street near the river and dive into Paine's pamphlet.

Scraping chairs and the opening of the doors to admit serving girls to clean up the litter of plates, cups and glasses indicated he might be getting his opportunity.

He judged the hour to be past nine. He hoped Alice wouldn't choose to spend the night with him. Her whims were unpredictable; dictated largely by how much claret she'd consumed.

She was a damned attractive wench, of course. A welcome diversion despite certain puzzling, even alarming quirks of personality, and a history that was a total enigma—

But he didn't want Alice tonight. He was eager to go to bed with no companion save Mr. Paine's *Common Sense*.

Reaching for his hat and stick as the gathering broke up, he was startled by a hand on his sleeve:

"Judson? A word with you—"

Tom Jefferson stood well over six feet. He met

his fellow Virginian's smile with a calm, almost remote expression. Judson's smile disappeared.

He had gotten on exceptionally well with Tom Jefferson ever since arriving in Philadelphia in mid-December. The other members of the Virginia delegation—the Lees, Ben Harrison, Jefferson's law tutor George Wythe, Braxton, Nelson—all were cordial enough. But Jefferson was closer to Judson's own age than the rest of them. Just a little over thirty, Judson guessed.

Not much for oratory, but reputed to be the best phrase-turner in Congress, Jefferson still spoke with a quiet directness that demanded a listener's attention. His laugh, when he was in the mood, could roar. Tonight he obviously wasn't in the mood—as Judson had noticed a while ago, when the wealthy young man gave him that odd look.

"By all means," Judson said with a slight bow. "Shall we go to the public room? I'd drink another ale before braving that rain."

Jefferson shook his head. "I believe enough's been drunk for one night."

Instantly Judson tightened up. The polite reply had delivered its barb—as he was sure Jefferson intended. Annoyed, Judson picked up a tankard left by someone else. He gulped the warm, flat ale remaining in the bottom.

That defiance out of the way, he wiped his lips with his lace-trimmed cuff and smiled engagingly:

"Then let's talk here, Tom. What did you want to discuss?" He suspected he knew.

Jefferson didn't avoid Judson's gaze. "You, Judson."

The smile stayed in place. "A fascinating subject! Go on."

"As you know, we've welcomed your presence and your liberal spirit in the Congress. In that sphere, you're as much a credit to Virginia as your brother."

Judson's smile soured then. "Shall we skip the preliminaries? I smell that compliment for what it is—a preamble to something less flattering."

Jefferson's lips thinned a moment. "Very well," he said. "We have received word of a rather distressing exhibition of patriotism at The Keg the other evening."

"It wasn't an exhibition of patriotism, it was a brawl." Judson cheerfully exhibited the bruises and healing scrapes on the back of his right hand. "I just went in the place for a drink. I had no idea it was the refuge of every young Tory in town. I had two or three, and then a couple of sweet-smelling chaps remarked that German Georgie would soon make the Congress regret it ever convened—by signing his treaties with the landgraves who are to supply him with German mercenaries."

Judson shrugged: "One thing led to the next, and when I got done with 'em, two of the pretty young gentlemen looked less pretty than when they first opened their mouths."

The lanky Virginian's nod was dour. "So it was reported. I only want to remind you, Judson—friend to friend—that we're engaged in deliberations of the most serious nature. Our every act will be scrutinized for years to come—"

"A lecture, then. This is a lecture!"

"Judson, calm down."

"No, by God, I won't listen to—"

"Yes you will," Jefferson said, so softly that Judson caught his breath. "Your private life is your affair. But publicly—"

"Publicly *what?*"

"We ask that you do nothing further to bring criticism to our cause." To ease the situation, he smiled a quick, glowing smile. "I don't doubt that in certain yet-to-be-written histories, we're damned beyond redemption as it is."

Jefferson seemed to relax then, the stiffness going out of his shoulders. But his clear eyes watched, awaiting a response. Judson bridled his temper with difficulty.

"You keep saying *we*, Tom. You're not speaking personally, then?"

"Not entirely."

"For the delegation?"

"And some others. Let's just say I was requested to pass the message along. I didn't relish doing it—in case that wasn't obvious. But I agreed because, in principle, the gentleman who asked me to do it was right."

Cheeks livid, Judson blurted, "Name the gentleman."

"Judson, there's no point—"

"*Name him!*"

Jefferson sighed. "Mr. Hancock—with the concurrence of Mr. John Adams."

"*Hancock!* That pompous dandy—!" Judson was sputtering.

But his anger cooled almost at once. The handsome and extremely rich Boston merchant, formerly the chief financier of patriot activities in Massachusetts, was the duly chosen president of the Congress. This was no mere slap on the wrist by a nonentity. For a blink of time, Tom Jefferson's lean face seemed to be replaced by that of Angus Fletcher—

Around the private dining room, shadows sprang up as the serving girls snuffed candles. All the other men had gone. Winter rain struck the window glass.

In a more temperate voice, Judson asked:

"You say John Adams also joined in the request?"

"You must understand why, Judson. What we're undertaking here in Philadelphia will be considered so heinous in some quarters of the world, our personal motives and behavior must be above reproach."

"In other words, we can drink and curse and whore as much as we like behind closed doors, just so long as the public face is hypocritically spotless?"

159

Jefferson looked upset. "If that's the way you care to phrase it, yes."

"That's the only way I care to phrase it!"

Jefferson sifled a sharp reply. Then:

"Judson, the central argument makes sense, if you'll just reflect on it a while—"

"I'll reflect on it while I'm having a drink somewhere else!" He turned and stormed out, leaving Jefferson in the shadows by the dying fire, a red-etched figure, vaguely accusing. All he could think of as he rushed from the City Tavern was that he had once more been found wanting.

ii

Winter rain slicked the brick streets and gathered in wind-riffled pools that reflected the butter glow of chimneyed streetlamps designed, people said, by Dr. Franklin personally. Muffled in his cape, Judson headed for Windmill Street, cursing fluently.

One minute he cursed Jefferson, deputized by Hancock and Adams to chastise him. The next minute he cursed himself, for again failing to live up to what was expected of him. Whatever the hell that was!

Jefferson's warning couldn't be ignored. Though still young, the red-haired Virginian had already made a considerable name for himself because of his grasp of diverse fields of learning, from the natural sciences to the law. That Hancock had assigned him the task of speaking to Judson was proof of his rising status.

And once he cooled down a little, Judson had to admit that Jefferson's argument was probably correct. The Congress *was* engaged in momentous and difficult work. The faction to which Jefferson and Judson belonged saw independence as the last available option in the face of the king's continuous refusal to protect American liberties. But time and again, Judson had heard John Adams state that although he considered independence a cause with high moral purpose, the idea lacked support among ordinary folk in the colonies. If it were noised about that members of the independence group were thugs who bloodied the noses of Tories in public taverns, the legitimacy of the cause could be seriously hurt.

And right now, the radicals certainly couldn't afford that.

Opposition to independence among the Congressional conservatives led by Wilson and the London-trained lawyer, John Dickinson of Pennsylvania, was formidable and determined. The conservatives would seize on every remark or incident that might change minds and ultimately swing votes. No, Jefferson couldn't be faulted—

Especially now that Paine's pamphlet had finally fired the imaginations of great masses of people, and begun to sway them toward the viewpoint of the radicals. All at once, Judson felt like a moral pygmy among giants.

By the time he neared Windmill Street and the plainly furnished rooms he rented from an elderly tinker, his sense of shame had deepened even further. He vowed he wouldn't embarrass Donald again—for he had certainly done that too, along with alienating himself from the members of Congress whose convictions he shared. He would have to work hard to repair the damage.

Judson had undergone subtle changes in attitude since coming to the city beside the Schuylkill river. At first, appointment as Donald's alternate had been little more than a welcome escape from the turmoil at Sermon Hill.

Then there'd been a period of confusion; a couple of weeks of familiarizing himself with the routine of the Congress; of sitting in on his first committee meetings, saying little. He was a junior member of two committees. One screened officer appointments for the twenty-seven new Continental regiments established the preceding November. The other supervised the newly structured Post Office Department, a Congressional creation which John Adams scorned as "frivolous" in view of the weightier matters to be considered.

Confusion and all, those first two weeks brought Judson a great sense of pleasure. He relished association with important men who had only been names before.

Then, because he did share Donald's politics, he began to take an active interest in the seesaw struggle between the conservative and radical factions. He was now definitely aligned with those who wanted independence but lacked the votes, or even an initial resolution to be voted upon. The conservatives were using every device and argument to block the introduction of the latter. Despite the king's rejection of the petition for conciliation, the conservatives and many of the moderates still believed that separation from England would not only be morally wrong for the colonies, but would also be economic suicide.

Judson climbed the rickety outer stair and let himself into the tinker's musty parlor. Flinging off his wet cloak and hat, he headed automatically for the sideboard, and the decanter of claret he kept for Alice.

Well, not only for Alice—

Midway there, he stopped, stung again with the conviction that, by his actions, he'd betrayed the men—and the cause—he supported without reservation. He ran his tongue over his teeth, scowled, turned away and lit a lamp.

He was again aware of some serious and fundamental flaw within himself. A weakness for the bottle was just one of its manifestations. Tonight, by heaven, he meant to start some corrective actions, however small. Such as forcing himself to leave the claret alone.

He took off his finely cut coat of plum velveteen, grateful that Alice wasn't on the premises. He carried the lamp to the bedroom and picked up Paine's pamphlet from the bedside table. Sprawling on the coverlet, he opened to the first page of text.

He read the whole book in less than an hour, relishing its polemical savagery. Then he went back to particular passages.

He laughed out loud at Paine's characterization of monarchy as *the most prosperous invention the devil ever set on foot for the promotion of idolatry.* He agreed with Paine's insistence on urgency: *The period of debate is closed. Arms, as a last resource, must decide the contest. By referring the matter from argument to arms, a new era for politics is struck; a new method of thinking hath risen. All plans, proposals, etc., prior to the nineteenth of April, i.e., to the commencement of hostilities, are like the almanacs of last year; which, though proper then, are superseded and useless now . . .*

He likewise concurred with Paine's assessment of the king's behavior:

Even brutes do not devour their young, nor savages make war upon their families.

And his scalp prickled when the journalist urged total separation from the mother country in phrases that rang like great bells:

The sun never shined on a cause of greater worth. 'Tis not the affair of a city, a county, a province, or a kingdom; but of a continent—of at least one-eighth part of the habitable globe—

Lying with the book resting on his hard belly, Judson thought of George Clark, wandering the western wilderness. Paine shared some of George's vision. He devoured the rest of the passage again:

'Tis not the concern of a day, a year, or an age; posterity are virtually involved in the contest, and will be more or less affected even to the end of time by the proceedings now—

Just what Jefferson had been saying.

Now is the seedtime of continental union, faith, and

honor.

Then, almost with reverence, he turned to the final page. Unblinking, he gazed at the seven superbly isolated words Paine had contrived to have set by themselves—his last tocsin and challenge to his readers.

Staring at the words, Judson's scalp prickled again. So rapt was his attention, he didn't hear the light footfalls on the outer stair, or the soft clicking of the latch.

But suddenly he was aware that the sound of the rain was louder. He jumped up, laid the pamphlet face down on the bed, open to that final, astonishing page. He walked toward the dark parlor.

He recognized the footsteps of his visitor. In a moment, she entered the perimeter of light cast by the bedside lamp. Alice—throwing back the cowl of her cheap cloak of gray wool. Just as lovely as she was every time he saw her.

And just as drunk.

iii

"Hallo, love," Alice grinned. She weaved a little, one sooty hand pushing back a lock of hair that might have been a tawny gold color if she had ever washed it. She was wearing her usual much-mended dark brown skirt, and a shabby low-necked blouse grayed by greasy smoke.

Judson concealed his annoyance. "Hello, Alice. I wasn't expecting you this evening."

"Meaning my company's not wanted?" Her smile, a shade malicious all at once, unsettled him. But that wasn't unusual.

She sidled forward, placed her roughened hands on his shoulders, bent to give him a teasing view of her naked breasts. "Ah, but yours is, love." The sight of her half-bared bosom started a familiar, tumid excitement.

She was a coarse girl; peculiar in many more ways than one. Maybe that was part of her fascination: she was a strange admixture of feigned refinement and gutter frankness.

At times she moved with the grace of the finely dressed ladies who took the air on Chestnut Street behind their jeweled vizards. But unlike those same ladies, she had a direct, unconcealed interest in matters sexual. She knew how to stir him. She wasted no time now, caressing his mouth with open lips.

Judson resigned himself, though not entirely unwillingly. He slipped an arm around her waist, smelling the tavern sweat mingled with the odor of the claret she drank from dawn to dusk—and later. He bussed her ear, murmured:

"You're still speaking of my company, correct?"

"Certainly, isn't that the dignified way to refer to this?" One hand crept below his waist to grasp and fondle.

Almost at once, her fingers produced the sought-for response. After she'd teased him a moment, she let go:

"Ah, but we have the whole night—I don't mean to go out in this damnable weather again. So how about a glass for a lady, Mr. Fine Fletcher of Virginia?"

He waved to the sideboard. "Lady you aren't. But help yourself."

"Not a lady? Don't lay wagers!" she laughed, flouncing off to the decanter with a peculiar look in her sky-blue eyes. He heard a mug clink. "Want some, love?"

He sank down on the edge of the bed, glancing with regret at Paine's pamphlet. "No, I don't believe—" Suddenly he saw Jefferson's face. "Hell, why not?"

He listened to the sound of claret splashing out of the decanter. She drank too much; much more than he did, and his consumption was far from moderate. On occasion, she used foul language, but it usually sounded awkward. She was ruining herself physically and mentally, and she couldn't be more than twenty-three or twenty-four.

Another curious thing: her cheeks were pitted. At one time she must have used the fashionable but ruinous cosmetics popular among highborn ladies. When and where had she been able to afford such concoctions?

Sometimes she made oblique jokes about a mysterious background in better circumstances. But Judson's questions about it always went unanswered. In fact he knew nothing about her except her one name, Alice, and that she worked serving the riffraff who frequented a particularly disreputable tavern near the docks. He'd stumbled into the place one night after Christmas, feeling especially blue with memories of Seth McLean's wife. In his stupor, Alice's flaunted body appealed to him. A direct proposition led to a quick coupling upstairs in a sleazy room under the eaves—for a fee. Half of it, she said, went to the landlord.

Still a bit drunk, he'd invited her to come to his quarters in Windmill Street some evening. For no fee. Two nights later, at two in the morning, she arrived. He'd seen her at least twice a week since.

Alice carried the cups of claret back into the bedroom, handed him one, neglecting her tugged-down blouse, a casualty of their embrace. The half-circle of one rouged nipple showed like part of a flower. Alice toasted him, drank what he guessed was a full cup in four quick gulps.

"No trade tonight?" he inquired, mildly cynical.

"Nothing Peggy can't accommodate."

Judson paled. "Who?"

"Oh, the other slut the old bastard's hired on—a stupid wench from Jersey. Peggy's this fat—" She pantomimed the measurements. Judson wiped sweat off his forehead and lay back on the bed as Alice went on, "When she's with a customer, you can hear her grunting all the way downstairs. Disgusting," she declared with a sniff.

166

Then she laughed, harshly. Judson studied her beautiful blue eyes and wondered again whether she was quite sane.

Alice plumped down beside him. "I give the customers something more refined, don't I, love?" Drinking with one hand, she teased his groin with the other. "It costs you nothing—and in exchange, I get to sleep in a bed that isn't crawling with bugs. A lovely bargain, I'd say—"

"If you despise that place so much, why do you work there?"

"Oh, reasons," she said with a vague wave of the cup. "Where else should a poor countryman's daughter work?"

"I've never been convinced you're just a poor countryman's daughter, Alice."

"Then what am I?" she teased, tossing her head. Her hair glistened with that greasy sheen he found repulsive—when he was sober.

"A very attractive young woman who, for some inexplicable reason, chooses to stay wretchedly dirty when she'd glow like the sun if she bathed—"

"Pooh," Alice replied thickly. "Bathing's for rich folk."

"—and who," Judson continued with mock seriousness, "drinks somewhat more than is good for her—"

"Now *that's* a fine comment from a chap who tosses it down the way you do."

"Well, I'm not trying to kill myself with it."

Alice's slightly glazed blue eyes glowed oddly. "You're not?"

"Alice, tell me who the hell you are. What are you running away from? A husband? An indenture contract?"

"Nothing." She repeated it, louder: "Nothing. Listen,

167

Mr. Fine Judson Fletcher—I could ask the same of you!"

He looked away.

"Oh, come on love," she said, more softly. "What's made you so cross with me this evening?" She reached past his thigh for the pamphlet. "Is this the reason for the chilly reception?"

"There!" he exclaimed. " 'Chilly reception.' Tavern trollops don't command such fine phrases—"

Examining the pamphlet's flyleaf, she ignored him:

"Oh, I see what it is. The book everyone's reading. We even had a helmsman tonight who had a copy. A lot of foolishness—just like the business with those dreadful old men at the State House. Why do you bother? Of course, if you hadn't come from Virginia to waste your time at that silly Congress, we'd never have met, would we, love? I'd still be tossing around in that nasty straw every night—instead of sharing a tidy bed. And sporting with a genuine gentleman—"

One hand between his legs, the other, with the cup, dangling down as she crooked her arm around his neck, she rubbed her mouth slowly back and forth across Judson's. Flicked her tongue along his upper lip. He smelled the wine, and her heat:

"We are going to make love, aren't we, Judson? You've improved your mind sufficiently for one evening, haven't you? Brains aren't everything—" Her hand grew bolder. "Master Cock-and-balls needs his exercise too—"

Damn, how she worked on him! Someone, somewhere, had taught her amorous skills in fine detail. He pressed his mouth tight on hers. They kissed a long, langorous moment, her tongue licking at his teeth, wet, sinuous—

But even embracing, he couldn't escape the past.

His hands constricted roughly on Alice's waist as he shoved her down on the bed. She dropped the empty cup

168

and wrapped her arms around his neck. The cup thudded on the carpet. He heard the pamphlet slide off as well—

He didn't care any longer. She'd slipped her blouse down so he could kiss her breasts. The smoky smell of her skin excited him beyond all reason.

"Wait, wait, love. A little more wine first," she gasped, darting away.

Flushed, he stood up. She found the cup and walked into the dark parlor, her blouse pushed all the way to her waist. He heard the decanter clink. He tugged off his throat-stock, his linen shirt. He really didn't understand why he wallowed with this girl who meant nothing to him. Nor did he understand her. Each had built a wall beyond which the other was not permitted.

But penetrating the wall wasn't necessary for their main amusement. He dropped his breeches, then his underclothes. Why the hell did it matter who she was? Physically, she hid nothing.

She had left her clothes in the parlor. She came out of the dark with long, langorous steps, her sky-blue eyes shining bright as the crystal of the decanter in her right hand. Her breasts bobbed at each step. Her lower belly glowed like finespun gold. Her body had a pale beauty that couldn't be marred even by the rings of dirt on her neck and forearms.

Standing next to the bed, Alice caressed the stem of the decanter in a lascivious way. She gazed at Judson's hips and smiled at the production of the desired response.

"I'm not the only one with mysteries, love," she giggled, seating herself on the bed. She cooed with mock disappointment as passion drained out of him suddenly.

"What do you mean, Alice?"

"I saw how you turned white when I mentioned the name Peggy."

"Like hell I did!"

"Who is she, darling? Your mistress in Virginia? A wife you're hiding from me? I don't honestly care, I'm just curious—"

His hand stabbed out. "Give me a drink."

"La, what a rude-tempered swain you are!" She held the decanter out of his reach. *Swain*, he thought. *Too educated by half to be only what she pretends—*

And yet, she played the part. She spilled some of the decanter's contents over her rouged breasts, letting the claret trickle down over her white belly. She sprawled back and uttered one of those wild, unnerving laughs that made him question whether she was of sound mind. What unhappy occurrence in the past had driven her to this unchecked, uncaring recklessness—?

Touching herself, she whispered, "Drink your fill, love."

Swiping the back of his hand across his mouth, he bent toward her.

Soon the rickety bed was creaking in steadily increasing rhythm. Alice raked him with her broken nails and cried her urgency with filthy street language. The decanter discarded on the carpet dripped the last of the claret onto Paine's pamphlet. The book lay open to that final page bearing just seven words, forgotten now; stained by the wine—

THE FREE AND INDEPENDENT STATES OF AMERICA

iv

The mild Pennsylvania winter faded under a mellow sun and the first balmy breezes off the river. Crowds on the streets grew more numerous as the temperatures moderated. Whether the Philadelphians wore the brocade of the wealthy or the craftsman's homespun, the livery of servants or the rags of youngsters hawking flowers or papers or fragrant bread up and down High and Chestnut Streets, chances were excellent that if they hadn't read Tom Paine's *Common Sense,* they had an opinion about it, or had heard of it at very least. As they'd heard the astonishing tidings couriers brought in from Boston:

By night, General Washington had fortified the Dorchester Heights with cannon brought from Fort Ticonderoga by his chief of artillery, a Colonel Knox. In a short span of hours between one sunset and the next dawn, two thousand men had performed the herculean task of digging earthworks and moving the weapons into place.

And just in time.

General Howe had planned to break out of the city. American intelligence had picked up definite word of an impending attack. But a violent storm prevented it. Then all at once, Washington's guns stared down on the rooftops. By the morning of the seventeenth of March, Boston was empty of the king's soldiers. All had been loaded aboard ships and evacuated to Halifax along with at least a thousand Tory families. From Halifax, it was said, a major British thrust would be mounted.

Among the patriot faction in Congress, there was jubilation. The Continental army, conceived and authorized by the Philadelphia body, had won its first significant victory. If not on a battleground, then in the hearts of its partisans.

But fear mingled with the elation. Where would Howe strike? There was little doubt that he *would* strike. America remained "in rebellion."

Even more reason to declare independence, the radicals argued in the large and lovely white room of the State House. It was time to unite the thirteen colonies for a concerted effort against the Crown; a war unhampered by hesitation. A war to secure American liberty forever.

The conservatives still shrank from it. What was needed, Judson's fellow radicals agreed, was a resolution to force the issue

V

Alice continued to visit Judson regularly. After that night in January, no more questions passed between them about the origins of the other, or about motives for the liaison.

Judson knew his own demons and strongly suspected that Alice had hers. But he decided that trying to force those demons into the light would probably serve no purpose. Would only cause trouble, in fact, since Alice seemed set on keeping them hidden. So he took pleasure in her highly sexed nature and at the same time worked to control his drinking. The results proved satisfactory. No more warnings were issued by Tom Jefferson, who treated him cordially again, though it plainly required effort. Jefferson's mother had died of an apoplectic seizure the end of March, and immediately, the tall Virginian began to suffer violent headaches that left his face bleached with pain.

For Judson, life was somewhat easier. When he held Alice in his arms after an hour of lovemaking, he slept deeply, free of dreams of Seth McLean's wife.

The Congressional committees labored from early morning till late in the day. One session in early April ran particularly long. Judson didn't arrive back at Windmill Street until shortly before midnight. As he opened the outer door, he saw a lamp burning in the bedroom—and Alice, standing in front of the ancient, flecked pier glass.

He called her name from the dark parlor but got no response. He started forward, heard her voice, pulled up short.

Quite drunk, Alice was watching herself in the mirror.

172

She touched her bare body now and then. Tears ran down her cheeks. Her slurred words stunned and frightened him:

"Philip? Why did you go? Why didn't you love me enough, Philip?"

He crept back to the outer landing. There he made sufficient noise to attract her attention before he re-entered. He didn't let on that he had seen her haunted face.

Or heard her speaking some lost lover's name as if her heart would break.

vi

From the south came alarming news. British vessels with troops aboard were cruising the coast of the Carolinas, obviously intending to launch an attack. The rebellion was no longer solely a Massachusetts problem, but an American one.

In Congress, the radicals continued to press their case in lengthy debates. Finally North Carolina empowered its delegates to support a declaration for independence. And at a meeting of the Virginia House of Burgesses in May, that colony followed suit. Even as riders on lathered horses brought word to Philadelphia that the British flotilla had dropped anchor off Charleston, South Carolina, and that an armed strike under the joint leadership of General Clinton and the newly arrived General Cornwallis was imminent, the ranking member of Judson's delegation rose to introduce a resolution.

Feeling a deep sense of pride because Virginia had finally provided the means for Congress to act, Judson sat with the other delegates and watched the handsome president of the body, John Hancock. On the wall behind Hancock's desk hung a drum, British swords and banners captured at Fort Ticonderoga. With appropriate protocol, Hancock recognized Richard Henry Lee.

Scowls appeared on the faces of John Dickinson and his fellow conservatives. They knew what was coming. To Judson, the morning light pouring through the chamber's tall windows had a luminous quality.

Having been recognized, the patrician Lee began to read the resolution modeled after the one adopted in his native state:

"The resolution embodies three propositions, the first being as follows. That these united colonies are, and of right ought to be, free and independent states. That they are absolved from all allegiance to the British Crown, and that all political connection between them and the state of Great Britain is, and ought to be, totally dissolved—"

The room was stuffy. Sunlight glared on the windowpanes, shone on the brass fittings of the chamber's two fireplaces. Men coughed, shuffled their feet, glanced at the narrow openings at the tops of the windows as if longing for more air. The windows were kept almost completely shut at all times, to prevent the frequently loud debates from being overheard in the street.

Despite the heat, the discomfort, Judson was suddenly aglow with a sense of purpose—of counting for something—that he had never experienced before.

While Lee continued to read, Judson glanced at Tom Jefferson. He sat hunched over, his palms pressed against his cheeks and his fingertips covering his closed eyes. Judson assumed he was suffering from another of the headaches that had afflicted him almost constantly since his mother's burial in Virginia. Across the chamber, Dr. Franklin kept his eye on John Adams, who sat with arms folded, taut, ready to spring up for the inevitable debate.

To Judson, never a religious person, the June morning had power to cleanse his soul. It was, somehow, a bright and sacred occasion—

Which rapidly degenerated into noise and rancor as

proponents and opponents shouted to be recognized in order to debate the issue posed by the resolution.

vii

"Damme, sirs, I'll prepare no document designed for approval by a group!" Benjamin Franklin declared three evenings later, over coffee and tea cups at The Sovereign near the State House. "I can forsee the surgery that'll be done upon it."

"Ben, don't be so confounded stubborn!" John Adams said.

"On this, I will be stubborn. Let me tell you a story—"

"I hope it's pertinent," Adams snapped.

"Extremely. I once knew a fellow here in Philadelphia who desired to open a hatter's shop. He put hours of energy and effort into designing and finishing the most important feature of such a shop—the signboard for attracting customers. He meticulously painted a hat on it, and the inscription 'John Thompson, hatter, makes and sells hats for ready money.' Then the poor fool consulted his friends. One said that because of the drawing, the word 'hatter' was superfluous. Out it went with a stroke of the brush! Someone else said that 'makes' should be deleted, since people who purchased hats didn't give a damn who made 'em. 'Ready money' was wasteful wordage—everyone knew Thompson never extended credit. Thus his precious board was reduced to 'John Thompson sells hats.' Ah, said another helpful soul, but who will be dunce enough to believe you'd give 'em away? So all the hours of work and thought produced nothing more than a worthless piece of wood with all of its legend brushed over, save for 'John Thompson' and the hat drawing, which was poorly done in the first place. Spare me from editorial congresses of any sort!" Franklin concluded cheerily.

"I'll yield the labor—and the later discomfort produced by the disemboweling of every other phrase—to our more eloquent and hardy gentlemen of Virginia."

"Not me, doctor," Judson declared when Franklin looked at him. He wished for a good drink of rum, instead of the weak tea he'd ordered. "I'm a poor writer at best."

"Then you, Tom." Franklin's curious spectacles with lenses of two different thicknesses flashed back the lamplight. "I'll be of what help I can, but you have both the skill for the writing, and the young man's vigor to withstand the editing."

Pursing his lips, Adams said, "But naturally you'll interject a few ideas."

Franklin beamed. "Naturally. Correcting others is easy. What do you say, Tom?"

Jefferson looked doubtful. From his waistcoat pocket he pulled a scrap of paper and laid it on the table. "My forte is composition of a particular and limited kind, gentlemen."

That produced laughter. Jefferson's spell of headaches had passed, and he didn't mind a joke at his own expense. His friends knew he was notorious as a maker of meticulous lists: the daily weather in Philadelphia; the delegates and where they stood on independence, day by day and week by week; or the list he'd just shown them. Leaning over, Judson saw that it itemized Jefferson's current living expenses.

As he put the list away, Jefferson added, "I'd really prefer not to carry the whole responsibility—"

"Damme, we have a committee, a committee!" Adams thumped the table. "Appointed this very day—!"

Franklin shook his head. "A committee never accomplishes anything save the wasting of time and the destruction of sound ideas. The committee can submit the draft, but one man must write it. Else we'll never

176

debate and vote by the first of the month."

From the corner, the scowling Adams declared, "And since a decision has been postponed until the Congress *is* presented with a document, a document we must have! *Ipso facto,* we require an author. Like Ben, I shun that role with a passion, and defer to you, Tom."

"Why?" Jefferson wanted to know.

"Reason the first—you are a Virginian, and a Virginian ought to appear at the head of this business. There is too much opprobrium attached to the name of Massachusetts. Reason second, because of my vehemence in favor of independence, I am suspected, unpopular and considered obnoxious." Adams sounded almost boastful, but Judson had to admit that the statement was correct. "Reason third—and the most important—you can write ten times better than I can."

"No more arguments," Franklin said. "You're elected."

Jefferson sighed. "Very well, I'll try it. But there are complex questions. What about the condemnation of slavery we discussed? Though I own slaves myself, I think we should include it. But it's certain to be disapproved by most of the southern delegates—"

The discussion continued until almost ten, with little settled except Jefferson's role in preparing the necessary statement for submission to the Congress. After the gathering adjourned, Judson walked slowly back to Windmill Street, savoring the balmy June air.

He hoped Alice would visit this evening. He was anxious to tell her what had happened today: the appointment of the committee to draft a declaration of separation. He knew she wouldn't be very interested. But his intense enthusiasm, fed by the mounting tensions in the elegant white room of the State House, had to find an outlet—

In the deep shadow on the corner opposite his lodging-house, he stopped. On another corner, he saw a man leaning against a brick wall. A very tall man whose features were hidden by the darkness. The man wore a cloak and tricorn and seemed to be studying the windows of Judson's bedroom—

There, a lamp burned. Had Alice already arrived?

Some warning instinct turned Judson's palms sweaty. He hesitated only a moment before making up his mind. He started across the intersection toward the tall watcher—

Who promptly wheeled and hurried off down Windmill Street.

But not before Judson had seen the man's cloak bell out as he passed under a streetlamp. The lamp revealed something that flashed dull yellow—

Metal-work. On a pistol in the man's belt.

Alarmed, Judson climbed the shaky stairs to his door. He was suddenly extremely thirsty again.

viii

Alice seemed in a gay, playful mood. He hesitated to mention the watcher. He wondered whether the man had been there before.

Judson and the girl drank, then tumbled into bed. An hour later, Alice slept restlessly in the crook of his bare arm. The fragrant air of early summer, turned even more ripe by the smell of the river, stirred the curtains.

Somehow the lovemaking had had an unusual effect on him. Ordinarily he went right to sleep afterward. Tonight he was tense; but not unpleasantly so.

Maybe it was the gathering momentum of events in the Congress. Earlier, while they tossed down claret, he'd described his day to Alice, ignoring her obvious boredom. He couldn't possibly be bored. One way or another, the issue should be resolved in early July when Jefferson's draft declaration was presented by the committee—

Musing, he was a fraction late in hearing the stealthy

footstep on the landing.

The door crashed in, the fragile latch booted to pieces by the hulking figure silhouetted against the moonlight.

"Stand fast in there!" a raspy voice commanded. Alice stirred. "I have a pistol."

And so the intruder did. It was the tall man Judson had seen earlier.

The man took a couple of steps into the parlor. "Light a lamp."

Judson hesitated, cold beneath the coverlet.

"I said light a lamp or I'll send a ball your way!"

Judson reached clumsily for the lamp and a sulphur match. In a moment a roseate glow lit the bedchamber. Alice rolled over on her back, muttering to herself. A section of the cover fell away, revealing her breasts.

Still in bed but with hands braced under him, Judson watched the tall man enter the room. Servant's livery showed under his open cloak. Lamplight gleamed on the brass-chased pistol. Judson didn't miss the way the man's supercilious eyes roved over Alice's exposed body.

"Get up and go to the inside wall," the tall man ordered. When Judson didn't instantly obey, the servant snarled, "Any further delay and it will be my distinct pleasure to kill you. A regrettable loss for the Continental Congress, eh, Mr. Fletcher?"

Naked and genuinely frightened, Judson pushed back the coverlet. He walked barefoot to the place indicated.

"It's taken a deal of searching to find her," the tall man remarked. "Months, in fact. We never imagined she'd go into the stews. Where you obviously took advantage of her. Ample cause for an accident, I'd say. However, if you remain quiet you'll come to no harm." He sounded as if he regretted the fact.

The tall man turned and called softly toward the landing:

"She's here, sir. It's safe to come in. Our Virginia
179

gentleman is pacified for the moment."

A portly, elegantly dressed man of middle age almost tiptoed through the parlor. He gazed at the restless girl, horrified:

"My God, smell the wine on her! No wonder she doesn't wake up—" Face mottled, he swung on Judson. "By heaven, sir, if you've debauched her—"

"*Debauched her!*" Judson guffawed. The nightmare had turned ludicrous suddenly. "She's a tavern whore! Just who the hell are you?"

"Careful how you address Mr. Trumbull," advised the servant.

"Yes, but you've got the better of me. Who—?"

"Never mind. We know who you are, and that's enough."

The portly man bent over at the bedside and began to chafe Alice's wrists. She groaned, thrashed her head from side to side as if resisting the hands on her flesh. *Trumbull, Trumbull,* Judson's mind repeated. He'd heard the name before. The Trumbulls of Arch Street were a prominent Tory family. The head of it—the portly man?—owned a large, prosperous ropewalk.

"Alicia, wake up. Alicia, it's Uncle Tobias come to take you home—"

"Alicia?" Judson repeated. "Her name's Alice."

The portly man directed another hateful glance at him. Judson realized he must have been followed for some length of time. Days; perhaps weeks. The naked girl just opening her sky-blue eyes and pushing back a strand of dirty hair was—as he'd suspected—someone other than whom she pretended to be.

All at once Alice's eyes focused. She sat upright as if she'd been slapped. Her voice was a mixture of terror and fury:

"What are you doing here, Tobias? Get away—get out!"

The portly man paled. "Alicia, cover your nakedness!

180

What am I doing here—?" A gesture to the servant with one ringed hand. The tall man watched Alice with quick alternating glances at Judson. "We have searched Philadelphia for months to locate you! What I am doing here is taking you back to Arch Street. To your aunt, who's been devastated—driven to her bed!—ever since you disappeared last fall. To find you working in a wharf den and consorting with a man who would destroy these colonies—!"

The sentence sputtered out. Tory politics and the morality of the well-entrenched made Mr. Tobias Trumbull speechless with outrage. But he managed to seize Alice's wrist again.

"I'm where I want to be!" She jerked her hand away. "Leave me alone."

"She's ailing," Trumbull gasped to his servant. "Robbed of her senses by grief—"

"Or by drink, and this lecher," the tall man said, pointing the pistol at Judson.

"Alicia, you must come home. We'll find the best doctors—restore you to health—"

"Get out of here!" Alice screamed in her best riverfront bellow. Then she began to curse Trumbull with oaths that bleached his reddened cheeks. Even the tall servant looked surprised—and in that moment, Judson moved with long, swift strides.

The servant swore, leveled his pistol. For one dreadful moment Judson stared down the muzzle. He grabbed the servant's wrist, cracked it over his leg, caught the pistol and drove his bare knee into the tall man's groin.

Judson jumped back as the tall man stumbled against the wall, teeth clenching. The servant recovered, lunged—

Only to halt as Judson took another long step back and aimed the pistol at his forehead. The servant glared.

Judson felt harrowingly sober, somewhat ridiculous—nude with a pistol in one hand—and not a little confused:

"Now before this charade continues, I want an explanation." To the portly man: "You claim to be her relative—"

"My wife is her aunt! She is Mrs. Alicia Amberly, widow of an officer in His Majesty's service and daughter of the Earl of Parkhurst."

"*Earl?*" Judson exploded, slack-jawed from this latest surprise. Alice had covered her breasts and was watching the scene like a trapped animal. She too was sober now, he judged. But still irrational. He had seen those sky-blue eyes glaze like that before—

He could hardly believe what he'd just learned. Still, if true, it would explain much about the girl's strange, contradictory personality—

Trumbull swung to Alice but pointed at Judson:

"Do you realize what sort of man you've fallen in with? One of those political cheapjacks who—"

"Now I understand why you know so much about me," Judson interrupted. "I've been spied upon."

"She has been hunted," the servant corrected, still furious.

"For the most humane of reasons!" Trumbull exclaimed. "Sorrow over the death of her husband, Lieutenant Colonel Amberly, caused her to run away. Sickness of the mind made her seek refuge in—squalor, in—"

Suddenly Alice screamed out, "I ran because my lover deserted me, you stupid old fool! My *American* lover. He turned his back on me—*that's* why I ran—"

Judson was horrified by the wild brightness in the girl's eyes. He remembered Alice standing at the pier glass. Was *Philip* the American she'd loved—?

Again Trumbull could barely speak: "Alicia—what you're saying—it's against all propriety, it's—obscenity—a symptom of your derangement—"

He lurched for her. "You will come home for care, for protection—"

She spat in the fat Tory's face.

Trumbull wiped the saliva from his jowl. For the first time, he turned pleading eyes to Judson:

"In God's name, sir—help me!"

Judson shook his head. "Why? The decision is Alice's."

"Her name is Alicia, you arrogant bastard!"

"The decision is still hers. You have no right to force her out of here."

The servant licked his lips. "He has debauched her, Mr. Trumbull. That's obvious now."

"I am here *by choice!*" Alice screamed again.

"Oh, God—child, please—" Trumbull was almost weeping.

Judson lifted the pistol, gestured toward the door open on the mellow June night:

"I think you'd better leave. At once. There is no law of which I'm aware that can compel her to go with you. I'm not holding her prisoner. So if she chooses to stay with me, there's not a damn thing you can do about it."

Livid, Tobias Trumbull said, "You'll do nothing to assist me when she obviously needs medical attention?"

"Nothing," Judson repeated. "Unless she agrees to it."

"No," Alice whispered, fingers like claws on the coverlet.

"I—" Trumbull swallowed. Then a bit more determination seemed to infuse his bloated face. "I do have one recourse in the face of behavior such as yours, Mr. Fletcher. Gentleman to gentleman—" The last word seethed with contempt. "I can demand satisfaction."

Judson's eyes raked the wheezing, overweight man. "Don't be an idiot. You're not up to a duel."

"Please—"

Alice was moaning now; moaning and swaying back

183

and forth. Judson knew Trumbull was right about one thing: something in the girl's past had damaged her mind.

Abruptly, she burst into tears:

"No more quarreling!" She covered her ears. "*Leave me alone!*"

The awful howl turned Trumbull's face pure white. He glared at Judson again. Behind Trumbull, the servant smiled sardonically.

"Then you'll deny me satisfaction?" Trumbull asked. "You're not only a traitor but a coward, is that it?"

Stung by the insult, Judson shouted, "Goddamn it, if that's what you want, send your second!"

Instantly, he regretted the outburst. It was the wrong thing to do on several counts. Trumbull was a pathetically weak-looking man. Yet accepting the challenge gave Judson a perverse satisfaction, somehow.

The tall servant bowed. "I will call on you in due course, Mr. Fletcher. Come, Mr. Trumbull—" Gently, he took the shaking Tory's arm. "—the matter is settled. When you've disposed of this gentleman, Mrs. Amberly can be brought home comfortably."

At the landing the servant glanced back, still amused:

"Keep the pistol for a time, Mr. Fletcher. I'll reclaim it after Mr. Trumbull puts an end to your life."

The door with its splintered latch closed.

Judson stared at the brasswork of the gun. Sick and furious, he flung the pistol on the floor. It skidded, struck the wall.

He sat down beside—what had they called her? Alicia Amberly? It didn't matter. He was consumed with terror and pity. Her sky-blue eyes had an almost infantile quality now.

One hand groped out to touch his chin. She said in a tiny, plaintive voice:

"No fighting, darling. There's been too much blood and hurt already, dearest. Promise me—"

Suddenly she pitched against him, her bare breasts cold; so cold. Her hands worked at his shoulder muscles:

"Promise me there'll be no fighting, Philip. Promise!"

"Alice, I—I'm not—"

No use. She was crying again. Wild, gulping sobs that told him just how fragile her mental balance really was.

He became aware of a noise that had intruded at the edge of his consciousness some time ago, but which he only now identified: a thudding from below. The tinker.

A faint voice demanded to know the cause of the uproar.

"Nothing wrong," Judson shouted over Alice's hysterical sobs. "It'll be quiet in a moment—"

"—tolerate no unseemly behavior in my house!" The voice faded.

Judson stroked the girl's filthy hair and stared over her shoulder at the pistol lying near the baseboard. Several times he repeated the name by which he knew her. She didn't answer or even respond, only kept kneading his muscles and crying like a sick child.

CHAPTER VII

The Thirteen Clocks

AFTER THE departure of the surprise visitors, Judson threw on a robe and persuaded Alice to drink a bit of the only remedy he had to hand—claret. She held the cup between her work-reddened hands, gulping greedily. She shuddered. Some of the glassy quality seemed to leave her eyes.

Mightily relieved, Judson saw that she recognized him, and her surroundings.

"Alice—" Though the name seemed awkward in light of Trumbull's revelation, he couldn't use the other with comfort. "—is that man really your aunt's husband?"

Her bowed head hid her face. "Yes."

"And you ran off from his home in Arch Street?"

"I was tending my husband who was—wounded while serving in Boston. He died and—please, no more, Judson," she finished in a whisper.

"But he said you were an earl's daughter. Is that true?"

"It was." Her mouth twisted. "Once."

"Who was Philip?"

"*Stop!*" she cried, hurling the cup at his head.

He dodged. The cup hit the wall, shattered. Once again the tinker thumped his ceiling and demanded quiet. Judson shouted ill-tempered assurances, then started pacing the bedroom. Alice had bundled herself in the coverlet as if she were extremely cold.

He saw how everything Trumbull said could be possi-

186

ble. The lines of her face were fine, delicate; or had been, before dissipation blurred them—

Alice stroked her arm. The flesh was prickled with tiny bumps. "Judson?"

He faced her, still dismayed by the information that had put a whole new perspective on their relationship. She'd meant next to nothing to him until the moment he discovered who she was, and what had driven her to her present state. Now he felt a new, deep concern. With it, he felt confusion about what to do.

"I heard a little of what they said, Judson. Talk of dueling—"

"That stupid uncle of yours wants satisfaction."

"Don't fight him—" She sprang naked from the bed, clutching at him. "Swear you won't! I've brought on too much ruin already—"

He caressed her hair. "Alice, I haven't much choice."

"You have the choice of saying no!"

Judson shook his head.

"*Why not?*"

"Because—" He could offer only one rather sour explanation. "—that's the way it is among gentlemen."

Although it was a truthful response, it seemed unsatisfactory. A moment later he understood why. He dared not admit the real truth. Deep in him, something wanted to lash out and maim—

He was ashamed and vaguely excited at the same time. Christ, how despicable he was!

"Then you won't promise—?" she began.

"The best I can do is try to get the poor fellow to reconsider and withdraw his challenge."

"If you face him, would—would you kill him?"

"He's fat, slow and twice my age. Yes, I think I would."

She stared into his eyes a moment longer, then limped back to the bed, covered herself and burrowed deep into the pillow. Her shoulders shook as she sobbed. The

187

sound of her voice reminded him of Peggy McLean's on the night of the slave uprising.

He poured more claret for himself—that seemed the only antidote to this muddled situation—and crawled into bed with her.

He pulled her close, tried to comfort her. Gradually her hysterical crying moderated and she fell asleep. Somewhere toward the hour when the stars paled, he did too.

When he awoke after sunup, his head aching, she was gone.

Every trace of clothing—every indication that she'd been in the room had disappeared, except two:

A strand of hair he found clinging to the still-warm bedclothes. And the tall servant's pistol gleaming in a ray of morning sun.

ii

News arriving in Philadelphia during June's balmy weather heartened the patriots. The British flotilla at Charleston had been repulsed and heavily damaged, thanks to the accurate, steady fire of the Americans entrenched in a fort of palmetto logs on Sullivan's Island in the harbor.

And members of Congress began to converse in whispers about *Roderigue Hortalez et Cie.*, a mysterious private trading company just organized in France. The company had one express purpose: to speed shipments of war materiel, including barrel after barrel of vitally needed black powder, to the colonies.

Some speculated that King Louis XVI, no friend of Britain, had callously seized an opportunity to strike at his country's traditional enemy via the Americans. If that were the real reason for the abrupt birth of the peculiar firm, no one loyal to the colonial side would quarrel. Dr. Franklin reported to a few confidants that similar covert assistance might be forthcoming under the auspices of Charles III of Spain.

But what heartened the patriots most was a hope:

If France had moved with such dispatch to aid the Americans in secret, perhaps, with careful diplomacy, the French might be persuaded to openly ally themselves with the rebels. Franklin thought it not impossible at all. And he expressed complete willingness to take advantage of the centuries-old European rivalry.

But whatever the outcome in that area, the long-term prospects for the war looked a shade less grim now that *Hortalez et Cie.* was operating under the personal direction of a most unlikely manager—the author and court wit, Beaumarchais.

Judson absorbed the news in the corridors of the State House, or in whispered conferences in the great white chamber that grew more and more sultry as the weather warmed. The windows still remained almost completely shut as the Congress labored on, awaiting the completion of the draft declaration by the committee.

Concern for Alice had somewhat lessened Judson's interest in the cause. He was drinking heavily again. He spent a large part of his time searching the city for the girl. But she had left the waterfront tavern where she worked and dropped completely out of sight.

The days dragged. There was no communication from the Trumbull household. Then Francis Lightfoot Lee took Judson aside and politely informed him that the challenge by the Tory ropewalk owner had become a choice item of gossip in the city. On behalf of Judson's friends among the delegates, Lee hoped—trusted—some settlement less scandalous than a public duel could be worked out.

Judson promised to do what he could. He penned a careful note which he dispatched to Arch Street. In the note, offered to entertain Mr. Trumbull's reconsideration of the challenge. A day later, Judson's landlord handed him an answer when he returned from the State House.

He questioned the landlord:

Yes, the person who had delivered the reply was tall; and damned arrogant for a servant. Judson broke the elaborate wax seal and unfolded the parchment. He read the note, then crumpled it and threw it away.

Far from accepting Judson's offer, Mr. Tobias Trumbull re-stated his demand for satisfaction more strongly than ever. The unfortunate Mrs. Amberly could not be located anywhere. The Trumbulls feared for her safety—and blamed him. Therefore Judson would please take steps to choose a time, a place and the weapons by which they would settle their quarrel.

iii

In the middle of the final week of June, there were signs of incredibly hot weather soon to come. On the afternoon Judson called at the rooms Tom Jefferson rented in a large brick house at High and Seventh Streets, the air had a hazy gray quality, minus any trace of wind.

The normally tidy parlor which Judson had visited on several occasions was a litter of crumpled foolscap. The young Virginian sat by a window, his beloved viola and some compositions by Purcell and Vivaldi gathering dust on a table nearby. One of Jefferson's arms was draped laconically over the back of his chair. A quill dangled from his inky fingers.

Across the room, Dr. Franklin occupied a settee. He acknowledged Judson's entrance with a cordial nod, then poked a finger at the sheet he'd been scanning:

"Tom, I find this wordy—'we hold these truths to be sacred and undeniable.' Wouldn't 'self-evident' serve as well?"

"Yes, that's good, scratch it in," Jefferson answered. He sounded tired and indifferent. Franklin picked up another quill, dipped it in a well and made the correction.

Noticing Judson's rather awkward pose at the parlor door, Jefferson laid aside the portable writing-box of highly polished wood that had been resting on his lap. He had designed the miniature desk himself, folding top and all. He lifted his long body from the chair, stretched, yawned.

"I only want to complete the damned thing and get on with the debate," he said. "Will you join me in tea this warm afternoon, Judson?"

"If you have it, I'd prefer something stronger."

Once more that vaguely accusing expression flickered across the Virginian's face, on which summer sunlight had brought out a considerable number of freckles. But he nodded politely, poured a glass of Madeira, his forehead glistening with sweat. Then Jefferson helped himself to tea from a pot.

Franklin tossed aside the foolscap sheet, pushed his spectacles up on his forehead, massaged the bridge of his nose:

"I would say we are approaching a finished draft." To the other man, with a smile: "What brings you here, Judson? Some additional thoughts for Tom to put in?"

"No, it's a personal matter."

"Well, before you launch into it, have you any final opinion about including a passage referring to slavery?" He indicated the discarded sheet. "Tom's still pushing for it."

Judson's brows hooked up as he sipped. The Madeira eased his edgy feeling. "You're talking about a passage condemning slavery?"

Jefferson nodded. "An instrument of oppression permitted, not to say encouraged, by His Majesty."

"It's going a bit far to blame the king for the blackbird trade, isn't it? He may permit it—but we practice it."

Jefferson stared out the window at the clatter of High Street. "Aye, a point. And my own hands—and my conscience—are dirty on that score."

"If we include it, I predict the declaration will be voted down," Judson said with conviction. "Dickinson and his friends are fighting us for every vote. Even stated in temperate language, an anti-slavery clause would sink us for good."

"I loathe the trade," Franklin said. "I organized the first anti-slavery club in the whole of this city. But I agree with your assessment, Judson."

"I'm still not prepared to strike it out at this stage," Jefferson warned them.

Franklin's eyes narrowed. "Nor ever?"

"Only if it becomes crucial to success or failure."

Heaving his bulk up from the settee, Franklin mopped his neck with a kerchief and picked up his coat of brown velour. He draped it over his arm, saying:

"It will, Tom, never fear, it will. Gentlemen, I'll leave you to your private business."

As Franklin departed, Judson helped himself to another drink. He felt sure the Pennsylvania scholar knew why he'd called—and had deliberately absented himself from the discussion. The entire Congress knew about Judson's predicament by now.

"Tom, I'll come right to it. I'm going to face Trumbull."

"Didn't Francis Lee speak with you?"

"Yes."

"And urge you to reconsider?"

"I sent Trumbull a letter agreeing to forget the matter. In reply, he insisted we go ahead. We've arranged it for the third of July, in the morning, someplace up the Delaware. I come to you as a friend, Tom. I know very few people in Philadelphia, and I need a second."

Unhappily, Tom Jefferson ran a hand over his clubbed red hair. With a look that sent Judson's hopes

192

plummeting, he answered:

"In other circumstances, I might do it. Now—it's impossible."

"Because of the reasons you mentioned back in January? The moral outrage it might cause—?"

Jefferson agreed with another nod. "You realize what may happen if you go ahead, don't you, Judson? President Hancock is well aware of the trouble. He has again made his feelings—his strong feelings—known to me. If you persist, in all likelihood you'll be quietly asked to withdraw from the Virginia delegation. I'm afraid I'd have to support that request. I'm sorry, Judson, but I fail to see how some tavern trollop is worth—"

White-lipped, Judson cut him off: "We needn't debate the details."

"Yes, we very much need to debate them. Damn it, Judson, no one among your close associates—least of all those of us from your home colony—can understand why you let yourself be drawn into such a shabby business. A futile, purposeless encounter over a woman who—"

"Tom, that's enough."

"On the contrary! You're being obstinate. You act damned near driven to this!"

Judson turned away. "Maybe I am."

"Well, it's a shameful waste. One day you're in the thick of things, working, debating, using your considerable intellect—the next, you're off swilling down so much strong drink you make Franklin look like a temperance lecturer! I puzzle over it, Judson."

Cold-eyed, Judson said, "Why bother?"

"Because—in a short time—" An eloquent shrug. "—you've become a friend. I try and try to understand what flogs you to these excesses—"

"So do I," Judson replied with a bitter smile.

"Have you found any answers?"

"Only one—and that not very satisfactory. I've con-

193

cluded that in this world, certain men are stronger than others. The weaker ones are unable to accommodate themselves to normal behavior—and finding themselves not fitting the pattern, they're destroyed by the situation. Or destroy themselves—"

"Are you sure that's not merely the wine talking?"

"No." He tossed off the rest of the Madeira. "My father. On numerous occasions."

"It's idiotic to surrender to that sort of defeatist philosophy."

"I'm a misfit, Tom. I always will be. Recognizing that, I've at least carried out one of my father's wishes." Judson's eyes grew bitterly amused. "He cautioned me against ever marrying, since if I did, I'd surely pass along my waywardness to generations of helpless, suffering grandchildren—"

"Nonsense. You're indulging in self-pity."

Judson smiled again, this time with utter charm. "But that goes with being a misfit."

Jefferson refused to be diverted: "If we bring about independency, Judson—if we can finish this war soon—"

"A pair of mighty tall *ifs*."

"Granted, granted. But think of what's to be won! All the chances you have to break out of this—this pattern you claim you despise—"

"I don't understand."

"Do you have any notion of the size of this continent, Judson? We're only crouching on the edge! It stretches from the Floridas to Hudson's Bay, and beyond. Out west, past the Ohio, the French fur traders have traveled a river that beggars the imagination! The Sieur de La Salle named it the Colbert but the Indians call it Big River. *Misi Sipi*." He was striding now, caught up in his vision.

"We're getting off the subject, Tom."

"No, no, we're not! This land mass is huge! Bountiful

as well. Who knows the full extent of the wealth it holds between that big river and the Pacific? I tell you the Spanish are doing their best to learn the answers—with their presidios and missions in what they christened the New Philippines. Imagine if even a portion of that territory were ours! If the foreign flags came down—the lions and castles of Leon and Castile flying right now in the southwest—the area they're coming to call *Tejas*— think of the opportunity for settlement! Agriculture and commerce! The general increase of human knowledge! All I'm saying to you, Judson, is that with such vast lands still contested in the west, no man should feel hemmed in by his immediate surroundings. By the Lord, I don't intend to be. Before I die, I mean to see a scientific expedition walk that whole wilderness to the Pacific!"

After a moment of silence, Judson said, "I understand a little of what you're saying. One of my good friends has already traveled past the Blue Ridge. Sometimes I've thought I belonged out there with him—"

"Who is your friend?"

"George Clark."

"George Rogers Clark?"

"That's right."

"He's already made a distinguished name scouting with the Virginia militia. But leaving the opportunity in the west aside for a moment—"

"Yes, because the idea's unrealistic. I'll never get there."

Judson's emphatic statement checked Jefferson before he could begin another sentence. His enthusiasm vanished, replaced first by a look of regret, then by an expression faintly stern and righteous:

"Very well, that may be so. But no matter what his condition or location, a man grown to adulthood is at least called to exercise self-control."

"That's another lecture I've received from my father."

Jefferson gnawed his lip. Then:

"In short, you won't try to moderate your behavior? Keep your eye on greater possibilities than what's up a skirt or down in the bottom of a glass?"

"I try." A pause. "I always fail."

"Does that mean you won't reconsider the Trumbull matter?"

"At this late hour—I can't."

"Not even in view of the probable consequences? Hancock will almost certainly insist you withdraw and return to Virginia."

"Let him."

"Judson, what are you trying to prove about yourself?"

"I beg your pardon?"

"To whom are you trying to demonstrate your independence? Your manhood—?"

Judson set the Madeira glass down, noisily. "I'm in no mood for subtle discourses—"

"Nothing subtle about it," Jefferson waved. "I see you as you can't see yourself. Sometimes you permit your essential nature to shine through. A good mind, moral courage of the highest order. Then you seem to lose sight of those qualities. Or quell them deliberately. I think only a man overcome with loathing for himself acts that way. You've mentioned your father—is he the one you're constantly—?"

"Good day, Tom." A muscle in his neck bulging, Judson started out.

"Wait! Listen to me! You'll destroy yourself, trying to prove something that doesn't need prov—"

The slam of the door shut out the rest.

Judson rushed down the stairs toward High Street, noisy with wagons rolling in from the country laden with farm produce. The astute Mr. Tom Jefferson had struck into depths Judson didn't care to plumb. Very uncomfortable depths—

As he walked through the hazy gray afternoon, ignoring several stares directed his way—the forthcoming duel was a town scandal—an image of Alice loomed in his mind.

The Trumbulls had driven her to her pathetic state. That angry conviction was validation enough for what he meant to do.

The image of Alice dissolved into another. His father—

Yes, Jefferson had struck much too close to the truth. Whatever the causes, he was poisoned by a frequent, almost wholly uncontrollable desire to defy convention, or any authority; to choose one road when he knew another was the accepted way—

Who was to blame? As if it mattered any longer! Or would change anything—

Instead of returning to committee session, he turned in at the first available ale shop and lost himself in the airless gloom, safe for a while from the reality of the world outside. It wasn't long before his inner world was similarly deadened and remote.

iv

Thunder shook the State House. Bursts of lightning glared like infernal fire let up from the bowels of the earth. The storm ripped across Philadelphia, slamming rain against the tightly shut windows and reverberating through the chamber where John Hancock again occupied the presidential dais.

The air in the room was boiling. Judson's face streamed with sweat. He swatted at one of the mammoth horseflies that had somehow invaded the chamber to bedevil the perspiring men listening to John Dickinson defend his position:

"—and I therefore cannot in conscience support the

197

resolution yesterday debated by this Congress sitting as a committee of the whole with Mr. Harrison as chairman—"

The fuzzy-sounding voice irritated Judson. He was starting to sober up, and didn't feel at all well. He wanted to leave, find a tavern, quench his thirst.

Exactly what day was it? He'd lost track—

With a jolt he realized it was the second of July. Tomorrow, unseconded, he'd face Trumbull. Perhaps the steady approach of the day of the duel was what had kept him in a constant stupor for the past week. That, and no word about Alice; she had utterly vanished.

He blinked, feeling more bilious by the moment. He changed the position of his chair noisily. He was aware of the disapproving stares of the Lees and George Wythe at desks nearby. Even Jefferson, nervously fingering a copy of his completed draft declaration, appeared less than friendly. Dickinson's damnably boring voice droned on.

Judson slouched, dull-headed, callously indifferent. To hell with all of them. He had no business in this lofty gathering. He was exactly what Angus Fletcher had always said he was. A wastrel—

What in God's name was that idiot Dickinson saying now?

"—I have long stood firmly against abuses perpetrated by His Majesty's ministers—"

A few canes rapped agreement. There was another crackle of thunder, then blinding whiteness outside the rain-rivered windows.

"—and in fact have publicly condemned those abuses in publications of which you are fully aware. But I see nothing save disaster in the resolution it is proposed we vote on today. To favor independency is akin to torching our house in winter before we have got another shelter. I beg you to consider the consequences of the total war which will surely follow such a declaration.

Think of great cities such as Boston not evacuated quietly by His Majesty's armies, but burned and razed to ruin. Already agents bring us reports that British officers are swarming across the frontier, rousing the Indian tribes as allies. What can that mean but butchery for the settlers who, for example, chose homesites in the western reaches of my own Pennsylvania? Furthermore, a war of long duration cannot but bankrupt both sides. Ruin England financially, and ourselves as well—"

"Dammit, this is tedious and insufferable yellow coward's talk!" Judson yelled, lurching to his feet. "I submit that we are not arguing what is or is not good business. We are arguing the choice of liberty or tyranny. Courage or cowardice!"

Shocked whispers ran around the chamber. Hancock glared and rapped for silence:

"If you please, Mr. Fletcher! You will be recognized in proper turn."

Flushing, Judson sat down. He felt queasy again. Received more than a few angry looks. Dickinson, obviously enraged, concluded with a single clipped statement:

"I cannot continue to be a party to these proceedings."

Stunned silence.

Upset, Hancock asked, "Are you indicating that you wish to absent yourself from further deliberations of this Congress, Mr. Dickinson?"

"I am."

In the pause, thunder boomed like cannon in the black sky. With an agonizing sincerity, Dickinson added:

"I am aware that my conduct this day will give the finishing blow to any brief popularity I may have enjoyed as a result of my defense of Englishmen's liberties. Yet I had rather forfeit popularity forever than vote away the blood and happiness of my countrymen."

John Dickinson sat down amid another flurry of cane-knocking, approval of his moral courage if not of his final stance. Judson stifled a belch. Thank God he wasn't burdened with such niceties of conscience —though he probably shouldn't have attacked Dickinson so rudely; should have waited his turn, framed a reasoned rebuttal—

A lightning-glare startled him. He whipped his head around as John Adams clamored to be recognized. On the white-shimmering surface of a tall window, he saw a ghostly image.

Lank hair.

Slack lips.

Haunted blue eyes—

Trembling, Judson covered his face. He broke out in a cold sweat, nauseous.

Tom Jefferson leaned close, whispering:

"Judson? Are you ill?"

"Drunk," someone else sneered.

"Spoiled sausage—" he said hoarsely. "Breakfast, I think—" His stomach began to churn more violently. Sourness climbed in his throat—

He stumbled up from his desk, hearing exclamations in the chamber. Hancock turned an unsympathetic eye on him as he ran toward the closed doors, afraid he'd be sick before he got outside.

His illness had nothing to do with breakfast. He'd eaten no sausage that morning, spoiled or otherwise. He'd eaten nothing. He had consumed four—or was it five?—pints of ale.

In the pouring rain in the State House yard, he vomited. When he tried to walk back inside, he slipped on the steps, seeing Trumbull's porcine face in a lightning burst. He sprawled on hands and knees, retching, delirious—

And then the step slammed up to strike his face.

Eventually he heard a voice. Familiar, somehow—

He rolled his head back; heard his name spoken again. Against the black sky he saw Tom Jefferson, rain-drenched. Jefferson leaned down to pull him to his feet:

"Stand up, Judson."

"Sorry," the younger man mumbled. "Sorry for the spectacle. Plagued bad sausage—"

Sadly, Jefferson glanced at Judson's befouled clothing. "Whatever the reason, it's the consensus of the delegation that you should withdraw. Immediately. I am sorry to tell you that, but you've exceeded reasonable bounds. Hancock is still in a fury over your interruption of Dickinson. Whatever his views, Mr. Dickinson is respected—and treated accordingly. Hancock would have come out and caned you if there hadn't been such important business before the chamber."

Thunder; roaring as if the earth would shake apart. The rain drove between them, and Judson hated Tom Jefferson's quiet power as much as he loathed his own weakness.

He wiped sourness from the corner of his mouth. "Sorry too. Wanted to be seated when the resolution—"

Jefferson shook his head. "It's done. You've been lying out here almost two hours."

"The voting's done?"

"Yes."

"How—?"

"Twelve for, none against, New York instructed to abstain. Tomorrow we begin work on the final phrasing of the document." Jefferson couldn't conceal his disgust. "But you have a more pressing engagement. You lent strength to this gathering for a time, Judson. I wish you'd had enough strength to see the venture to its end."

He turned and disappeared into the State House. The door closed loudly.

Judson felt humiliated; unclean. Still sick to his

201

stomach, he stood with the rain pouring over him. It had washed the worst of the mess off his clothes but it could do nothing to cleanse the stench in his mind and soul.

V

At first light the next morning, Judson faced Tobias Trumbull and the tall, smirking servant in a maple grove beside the Delaware River. Judson's horse was tethered nearby. Further away in the mist, a large, splendid coach-and-four showed blurs at the windows: a few well-wishers come to offer Trumbull encouragement.

Nervously tapping a thumb on the side plate of his pistol, the Tory wheezed:

"I ask you one more time, sir. Where is Alicia?"

"I haven't seen her and I don't know." Judson felt abominable. Hung over. His stomach was still unsettled. His hands shook.

"Liar," Trumbell said. *"Damned liar!"*

Judson almost struck the fat fool. Instead, he turned to the servant:

"Let's have done."

Pleased, the servant indicated a fresh slash on the muddy ground:

"Start back to back from this line. At the count, begin your paces. At ten, turn and fire."

Pistols held muzzle up, the two men took their positions. Judson was worried about his powder and the priming in this damp weather. The tall man called out:

"One."

Both duelists started forward, walking away from each other. Judson consciously tried to steady his gun hand.

"Two. Three."

Trees along the murmuring river dripped from yesterday's storm. Rising before daylight, Judson had found the streets already crowded. People were turning out to learn more about the incredible action taken in the State House. Independency had been voted, so everyone said—

"Four. Five."

Judson fingered the cock of his pistol, aware of his own raspy breathing. *What had happened to Alice?*

"Six. Seven. Eight."

Judson's boots squashed the sodden ground. Muggy with mist, the morning seemed funereal. An appropriate day to die—

Goddamn it, stop thinking that way! He had only to take his time; remain calm. Trumbull would surely miss—

"Nine."

All at once, a torrent of rage against everyone and everything ripped through him, threatening to loosen the hard-won control of his pistol hand.

"TEN."

Fighting to stay steady, he pivoted. Watched the Tory ropewalk owner raise his pistol, aim—

Judson stood motionless, presenting the right side of his body, a narrow target. The tremor in Trumbull's forearm already spelled the outcome. The pistol discharged with a spurt of red, a lick of smoke. Trumbull took a backward step as Judson listened to the ball whiz past a good yard from his chest.

The stupid wretch, to push it this far—!

He could aim to wound and the affair would be settled. That would be the sensible way. Slowly, Judson swung up his dueling pistol, extended his arm full length, sighted down the muzzle. The tall servant tensed, clearly afraid his master might bolt.

Trumbull stood his ground, but only with obvious difficulty. Judson's face wrenched into vicious pleasure as he noticed a wet stain at the crotch of Trumbull's trousers. He sighted for Trumbull's left shoulder, started to squeeze the trigger—

And saw not some ridiculous, craven Tory, but his own father, a spectre in the river mist—

Without conscious thought, Judson swung the muzzle slightly left and fired. Trumbull squealed, tried to dodge. But he wasn't fast enough. The ball caught him in the side of the temple, opening a splintery hole that looked black in the bad light.

Cries of shock and horror sounded from the coach. The tall servant fanned his cloak aside, his right hand diving toward his belt. Judson enjoyed a brief moment of self-congratulation. He had anticipated some such treachery. The tall servant drew a pistol as he stepped across the body of his fallen master—

But Judson had already produced a second pistol himself, from a hiding place under his coat. He held the pistol at full cock:

"My duel was with him. I shot fairly. Walk to the bank and throw your gun in the river."

The tall servant didn't move.

"Throw it away or I'll kill you," Judson shouted. "With those fine gentlemen in the coach as my witnesses that I was attacked first."

The bluff worked. Fuming, the tall man strode through the mud to the high grass along the shore. He flung his weapon into the water. Judson laughed, his face as white as a skull in the murk. He aimed the second pistol at the ground, fired, and when the explosion died away, tossed the weapon to a point halfway between himself and the servant.

"That's the one you promised to take back," he yelled. He walked to his horse, mounted quickly and booted the animal toward the rutted road leading to Philadelphia.

Despite the fairness of the duel, Judson had no illusions about the stories that would be circulated. He'd had no seconds—no witnesses of his own. Philadelphia would be hot for him now. He could become the victim of much more than slanted gossip.

The horse's hoofs shot up great sticky slops of mud on the road to the city. Feeling the aftershocks of the duel at last, Judson sweated and trembled and wondered numbly who, after all, he had shot to death beside the Delaware.

vi

Weary, he unlatched the door to his quarters on Windmill Street—and pulled up short just inside the entrance:

"Alice! My God, what's happened to you?"

All filth and rags, she swayed in front of him.

"Judson—this was the morning when—"

"Where have you been? *Where?*" he exclaimed, rushing forward.

She fended his hands. He realized with a second shock that she was feverish. Her eyes failed to focus properly. Her shabby clothing was brown with mud; ripped in half a dozen places. There were ugly moist sores at each corner of her mouth.

"Never mind," she said, with an expression of such utter misery Judson could barely bring himself to look at her. "Is my aunt's husband—?"

"Dead." Judson swallowed. "I gave him a fair chance. Alice—" He walked toward her. "Let me get you into bed. Clean you up. You're ill. Christ, girl, have you just been wandering the streets—?"

As he reached for her, she uttered one short, wild wail and dashed past him, out the door and down the stairs.

He ran after her, shouting her name. But she eluded him in the morning mist.

He ran a block up Windmill Street in one direction, a block the other.

She'd disappeared.

Knowing that he could have done little to correct her

unbalanced mental condition, he still felt a deep sense of responsibility for her safety. Not love; nothing like love. It was just that she had no one else to protect her against herself. As he had no one else.

He pondered alternatives. Should he take his horse and search again? No, he'd tried that before, with no success.

But he couldn't simply abandon her when she was clearly in a deranged state. Starting up the steps to get rid of his damp, mud-fouled clothes, he looked down, struck by something he'd missed before—

Marks of bare feet on the bleached plank steps. A toe; an instep; traced in something damp and reddish-brown.

He crouched, fingered it.

Blood.

How long had she been walking like that? In pain? He bent his head and wept his grief.

vii

He searched for her the remainder of the day, unsuccessfully. At dusk, exhausted, he found a tavern. He barely heard the animated conversation—and loud arguments—that seethed over the latest rumors from the State House. Yes, the Congress *was* close to adopting a final draft of its declaration—

Uncaring, Judson drank himself steadily deeper into darkness—

And woke with a lump on his head, and his purse empty, in an alley two blocks from the establishment where he'd passed out.

Stumbling up, he staggered into the nearest street. A newsboy was ringing a handbell. Judson walked by, then caught the lad's cry:

"—*alarming death of relative of Trumbull family!*"

He snatched a sheet, read it over the boy's whining protests. The story was brief, the ink still wet:

A woman had been discovered floating near one of the river piers the preceding evening. A Mrs. Alicia Amberly, widow of the late Lieutenant Colonel Amberly of His Majesty's army, and niece by marriage of Mr. Tobias Trumbull who had likewise met his death the same day in an affair of honor. Trumbull's distraught wife had identified the drowned girl, apparently a suicide, as heiress to the fortune of the Earl of Parkhurst of Great Britain.

Judson flung the paper back at the boy and strode on, too drained to hurt any more. Now the issue was whether he himself wanted to survive amidst the wreckage he had created.

viii

But that was another weakness among the countless ones afflicting him: he lacked the strength to expunge his guilt by doing away with himself.

He thought about it many times in the next couple of days, sitting alone in the silence of the rooms at Windmill Street, drinking. Outside, bell boys passed frequently, shouting that the text of the independency declaration had finally been approved by the Congress.

That finally stirred Judson out of his torpor. He found a coin, went into the street and purchased a broadsheet—another quick print job, he saw from the bleary type. Going back upstairs, he read the news:

On Thursday, the fourth, the *Unanimous Declaration of the Thirteen States of America* had been duly agreed upon, and signed by the Congressional president, Hancock, "in a hand big enough for John Bull to read it." Judson reckoned this to be Saturday morning already. Quickly he read on.

Official signing of the declaration by all the Congressional delegates would not take place for at least a month. A much-corrected copy of Jefferson's text had been turned over to a printer named Matlack for proper engrossing on a clean sheet of parchment. Additional copies were being rushed to the army and other major cities. On the eighth, the broadsheet declared, the people of Philadelphia would be made aware of the document's contents by a public reading in the State House yard.

Judson suddenly felt hungry. Hungry and awake. In no better spirits, but stubbornly alive. The high drama had reached its conclusion. He reckoned he'd go along to that reading and learn how it had all come out. As he poured himself still one more drink, he decided that a minor actor who had botched his small, almost insignificant role still had a right to be present for the denouement.

Despite the horrors of the past days, Judson couldn't help feeling a shiver of pride at the thought of what had been done in Philadelphia City. If he was of no consequence on the world's stage—and he knew he wasn't—at least he had been privileged to share a bit of the last act. The thought was enough to make him put the decanter aside and think of hunting up a bite of food to renew his strength.

Monday he would be in the Yard. Time enough after that to let the circumstances of his dismal existence reclaim him.

ix

A thousand people or more jammed the area around the State House on Monday morning. The crowd packed the Yard and spilled out into the streets, everyone talking excitedly. Some looked fearful. Others boasted that now the colonies would whip King George's soldiers for fair.

Judson tethered his horse at a crowded hitch-post, wormed his way to the Yard entrance and gained a favorable position with some shoving and scowling. The attention of the crowd was focused on a circular platform normally used as a base for the telescopes of the Philosophical Society. But this morning, the person clambering up with parchment sheets in hand was no scientist bent on studying the heavens. Judson recognized a man he'd seen around the State House before: John Nixon, of the local Committee of Safety.

Judson scanned the faces, smiled in a weary way. Very few well-to-do people were present. Mostly plain folk of the working classes, to judge from their garb.

Then, a row or two ahead, he noticed three familiar backs: Tom Jefferson, Dr. Franklin, John Adams. They were talking in an animated way. Judson didn't want to be seen by them. Yet something compelled him to edge forward sufficiently to pick up some of the conversation.

"—and it ought to be celebrated by succeeding generations as the great anniversary festival!" Adams was saying. "It ought to be commemorated as the day of deliverance! Solemnized with pomp and parade! With shows, games, sports, guns, bells, bonfires and illuminations from one end of this continent to the other—from this time forward!"

Judson heard Jefferson answer, "You have a good right to be proud and thrilled, John. You were its chief architect."

"I never thought I'd see the hour come," Franklin said with a deep sigh. "Remember what I observed about the clocks?"

"Certainly," Adams told him. "That pulling thirteen colonies into concerted action was like trying to force thirteen clocks engineered by thirteen distinctly dissimilar clockmakers to chime all at once. Improbable indeed!"

"But not impossible, as it turned out," Franklin said. "We've done it, by God."

Said Jefferson with a wry smile: "Let us devoutly hope we survive the consequences."

"Come, come, Tom," Adams chided, "no flagging
209

now! We must all hang together—"

"Or surely we'll all hang separately," Franklin said, amused.

Nixon clamored for the crowd's attention, finally got it. A wave of silence rippled outward from the round platform. The man's clear, strong voice sent each word through the gates and into the mob thronging the street:

"Herewith the unanimous declaration of the thirteen United States of America, voted upon by the delegates of the various states in congress assembled last July fourth—"

Applause, some cheering. Nixon waited. In the interval, Judson heard Jefferson say to Adams:

"I've seen some of the copies run off from the one at Matlack's. My God, what they'll think of us when those copies arrive in Boston or Richmond—!"

"What's wrong with them?" Adams asked.

"The spelling! The punctuation! They follow neither the approved draft, nor reason, nor the custom of any age known to man—"

Adams laughed, then shushed the young Virginian as Nixon resumed:

"When in the course of human events, it becomes necessary for one people to dissolve the political bands which have connected them with another, and to assume among the powers of the earth the separate and equal station to which the laws of nature and of nature's God entitle them, a decent respect to the opinions of mankind requires that they should declare the causes which impel them to the separation—"

Total silence now, the throng hanging on each syllable. Judson had the eerie feeling that he was being watched. He turned his head slightly, saw the tinker from whom he rented his rooms clinging to the top of the Yard's brick wall. The little old man frowned, his white locks blowing in the July breeze. He seemed to be trying to communicate something to Judson with his glance. Exactly what, Judson couldn't fathom. He returned his attention to the reading:

"We hold these truths to be self-evident, that all men are created equal—"

Cheering.

"—that they are endowed by their Creator with certain unalienable rights, that among these are life, liberty, and the pursuit of happiness. That to secure these rights, governments are instituted among men, deriving their just powers from the consent of the governed. That whenever any form of government becomes destructive of these ends, it is the right of the people to alter or to abolish it, and to institute new government, laying its foundation on such principles and organizing its powers in such form, as to them shall seem most likely to effect their safety and happiness—"

The crowd began to grow restive. Jefferson's stirring phrases were just a bit lofty for the common man's taste. But shortly, Nixon reached a section that stirred the people to frenzied huzzahs and hand-clapping. The speaker read off a lengthy bill of particulars accusing *the present king of Great Britain* of a host of *injuries and ursurpations.* Each new accusation was greeted with an outburst more enthusiastic than the last; clearly, this was the section of the declaration that would prove the most popular, and be quoted most frequently in years to come:

"He has called together legislative bodies at places unusual, uncomfortable, and distant from the depository of their public records, for the sole purpose of fatiguing them into compliance with his measures. He has dissolved representative houses repeatedly, for opposing with manly firmness his invasions on the rights of the people—"

Judson's attention wandered a little, his eyes drawn upward to the bell tower of the State House where he thought he saw a figure scrambling against the blue summer sky. Again he swung to peer at the tinker perched on the wall. But the man was watching Nixon:

"For imposing taxes on us without our consent. For depriving us in many cases of the benefits of trial by jury—"

Judson began to be troubled by the tinker's earlier look. It had seemed to contain a warning. Of what? he wondered. When the reading concluded, he must find out.

"He has plundered our seas, ravaged our coasts, burnt our towns, and destroyed the lives of our people—"

As the sonorous accusations rolled on, Judson again felt the humiliation of having failed to carry out his role which his brother had arranged for him in good faith. *If only he'd sat through with the Congress to the end!* The Fletcher name—his name; and Donald's—would have gone down with the names of all those others who would eventually sign the clean copy—

Judson's mouth twisted. As he'd suggested to Tom Jefferson, not all men in the world could be great or important men. Some had to be flawed; failures—

The dreadful self-hate filled him again, relieved only by the rising volume of Nixon's voice. He had evidently reached the document's conclusion:

"We therefore, the representatives of the United States of America, in general congress assembled, appealing to the Supreme Judge of the world for the rectitude of our intentions, do, in the name, and by authority of the good people of these colonies, solemnly publish and declare that these united colonies are, and of right ought to be free and independent states. That they are absolved from all allegiance to the British Crown, and that all political connection between them and the state of Great Britain is and ought to be totally dissolved. And that as free and independent states they have full power to levy war—"

The crowd grew hushed at that sentence.

"*—conclude peace—*"

A stirring; whispers here and there; perhaps the conflict could be speedily resolved.

"*—contract alliances—*"

France, Judson thought. If only France could now publicly come to the aid of the fledgling country.

"*—establish commerce, and to do all other acts and things which independent states may of right do. And for the support of this declaration, with a firm reliance on the protection of Divine Providence, we mutually pledge to each other—*"

Judson glanced up, saw more activity in the bell tower; ropes bobbing.

"*—our lives, our fortunes and our sacred honor.*"

Bedlam broke loose. People shouted, stamped the ground, wept and clapped. Judson was punched, nudged, buffeted from every side as the crowd roared approval of all it had heard. He wanted to leave the Yard.

As he turned, so did Tom Jefferson, his red hair bright as fire in the sun. Their eyes met. Jefferson's looked abruptly sad.

He seemed on the point of trying to speak through the rising tumult, a tumult heightened by the first clangorous peals of the huge bell in the State House tower. Ashamed, Judson turned away.

Clang! Clang! The bell sang, each peal reverberating. As Judson struggled through the crowd, he thought he'd suddenly been afflicted with some malady of the ear. He heard echoes begin, sweeping from one end of the sky to the other. Bells of different pitch and volume, all responding to the signal of the first bell proclaiming liberty, filling heaven with their brazen music—

CLANG! CLANG!

The free and independent states of America. Judson wasn't embarrassed to wipe tears from his eyes. He

213

would be forgotten. But he had been here.

CLANG! CLANG! CLANG!

Clambering down from the wall, the old tinker fought toward him, looking decidedly out of sorts:

"Mr. Fletcher—stop pushing, woman, this is important!—Mr. Fletcher, you left Windmill Street ahead o' me—"

"That's right, what of it?"

"Just 'fore I come down here, a party of gentlemen arrived. Huntin' for you." The tinker was obviously unhappy about this latest disturbance of his quiet life.

Judson scowled, his gray-blue eyes hardening. "I know of no gentlemen who'd seek me out."

"Not a one but didn't have a mighty ugly phiz. And a couple o' pistols, too. Tory gentlemen, I think they were."

Trumbull's crowd. He'd been lucky to avoid them thus far.

"I want no trouble, Mr. Fletcher! If you go back to the rooms, I'd at least wait until dark. I just won't abide any more rows, or damage to my property—"

Judson's decision was almost instantaneous. He shook his head:

"I don't believe I'll go back. I've no belongings of value there. And my account with you is in order, isn't it?"

"Yes, square. But what do you want done with 'em things of yours?"

"Sell them, burn them, I don't give a damn." He turned and strode swiftly through the crowd as the bells pealed across the sky. In moments, he was mounted and lashing a path through the celebrating mob, heedless of whom he struck with his flying crop.

x

By early afternoon on the eighth of July, 1776, Judson Fletcher was riding southwestward along the

Delaware, bound home for Virginia.

He knew his father's strength of will. There would be no place for him at Sermon Hill. But he'd face that problem later. Virginia was the inevitable choice. It was the only land he knew.

Ah, but what did it matter where you lived when your only course seemed to be uncontrollable destruction of yourself and everything around you?

Still, as Jefferson had said, it seemed to him that there should be a place in the world—in this country—where a man could find contentment. An ordered existence. Peace for a troubled spirit. Unfortunately Judson had no clear and positive idea about where such a place might be.

The brief exhilaration of the morning faded under the wearying rhythm of the horse. Tom Jefferson was right about something else. The patriots who had gambled their futures and their very lives on a sheet of parchment—the men who had pulled and hauled with such dedication to create union out of disunion—would want no name like Judson Fletcher's on their declaration. They would want no part of a man who was dishonorable and damned.

But why damned? *Why?*

Was he, as his father contended, the bearer of some contaminant impossible to overcome? Some fatal flaw of body and soul?—providing, of course, such a commodity as a soul existed! The old man termed it the devil's blood, but Judson reckoned *Fletcher blood* would be more accurate.

Whatever the name, was he absolutely powerless to escape the disastrous effects? Sometimes—as now—he felt so. But he could never puzzle out a certain answer. And just thinking about it was laborious and hurtful—

Do you suppose there's an inn at the ferry crossing ahead? I'm plagued thirsty—

Gradually, as he rode on, the last distant ringing of

215

the bells of Philadelphia died away beneath the murmur of the hot July breeze.

What would become of the new nation? he wondered, trying to dismiss a sudden picture of Alice from his mind. What would become of him—?

Godamighty, he was thirsty!

And a great fool. The first question was certainly the only one of importance. The second—and its answer—counted for nothing at all.

Book Two

The Times That Try Men's Souls

CHAPTER I

The Privateers

FEBRUARY ICICLES hung outside the parlor windows, fiery crystal that dripped in the bright sun. The light spilling into the room sparkled the dark eyes of the baby Philip Kent swung high over his head, then down again.

"Philip, you'll frighten him!" Anne said as she came in. The child, stocky as his father, and with the same thick, dark hair, disproved it with a delighted gurgle as Philip set him down gently, then brushed out a fold in the homespun smock Anne had sewn herself.

"He enjoys it," Philip grinned, moving two paces backward. He stretched out his arms. "Walk to me, Abraham. Walk to Papa."

Gurgling again, Abraham took three unsteady steps. He stumbled and sprawled, wailing.

Philip rushed forward. So did the two visitors. But Anne reached the baby first, snatched him to her breast and started out of the room:

"You're so used to tossing muskets around at top speed, you've forgotten how to handle something more delicate," she teased Philip. "I'll put him in the crib for his nap. Then we'll eat."

When she'd gone, George Lumden packed tobacco into his clay pipe and said, "A fine, strong boy, Philip. How old is he now?"

"Just turned sixteen months."

"I hope we're similarly blessed this spring."

Lumden was a soft-spoken, gray-eyed man with a large mole on his forehead. Formerly a British infantryman garrisoned in Boston, he had deserted to the American side—and an American bride—with Philip's assistance.

Reveling in the warmth of the two logs popping in the fireplace, Philip said to Lumden's visibly pregnant wife:

"So this will very likely be your last trip to Concord before the baby's born, eh?"

All vivid red hair and winter-pinked cheeks, Daisy Lumden nodded. She sat beside her husband, clasping his hand. "I wanted to see my father before it became impossible to travel."

Early in 1775, Philip had stayed at the farm Daisy's father owned out beyond the Concord River. The red-haired girl had been the cook in the Ware home in Boston. Lumden had been quartered there, as soldiers were quartered in houses all over the city, by royal decree. Romance had spurred his decision to join the hundreds of other redcoats who stole away, unwilling to take part in a war against people they considered fellow Englishmen.

"Even with the thaw, the trip up from Connecticut is difficult," Daisy added.

Philip stretched his cracked boots toward the flames of the hearth. How well he knew.

"I'll spend half my leave just riding to and from Morristown." A pause. "But you haven't told me how you're finding life in Connecticut, George."

"Satisfactory, more than satisfactory!" the ex-soldier smiled. "I obtained a small loan from my second cousin in Hartford, and I've put the training I got at my father's smithy in Warwickshire to good use—"

From a traveling valise, he produced a long, slender oiled-paper package.

"I'll never make a Continental soldier," he said. "But at least I can do my share in other ways. Here, I brought this for you."

Pleased and surprised, Philip unwrapped the package. Sunlight flashed on the gleaming metal of a new bayonet.

"I opened up a small forge, and I'm supplying them on contract to the army," Lumden explained with pride.

"A beautiful instrument." Philip balanced it on his hand. "And appreciated—as they weren't when we tried to hold Breed's Hill. I'd say a fourth of our men are equipped with bayonets now. More are getting them every day. Thank you, George."

Daisy patted a loose curl of coppery hair. "When Anne wrote that you were coming home, we thought it might be permanently, Philip."

He clucked his tongue. "I wish it were. But in January, I rejoined for three more years."

"You very nearly had no army left to rejoin," Lumden commented.

"That's true."

"In Connecticut, the criticism of General Washington has been bloody scandalous. Or it was until last month. People claimed he was such a poor commander, men kept sneaking away home by the hundreds."

"It's not the general who's lacking, it's the troops," Philip replied. Yet he had to admit that during the grim days of the autumn of '76 just passed, he too had again questioned the leadership ability of the squire from Fairfax County, Virginia. Now that he was home for a bit, the agonies of the preceding months had a dim, unreal quality; but the net effect lingered. The American army had failed miserably.

Washington had lost Long Island in August. Then came the humiliation of the British capture of New York City, as the Howe brothers—General Sir William

221

in charge of the ground forces, Admiral Lord Richard commanding the naval squadron blockading the rivers and landing the regiments—forced Washington's army into retreat after retreat.

Lumden said, "We understood Sir William and Black Dick Howe had the king's authorization to pardon the colonials."

"Yes, I think that's correct. But that was *before* Long Island. And of course the effort came to nothing because they had no authority *except* to pardon us for our supposed sins. No power to deal with the issues that caused all this."

Philip chuckled. "The whole rigmarole does have its comical side sometimes. The Howes tried to open negotiations with Washington but they refused to address him any other way than *Mister* Washington. To have called him general, you see, would have acknowledged that he had some authority! And that, in effect, would have recognized last July's declaration. Well, *Mister* Washington rejected all such correspondence—so the Howes tried 'George Washington, Esquire, *etcetera*' —arguing that *etcetera* could mean anything the recipient wished! Washington rejected those letters too. Finally the Howes got tired of dallying offshore and landed on Long Island."

"And the soldiers ran!" Daisy said, disgusted.

"In some cases," Philip agreed. "But for every one of those incidents, I could tell you three where little groups of men stood and died. Still, the problem of lack of training is having its toll. The majority of men just don't understand military life. God knows I don't enjoy obeying some fool's orders! A friend of mine who's in charge of the artillery once prophesied the problem. He said farmers and artisans probably couldn't be turned into a disciplined fighting force. And whenever it proves to be true, it's a disaster. When the British crossed to New

York island and landed at Kip's Bay, for instance, the militia turned tail. Washington arrived on that beautiful white horse he rides. He swore like I've never heard a man swear before. And he laid about him with his own sword—"

"Attacking the enemy personally?" Lumden asked.

Philip shook his head. "His own men—who were running. He was in such a state, one of the staff officers had to lead his horse off the field. That kind of thing poisons the air. By the time we were pushed back across the Hudson into Jersey, and then marched south, the army was ready to fall apart. I think it would have if the general hadn't turned us out on Christmas to cross the Delaware."

"People began saying better things about Washington after that," Lumden commented. "It was a splendid victory!"

"George, you're acting and sounding like a patriot these days," Philip laughed.

"I am, a bit," Lumden said, reddening. "Loyalties do change. How many of those damned German mercenaries did you capture?"

"Over nine hundred. They're not the beasts they've been painted. They're hired to fight and they do it, that's all."

Lumden was correct in one comment, though. Public opinion of Washington had altered radically in the preceding thirty days. Only the general's desperate decision to attack Trenton's Hessian garrison—a garrison placidly celebrating Christmas and totally unprepared for attack—had kept the American army from collapsing under wholesale desertions brought on by demolished morale. Philip vividly recalled the cheerless cold of the December weather; the stomach-turning passage over the ice-blocked Delaware in open boats piloted by the men from Marblehead; the fast march to Trenton

223

with his boots all but rotted away; kneeling and firing at the Hessians charging along Trenton's main street while the sleet slashed over his bare, bloodied feet. Sent to the rear of the lines because he could barely walk, Philip had missed taking part in Washington's second small but decisive rout of the British at Princeton.

Though the memories, once called up, came back in detail, he could contemplate them with a certain hard calm. He had faced death often in the past year. And though he was always afraid before an engagement, his earlier morbid concern for his own welfare had disappeared. He supposed that was a result of experience; the toughening process of combat. Like Colonel Johann Rall's Hessians at Trenton, he did his job and hoped for a speedy end to it, so that he could come home for good to the little house Anne had rented here in Cambridge.

But the return wouldn't be immediate. At the moment Washington's army was in winter quarters, as were the forces of the king. Spring was sure to bring new campaigns. Against York State, some said. Against Philadelphia, others claimed.

Along with the Trenton and Princeton victories, the discovery that the Hessian mercenaries could be defeated had somewhat stiffened the army's backbone. But not enough, Philip had decided. As Knox had predicted, the Americans had not become an army in the true sense—

Anne brought cheer back to the room as she announced:

"Come, the meal's ready. I'm afraid the fare isn't very elegant."

"Seeing you both again is worth ten banquets," Lumden smiled, an arm around his pregnant wife's waist.

"But we must be off by mid-afternoon, George," Daisy said. "I want to be in Concord before it gets too dark."

"Of course, love," Lumden murmured. Anne and Philip exchanged amused glances over Lumden's domestication.

For a while, accompanying his wife to the carefully set table in the dining room, Philip could forget the squalid garrison life at Morristown, and the constant speculation about a spring offensive. He surrendered pleasurably to conversation with old friends, and to the costly but slightly gamy chuck of beef Anne had purchased for the occasion, doctoring it with a thick brown gravy to make it palatable.

ii

Farewells were said on schedule, about three. Philip and Anne waved their visitors away from the front gate. Lumden's hired carriage lurched out of sight up the rutted street.

Philip took his wife's hand, started back along the walk almost melted clear of snow. He noticed a curtain stirring at a downstairs window of the clapboard house next door.

"Old busybody's watching us again."

Anne laughed. "Mrs. Brumple is a dear lady, Philip. Eccentric, but dear."

"There's nothing more pestiferous than a widow with time on her hands. I know she spies on us in the evening—especially when we shut the curtains early and go to bed. Frustrated biddy!"

"But she's been very kind and helpful. She fixed a poultice when Abraham had the croup at Christmas."

"She's asked me twice how much money your father left us."

"Only twice? I've lost count of the times I've heard the same question—" Anne's brown eyes shone merrily. "I fend her off."

225

"I'm afraid I just act rude and say nothing."

"Oh, Philip, you mustn't. It's ever so much more satisfying to Mrs. Brumple if you hint that Papa left a fortune. That way, she has something to discuss when she visits the market, or sews uniforms with her church group—"

"I suppose." He wasn't convinced.

Back in the parlor, he warmed his hands at the fire. On the mantel rested his mother's casket and the little green bottle of tea. Above, on pegs, hung Experience Tait's Kentucky rifle and, higher still, the sword given him by his friend Gil.

"Would you like to rest a while till Abraham's done napping?" Anne asked.

He yawned, said, "I would, but there's work that needs doing." Somber, he kissed her mouth gently. "It's time I answered my father's letter."

Her brief nod and quick caress of his cheek said she understood.

iii

Seated at a desk near their bed, a candle lit against the fading light of the winter afternoon, Philip unfolded the neatly inked pages of thin vellum.

The letter had been delivered in January to the Cambridge office of the postal service, after months in transit. It had been written in the early fall, and had reached Boston on a French packet that slipped past the British squadrons ranging the coast. When Philip had initiated the correspondence the preceding summer before marching south to New York, he had never imagined his letter stood much chance of being delivered to Kentland, his father's country seat, let alone a chance of being answered.

But now, re-reading the reply, he felt the same emo-

226

tional tug as he had all the other times he'd pored over the words since his return home. His eye was drawn to the passage toward the end:

It is a wondrous thing—nay, I may say a miraculous thing—to hear, after years of silence, that my well-loved son Phillipe Charboneau is alive and grown to manhood. Your brief missive to that effect burst like a sunrise into what has become a gray and tedious existence. My wife is ten months in her grave, and my other son, Roger, perished in Philadelphia, of wounds incurred in Boston Town, where he was serving with the army. The exact details of his fatal encounter remain elusive to this day.

Philip wiped his perspiring upper lip. Last summer he had written his father out of some deep, almost mystical complusion to communicate with the man who had given him life. But that first letter to James Amberly had been guarded; had done little more than establish his existence in the colonies under a new and different name. He'd mentioned Marie Charboneau's death on the voyage to New England. But he'd said nothing about Lady Jane Amberly's treacherous hoax to cheat him of the inheritance his father had promised. Nor would he, ever.

And the identity of the slayer of Amberly's legitimate son would likewise remain his secret; his guilt.

To know, however, that Phillipe Charboneau has become Philip Kent—I do not overlook the significance of the last name; to know, I say, that he is happily wed, and has presented me with a grandson, cheers me as nothing else could. I am only regretful that circumstances, including my untimely illness when you were at Kentland, conspired to rob you of

227

the portion I meant you to have from my estate. Your remark that you had burnt the letter to your beloved mother—the letter in which I pledged you that portion—was momentarily distressful. Yet on reflection, I grew to appreciate your act, drawing from it many favorable assumptions about the man you have become. With an ocean separating us, and a d——d debilitating war whose causes are better left undebated between father and son, I send you my warmest affections, a full measure of pride, and my renewed expression of astonished joy at hearing from one I had presumed dead. I hope conditions will not prevent the happy occurrence of communication from repeating itself.

With eternal fondness,
Jas. Amberly.

His father had omitted his hereditary title.

Philip found a fresh sheet, whittled a sharper point on the quill, then hesitated. He was still unsure how a duke was properly addressed.

At last he gave up speculating and again wrote *My dear father* as the salutation.

I too experienced great joy and pleasure when a French vessel succeeded in delivering your letter to our shores. Let me tell you at once that I wish only for your good health and fortune, despite the opposite positions in which we find ourselves as a result of the strife between our nations. Along with most of my countrymen, I hope that the trouble will be resolved, with due consideration to the interests of both sides, before much more time elapses——

Though wholly dedicated to the patriot cause, Philip could write that honestly; it was the prevalent view. Most men he knew looked forward to a resumption of amicable relations with England not to mention trade. Provided, of course, the Americans didn't lose the war.

In regard to your statement about the inheritance, I must say to you that I have no regrets about destroying the letter in question, as I determined at the time to renounce all claims except the one, most meaningful of all, whose renunciation circumstance, pride, and love would never permit. That I may address you as my father is reward enough, as many persons I met round about your estate, and also in London where I stopped briefly, spoke excellently well of your virtues and character. Not the least of these was the famous American savant, Dr. B. Franklin—

The quill scratched on as the candle burned down. Philip described his wife in glowing terms, then his son Abraham. After deliberating, he included one carefully phrased line about his service under General Washington.

He signed the name *Philip,* folded the closely written sheet and waxed it shut. He owned no special seal to mark the wax. He addressed the outside to his father at Kentland, Kent, Great Britain, not knowing Amberly's London residence.

Then he went to the kitchen. Anne was using the remains of the meal for the Lumdens to create a kettle of marrow soup.

Walking up behind her, he kissed her ear. She clasped his hand where it circled her stomach, pressed his forearm up against the softness of her breasts, leaned her head back a moment, her eyes closed.

"Annie," he said, "do you suppose we—?"

Mischievous, she gave him no time to finish, spinning around and kissing him soundly on the lips. "The answer is yes. The soup can wait. Your leave's too short as it is, and Abraham won't wake for a while yet—"

Laughing, he hugged her. "That wasn't precisely the proposition I had in mind—though it's a very good one. Would you like to go to Boston?"

"Now?" she exclaimed.

"Oh, we've things to do now," he smiled. "Tomorrow, perhaps. You could market while I look up Ben Edes and see whether letters can be posted to England."

"I'd love to! I'm sure Mrs. Brumple would care for Abraham for the day."

Philip grimaced. "I'm glad she's good for something besides asking impertinent questions and peering at our closed curtains." He tugged her hand. "Come on, let's pull 'em shut and give the old soul her evening's titillation."

iv

The excursion to Boston, though undertaken on foot along slushy roads, proved fortuitous in several ways. At North Square, Anne was able to fill her basket with two reasonably fresh loins of pork. And at another of the market booths there, Philip spent a few shillings on a brightly painted toy drum and sticks for Abraham. He ignored Anne's tart comments about disliking playthings that reminded her of the war.

Ben Edes' former shop had been looted and burned out by the British. But he had returned to a new location a few doors further down in Dassett Alley. There the young couple found their old friend busily working his hand press. He was once again publishing the *Gazette*, though without any assistance.

As soon as Philip and Anne arrived, Edes closed up shop and took them to the Green Dragon for tea and biscuits. At the table, Philip asked about outgoing mail.

"Oh, it'll take a spell for it to reach England," was

Edes' reply. "But it should get there eventually. Here, I'll see to the posting—" He plucked the letter from Philip's fingers.

"I must pay you—" Philip began.

"No, it's a patriotic service to one of our army lads. Just like buying the tea and biscuits."

"You think the letter'll get through, then?" Philip asked.

"Well, I'm not positive. But there are plenty of New England privateersmen coasting down south hunting for British ships to plunder. They drop mail for Europe in the Indies. From there, neutral ships carry it to the continent, and it crosses back to England. We might get lucky and make a more direct connection on a Frenchman going home light after dumping powder here."

"The harbor is certainly crowded," Anne remarked. "On the way back from the market, we walked by the Sawyer Yard. I've never seen it so busy."

Edes said, "These days the slogan is—if it floats, arm it. A new privateer puts out practically every day, seems like. Only problem is finding money to build and equip 'em. And men to sail 'em."

He unfolded the copy of the *Gazette* he'd brought along, pointed to an advertising notice headed in bold type. Philip had heard that the launching of privately owned war vessels under letters of marque issued by the Congress was a move to help offset America's virtual lack of a navy. But something much more personal about the notice captured his attention:

An Invitation to all brave Seamen and Marines, who have an inclination to serve their Country and make their Fortunes.

The grand Privateer Ship ECLIPSE
commanded by WM. CALEB, ESQ., and prov'd to be a very capital Sailor, will shortly Sail on a Cruise

against the Enemies of the United States of America. The ECLIPSE is excellently well calculated for Attacks, Defense, and Pursuit—This therefore is to invite all those Jolly Fellows, who love their Country, and want to make their Fortunes at one Stroke, to repair immediately to His Excellency Governor Hancock's Wharf, where they will be received aboard ECLIPSE with a hearty Welcome by a Number of Brave Fellows there assembled, and treated with that excellent Liquor call'd GROG, which is allow'd by all true Seamen, to be the LIQUOR OF LIFE.

The moment he'd finished reading, Philip said, "Annie, look at this. *Eclipse* is the ship that brought my mother and me from England."

Edes' eyebrows lifted. "You know Will Caleb?"

"If it's the same man—"

"First-class captain. From up Maine way."

"That's the one," Philip nodded, warming at the memory of Caleb's kindnesses to him aboard ship after his mother's burial at sea. "As I recall, though, Captain Caleb didn't take to sailors drinking—"

"Can't attract a crew without grog," Edes commented. "And Caleb needs more crews than one. He's going into privateering in a big way. Got *Eclipse* and another ship armed already. He's trying to raise money to build two more. Depending on his luck at sea, he and the people who buy in stand to lose a lot—or get rich."

Anne glanced up from the paper. Her brown eyes took on a speculative look:

"Does this Captain Caleb have his commissions in order?"

"Think so. Two from the Congress on the vessels already afloat. Two more are supposedly guaranteed by the Massachusetts legislature soon as his new ships
232

are built. A real enterprising fellow, Caleb is."

"Where is his office?" she asked.

"The head of Hancock's Wharf, a little further up from where the ship's berthed."

Crisply, Anne swung to her husband. "Philip, I think we might go along and look up your old friend."

"Whatever for?"

"To see whether we might put a bit of Papa's money to work for us."

"Annie, we're saving that!"

"So you can turn into my competitor one of these days," Edes joked.

"The money's just sitting there," Anne said. "And we don't need every last pound to live. If we had an opportunity to help the cause and make a modest profit at the same time—"

Skeptically, Philip cut in, "We're more likely to see that kind of investment sunk in the ocean and gone forever."

"At least it's worth investigating, don't you think? I do." Her emphatic nod left Philip smiling in spite of himself:

"Annie, sometimes you are the most surprising woman—"

"She's a woman," Edes said. "That explains it all."

Philip said to him, "I think she's just making up for her mother not being able to stay in the ship-building business because it wasn't permissible for women. Her grandfather owned Sawyer's—"

"Enjoy your fancied male supremacy, gentlemen," Anne said cheerily, rising. "I intend to look out for the interests of Kent and Son."

"Is that the name of my competition?" Edes asked.

Anne smiled her sweetest smile. "It will be."

"If she's your business manager, Philip, I might as well quit right now. There won't be a printing house in New England can stand up against the combination of

233

you on the press and your wife on the ledgers."

"I think you could be right," Philip grinned as he rose to join Anne, who was obviously impatient to leave the smoky taproom. "Goodbye, Mr. Edes."

The printer looked mockingly mournful. "Remember me when I'm bankrupt and need a loan, will you?"

"How much interest can you pay?" Anne asked.

Edes laughed, then she did too, as she and Philip left.

They walked into the February sunlight. Melting snow ran in the street channels. Philip shook his head:

"Annie, I repeat—you are a damned astonishing woman."

"Why should you be astonished, darling?" She settled her market basket over her arm. "You know our plans as well as I do. You're going to get through this detestable war, which we're going to win, and you might as well open your shop with two or three presses instead of one—and have something left to hire a couple of apprentices. Captain Caleb just might make that possible. So it's all settled."

"Yes, I had that feeling a few minutes ago," he laughed, admitting privately with some chagrin that he wished he'd thought of the idea himself.

V

In a tiny loft office at the head of Hancock's Wharf, Philip introduced his wife to a momentarily dumbfounded Will Caleb:

"Lord, you were barely more than a boy when you crossed on *Eclipse*. I hardly know you!"

"Well, a good deal's happened since that voyage, Captain Caleb." Philip moved a chair into position for Anne beside the Maine seaman's cluttered work table. "Right now I'm on leave from a Massachusetts regiment down in Jersey."

"The army?"

"Yes."

Caleb had really changed very little, Philip decided. He had to be approaching sixty now. But he was still as trim and tanned as when Philip had sailed with him from Bristol. His beak nose and flowing white hair reminded Philip of the prow of one of the swift New England merchantmen on which Caleb had spent his life.

Caleb said, "If you're in the army, then you sure as hel—uh, your pardon, Mrs. Kent. You surely didn't come here to sign aboard one of my privateersmen."

"No," Anne put in, "Mr. Ben Edes mentioned that you were searching for investors to help underwrite the construction of two additional vessels."

Caleb's eyes narrowed. "You've money to put into such a venture?"

"Possibly—under a captain with an outstanding record," Anne told him. "Both Philip and Mr. Edes say you're every bit of that. We might be able to raise a sum of two hundred pounds if the proposition was suitable."

Philip almost strangled trying to protest. Two hundred pounds sterling represented just about two thirds of the total bequest left them by Anne's father. He'd been thinking more on the order of fifty. It was painfully evident—again—that his business affairs were now securely in the hands of his wife.

Captain Caleb likewise nearly broke out in a sweat at the mention of the amount. At once he unlocked a lower drawer of his desk and produced a bottle of rum and rolled-up plans. Anne declined the offer of strong drink but Philip, still nonplused, helped himself to a bracer. Caleb eagerly spread the inked drawings:

"You know anything at all about seagoing vessels, Mrs. Kent?"

"A little. My grandfather founded Sawyer's."

"The devil! That's where I'm going to have these two

235

beauties built. Here, let me show you—"

Anne bent forward with interest. To Philip the drawings resembled a confusion of spiderwebs. He recognized a hull plan and elevation, but not much else. He rapidly became lost in Caleb's nonstop references to fore-and-aft rigging, hull displacement, sharper deadrise for greater speed and reduced tumble-home thanks to smaller-bore cannon, another weight-saving scheme.

"All the newest designs, Mrs. Kent. And the best long guns we can purchase. The idea's to crack on as much canvas as possible, for short cruises. Carry fewer provisions, less ammunition—speed, speed! Catch those lumbering Britishers! If we hit, we'll hit big."

"What are the financial arrangements if you do seize an enemy merchantman, Captain?"

"Works like this. A prize crew brings the ship back to an American port—I can't afford agents in France and the Indies. Besides, the owners lose out if the prize is sold in a foreign port. That's standard in the Articles for any privateer."

"All right, that's clear."

"We publish the captured ship's name in the papers and wait fifteen days. There's a trial to determine whether she's legally a prize—formality, mostly. Don't imagine any Britishers are going to hop across the Atlantic to appear in court and fight the claim. Soon as the jurors condemn the captive as a prize, we pay off the trial costs and put her on sale—cargo *and* vessel. There's auction expense to be deducted, but that's a pittance. Whatever the auction brings, the Articles for each privateer of mine state that no more than a third is divided among the captain and crew. The remainder's to be paid to the owners, in proportion, according to how much they put in."

Anne said, "I'd want all of that in writing. I mean the exact amount of ownership in each vessel."

"*Each*? You'd want to invest in both?"

She nodded. "A hundred pounds per new ship. The designs are excellent, so by dividing the investment we double the chance of a return, and halve the chance of loss."

"Anything you say!" Caleb beamed. "I've papers here to completely describe the agreem—"

"No, we're not prepared to negotiate today. But you're welcome to call at our home in Cambridge with the documents. Also your letters of marque which I'd of course like to see personally."

"I'll be there inside of a week! With two hundred pounds promised—"

"Not promised," Anne warned. "Available."

"Yes, yes, understood. But still, that'll be a big help. Enough so that I can pretty near raise all the funds for at least one of the new ships right away."

Anne rose and extended her hand in a business-like fashion. "Then do call at your convenience, and let's discuss the terms."

"Yes, ma'am, I surely—"

Footsteps on the stairs leading up from the wharf distracted them. A tall, swarthy man in a blue wool captain's jacket stalked into the office, carrying documents. The man was perhaps ten years older than Philip; in his thirties. He had dark, tight-curling hair, heavy brows and a small white scar at the outer corner of his right eye. The scar pulled the skin downward to lend the eye a peculiar slitted look.

Despite that, the man exuded cockiness. His expression had a certain arrogance that repelled Philip completely.

"Pardon me, Will. Didn't realize you had visitors." The man's nasal voice identified him at once as a New Englander.

"Potential investors, Malachi," Caleb said. "Mr. and Mrs. Kent of Cambridge—my associate, Captain Rackham, in command of *Nancy*, the other privateer

I've already got on the water. I'll be skippering *Eclipse* till the new ones are built."

"Pleasure," said Rackham, bowing but obviously unaccustomed to it. Philip noticed how the man's eyes worked their way from Anne's face to the outline of her breasts. Uncomfortable, Anne fiddled with the cloth cover on her market basket.

Caleb didn't appreciate Rackham's somewhat brazen interest either. To divert him, he asked sharply:

"You've something for me, Malachi?"

Rackham showed the papers. "A good morning's work. Two more prize masters for *Nancy,* plus the cooper and the sailmaker you've been hunting for *Eclipse.*" He tossed the articles of agreement on the desk, then helped himself to rum. "But it can wait while we entertain our guests."

"We're leaving," Philip announced, taking Anne's arm and steering her toward the captain, whose rakish figure blocked the head of the stairs.

Rackham stared at Philip—considerably shorter—for a moment or so. Then he smiled with insolent charm:

"Shame. Thought we might all become better acquainted, seeing as how you're planning to join our venture." He took account of Philip's tricorn hat with its black army cockade. "Serving with the troops, are you, Mr. Kent?"

He met Rackham's gaze without blinking. "That's right."

"Stationed where?"

"Jersey. I'll be going back soon."

He said it without thinking. An instant later he regretted the damnable frankness. Captain Rackham seemed to have become extremely interested in the contents of his mug of rum. But Philip saw the seaman's eyes flicker toward Anne with renewed interest.

Or was he only letting his imagination get the better of him?

Captain Caleb remained perturbed by the minor confrontation: Philip and his wife at the stairs, Rackham casually pretending he didn't realize he was blocking their way. Caleb reached out, gently but firmly pushed Rackham's shoulder.

The taller captain stiffened, his quick glare giving Philip a clue to his temper. Caleb, however, was clearly in charge. Rackham took the shove and stepped aside without protest.

"Philip, I wish you safety in Morristown," Caleb said.

"Thank you, Captain, I'll take that wish. Things may get pretty lively when the weather breaks. General Howe is slow-moving. But Lord Cornwallis is turning out to be fast and foxy—"

Caleb saw them part way down the stairs:

"Mrs. Kent, the pleasure's entirely mine. Be assured I'll call on you promptly with my proposal."

"I'll look forward to it."

From above, Captain Rackham called, "We'll both come if you wish."

Philip said harshly, "That won't be necessary."

Caleb glared at the other captain. Ignoring him, Rackham lifted his mug in a wry salute:

"Whatever you say, sir."

As they left the head of the noisy wharf, Philip said, "Anne, I disliked that Rackham fellow on sight. A low, scurvy sort."

"I agree. I didn't care for the looks he gave me."

"Stay clear of him."

"I intend to. I'll make sure I deal only with Captain Caleb. He's obviously a man of good character. If we're lucky, we stand to make a great deal of money."

"Yes, aside from associating with Rackham, I think the gamble could be worth it. And I'm not saying that just because I have no choice."

Despite his smile, he was troubled. In minutes, he had become less concerned about the financial risk than about Caleb's partner—who would be within a few miles of his wife after he had gone back to Morristown.

Anne sensed his worry. "Don't fret," she said, tucking her free arm around his. "I've handled worse than a ruffian sailor before. I can do it again if need be."

Still, the February sun seemed a mite more chilly, and the prospect of financial gain from privateer shares much less appealing.

But he knew his wife. Anne was a determined woman. So he said nothing more about it.

CHAPTER II

Deed of Darkness

SOMETIMES WHEN the summer's heat of Caroline County weighed too heavily in the cabin, Lottie liked to start their lovemaking outdoors. Tonight was one of those times. Judson heard her call from the darkness under Tom Shaw's apple tree that had failed to come to bud in the spring:

"Darlin', hurry up!"

Leaning in the cabin door, Judson tilted the jug of corn across the back of his thin forearm and drained the last of it. He dropped the jug beside the lolling yellow hound. The dog's tongue dripped moisture drop by slow drop.

A red-hued, steamy moon hung three quarters up from the horizon. Judson could hear Lottie preparing for him; soft sounds of her skirt and blouse being put aside counterpointed the harping of night insects. By now Judson had tired of Lottie. But he'd had no place else to live when he rode home from Philadelphia the preceding summer.

He hadn't even considered stopping at Sermon Hill. Simply out of the question. To postpone the return to Caroline County even further, he'd bypassed it and spent a week in the stews of Richmond. There, in a brothel, he'd encountered an acquaintance from his home county. Once the red-faced young squire had gotten over his embarrassment at being recognized, he and Judson fell to drinking, and thus Judson picked up word

241

that Lottie's marital status had changed while he was away. She couldn't go home to her mother and father; they had married her off solely to get rid of her and create a little more room in a squalid shanty still crowded with six smaller children. So, Judson's acquaintance related, Lottie had been forced to set herself up in business, accommodating any planter's boy with a few shillings and a randy feeling in his breeches. Judson went to see her and they reached an accommodation; an accommodation helped along by Donald's sense of responsibility.

Early on, Donald visited the cabin—Judson having made no special effort to conceal his presence. Donald politely asked his younger brother to go somewhere else besides Caroline County. On that occasion, Judson—as usual—was half drunk. He bluntly refused Donald's request, offering the very reasonable explanation that he had nowhere else to go.

That stoked Donald's anger:

"I don't care—and I don't want any of your damned impertinence. You've disgraced yourself, Judson. In Philadelphia you completely betrayed the trust I placed in you—"

"Oh, so you heard. I wondered."

"You've been back home three weeks. Express letters from Pennsylvania travel almost as quickly."

"Who wrote you?"

"It doesn't matter."

"Well, I hope you're not going to lecture me about killing that damn Tory—I assume you know about that too?"

"That information was also contained in the letter—" Judson's older brother sighed. "But I won't lecture. It seems you've gone far past the point where mere words will avail—"

"For Christ's sake stop talking like the old man."

In that wheezy, unhealthy voice, Donald said,

"Nastiness seems to be your stock in trade, Judson. Let's get back to the issue. If you insist on spending your days here—"

"I told you I've no place else!"

"—then be so good as to be reasonably discreet. Keep yourself and your whore out of sight as much as possible."

Judson shrugged. "That won't be hard. I don't have a penny left. Before I came back and made my arrangement with Lottie, I spent my last on a little—ah—holiday in Richmond."

"Very well, then. I'll make a bargain with you. Don't flaunt yourself all over the county and I'll return from time to time—" He fished in his coat, pulled out a small purse that jingled in his hand.

Judson grinned suddenly:

"You came prepared for a little bribery!"

"Because I suspected you wouldn't go away," Donald admitted.

"Shrewd. You always were the clever one of us, Donald. The one Father half admired—"

"Have the decency to let that subject drop. I am sick to death of what you've permitted yourself to become. I should turn my back on you—just as every respectable citizen in this county will do—"

"When it's a chance encounter in public," Judson smirked, recalling the young squire in the Richmond brothel. The point escaped Donald. He went on:

"I should abandon you, but I find I can't. Not completely, anyway."

This time, Judson laughed aloud: "Then the bloodline *is* improving from father to son! The old man takes the opposite view. At least where I'm concerned."

"Spare me your hatred, for God's sake!" Donald flung the purse on the ground. "I will see you again—here—*if* you've kept your distance. As I say, I can't properly explain why I should take the trouble

243

when apparently all you want is to go down to ruin—" The puffy face wrenched. "It's my curse to be unable to forget we're brothers. But believe me, Judson—any public scandal and I will forget. Forever."

Scooping up the purse, Judson bowed low. "You, Donald, have the misfortune to be an honorable man."

"No, damme—only a very weak and foolish one."

With that he summoned the black who'd been sent to wait out by the road. The black helped Donald mount and the two rode away—

The conversation came to mind this July evening in 1777 because Judson suddenly recalled that his most recent purse from Donald was almost empty. He took an unsteady step into the dooryard, wondering if his brother would pay another call soon—

More immediate concerns re-focused his thoughts. Lottie's voice whined in the shadows under the dead apple tree:

"What the devil are you doin', Jud? Stop thinkin' about it and come do it, sweet—"

How many Virginia gentlemen have their own private whores? he thought mockingly as he shambled toward her in the humid dark. *Raised from the depths of her foul degradation courtesy of my soft-hearted brother, she accommodates my every wish here on my splendid private estate—*

He glanced past the corner of the cabin, saw the white puff of a rabbit's tail. The rabbit was hunting edible leaves in the pathetic garden patch Judson had tried to plant in the spring weather. Hardly any of the seeds had sprouted.

Dying. Everything dying—

In a year Judson had lost about twenty pounds. Gone from fashionable slimness to near-emaciation. His unkempt beard had sprouted fairer than his hair. His mouth, moonlit as he crossed the yard, looked softer than ever. Sweat ran down his bare chest toward the first

244

swelling of an old man's belly. He wore only ragged trousers—

Well, what difference did it make? He had nothing to dress for; no purpose beyond sheer, perverse continuation of his existence. His days and nights passed in a haze that was like the haze of the summer moon. Indistinct, vaguely unreal—

For a year he'd roamed the back roads with the yellow hound; fished in creeks; worked as little as possible, and slept a lot. When he tired of that, he played one-hand card games with a worn deck he'd bought from a peddler's wagon. When his need or Lottie's grew too fierce, fornication brought a moment's release. But not much more.

And of course Donald's money bought distilled popskull from the dirt farmers in the county—

"Wish you'd saved a drop of that corn for me," Lottie complained as he reached the tree. "I'm so damn dry—"

Judson dropped his breeches and squatted beside her, his hand reaching out to begin the wearying routine.

"Oh, we'll have that fixed in a minute, Lottie—"

She giggled, widening the spread of her legs to allow him a freer access. He ran one palm down the slope of her breast, aware of the premature sag of her flesh. Very quickly he tired of the fondling. He dropped over her and began to work.

Somehow, rolling and clutching at one another, they moved a short distance from the dead trunk of the apple tree. All at once, braced above her on his hands, Judson realized where they were. He wrenched away, sickened—

On coming home to Caroline County, he'd learned that Tom Shaw had been killed one night riding patrol. A fox had spooked his horse. He'd tumbled off the runaway, breaking his neck. Lottie couldn't afford to bury him anywhere but on his own property.

Now, seeing Judson's stark eyes blazing in the moon, Lottie giggled again. She reached between his legs:

"Come on, darlin', you don't believe all those church stories about souls flyin' around once the body's planted. The old fool don't know we're doin' it right on top of him—"

His face almost demented-looking, Judson stared at the crude wood cross just beyond Lottie's tangled hair. Lottie jerked her hand back:

"Listen, Judson Fletcher! You got me all worked up. You got to finish what you—"

He slammed at her cheek with the back of his right hand. Her head snapped over. She yelled, a low, hurt sound. He jumped up, ran from the grave to the far side of the dead apple tree, leaned his forearm on the rotting trunk, and his forehead on his arm.

Behind him, Lottie was panting, half frightened, half furious:

"You're turnin' into a crazy man. *A crazy man!*"

In the stillness of the summer dark, he said nothing to deny it. He was sick of her sluttish voice and sluttish ways—because of what they told about him.

His refusal to answer only angered her more:

"You gonna talk to me, or you gonna stand there staring like some stupid, moonstruck—?"

He whirled on her. She'd clambered to her feet, rushed at him, one hand lifted as if she wanted to use her nails on his cheeks; his eyes. When she saw his ugly stare, the hand lowered quickly.

"I've had enough of you, Lottie. Leave."

"*Leave?* This here's my property, not yours—"

"You want to be buried on your property, Lottie? That's the only way you're going to stay around here—buried beside that poor wretch lying yonder. I'll give you till dawn to pack up and get out."

He flung her hand away like some befouled object, snatched up his breeches and hurried toward the road.

He didn't have a notion of where he'd spend the rest of the night. But he couldn't stand to spend it with her.

He heard her screaming at him:

"You'll be sorry you treated me like this, Mr. Judson Fletcher. You'll be goddamn sorry, I promise you—!"

He walked faster, pausing only long enough to tug on the filthy trousers. Threatening him, was she? Maybe that meant she was going to respond to his own, completely honest threat of physical harm—and get out. It was some small encouragement—

But he had to suffer the sound of her yammering voice for a good quarter mile before distance and the racketing night insects finally stilled it.

ii

Three mornings later, Judson groaned and rolled over on the straw pallet in the cabin. The yellow hound was licking at his arm.

Judson heard rain through the hole in the roof near the fireplace, *plip-plop,* then another sound—the splash of the hoofs of a horse in puddles in the yard. Before he could stand up and pull on his breeches, the cabin door opened.

Supporting himself on his cane and favoring his bandaged left foot, Donald hobbled in. Outside, standing with two sets of reins in his hand—and getting soaked because that was his function at the moment—Judson recognized the house slave who always accompanied Donald on his trips from Sermon Hill. The young black had charge of Donald's horse and his own pony. His eyes shone, big and white in the steamy gray of the morning. He was peering toward the cabin, perhaps hoping for a glimpse of its notorious inhabitant.

"Shut the goddamned door," Judson said, holding his head.

"I will if you put your pants on and try to behave like

something halfway human." Donald pushed the squeaking door closed with his cane.

Climbing into his trousers, Judson let go with a sour-tasting belch. "A little moral remonstrance before I get the monthly dole? Well, you can keep 'em both!"

Donald colored. But he refused to be provoked:

"The Shaw woman's left you?"

"That's right, I got a bellyful of her and told her to pack up."

"Certainly cavalier of you—considering it was her husband who owned this place."

Judson spat one quick epithet to show what he thought of that sarcastic quibble. He rubbed his eyes, yawned, asked:

"How'd you find out she was gone?"

"Very simple. She's already selling her fine wares in Richmond. A friend of mine came back from there yesterday. He said Lottie's informing everyone that you've lost your mind."

That brought a smirk to Judson's mouth. "Could well be, Donald, could well be. How's the lord of Sermon Hill taking the news?"

"I've been at some pains to keep it from him. That's not too difficult. He knows you're back but he doesn't talk about you."

"Never?"

There was a hesitation before Donald replied:

"No. Never."

"Jesus," Judson said, very softly.

Donald frowned. "Judson, this place is a sty. Since that slattern's gone, there's no reason you can't clean it up."

"Oh, God, don't start—"

"Why not? Some time, you're going to have to put an end to reveling in filth—indolence—"

"Right you are. The moment I find something for which I'm better suited—" Judson yawned again, then

248

shambled toward the crock where he kept the cabin's supply of mealy corn cakes. Lifting the lid, he found the crock empty. He remembered that he'd fried the last cake for his only meal yesterday.

Donald reached for the inevitable purse whose drawstring hung from his coat pocket. Fingering the string, he asked, "You do know they're constantly in need of men for the Virginia militia levies—?"

Judson scratched his navel. "The last thing I want to be is a Virginia soldier."

"Then what the hell do you want to be?—other than a drunken fool bent on slow death? You seem totally dedicated to rebelling against everything ordinary people consider normal or decent or—"

"Get out."

"No. You've got to look at yourself, Judson."

"Damn," Judson said with a weary shudder, "what's provoked you this morning? I've never begged you to come here, remember. I'd just as soon you leave."

Donald bit his lip. "Well—you ask what provoked me—the truth is, I had a most distressing note delivered to me at Sermon Hill last night. It upset me because I don't know how to reply to it."

"A note from who?"

"From Seth McLean's widow."

Rigid, Judson swallowed. "She's back home?"

"For nearly a month. With the assistance of Williams, she's gradually taking over affairs at the plantation. I haven't seen her. But I'm told her health and composure have been reasonably well restored. Unfortunately she heard some talk about you. Your—" A weary wave of the hand. "Present condition. She asked whether there was anything anyone could do to help." Donald's mouth pursed, sour. "You see why I'm in difficult straits regarding a reply? Obviously the answer is no."

Judson seized his brother's arm. There was a strange, prickling alertness tearing through the lethargy of sleep and hangover:

"Maybe I'll answer in person. I haven't seen Peggy since Seth was killed. I should call on her—"

Donald shook his head sharply. "I'm not certain that would be wise." Yet his skepticism seemed a trifle artificial.

"Dammit, listen—I'll behave myself. I swear I will. Just a brief visit. I owe it to her!"

Still doubtful, Donald said, "There's no guarantee she'd receive you."

"I think she would."

"Well, you certainly couldn't go in your present state."

"Are any of my old clothes stored at the Hill?"

"I believe so. In the attic—"

"Get one of the nigras to bring me an outfit. Sneak it out after dark if you have to—" Judson whirled to a wall peg where a scrap of pot-tin served as a bleary mirror. He raked his fingers through his fair beard. "I'll scrape this off. Clean myself up decently—"

"*Only* to pay your respects and express your sympathies about Seth."

The concern in Donald's voice spun Judson around again. Vaguely fearful and yet excited, he answered:

"Yes, what else did you think? I'll stay only ten or fifteen minutes. Just long enough to—*what the hell are you grinning about?*"

"Nothing, nothing. I'll see what can be done about the clothes—" He gestured to the young black being drenched in the dooryard. "Lemon can be trusted. But we'll need to take care that the old man doesn't find out. It may require a day or two—"

"As soon as you can!"

Donald nodded, started out. Then he turned back:

"I hope it isn't necessary to remind you that she is a widow. Her status demands special courtesy."

"Stop worrying! I'll behave! I just want to see her, tell her—dammit, what is it now?"

With surprising gentleness Donald said, "You love

her very much, don't you?"

After a moment Judson said, "I always have. Hopeless. But I can't help it."

All at once Donald seemed brisk; almost cheerful: "A visit might hearten her. And perhaps have a salutary effect on you as well."

Sudden understanding made Judson laugh aloud:

"*That's* why you came here today. For my benefit, not hers. Admit it!"

"Yes, you've caught me. I thought that if anything could pull you up out of your sorry state, it might be the name of Peggy McLean."

"Well, you were right. Though I continue to be astonished that you'd concern yourself."

Donald's smile faded. "I continue to be astonished myself. I don't suppose anyone can fully explain how it's possible to despise and love a brother at the same time. Or why one woman out of all the women in this world has the power to redeem a man."

Or ruin him, Judson thought as Donald went out into the rain.

The brief flash of despair passed almost instantly. Before Donald and the slave Lemon rode away from the dooryard, Judson was at work in front of the scrap of pot-metal. Teeth clenched, he hacked and chopped at the yellow growth with his hunting knife. In the process he cut himself three times, and scraped his skin nearly raw.

But he couldn't recollect any discomfort he'd ever enjoyed quite so much.

iii

Reasonably presentable, and mounted on a gray gelding Lemon had smuggled out of the Sermon Hill stables for his temporary use, Judson Fletcher rode up the lane to the McLean plantation the following Tuesday.

251

Twilight etched the western horizon gold below bars of dark gray cloud. The rainy, stifling weather had passed in favor of a cooler spell. That too had a certain restorative effect on Judson's spirits.

He was infernally nervous, though. His belly was as fluttery as a young man's at his first plantation ball.

He was still determined to keep his promise to Donald. He would make the call a short one—

Provided Peggy McLean would let him in the house!

He cantered up the drive past lamp-lit windows, listening to the trees rustling in a light breeze. The sound lent a certain enjoyable melancholy to the occasion. As he crossed the veranda, he realized he hadn't been on this same spot since the night of the uprising. He almost dreaded the opening of the front door, for more than one reason.

He fussed a moment with the lace stock at his throat. He smoothed his ruffled cuffs, rubbed both hands back across his combed temples, checked the knot of the ribbon with which he'd clubbed his hair. Then he raised the knocker.

The shiny black face that appeared a moment later belonged to one of the house girls who'd sent him upstairs the night Peggy was raped. Astonishment, then delight registered in quick succession:

"Why, Mist' Fletcher! Good evening, sar."

"Good evening, Melissa. Is—is Mrs. McLean at home?"

"Yes, sar, she be out in the summerhouse."

"I wonder if I might speak with her?" With effort, he kept his eyes on the girl's, avoiding the parquet beyond. Even so, his mind saw grisly images of Seth's butchered body.

"Why, yes, sar, I think she'd be right happy to see you."

"I understand she's well and in good spirits?"

"After a long time home with her kin. Mist' Williams,

he took good care of the place while she was away. But we mighty glad to have her back."

Melissa stepped onto the veranda, pointed toward the corner of the house.

"Why don't you walk 'round and right on up to the summerhouse, Mist' Fletcher?"

That was precisely what Judson wanted to do. He wiped his moist palms on his trousers, forced a shake of his head:

"I believe it might be better if you told her who was calling. She might not wish company this evening."

Puzzled, the black girl said, "All right, sar." She started away along the veranda.

In the west, beyond the trees where the last light was fading to amber, a flight of swallows sailed gracefully. "I'll wait right here," Judson called. Melissa vanished.

He began to pace back and forth. Remember—a brief visit. *Brief!*

The darkness along the lane seemed to deepen. He kept peering toward the veranda's end. The black girl didn't return. His hope started to disintegrate—

"Mist' Fletcher?"

Surprised, he whirled. The girl had returned through the rear of the house. She stood in the open front door. For a long, dizzy second, Judson hung between wild hope and what he felt was certain refusal.

"Yes?"

A dazzling smile.

"Mrs. McLean, she say she pleased to see you. So you go right on 'round."

It was all he could do to keep from running.

iv

The McLean summerhouse, a white-painted structure with a cupola and pine louvers to admit the breeze, perched on a knoll at some distance from the main house. As Judson hurried up the lawn, he saw lamps

253

gleaming in the slave cabins at the rear of the property, blacks gathered in groups in the street between. Someone was clicking out a rhythm with beef bones. Someone else chanted a wordless melody. Up at the far end of the cabin street, a portly figure sat in a rocker that moved slowly back and forth to the tempo of the music.

Judson thought he saw the overseer wave, lifted his hand in response. To make such a small, ordinary gesture somehow filled him with a warmth and satisfaction he hadn't known in a long time.

A lantern glowed inside the summerhouse. But the louvers hid the interior. The closed door intimidated Judson all at once.

Inhaling the fragrance of the freshly cut lawn, he approached, straightened his stock again, knocked softly.

"Come in."

As he closed the door behind him, Peggy Ashford McLean rose from a wicker chair, putting aside a newspaper. Several more were neatly stacked at the foot of the chair. The sight of Seth's widow, her creamy skin given warmth and luster by the shaded lantern, almost petrified him.

Peggy wore white silk. The mourning period was over. Her flawlessly done dark hair caught the lantern's gleam. She was still slim; elegant; heartbreakingly lovely. Only her eyes had changed. They lacked the vivacity he remembered. Well, there was good reason for that—

Peggy's cheeks took on more color as she extended her hand. Her skin carried a faint tang of sweet balsam oil.

"Judson, how good to see you!"

"Peggy—" Words came hard. "You're looking exceptionally well."

"Thank you."

"I—I understand you're taking over the plantation."

"Yes, I'm finally learning something about it. Not without a good deal of struggle, I must confess. I'm afraid I never concerned myself before—"

She held back the rest of it; he thought he saw the horror of memory stain her eyes for an instant.

"Oh, but please sit down, Judson. It's terribly rude of me to keep you standing—"

"I can't stay long. I only wanted to call because I hadn't seen you since—" Inadvertently trapped, he got out as best he could: "—since Seth's passing."

"I remember very little of that night," Peggy said in a calm voice. She sat down, folding her hands in her lap. "That's turned out to be a blessing."

"Yes, I can see how—"

Again he faltered. To conceal how ill at ease he was, he took the indicated seat, a wicker lounge. He sat perched on the edge. Peggy picked up the conversation:

"Still, I know very well what you did to help. The debt can never be properly paid."

Another awkward silence. He suddenly felt he'd made a serious error in coming here. He'd wanted to see her; look at her a moment. But it was too painful. The sweet lines of her figure, the grace of her finely wrought face still had the power to torture him. But reopening the old wounds served no purpose—

Again it was Peggy who broke the silence:

"Would you care for refreshment? There's port on the table."

Even though his mouth felt dust-dry, he shook his head. "I don't believe so, thank you."

"I hope you don't mind if I pour a glass. I've grown to like a little something this time of evening."

"All right, I will join you," he said impulsively, standing and walking over to pour a crystal goblet for each of them. As he handed Peggy's to her, his hand accidentally touched her fingers. A shock vibrated through him. Damn, he'd better leave. And quickly.

He tossed off half the port much too fast. Peggy noticed. The lantern's flame cast shifting shadows. With night's coming, the breeze between the half-closed slats had grown a little more chilly.

"I'm told you've been home almost a year—" she began.

Another piece of touchy ground! How much did she know about his present situation? And Lottie Shaw? He inclined his head, trying for casualness:

"Yes, I spent a while in Philadelphia."

"But you're not living at Sermon Hill."

"No. No, I'm not."

"I did hear the sad news that you and your father had quarreled—"

He finished the port, felt sweat on his palms. The balsam scent teased his senses in a disturbing way. A ghost of his old, charming smile hid his turmoil:

"Oh, I think it was to be expected sooner or later. I've never fit in with this sort of life. I guess I'm too ornery to be tamed down by anyone, especially a father."

"But that's always been one of your chief charms," she smiled. Then she took a quick sip of wine, as if embarrassed. She set the goblet aside and lifted one of the papers from the floor, finding a refuge in safer subjects:

"I've been trying to catch up on the war news. The Richmond *Leader* reports that we have a new flag for the thirteen states."

"I hadn't heard. What sort?"

She tapped a finger against one of the narrow columns. "Thirteen alternating stripes of red and white, and in the corner, a blue field of thirteen white stars. The Congress approved the design in June."

"Sounds appropriate." Yes, dammit, he'd best get out. The intimacy of the sequestered summerhouse was too upsetting. He rose from the lounge, walked quickly to the port. "May I?"

"Of course." A pause. "The paper says things aren't

going well for the army in the north—"

"Honestly, I'm all but out of touch—" His hand was shaking. He spilled some of the wine as he filled the glass.

"And we now have commissioners in Paris. Mr. Deane, Dr. Franklin—"

"I met Franklin in Philadelphia. A genius. Damned—uh—very jolly gentleman, too."

"So far, he and his associates haven't been able to promote direct assistance from any of the European countries."

"I suppose such negotiations take time," Judson answered in a lame tone, feeling more and more trapped by the moment. He could barely keep his eyes off the sculptured neck of Peggy's gown. Sweat filmed his forehead. His mind's eye flickered with images of her naked body on the bedroom floor.

He fought the memories, sipped the port in silence. Again she came to his rescue:

"That British general—the one they call Gentleman Johnny—"

"Burgoyne, isn't it?"

"Yes. The paper reports he may bring a great force of Germans and those terrible Indians down through York State this summer. There's turmoil in the west, too."

It had been months since Judson had thought of his friend George Clark. He brought up his name, said, "I wonder how he's faring."

"I understand he was back in Virginia last fall."

"He was? For what purpose?"

"My father told me he came to see Governor Henry in Williamsburg. He was asking for several hundred pounds of powder to defend the Kentucky settlements. The Indian tribes are raiding there, incited by the British at Detroit. There's an officer in charge at Detroit who pays silver for American scalps."

With genuine astonishment, Judson studied Peggy

McLean again. He really hadn't appreciated how much she'd changed. The young woman he'd courted would never have been so matter-of-fact about a subject such as the Indian threat to American settlers on the frontier. In fact the Peggy of the past might have made a gay, tasteless joke about it—if she mentioned it at all. Perhaps the slave uprising hadn't been without some saving effects. There was a new, assured firmness in her manner. She had passed out of girlhood forever.

Pondering the change while he finished the wine helped relieve his disappointment on another score: not having seen George Clark the preceding autumn.

Ah, but George had probably been warned off:

Don't bother with Judson Fletcher any longer. He's ruined. Drunk all the time. Rutting with a white-trash woman—

He set the empty goblet on the table, a sudden, jerky motion. His head was buzzing a little. The summerhouse was confining; dangerous. Peggy was too lovely. He damn near ached for her—

"Yes," he said at last, "Donald did tell me the situation in Kentucky is very perilous. All the settlers have taken to the stockades for fear the men will be shot and the women rap—"

He closed his mouth abruptly. Then:

"Peggy, I believe I should be going."

She rose, hurrying toward him. Again he thought he saw something unusual in her eyes. Embarrassment over her own quick reaction—

She lifted one slender hand, as if to hold him:

"You mustn't leave without telling me what plans you have for the future."

The wine had gotten to him. "None at all. Donald sent me to sit in his stead in Congress. If you listen to the county gossips, you know I botched that. I humiliated Donald—and since returning, my life has been even more distinguished."

"Judson." Her cool, gentle voice caught him up short. "What?"

"You needn't sound so bitter. You can't shock me. I've heard everything."

Something drove him to ask, "Including my relationship with Lottie Shaw?"

"Yes, that too."

"And you still permit me to come here?"

"Oh, I suppose by custom, I shouldn't—" She turned away, her cheeks coloring again. From the wine—or something else. "But much as I love my parents, I hope I'll never be so narrow and unforgiving as they are on occasion. Being married to Seth for even a few years was a blessing. I learned a great many things from him. Things you'd understand because you were his friend. Above all I learned kindness. Love—" Head bowed suddenly, she said, "I only grieve for the waste, Judson. The terrible waste of yourself."

Without knowing how it happened, he touched her.

Perhaps it was the isolation of the summerhouse; or the wine; or her loveliness and the haunting balsam tang that drifted in the soft lamplight. But standing close behind her, he touched the shoulders of her gown.

Leave, damn you! Before you do something you'll regret!

He didn't leave. He said:

"It was the only possible outcome after I lost you, Peggy. Though I didn't want to, I stayed away because I cared for your husband."

Head still bowed, she whispered, "Yes, I know."

"Of all the people along this river, I cared for George Clark and Seth McLean—and so I stopped caring for you. Or tried. You know I came to the house too often. Everyone knew it. I'm sorry for that, and I'm sorry for bringing it up now, but I can't help it—"

He was drowning in the scent from her skin. Against

259

all prudence and judgment, he leaned down to kiss the back of her neck.

Instantly he realized his mistake. He let go of her shoulders—

The rest would never have happened if some impulse hadn't caused her to weaken just one instant. Swiftly, she reached down with her right hand to grasp his and pull it around to violent, startling contact with her breast. Her eyes were closed:

"I was a good wife to Seth. I couldn't be anything else. But there was only one man I really loved, ever."

The flesh beneath her gown seemed to heat his hand; then his whole body. She felt him stiffen. Her eyes flew open, alarmed. She broke away:

"Judson, forgive me—"

"There's nothing to forgive, Peggy."

"Yes—what I did just now—taking your hand that way—"

He saw how deeply it disturbed her. Peggy Ashford McLean had always lived by the moral code of the tidewater. Not welcoming it, perhaps. But accepting it. And that code, of which her parents were the symbols, explicitly forbade certain behavior—and a relationship with certain men. He was one of those men and always would be.

Shame reddened Peggy's cheeks now:

"Perhaps we had better say good evening—"

"Kiss me, Peggy."

"Oh dear God, don't—"

"No one will see. We're far away from the house—"

"Please go. In your presence I'm not as strong as I should be—"

And he had no strength at all, save the special kind she'd roused in him suddenly. If only he hadn't weakened! Hadn't indulged his habit; drunk the wine—

But it was too late for ifs. She was far too beautiful. And they were alone—

260

Clumsily he pulled her into an embrace. She fought back, tried to push him away even as his mouth crushed hard on hers, taking from it all the warmth and sweetness that had been denied him for so long. He felt himself roused again. So did she. With a small, terrified moan she wrenched her head to one side:

"It's wrong, Judson—this is wrong—"

"Admit you want what I do, Peggy." His voice was already slurred from the wine. He pressed her backwards, hands caressing her shoulders. Something savage was loose in him, mastering every thought but one; every intent but one—

"I don't dare admit that. If we were husband and wife—"

"We'll never be husband and wife. You know that."

"Yes. Yes."

"But at least we can pretend—"

This time he literally took her prisoner, his arms around her waist. She struggled very little as he kissed her. But for a moment her lips gave no response. Some dim corner of his mind comprehended what he was doing to her. Yet the stark, undammed forces within him overrode conscience. He kissed her cheeks, her eyelids while she whispered her fear, all the old morality of her upbringing crying out against the touching of their bodies, the increasing heat of flesh against flesh with confining clothing between—

Suddenly she clasped her arms around his neck. Her mouth came open under his. He picked her up—she was so light; so airy-light—and bore her to the lounge, his boots trampling the Richmond papers with their news of meaningless distant battles. She resisted hardly at all; a fist against his shoulder for a moment. Then it opened, defeated. The fingers slid to the back of his head—

To have put out the lantern would have betrayed too much. But as he lowered her gently to the lounge, he managed to shut the louvers on the side of the summerhouse facing the plantation buildings. He sat beside her, hands fondling her breasts free of the corseting—

Her gown a tangle around her hips, she let him bare her lower body and kneel over it. A terror filled her eyes all at once. She pushed her palms against him:

"I don't think I can. Not since—"

"Yes you can, love. Of course you can—"

"No, I'm afraid, I don't—*ah!*"

She uttered the cry as he pierced into her, aware of her fear but unable to stop himself. Tears ran down her cheeks.

She tried to feign feeling; response. But it was as if her body had locked into rigidity. The quick, almost brutal thrusts skidded the lounge back and forth an inch, then two, each motion painful to him but doubly so for her. He saw that in the stricken face pressed close to his; felt it in the taut, abruptly cold body. Who was she seeing with those staring, tear-brimming eyes? Not him. Another man who had stalked up to her bedroom on a night of fire and murder and taken her the same way. *Christ, almost the same way*—

Mercifully, it was soon over.

Panting, he drew back, realizing much too late the kind of choice she had made: on one hand, the impulsive thrust of her emotions; on the other, her scruples and —more important—a fear from which, God help her, she might never recover.

And it had been the wrong choice.

She wouldn't look at him. She kept her head turned aside on the lounge cushion, tears shining tracks down her cheeks. Drained and hating himself, he brought up one hand to brush at the tears. She pulled her head away as if his fingers were fouled.

"Peggy—"

"Don't say anything. Don't speak."

"I lost control, I—"

"It doesn't make any difference. You—you

felt—how I couldn't—how—"

"That'll pass with a man who's gentle. I wasn't. I'm sorry. God, believe me, I'm sorry—"

"The sin's mine as much as yours. Please go."

"Peggy, there's no sin if two people want—"

"*Yes there is!*" she cried. "I've dishonored Seth!"

"Seth's *dead!*"

Her eyes flew open. For one blinding moment she gazed at him with absolute revulsion.

Then she said in a voice whose softness terrified him: "*I am still his wife.*"

Struggling to conceal her exposed body, she stood and turned her back, tugging her underthings into place to hide the staining evidence of their mutual weakness. He heard her weeping, and that was how he left her—

He ran down the lawn through the darkness, mounted the gelding, booted it along the lane. The weakness was his; *his!*

He'd vowed nothing like this would happen if he called. But he'd made a hundred vows in the past—a thousand!—and broken every one. Whatever he touched became wreckage. And now he'd wrecked the dearest object of all.

Forever, he was certain.

v

Pacing the Shaw cabin all that long night, Judson seethed with conflicting emotions. Shame. Condemnation of Peggy for leading him on, permitting him—

No, goddammit! *He* was responsible! He had virtually raped her.

Yes, of course, she'd wanted it—at first. But if he'd had the sense to remember the uprising—the strength to call a halt at any of several stages—

The yellow hound licked at his bare foot. Judson kicked the dog's ribs. The animal fell, yelping, then crept into the cabin corner, its tail curled under its hindquarters.

Judson couldn't sleep. It was agony for him to imagine what Peggy must be feeling as the sun rose on Caroline County. The deed of last night would probably blot her conscience for a lifetime. She was that sort of person.

Yet he'd gone ahead. *Gone ahead!* Just as he went recklessly ahead with any headstrong wish, no matter the havoc it caused—

He found a quill, a little ink, tore a scrap from an old ledger Tom Shaw had used for keeping a record of his pathetically small purchases of seed and other staples. In the dawn, Judson wrote a single sentence:

I abjectly beg your forgiveness.

He signed his initial, folded the scrap twice, put on his shirt and boots and rode to the McLean house where hands were already heading into the fields. He knocked at the front door. This time a different house girl answered.

"Please give this to Mrs. McLean at once."

The girl shook her head. "Mrs. McLean, she still in bed. She was up mos' of the night feeling poorly."

"Then give it to her when she wakens."

"Yes, sar, Mist' Fletcher, I will."

Destruction on destruction, he thought as he galloped down the lane. He had to escape. But the very hope was futile. There was no escape from the failures that were built into the flawed framework of Judson Fletcher. Perhaps old Angus was right after all; perhaps some poisonous perversity raged in his blood, uncontrollable. He wondered if some learned physician might explain it; doubted it. At any rate, if the lord of Sermon Hill was correct—and mounting evidence seemed to indicate he was—it might prove fortunate in the long run that Peggy's parents had chosen childless Seth over her other suitor—

At the cabin Judson found some corn left. He kicked

the hound outside, latched the windows and the door and started drinking. When he woke up hours later, the hound was gone.

vi

A few days later, a McLean black rode over with an answer to Judson's note:

All shame and responsibility must be shared equally between ourselves. I deem it wisest—and safest—that we do not ever see one another again. P.

So Judson didn't venture anywhere near the McLean plantation again that summer. He could never quite decide whether he was doing penance or suffering punishment.

But then, weren't they supposed to be the same thing? It certainly felt like it.

The yellow hound never came back.

CHAPTER III

Reunion in Pennsylvania

"LET GO, Adams! Damn you, I say let go—!"

"Ah, come on, Royal. I only want to try your little cap."

"You stay away from me!"

In response, Philip heard a low, rumbling laugh.

Philip jumped up, spilling his wood trencher and the utensils—wood-handled knife and spoon; wrought-iron fork—into the dirt beside the four-legged brass cooking pot. Uneaten slices of fried salt beef were trampled as he and chubby-faced Lucas Cowper dashed for the flapped entrance of the wall tent assigned to their mess. At least the infernal salt beef ration, as appetizing as burned gunpowder, was no loss—

Philip whipped up the flap to see Mayo Adams backing the small-boned, dark-eyed Rothman toward the rear of the six-foot-square tent. Rothman's feet tangled in the bedrolls arranged on the ground. With an explosion of breath, he sat down heavily on the packet of new books his parents had shipped him. Philip was very nearly as alarmed over the welfare of the precious books as he was about that of the young man; the books provided Philip's only means of keeping abreast of trends in the printing trade.

Chuckling, Adams watched Rothman flounder. When the younger man diverted his attention to the book packet for a moment, Adams shot one hand toward the small knitted cap of black wool that Rothman wore fastened to the top of his head with pins:

"Don't be so skittish, Royal. Here, alls I want to do is try it on—"

Rothman bobbed his head to avoid the bigger soldier's hand. Scrambling to hands and knees, then crouching, he panted, "You can't. It's part of my religion and nothing to do with you!"

"Yeh, but I only seen a few Israelites in this army, and you're all a mighty sanctified lot—" He snatched again with one huge hand; again Rothman ducked just in time.

Adams claimed to have been a brewer's apprentice in Boston. The bunched muscles of his forearms showed he was accustomed to heavy work. His oafish face and squinty eyes indicated that the work didn't require much brainpower. Royal Rothman was nineteen, and frail. He had formerly clerked for his father, a prosperous Boston chandler.

"Listen, I'm gettin' peeved, Royal. I want to try it on—now gimme!"

A third time, Royal's agility saved his skullcap. Philip and Cowper grabbed the bull-shouldered Adams and spun him around.

"Leave him alone, Mayo," Cowper said, though it obviously required some courage because of Adams' size.

"Go on back and eat them slops they call food around here," Adams warned, his eyes smoldering suddenly. In the heat of the early August evening, the inside of the tent was as hot as a furnace. "This ain't none of your affair."

"Certainly is," Philip said, glancing past the big apprentice to the wooden horses; the racks where six muskets leaned. He judged the distance, adding, "When six people live together in one tent, everybody needs to tread a little easy. You've been ragging Royal ever since he came to camp."

Adams, who was fond of bragging about kinship with

Mr. Samuel Adams—a lie already identified by the messmates for what it was—spat on the ground:

" 'Cause he's been nothin' but a nuisance. I'm gettin' a bellyful of livin' with a feller who jabbers half the goddam night, keeps a lantern lit the other half—"

"There is nothing wrong with praying *or* reading!" Royal protested.

"—*and* sports a fancy British monicker on top of it!"

On the defensive, the dark-haired young man shook his head. "I've informed you a dozen times, Mayo—my father gave me the name Royal when the colonies were still friendly to His Majesty."

"No damn skin off me," Mayo Adams grinned ill-humoredly. "I just plain want to try on your cap. Want to see if it'll make me as all-fired holy as you are."

"Nothing would do that, Mayo," Philip said. "Absolutely nothing."

Wearily, the big-bellied Cowper asked, "What's got you up, Mayo? Did you bribe one of your friends at the sutler's tent to give you more than your half pint of spirits for the day?"

"Go fuck a sheep, farm boy."

Lucas Cowper turned scarlet. But he kept his temper. "You wait outside, Royal," he ordered.

The dark-haired private scrambled past Mayo Adams' tree-like legs and disappeared with one hand still clutching the little black cap on the top of his head.

As Adams glared, Cowper said, "Now calm down and that's the end of it."

"Not by a damn sight! I'm tired of the rest of you treatin' me like I'm nothin'—"

"You act like something else, we'll treat you that way," Philip snapped, pivoting to escape to the slightly cooler air outside.

A massive hand crashed on his shoulder, the fingers constricting, jerking him around. From Mayo's breath it was evident that he'd consumed much more than the

268

permitted quantity of gin. The huge apprentice towered over Philip, enraged—no novelty in these steamy days of inactivity:

"Suppose you say that where we got some wranglin' room."

Philip wriggled free of the hand. "For God's sake, Mayo, we're supposed to be fighting Howe, not each other!"

"Yeh, but nobody knows where old Billy's got to since he sailed out o' New York—and you're right here, Mr. Sassy Kent." Fists up, he lunged.

Frightened out of an earlier impulse to laugh in Adams' face, Philip barely had time to sidestep. He blocked the bigger man's fist on his forearm, ducked under the windmilling arms while he signaled Lucas Cowper with one quick glance. Adams grabbed Philip's throat. He shoved Adams' slab-like chest with both hands. Cowper bent just enough so that Adams fell over him backwards, cursing blue.

By that time Philip had reached the storage horses. He jerked out his Brown Bess with Lumden's bayonet locked to the barrel stud. Philip was the only man in the mess who owned one of the weapons. Now the way the bayonet extended his reach was a definite advantage. Leaning forward and down, he brought the tip to within a couple of inches of Adams' bobbing throat-apple.

Soaked with the sudden sweat of danger, Philip still tried to speak reasonably:

"Mayo, if you don't back off, and right now, I'm going to send you up to the hospital tents. You've got better things to do, don't you?"

Sprawled on his back, Adams eyed the steel under his chin. Some of the hate went out of his eyes. Some, but not all:

"Well—I guess I do. Let me up."

"Only if you go outside and walk around till you're sober."

Cowper put in, "And stay away from Royal, he does you no harm."

"I didn't sign up to serve with no damn Israelites!" Adams exploded as he clambered to his feet. "Robbers, usurers, every stinking one—"

"Outside," Cowper sighed, summoning courage to add a shove.

Huge and stooping, Mayo Adams swung his massive head around as he reached the tent entrance. His glower was no less unpleasant than it had been when he was baiting Rothman:

"This time you got me two for one. But I remember pretty good. Soon as we see some action, you boys are gonna have more to fret about than Tommy's musket. You better watch your own backs, too."

He clumped out, leaving Philip and Cowper exchanging uneasy looks. Lucas Cowper wiped his forehead.

"Lord, Philip, I think the big fool's serious."

"I know he is," Philip said as he returned the Brown Bess to the horse.

There had been arguments with the dull-witted Adams before. But they'd never climaxed with such an open threat. Damn, it infuriated him. As if they didn't have enough to wring out their nerves these summer days—!

He followed Cowper outside. Mayo Adams had disappeared down the noisy street that ran between the Massachusetts tents. Royal Rothman was righting the overturned cooking pot in which the six-man mess prepared its meals. He glanced at Philip and Cowper, almost apologetic:

"I thank you both for helping me."

Cowper waved it aside as he retrieved his trencher. "Royal, keeping a bridle on that straw-head is to our own benefit. Just as Philip said—men who have to fight together should stick together."

270

"That's granting we ever fight," Philip said with a nervous eye on the steaming August sunset.

All across the hillsides near the Neshaminy Bridge northeast of Philadelphia, heavy blue smoke from hundreds of cook fires hung in the humid air. Regimental pennons in the tent city drooped on their poles. Eleven thousand men were camped in the prescribed rows—and had been for weeks. A sea of canvas shelters—the largest belonging to the officers—rolled from horizon to horizon. There was constant din: men arguing or laughing or singing; the rumble of baker's wagons delivering the next day's ration of fresh bread; the rattle of musketry as some unit staged a sharpshooting contest to pass the time.

Philip picked up his trencher and utensils, then forked the dirt-covered salt beef and held it up:

"Want this, Lucas? Might taste better with some Pennsylvania grit on it."

"Nothing would make it taste better," Cowper said, throwing his own half-eaten slices into the coals under the cooking pot. Philip started off to dispose of his garbage, stopped when he recognized two men coming along the smoky, teeming street—the other two members of their mess.

One was Breen, a man from the village of Andover. He was about thirty-five, a lackadaisical tosspot who maintained that all his life, he'd had no occupation other than "unemployed." Breen wasn't his real name, he'd confided once. He'd used it to join the army and escape creditors and a common-law wife.

Breen's companion, Pettibone, was a short, spectacled man in his middle twenties. Before enlisting he'd taught school in Roxbury. It was to the somewhat prim teacher that Philip hurried:

"Did you stop to see about mail?"

Pettibone showed a letter. "I've one from my Patsy.

271

Nothing for the rest of you, I'm afraid."

Philip was disturbed. He hadn't heard from Anne in over a month.

He knew that freighting the wagon-loads of mail to the army was a slow process. Sometimes a sack split and weather ruined hundreds of addresses. Many letters took months to be delivered, or got lost altogether. That didn't change the fact that he wanted word about Anne's well-being, and Abraham's. And about the progress of construction on Captain Caleb's two new privateering vessels.

In the first of two letters he'd received since his departure from Cambridge, Anne reported that Caleb had called—without Captain Rackham; a relief. She had gone over Caleb's proposal, satisfied herself about the details and invested their two hundred pounds. But her second letter, posted in June, said nothing more about the venture.

After supper, Philip occupied himself with the little sewing kit Anne had prepared before he left. Seated cross-legged on the ground outside the tent, he stitched up a tear in the sleeve of his long hunting shirt. He was becoming an expert with thread and the steel needle and the open-topped pewter thimble. In the field, there was no other choice.

Royal Rothman had already gone inside, lit a lamp and started opening the packet of books from his parents. His collection thus far included an assortment of political pamphlets, a tattered copy of *Common Sense* which he claimed to have gone through over fifty times, and an edition of one of the most popular books of recent years, *Night Thoughts on Life, Death, and Immortality.*

It was a work of the so-called "graveyard" school of poets. Philip found its blank verse uninspiring, and its themes somewhat too morbid for present circumstances.

What did continue to amaze and confound him was the popularity of English authors such as Reverend Young who had produced *Night Thoughts*. The war didn't seem to dampen American enthusiasm for British literature.

Momentarily, Royal came out again with his new arrivals. Philip looked enviously at a richly bound volume whose title he recognized at once. John Milton's century-old metaphysical epic, *Paradise Lost*, was enjoying a new burst of popularity; it was, Royal reported, the year's best seller in Boston. And the new edition which the younger man showed enthusiastically was one of the handsomest Philip had ever seen.

He ran his hand down one page, experiencing a pleasure that was almost painful. For a moment, bitterness swept over him, coupled with another intense wish that he could be home, free to pursue the trade he'd come to love. He voiced his feelings to Royal, with whom he'd discussed his ambitions before:

"If I had the money and equipment to print fine books, this would be the sort I'd want to bear my name."

"I'm sure you'll publish books like this one day, Philip."

Philip's shrug expressed his uncertainty. Royal laid the Milton aside, knelt beside his messmate, fanned out three inexpensively produced pamphlets.

"Here are the real treats—a new series by Mr. Paine."

Philip took the trio of pamphlets, noted that they all bore a common title—*The American Crisis*—and were numbered sequentially. He opened the first; it was just a few pages long. He flipped to the end, where the date appeared—December 23 of the preceding year—along with the author's pseudonym, *Common Sense*. Philip had heard that the famous pamphleteer was now employed as secretary to the committee of foreign affairs of the Congress. From that vantage point, he continued to use his pen to praise and encourage the patriots—and damn all Tories, British and domestic.

"Read the opening paragraph," Royal urged.

"I'd like to read the whole of all three when you're finished with them."

"Of course you may. But do look at the opening of the first. Some of the phrases are worthy of a Milton."

Philip turned back to the passage indicated:

These are the times that try men's souls. The summer soldier and the sunshine patriot will, in this crisis, shrink from the service of their country, but he that stands it now deserves the love and thanks of man and woman. Tyranny, like hell, is not easily conquered; yet we have this consolation with us that, the harder the conflict, the more glorious the triumph. What we obtain too cheap, we esteem too lightly; it is dearness only that gives everything its value. Heaven knows how to put a proper price upon its goods, and it would be strange indeed if so celestial an article as freedom should not be highly rated.

At that point, Philip stopped and returned the paper-covered essay with the other two, saying:

"Mr. Paine certainly has a grasp of the mood of an army camp. He's doing his best to keep spirits up."

And my own need it badly, he added in the silence of his mind. He wondered again whether he would ever live to embrace Anne; hold his child; or pull the lever on a flatbed press and watch a sheet come forth, miraculously inked with the thoughts of the author.

Royal said, "My father's letter reports that Mr. Paine is planning a whole series of these *Crisis* articles— written as the need arises. Someone will certainly put them together in a book one day. Why shouldn't it be you, Philip?"

Philip smiled wearily. "Well, it's a mite early to consider that, seeing as I have no press, no pressroom and precious little money."

But his eyes had brightened a bit; the suggestion had caught his fancy. Reality quickly took control again:

"Very likely some printer who isn't with the army will seize on the idea first."

"Yes, but a Kent edition could be finer and more handsomely prepared—and I'm sure it would have a guaranteed sale. Look at all the different versions of *Common Sense* that are circulating."

Philip nodded, enjoying the fantasy of a collection of Paine's essays offered under his own imprint. He didn't even think about the legality of it. Every respectable printer practiced piracy, despite copyright statutes of various sorts in force in the former colonies. Massachusetts Bay's law had been enacted in 1672, Ben Edes had told him once. But it was largely ignored, and the penalty was relatively paltry: a fine three times the manufacturing cost of the illegal edition. Anyone could reprint foreign authors such as Milton and the Reverend Young with absolute impunity. Existing copyright laws didn't apply to works by non-Americans.

"All right, Royal," Philip smiled at last, "I'll consider an edition of Mr. Paine one of my first priorities. But don't pin me to a calendar, please. Who can be certain when we'll be back in Boston?"

Royal's somber nod showed that he caught the undertone of resignation and apprehension. He scooped up his shipment and headed for the tent.

"I'll get busy reading so you may have these quickly—"

Philip barely heard the remark. He was staring into space, seeing the title page of the Paine book as he

275

would compose it.

Lucas Cowper, not the least interested in matters literary, had paid no attention to the conversation, occupying himself instead with an ox horn he'd obtained at the camp slaughterhouse. He was fashioning a new container for his powder. Left-handed, Cowper needed a horn that would fit snugly on his left hip; an ox's right horn would have done him no good.

While Philip and Royal talked, Cowper worked away with the tip of his knife, carefully chipping letters from the bony surface. Now he held up the horn and displayed its legend to Philip:

Lucas Cowper, His Horn, August 1777

"A handsome job, Lucas," Philip told him.

"I don't know about that," the other grinned. "But maybe it won't be stolen like the last one." He applied himself to a few finishing cuts to smooth rough edges of the letters.

Paine's phrase kept stealing back into Philip's mind. *Times that try men's souls.* It was certainly apt. Fear and frustration combined to harry the strongest man's nerve; erode his will; fill him with anxiety. In a few moments, Philip was almost regretting that Royal had brought up the subject of an edition of Paine. The tempting idea only reminded him of the impossibility of fulfilling any dreams or ambitions in the immediate future.

Stretching, Pettibone emerged from the tent to take the air after completing his letter to his wife Patsy. Breen appeared, having vanished to the sutler's for a while. As the regimental drums began to beat the night's tattoo, Breen announced disparagingly:

"More of them goddamn Frenchies comin' out tomorrow."

Philip looked up from his unfinished sewing. "Officers?"

"Fortune-hunters, more like. Figger to make a killin' sellin' their fancy selves to lead us poor ignorant clodfoots. Feller told me the Congress is gettin' mighty sick of them monsoors paradin' off the ships and askin' for high rank and lots o' pay."

"If there are more coming out tomorrow, I imagine we'll have an inspection," Philip said. "Maybe even a grand review. That'll break up the day, anyway."

Anything to break up the day—!

And the waiting.

ii

Mayo Adams hadn't come back by the time the last drumbeats died out across the Pennsylvania countryside. Philip lay sweating in his underdrawers, on top of his bedroll instead of in it. Breen's loud snores, augmented by the click of his wooden dentures, added to the other irritants—the heat; the boredom; the uncertainty about what might lie ahead—that kept Philip awake and restless.

Eventually he dozed off. A sudden clumping and heavy breathing shot him upright:

"Who is it?"

"Adams." Crawling past the other sleepers.

Adams still reeked of gin. General Washington believed that a certain amount of alcohol was necessary to a soldier, but that too much was disastrous. A man could only obtain more than the daily ration if he had a friend. Adams did.

"You gwan back to sleep, Kent. Let's hope you wake up tomorrow, huh?"

Chuckling, Adams passed on, a dimly seen bulk in the stifling gloom of the tent. He took his place on his roll at the rear corner. Philip settled down again, tense.

Not a sound came from Mayo Adams. But Philip had

277

the uncomfortable feeling that the brewer's apprentice was still awake.

Staring at him.

Watching him.

And maybe thinking secret thoughts——?

iii

Two things plagued the Americans encamped above Philadelphia. One was in the past, the other yet to come.

The first was the devastating plunge in morale produced by news from the north. Practically on the anniversary of the declaration of a year ago, the American defenders of Fort Ticonderoga had been forced to evacuate the position as untenable. Gentleman Johnny Burgoyne was marching south from Canada with eight thousand British soldiers, Canadians, and Iroquois tribesmen recruited by the king's agents.

Word of Ticonderoga's recapture had arrived in the Pennsylvania encampment in mid-July. Virtually every man took it as a grim sign. Horatio Gates, a capable American general, was supposedly moving to blunt Burgoyne's thrust. But there was no guarantee he could do it. God knew what bloodshed was being perpetrated in northern York State this very moment.

Then there was the second worry—the future.

The uneasiness sprang directly from no one knowing the whereabouts of General Sir William Howe, His Majesty's commander-in-chief in America.

For months, Howe had dallied at New York. First there were reports that he intended to go north to link up with Burgoyne. Then other reports said his objective was Philadelphia. All the while, his troops remained garrisoned in New Brunswick and Amboy, supplied from across the Hudson and capable of retaking the whole of Jersey—*if* they received orders.

Howe was too busy to issue orders. He was occupied

with balls and fetes in the captured city. And, so the story ran, with his new blonde mistress, one Mrs. Loring.

The charming lady's husband, a fervent Boston Tory, had been appointed commissary-general in charge of American battle prisoners. The position permitted Loring to fatten his own purse by selling off prisoner rations at a profit. The scoundrel seemed happy with his lot—and not the least jealous when General Howe commandeered his wife for a bed-partner. Perhaps, in some bizarre way, he considered her surrender a duty to the Crown that was making him rich.

At last, in late July, Howe had moved—but in an unexpected direction. He and his Jersey army disappeared into the Atlantic aboard the three hundred ships commanded by Howe's brother. Somewhere on the ocean, that armada cruised out of sight of shore—and no one could say where the eighteen thousand British and Hessians would ultimately land. Nearly every day, new rumors reached the Pennsylvania camp—

Howe had been sighted off the Virginia capes—

No, he had not.

Yes he had, but the fleet was gone again.

Whatever the truth, it seemed obvious to Philip and his messmates that the plan to relieve Burgoyne had been abandoned. So what would be Howe's objective? A southern port? Philadelphia, where a nervous Congress was receiving a stream of foreign officers who had sailed to America bearing papers from Silas Deane, the commissioner in Paris? The papers guaranteed the foreign officers high ranks in the Continental army in return for their services. *Guaranteed it!* Their American counterparts complained, with justifiable bitterness.

Some of the soldier-adventurers were reasonably well qualified. Washington had already appointed a skilled Polish engineer, Kosciusko, to a colonelship in that "learned" branch of the service. But many of the officers were not qualified for much of anything, and had only come to the new country in hopes of deposing some native-born officer—for profit.

And tomorrow, Philip thought, dozing again, a new contingent of Europeans was due to arrive.

Well, it *would* provide diversion. Something to break the endless tedium of the days spent waiting and wondering when Howe's flotilla would appear again; and where.

iv

The drummers hammered in the blistering sun. The fifers tootled the melody of *The White Cockade*. Standing in the ranks on the parade field, his musket held at shoulder firelock position, Philip squinted across the sere grass toward the approaching horsemen. Out in front of Philip's company, the commander, Captain Walter Webb of Worcester, stood as straight as the spontoon he gripped in his right hand.

Philip wished he could wipe the sweat off his forehead. It trickled down both sides of his nose and into his eyes. He had trouble seeing the brightly uniformed officers cantering toward the Massachusetts companies.

Of course Washington was immediately recognizable because of his white mount and his customary blue and buff. But the two men beside him, riding out ahead of the staff officers, were unrecognizable blurs—

Until they drew up opposite Philip's company. Suddenly one of the two with Washington reined in. Philip gasped aloud at the sight of a long-forgotten face.

A youthful face. Aristocratic. Crowned under a tricorn by red hair far brighter than the commanding general's. But Philip was sure his own eyes were playing tricks—

No, no, there could be no mistake. It *was* the same

face; a face he'd first seen in a howling blizzard near his mother's inn, when he'd come upon a thirteen-year-old boy struggling with two would-be kidnappers. The boy had been born to the French nobility; destined for a military career—

The Marquis de Lafayette caught Washington's attention, pointed. Next to Philip, Lucas Cowper said under his breath:

"My Lord, he's singling out somebody in this company!"

Washington stood in his saddle, spotted Philip. The general's face seemed to register recognition too; perhaps from that night in Vassall House before the expedition with Knox.

Washington said something to Lafayette. Instantly, Gil's face burst into a smile.

Royal Rothman, his cap concealed under his round-brimmed hunting hat, hissed from the front rank where the shortest men stood:

"It isn't me. It's somebody behind me."

"Damn if that froggy ain't wavin' at you, Kent," Mayo Adams said from directly behind. "How'd you git your ass in trouble this time?"

Unbelievably, Washington himself had now ridden back to consult with a staff officer. The main body of the inspection party rode on, Lafayette casting one glowing smile back across his shoulder. The staff officer wheeled his horse toward Captain Webb, who appeared ready to fall over in a faint from the sudden flurry of attention.

The staff officer dismounted, spoke with Webb. Philip could hear their voices but not the words. Then Webb's eyes literally bugged.

As the staff officer re-mounted and cantered away, Captain Webb turned to give Philip a disbelieving stare. Lucas Cowper whispered again:

281

"Philip, do you know that officer who went by?"

"Yes, I do."

From behind, Mayo Adams sneered, "Way it's goin', Kent's liable to be suppin' with old George 'fore long. My God, I didn't know we were in such highfalutin company."

But Adams' jibes couldn't unsettle Philip now. He was too stirred by memories, by excitement, by the astounding reappearance of the young man who had given him the treasured sword—

The young man Philip had never expected to see again in all his lifetime.

Then he recalled something the young marquis had said the last time they met at Marie Charboneau's inn, just before Gil returned to Paris for more military training. Something about comrades in arms always encountering one another again on battlefields.

Comrades in arms. Gil had said they were exactly that because Philip had saved his life—

And the prediction had come true.

Officers began to shout orders to break up the review formation. Captain Webb barked Philip's name and headed straight for him:

"Kent, are you aware of the identity of that Frenchman? The one who singled you out?"

"Yes, Captain, I am. Let's see whether I can give you all his names—"

Philip's friends crowded around, listening. Even Mayo Adams lingered, a disgusted curiosity on his face. Philip recalled the names one by one:

"Marie Joseph Paul Yves Roch Gilbert du Motier—"

Webb continued to look utterly stupefied as Philip added:

"His hereditary title's Marquis de Lafayette. I always called him Gil."

"Pretty damn familiar!" Webb exclaimed.

"I was born in France, Captain. I knew him there. His family home was in the same province as mine."

"Well, I don't care what you called him then, you're going to have to call him sir when you go to supper."

"Supper?"

"Why d'you suppose that major rode over here? You're to clean up and report to the marquis' pavilion at six on the dot. And you'd better not forget the Congress just appointed him a major general."

That touched off an explosion of exclamations. Philip joined in:

"He can't be more than nineteen!"

"Looks younger, if you ask me. But he's still a general attached to Washington's personal staff. And the major passed the word that the old man's taken a strong liking to him. You'd best be on your good behavior."

Abruptly, Philip was overcome with apprehension. He was excited at the prospect of a reunion with his boyhood friend. But a meeting between a common private and a freshly commissioned major general—that was something else entirely. He spent the rest of the afternoon nervously washing, shaving, sewing all the ragged places in his best shirt and trousers—and withstanding jokes from the men in his mess.

There were no jokes from Mayo Adams, though. He treated the whole business with silent contempt.

V

"Uh—sir?"

The young Frenchman seated inside the spacious officer's tent jumped up from his camp chair and ran around the table where exquisite china, silver and glassware had been set for two. The orderly held the entrance flap aside, but Philip hesitated, uncertain as to whether he should salute.

Gil seized both his shoulders, his face almost glowing as he exclaimed in French:

"My God, Phillipe—it is you! Ranks and titles are forgotten here. It is Gil and—no, no, I was told you were someone else! A new name?"

"Yes. Philip Kent."

"Gil and Philip, then! Long-lost comrades reunited!"

He embraced Philip so ardently, kissing him on both cheeks, that the orderly blushed.

Gil took Philip's arm. "Come in, come in—we will dine and talk. But what shall it be? French? Or the English I speak so badly?"

"My French is pretty well forgotten," Philip said with an apologetic smile. Though several years older than the handsome nineteen-year-old, he still had a feeling that he was the junior in the relationship. Even at thirteen, Gil had been a commanding presence; the tutor who gave Philip his first rudimentary lessons with the musket and spontoon. "But we can try, if you wish—"

"It's easier, easier," Gil continued in French as he pulled back a chair for his guest. "Be seated! Tell me everything! Where you live, your fortunes—everything."

"I'd like to. But honestly, Gil, it—it isn't necessary for you to entertain me this way—" He indicated the elegant table. "You're a high-ranking member of the staff. I'm only—"

"Only my friend. My savior," Gil said with utter seriousness. His hazel eyes held Philip's. "I remember very distinctly that I would not be here in the glorious new land of freedom if you hadn't happened along that road near Chavaniac when I was in danger. I'd be a major general of the worms, very likely. So let's have no more folderol about rank—" He grinned. "That is a direct order."

Philip laughed. "All right—General. I still have the sword you gave me. It hangs over the mantel in our

284

home in Massachusetts—" The language was slow going, but Philip took his time, translating each phrase carefully out of the more familiar English. Gil's sandy eyebrows hooked up at the last remark:

" 'Our home.' You are married, then?"

"Yes, to a girl I met in Boston."

"Children?"

"One son. He'll be two in September."

"How marvelous, wonderful!" Gil reached under the bosom of his uniform, pulled out a golden locket on a slender chain. "This is rather a delicate ornament for a soldier. But my own dear heart insisted I bring it with me—"

Proudly, Gil thumbed the locket open to display a beautifully done miniature of his attractive, fragile-looking wife. Philip judged her to be little more than fifteen or sixteen.

The marquis snapped the locket shut, signaled to the orderly, said in heavily accented English:

"Set the meal, please—and the wine. Then leave us." The orderly wheeled and hurried out.

"Gil, how in God's name did you get here?"

"Well, service to your new country has become popular in many parts of Europe. The splendid declaration against King George last summer—you've no idea how it fired the minds and hearts of Frenchmen!"

"And inspired some private help from your king."

"The bogus trading company? Yes, I've heard of it. Officially, of course, France takes no position in the war. As yet," he added in a significant way. "One may hope—"

He shrugged. "For the present, it's enough that volunteers may cross the ocean to offer their swords. In my case, I'm afraid King Louis felt the Lafayette name a trifle too prestigious for even that to be allowed." He made a face to demonstrate his displeasure.

"You mean it was suggested you shouldn't come?"

"Suggested hardly covers it. I was on garrison duty in Metz when word reached me about the noble declaration. I have never been so overcome—so moved. I decided at once to speed here to support your cause."

Finally relaxing a little, Philip smiled. "I also recall you didn't think too highly of the British."

"That's true—as well as an understatement. Unfortunately, members of my family were determined I should not risk my career in this venture—nor lend the Lafayette name to what remains, in official circles, an illegitimately conceived nation. King Louis even issued a writ forbidding my journey. Had the paper ever caught up with me, I'd have been clapped away in the Bastille until my enthusiasm for America cooled. As it was, I rushed overland in secret—I took ship at *Los Pasajes* in Spain—and I landed early in July in your Charleston."

"South Carolina?"

"Quite so. Then I traveled nine hundred miles more —in carriages I paid for myself—also on horseback when the carriages broke down. When I reached the Congress in Philadelphia, I was given a decidedly rude reception, at least in some quarters. A Mr. Lovell of that body remarked that French officers had a great fancy to enter American service without being invited. In short, I was treated like the rankest freebooter."

"We've had some of those show up, though."

"Nevertheless, it was an insult. Since I had come here out of the purest motives, and at my own expense, I demanded two favors of the Congress. To serve at my own cost, and entirely as a volunteer—requiring no rank or command. Though naturally I hope to have the honor of field command at some time in the future. I am well trained for it, after all." He still sounded a bit miffed. "And training seems sorely needed in this army.

I was agog this morning. That is the only word—agog. No uniforms! Merely—forgive me!—those peculiar shirts such as you're wearing. Then I watched a bit of drill. An absolute shambles! A drillmaster's badly needed—"

"Gil, I'm afraid Washington has neither the money nor the talent to put together the kind of army you're accustomed to."

"Aha, but European officers are arriving who can do something about that! They must be given the opportunity! Else your cause—our cause—is surely lost."

Glum, Philip told him, "I don't doubt the general would welcome really good assistance."

"Yes, a magnificent man, magnificent! I told him I wished for nothing more than to be allowed to serve near his person till such time as he thought it proper to entrust me with a division." With an emphatic flick of one of his epaulettes, he added, "I did not *insist* upon a major generalship. However—" Another shrug, and a wink. "It is certainly a step in the right direction."

Philip smiled again. So did his friend. The orderly returned, followed by two Frenchmen: one a cook in a white smock, pushing a wood-wheeled serving cart, the other a liveried waiter who proceeded to serve the meal and decant the wine. Philip discovered that Gil wasn't exaggerating about paying his own way:

"I want no one in this command to think I am living in my accustomed style at their expense, Philip. Everything you see, I purchased. The venison, the wine—this uniform, the tent, even my horses and wagons. I am of the opinion that perhaps I have more dedication to the American purpose than some of your own rude Congressmen."

"I don't doubt it. More money, too."

"A hit, a most accurate hit!" Gil cried, clapping one hand over his heart in false pain.

There was no longer any barrier of hesitancy between them. Philip's uneasiness had completely vanished, and he fell to enjoying the excellent meal, the wine and the conversation with unashamed gusto. The talk was virtually continuous because both friends had much to tell.

Philip related all of his up-and-down history since Gil had ridden away from Auvergne that long-ago day. He only omitted the most unflattering parts—his killing of Roger Amberly and his dalliance with Alicia before he finally made up his mind about Anne Ware and the American cause.

For his part, Gil was ready with anecdotes about military life, as well as acid comments about the American commissioner in Paris, Mr. Deane, who was "frantically" issuing letters to European officers, promising them exalted posts and high wages—without specific authorization from the Congress. Presently, when the table had been cleared and a lantern lighted and hung at the open end of the tent, Gil offered a toast with brandy:

"To my comrade Phillipe—ah, I forget so easily. Philip! May he and his country live in liberty forever."

Unable to think of any appropriate sentiment to offer in return, Philip smiled, raised his glass and drank, supremely content for a few hours in the renewal of a bond that defied explanation or—seemingly—geography.

With a little more of the brandy under their belts, the friends could talk even more frankly:

"Gil, I don't want to sound pessimistic, but it strikes me that the outcome of this war is as much up to men like Johnny Burgoyne and General Howe as it is to us."

"Exactly! There has never been an engagement of forces in which that wasn't so. However, don't worry— the enemy will make all the incorrect moves, and we shall make all the proper ones."

Philip sighed. "I wish I shared your confidence."

Gil grew solemn. "Sham confidence—and a poor joke. Truly, I wish it were so simple. There is much tension and impatience on the general's staff because of the uncertainty in regard to Howe's position."

"He can't stay at sea forever."

Gil clapped him on the shoulder, breaking the dour moment:

"He'd better not, with two such stout fighters waiting to engage him!"

The boast was cheerful enough. But Philip was already certain his friend placed little or no confidence in the disreputable-looking American troops he'd reviewed earlier in the day. Philip couldn't much blame Gil, either.

The two talked late into the night. Tipsy, Philip finally meandered back toward the Massachusetts tents. On the way he took great pleasure in displaying Captain Webb's signed order to the guards who questioned a private's right to be abroad after tattoo.

He yawned as he neared his own tent. He was anxious to climb into his bedroll and sleep. But it wasn't to be. His messmates were still awake, and fired questions at him almost until dawn. They wanted this or that bit of information about Lafayette; a history of his experience; an explanation of how he'd gotten to be a general at age nineteen; his views on the possibilities for victory.

The only one who sat sullen, cursing frequently because he couldn't sleep, was Mayo Adams. Philip's evening out with his celebrated friend seemed to have increased the man's hostility all the more.

vi

On Saturday, August twenty-third, the drummers beat out a different rhythm. The signal to strike camp.

Immediately, the tent city began to come down; the

artillery and the Conestoga wagons began to rumble; work replaced indolence. Admiral Howe's fleet had been sighted off Chesapeake Bay. If the enemy troops landed, less than a hundred miles separated them from the much smaller American force. In between lay Philadelphia, where the Congress still sat in session. Every man in that body was a candidate for a hangrope if he were caught.

The Americans marched south. Philip was in low spirits because he still hadn't received any new letters from Anne.

vii

On Sunday morning, it rained. But the clouds cleared by noon, in time for a good percentage of the forty thousand people now living in Philadelphia to turn out and watch the American companies march through. Philip didn't see Gil; he would be riding at the very head of the column, with Washington, and Henry Knox, and other senior members of the staff.

Captain Webb's command lived up to Gil's original horrified assessment of it. They were just as ill-clad as the rest of the units from the other states represented in the huge parade of eleven thousand men.

But one visible feature united them—a sprig of greenery, fresh-cut the night before by the carpenters and placed in each man's hat to signify the army's vitality—on direct order of the commander-in-chief. Quite a few grumbled that more than a couple of leaves on a twig would be required to bring the quarrelsome, heat-weary citizen-soldiers up to fighting trim.

Webb's company, where Philip marched, was at present a fifty-man unit, the second in line among four such companies forming the battalion. Two battalions comprised the regiment. And throughout its shambling ranks—marching was too dignified and precise a term—disorder in formation accompanied disorder in costume. Seldom did anyone step exactly in time with the drumbeats. And whenever the fifers struck up one of the popular marching songs of the day, the men bellowed out the words if they felt like it:

> *"We are the troop*
> *"That ne'er will stoop*
> *"To wretched sla-ver-ee—"*

People leaned from windows, huzzahing, fluttering handkerchiefs. They lined the walks of Front and Chestnut Streets that Philip remembered so well from the weeks he'd spent in the city. Now circumstances were much different. Burdened with the equipment of war—canteen, cooking gear, hand-carved wood drinking cup, sheathed hunting knife, cartridge box, lead, ball mold and, most important of all, his Brown Bess with the bayonet in place—he was leaving the great city not to return to Anne but to confront the immense might of Howe's army. He imagined the foe as a scarlet serpent a thousand times longer than the British columns he remembered from Concord and New York and Jersey.

Next to Philip was Lucas Cowper. Although he had a deaf ear for music, he tried to improvise the marching airs anyway—whistling them off key. Philip stared up at the housepeaks and the clearing sky, singularly uninspired. No doubt it was partly due to the long, worrisome silence out of Cambridge. Surely Anne would have written if anything had gone wrong—

The singing and the cheers didn't help his mood either. A dedicated enemy lurked to the south. His job—every man's job—was to obey orders and destroy that enemy. Philip was sure Gil would be all dash and zeal on a prancing horse somewhere up with Washington. He was glad his friend couldn't see him, or the rest of his company, as they struggled to keep time with the Massachusetts drummers and fifers.

Marching immediately behind Philip and Cowper were Mayo Adams and Royal Rothman, the latter looking extremely nervous. But no more than ex-schoolmaster Pettibone just ahead. Pettibone gazed wistfully at the faces of the young girls cheering themselves hoarse on either side of Chestnut. He was no doubt wishing one of them was his dear Patsy.

Only Cowper, whistling in his monotone, seemed phlegmatically content. And of course Breen, staggering next to Pettibone. Breen was drunk.

The older man had somehow wheedled an extra ration of rum which he had proudly poured into his canteen before the march began. Now he found it necessary to slake his thirst frequently—no unusual sight among the soldiers. But Breen's step grew more erratic by the moment. Finally, swearing under his breath, Captain Webb dropped back and ordered Pettibone to hold Breen up.

Breen gladly accepted the support, doffing his filthy hat to the captain. His sprig of green fell off and was trampled.

Breen paid no attention, putting his hat back on, then extending his canteen to Webb. The captain slapped it down, colored when he saw people on the sidewalk point. He about-faced, returned stiffly to the head of the company. All jollity, Breen made an obscene gesture and continued to loll with his arm over the shoulders of the scowling schoolteacher.

Philip wasn't amused. It seemed bitterly clear again that a victorious army would never rise from such a disorganized collection of hooligans, malingerers and sometime-patriots yearning for home. Yet if there was ever a day when an army in the true sense was needed, that day had arrived.

The complainers were right. Twigs worn on the order of the commanding general weren't enough to work the miracle.

Some of the men started a new song:

> *"Over the hills with heart we go,*
> *"To fight the proud insulting foe—"*

"Kent?"

The voice brought Philip's head around even as he tried to keep in step with the drums. Mayo Adams gave him a coarse wink. His eyes glittered like polished stones in the August sun.

"You doin' all right, Kent?"

"I'm doing fine, thanks."

"Well, good, good. Just don't want you to forget I'm right behind you, boy. Right behind you every step."

> *"Our country calls and we'll obey—*
> *"Over the hills and far away!"*

CHAPTER IV

Retreat at Brandywine

"JEHOSHAPHAT, Philip—look there in the ditch!"

Staggering along the road among the hundreds of men fleeing through the early autumn dusk toward Chester Creek, Philip wiped sweat from his eyes and followed Lucas Cowper's pointing hand. Of the men from his mess, Cowper was the only one he'd seen since the full retreat began an hour ago.

Now he saw another. Pettibone, lying on the slope of the roadside ditch, a bloodied hole shot through the left side of his chest.

The schoolmaster had apparently come this far when the lines broke, only to drop and die. Through the dust and smoke billowing over the road, the last, almost horizontal beams of September sunlight pierced here and there; sufficient light for Philip to have a swift, harrowing glimpse of a fat green fly landing on Pettibone's lip. The fly crawled over Pettibone's lower teeth and into his mouth.

"Somebody's got to let his poor wife know," Cowper said, shaken.

Philip tugged Cowper's arm. "Later. Come on! Staring won't help him—or us." He had to shout to be heard above the noise.

All around them, men limped or ran through the mellow evening. Cursed or complained as they dragged themselves along, slowed by wounds or the plain disgust and bitterness of defeat. Cowper surrendered to the pull of Philip's hand. The two returned to the center of the road. Behind them, musketry rattled.

For most of the day the American center had held Chad's Ford on the east side of Brandywine Creek, against the fire of Knyphausen's entrenched Hessians. Then, late in the afternoon, red jackets began appearing on the wooded hills to their rear, northward, where the right wing was stretched out in a long defense line. The bulk of the British army, mysteriously absent from the field for hours, had somehow gotten around behind the American positions. Three divisions under Cornwallis streamed down the hillsides to attack.

General Sullivan's brigades vainly tried to hold them back. Knyphausen's Hessians moved at last, eastward, to ford the Brandywine. From that hour, when the sun was already starting down, the outcome was certain. The Americans had been prepared for an assault from the west, not for a two-pronged attack from both front and rear. Around Philip and Lucas Cowper was the terrible result—a retreat more clamorous and confused than the one at Breed's Hill. A retreat that might prove even more devastating than the steady withdrawal of Washington's troops at Long Island and New York—

Philip knew the battle was lost. Cowper knew it. So did all the other men on the road. Fright and humiliation showed on every face.

As the light kept fading, Philip thought he saw the shapes of soldiers moving among the trees on his left, about a hundred yards north of the road. More Americans retreating, he assumed.

He was so tired, each step almost required a conscious act of will. His shoulder ached from returning Hessian fire with the Brown Bess. He'd had no food since early morning. At three, he'd drained the last tepid water from his canteen.

"Where in Christ are we supposed to be going?" he

yelled at Cowper, above a din of hoofs and wheels coming up behind.

"We're to cross Chester Creek, that's what Webb said."

"Then what?"

"I don't know, maybe they'll tell us at the creek—"

"Clear away, clear away!" men shouted. Hastily Philip pushed Cowper to the shoulder. The heads of charging horses loomed, great silhouettes against the sunset light piercing the smoke. At full gallop, the horses dragged a pair of jouncing howitzers.

The men nearby broke for both sides of the road. The horses and wheeled guns thundered past. Above all, it was necessary to prevent the capture of artillery. Men were expendable.

Back on the road, yearning for just one good breath in the smoke and dust, Philip grabbed at a skinny soldier loping toward the east:

"Who are you? What unit?"

"Pinter's Marylanders—"

"Is the whole line broken?" Cowper shouted.

"Damn right it is. Howe's liable to whip us all the way back to Philadelphia—"

Then the Marylander was gone, dodging and darting around less speedy soldiers. The man was plainly determined to save his own skin. Maybe he had more brains than the rest of them, Philip thought. More brains than any of the spectral pairs and trios stumbling east in the lowering gloom, too worn out or hurt or disheartened to run.

More artillery roared through. Horse-drawn field cannon this time. One soldier failed to heed the shouted warnings and fell in the path of the slashing hoofs. Sourness rose in Philip's throat as the horses, then the iron-tired wheels, kept straight on over the flailing victim, muffling his shrieks, leaving him twitching in the road, all blood and broken bones.

Cowper kept looking back. Philip jerked his arm again:

"Damn it, Lucas, you can't stop to help every man who's hurt or you'll wind up the same way yourself."

Resigned, Cowper resumed the shambling pace. And despite the seeming callousness of his words, Philip was just as sick over the carnage as the young farmer was. It seemed to him that those in command—Washington, the staff, even his friend Gil who was supposedly on the field today—must have trained themselves never to view a battle in terms of individuals, only in terms of units, tactics, strategy. If they ever looked at the soldiers one by one—looked at the Pettibones lying dead in the ditches—they could never remain strong enough to issue orders for the next battle. Their hearts would break with despair.

Bitter fury welled up in Philip then. Fury born of the chaos and his exhaustion; fury over the human loss and the scandalous defeat—

Why hadn't someone caught the surprise flanking movement of Cornwallis? Was Washington asleep? Or was he simply the bungler he was so often accused of being?

Letting his emotions blur his already failing alertness, Philip wasn't ready for the unexpected crackle of musket-fire that raked the road from the left. Men yelled, dove for the ditches. Philip and Cowper crouched down, fumbling to load their weapons. The men drifting through the trees north of the road had right-flanked suddenly. They weren't American stragglers at all. Philip glimpsed florid faces, mitre-shaped hats—

A jaeger company. Hessians who had thrust forward parallel to the retreat route and were now turning to attack.

Running for the ditch with powder trailing from his horn, Lucas Cowper's legs suddenly gave out. Only an

297

instant later did Philip realize what had happened. The young Massachusetts farmer had been hit.

Cowper pitched head first into the ditch, musket fallen, horn fallen, bellowing in pain as blood poured from the place where a Hessian ball had shattered his upper left arm.

The Hessians were kneeling among the trees nearest the road, firing their rifles with precision. Philip jumped into the ditch, ducked as a ball hissed by, completed the loading of his Brown Bess without conscious thought. He raised it into position, shot, absorbed the slam of the stockplate against his already bruised shoulder, squinted through the failing light. A blond-haired German boy slumped against the trunk where he'd been kneeling. Philip hoped it was his ball that had opened a gushing hole in the boy's throat.

Cowper was moaning. Philip took a moment to look at the wound. He saw grisly muscle and bone showing through the blackened rent in Cowper's sleeve. The Hessians began advancing toward the ditch, where no more than a dozen men had taken cover to fight off the attack. The last of the September light glared on the steel of German bayonets.

On the road, Philip could still hear many more men running. He knew what they were thinking. Why risk your life in a skirmish that couldn't possibly change the day's outcome—?

"Into the ditch! Turn them back! *Blast you for a pack of yellow dogs—!*"

Struggling to re-load, Philip twisted his head to see who had shouted. An officer who had evidently come up from the west dismounted and pulled his saber. Whacking back and forth with the flat of the blade, the officer drove men into position to defend the ditch.

The officer was young; in his thirties. He wore a dingy assortment of clothing. A soiled dark red coat; a sweat-blackened cravat; limp, frowsy lace on his tricorn.

He might have been good-looking, except for the wrath that disfigured his features.

He smacked heads, backsides, thighs, succeeded in forcing ten or twelve more soldiers to the ditch. Philip got off another shot but saw no direct result. The Hessian company was advancing through tall weeds across a long, ragged front.

The American officer leaped into the ditch near Philip, one of his boots accidentally slamming Lucas Cowper's right leg. Disgusted with the man's almost maniacal bravado—some promotion-hungry subaltern, undoubtedly—Philip turned on him:

"The man's wounded, you damn idiot!"

"Then he can't turn back the jaegers. But you can. Charge 'em with me!"

In other circumstances Philip might have struck the officer. But there was no time. Bent over, the man ran along the ditch, shoved the crouching Americans up over the lip toward the Hessians. When he'd gotten half a dozen of them started, he jumped out of the ditch himself, a grin of bestial glee on his face.

My God, he's serious! Philip thought, caught between an impulse to follow and another that urged him to tend to the fallen Cowper, who was weeping in delirious pain.

A yard or so out from the ditch, the young officer turned back:

"Are you all weaklings? *Come on!*"

He ducked as if instinct had warned him of a ball from the Hessian rifles—he was facing toward the road—then spun and went storming toward the mercenaries. He uttered such a bloodthirsty howl that Philip's spine crawled. The officer was either a complete madman or entirely without fear.

But here and there along the ditch, a few more men climbed out to follow the half dozen others. The Hessians immediately stopped their forward march, knelt to re-load—

299

Philip hadn't had time yet. But he had his bayonet in place. He watched the officer an instant longer. Out in front of all the others, the man was actually charging right toward the Hessians, ducking and dodging as the German rifles cracked and flashed.

Miraculously, the officer avoided being hit. He brandished his sword and kept up that worldless screeming that brought all of the Americans out of the ditch at last—Philip among them. The first ranks of Hessians started scuttling back toward the trees.

Across a front fifty or sixty yards long, two dozen Americans followed the officer in his crazed charge. A Hessian stumbled. The officer sabered him through the chest. A cheer went up from the Americans. Suddenly Philip caught the mood of savagery, found himself running as fast as he could, just like the others—

The Hessians—perhaps thirty in the company —completely abandoned any pretense of orderly formation, retreating from the wave of attackers who began howling like the officer. Philip sped through the tall weeds between the ditch and the trees. Almost all the mercenaries had already melted back into the forest.

One sergeant, his belly bulging the tunic of his uniform, didn't quite make it. He stepped into an animal's burrow and sprawled. Philip reached the sergeant just as the man pulled his foot from the hole, supporting himself on his hands and one knee.

The Hessian heard Philip coming, turned his bulky body, raised a forearm to protect his face, shrieked:

"Himmel—"

Philip bayoneted him in the stomach.

In the near-darkness, American muskets spouted orange fire. Philip stepped on the Hessian's head, plunged on toward the trees where the saber-wielding officer had disappeared. But the light was so poor, he could find no more targets.

He passed a Hessian corpse just this side of the woods, saw another man running toward him, whipped up his Brown Bess to stab defensively—

A saber flashed as another musket glared to Philip's left. The saber clashed on bayonet steel, striking sparks. Philip absorbed the blow, dropped back a step, prepared to fight hand-to-hand—

Then he recognized the man who'd knocked his bayonet aside. The shabbily dressed officer.

Philip couldn't see the man's face clearly. But his voice was enough to suggest his pleasure:

"A little spirit and they turn tail. That's all it took, a little spirit—"

He breathed hard a moment, then shouted to those who had followed him:

"Well done! Well done!"

To the right and left, the Americans who'd joined the charge, voluntarily and otherwise, offered each other loud congratulations. The officer's saber clacked back into its scabbard. The whole action had taken no more than three or four minutes.

Philip thought of Cowper, headed back for the ditch. The officer strode beside him through the tall weeds:

"Damme, if we'd had this kind of spirit at the creek, we might have carried the day."

Quite without thinking, Philip said an obscene word. "We don't need more spirit. We need some commanders who know where the hell the British are hiding. If intelligence had been proper, we wouldn't have lost."

The officer stopped suddenly. His voice iced:

"I'll convey your opinion to the commander-in-chief. But perhaps I should also convey the name and unit of the man making the statement."

"Philip Kent. Private, Massachusetts infantry."

"You've a ready tongue, Mr. Kent."

Beyond caring whom he offended, Philip shot back,

"Maybe so. But I'll stick by what I said. We wouldn't be retreating if we'd known Cornwallis was coming at us from behind."

"I am well aware of that, soldier! Do you think I like it any better than you?"

The officer's tone brought Philip up short. He rubbed his eyes.

"No, sir, I suppose not. I'm sorry I spoke out."

The officer too seemed less angry:

"Don't be. What you said was blunt but correct. And I spoke too sharply. You fought well a few moments ago. All these men fought well—"

His hand lifted to indicate the little band he'd rallied to rout the Hessians. All at once he realized the men were gone. As quickly as they'd assembled, the anonymous soldiers had disappeared back to the road, rejoining the columns trailing east. The officer concluded:

"Let's put the whole conversation out of mind and just remember the engagement, eh?"

In the darkness a voice shouted, "General Wayne?"

"Here," the officer barked.

"I've caught your horse, sir."

"Right with you. Mr. Kent—" A hand clapped Philip's shoulder. "Bravely done."

And he tramped off toward the ditch, leaving Philip stunned and speechless.

Because of the man's sorry-looking uniform, Philip had had no idea he'd been following one of Washington's top field commanders. General Anthony Wayne, a young squire of this same Pennsylvania country through which they were fleeing, had a reputation for recklessness and quick temper. Philip was grateful that temper had moderated while they talked. Otherwise he'd certainly have been a candidate for disciplinary action.

He heard Wayne's horse pound away in the direction

of Chester Creek. Again he remembered Lucas Cowper, started running.

There seemed to be fewer men on the road. Perhaps the main body of the retreating army had passed. He was uncomfortably conscious of the quiet of the night-shrouded countryside as he reached the ditch, clambered down to the bottom, oriented himself as best he could—

He had charged the Hessians on an oblique line from the point where Wayne first joined him. That meant Cowper should be somewhere to the left as Philip faced the road. He headed that way.

He'd gone no more than a yard or so when he heard sounds made by two other people. One was unmistakably Cowper; groaning. Another man was breathing hard. The man heard Philip coming along the ditch:

"Who's that?"

Sudden fear wrenching his stomach, Philip answered:

"It's Kent. What are you doing, Mayo?"

Mayo Adams stood up beside Cowper's shuddering body, a black hulk against the first stars. There was a vicious undertone in Adams' voice:

"I come across Lucas and decided to help myself to his canteen and cartridge box. Lost mine back at the crick."

"Don't touch him. He's hurt pretty badly."

"Shit, he's dyin'. He won't miss them things."

"I said get away from him and get back on the road." Philip raised his empty musket. The metal of the bayonet glimmered in the starlight.

Mayo Adams chuckled.

"Why, you still got a musket! Think I'll take that too."

"What happened to yours?"

"Dropped it a ways back, accidental, and couldn't

303

find it again. And a feller can't get by without a musket, now can he? Sure glad I bumped into you this way. Nobody's gonna know whether the redcoats kilt only one of the bodies in this here ditch, *or two—*"

The sudden explosion of Adams' breath gave Philip forewarning that the bigger man was moving. But tiredness slowed his reaction time. His bayonet-thrust was poorly aimed.

Mayo Adams sidestepped, safe, and clamped both hands on the muzzle of the Brown Bess. He jerked hard. The musket tore out of Philip's fingers.

Adams swung the musket like a club, his meaty face awash with starlight for a moment. The little eyes shone. Desperately Philip wrenched back out of range of the stock arcing toward his head—

Adams cursed when the blow failed to land. Philip dove forward, both hands fastening on the stock. He kicked Adams' shin. The bigger man swore and kicked right back. Philip almost let go under the painful impact. Adams wrenched and Philip lost his hold a second time.

The stock came hurtling toward his jaw. Once more he started to dodge. His left boot skidded on the slope of the ditch. Off balance, he fell. He landed on his spine, the wind knocked out of him.

Laughing, Adams dropped the Brown Bess in the weeds.

"Well, Kent, guess this here's as good a time as any to settle things, what d'you say—?"

Philip yelled as Adams' huge weight crushed his belly; Adams had simply dropped down on both knees. Big hands stinking of powder closed on Philip's neck.

Suddenly he felt something rigid under his right hip. His hunting knife, still in its belt sheath. If he could only reach it—

To do it, he first had to stretch out his right arm. And he was close to passing out because Adams' fingers were digging deep, cutting off his wind. The Boston apprentice squeezed, then let go; squeezed and let go. He hummed as he knelt on Philip's midsection, sporting with him.

Philip heard several men passing along the road only a short distance away. But they were moving fast in the darkness, making noise themselves. They'd never hear Adams' little hum of pleasure—

Philip got his arm straightened out. Then he doubled his right hand under; bent it so far he thought the bones in his wrist would snap. Almost as if the hand were a separate thing, he groped back toward his right hip. Pushing his knuckles against the ground, he forced the hand along until he touched his own body.

He extended his fingers—stretched them toward the hilt of the knife—

He couldn't reach under and free it. Adams' weight was too great, pressing him flat. The huge fingers worked on Philip's throat while Adams hummed. Dig and release. *Dig and release—*

"Your poor wife's sure gonna wonder what happened to you, Kent. She'll think some Tommy kilt you. Maybe I'll call on her one day and tell her what really happened. Tell her how you got smart with the wrong man—how you feel about that?"

Abruptly, Adams released his grip.

"Come on, you snotty little bastard, say somethin'!"

Waiting, Adams slid off Philip's belly. Philip could only make raw, retching sounds. He tried to raise his right hip a little. He was too weak.

Adams seized his hair, yanked his head up.

"Listen, I told you to say somethin', you son of a bitch!"

Adams pulling him up was the mistake. Philip's tortured right hand closed on the hilt, freed the knife, brought it whipping up, the blade turning toward Adams' throat—

Adams saw the glare of the stars on metal. He
305

stabbed his free hand at Philip's wrist——

Too late. Philip raked the knife edge over Adams' neck, pushing———

One startled, gurgling cry. Then blood spewed like a fountain.

The blood drenched Philip's forehead, his eyes, his cheeks. He rolled away as the dead hand came loose from his hair. The warm, meaty stench of the pumping blood sickened him.

He flattened on his belly, burrowed in the grass of the ditch bank, wiping frantically at the mess on his face. He heard Adams fall.

Minutes went by. Philip lay panting, wanting to vomit. Gradually the nausea passed. He tried to stand. Still too tired. He'd had too much. He'd just lie here, forget it all—

He thought of Lucas Cowper.

He fought the shock and the overpowering lethargy as if they were enemies as real as Adams had been. At last he was able to stand up. Weakly; dizzily. But he was upright. He made four passes at the belt sheath before he got the knife back in place.

Clenching his teeth and shuddering, he forced himself to step over Mayo Adams' corpse, walk toward Cowper till he found him.

He knelt, touched sticky fingers to Cowper's lips. He felt faint breath.

"Lucas? Lucas, I'm going to pick you up—"

One hand curved under Cowper's neck. As he raised Cowper's head a few inches, the young farmer screamed and thrashed. The starlight whitened exposed bone in Cowper's ruined upper arm. Philip knew he had to get Cowper on his feet and moving or his friend would surely bleed to death. The responsibility somehow helped him find strength:

"We'll get to a hospital, Lucas. They'll have a hospital set up someplace ahead. Chester Creek, maybe.

Don't worry, we'll get you there and get you fixed—"

He literally dragged Cowper to his feet. The young farmer cried out again as Philip maneuvered him. Finally Cowper's right arm was draped over Philip's neck.

Left arm around Cowper's waist, Philip crouched and retrieved his Brown Bess. Supporting Cowper's limp body, fighting the pain and dizziness in his own, Philip started to walk. Step by labored step, he climbed to the road and turned east in the September darkness.

ii

At Chester Creek bridge, he caught up to a Conestoga wagon that had broken an axle. The teamsters struggling to repair it stopped long enough to help raise Lucas Cowper, unconscious now, to a place on top of the rolled-up command tents. When it became apparent that the battle was lost, the tents had been struck at headquarters not far from Brandywine Church.

The teamsters told Philip to pull himself up into the wagon too, and ride the rest of the way. He was glad to do it.

Only half aware of the repaired wagon starting to roll again, he leaned his forehead against the plank side and laid one hand on Lucas Cowper's feverish forehead. The wagon swayed and bounced as the drivers negotiated the rutted road. Each jolt made Cowper writhe, though he never woke up completely.

It took the wagon over an hour to travel beyond the village of Chester and reach the temporary night camp—and the hastily erected tent that resembled a corner of hell more than a hospital.

iii

"Raise his head so he can take the rum. That's good. Son? You awake?"

Stretched out on bloody planks placed on wood tres-

307

tles, Lucas Cowper shivered and opened his eyes. Philip stood directly behind Cowper's head at the end of the crude operating table. An orderly was already at work ripping away Cowper's shirt.

Philip hardly dared look at the arm. It was a ruin of blood, severed muscle, bone slivers. Any time the orderly touched it, Cowper grimaced.

The surgeon was middle-aged. He wore a white apron stained as red as a butcher's. He pressed a brown glass bottle to Cowper's lips. Cowper choked. But some of the liquor got down his throat. Gradually, a little of the glaze left his eyes.

He heard the sounds of the tent. The sounds Philip tried not to hear—

The cursing of the overworked doctors. The grisly grind from the next table, where two surgeons twisted the wood handles of a T-shaped cylindrical saw whose toothed bit was boring a hole in a casualty's shaved skull.

And above all, there was the screaming.

The tent stank of urine, excrement, sweat, putrefying flesh. In the aisle to Philip's left, a severed foot and a length of intestine floated in a tub of pink-tinted water. Although exhausted, the surgeon treating Cowper tried to speak gently, patiently. His voice carried the soft rhythms of one of the southern states:

"Can you hear what I'm saying to you, son?"

Feebly, Cowper answered, "I—I can."

"You feel anything in that arm?"

"Hurts—plenty. Can't—move it—"

"Well, the ball destroyed too much muscle and bone. I'm going to have to take it off at the shoulder."

The surgeon held out one hand. An orderly dropped a new musket ball into the dirty palm. Grasping the ball between thumb and forefinger, the surgeon held the ball up where Cowper could focus on it:

"I'm going to put this between your teeth. I want you

to bite down hard. Then you won't feel it so much." The surgeon's pale, stubbled face showed the lie behind the words.

All at once Cowper tried to struggle up:

"What did you say about my arm, doc—?"

"That I can't save it, son. I have to saw it off."

"Please don't. Oh God, *please!* I'm left-handed, doc. I need both hands to work a plow—I'm a farmer, *I can't run a farm with one arm gone—*"

Cowper was shrieking now. Philip turned away, closed his eyes a moment, tightened his hands on Cowper's shoulders as the wounded man tried to wrench himself off the bloody table.

"Goddamn it, you've got to hold him down!" the surgeon shouted to Philip. The orderly shoved the rum bottle between Cowper's teeth, up-ended it until Cowper fell back gagging and slobbering from the liquid gushing into his mouth. Against his will, Cowper swallowed several times. The wild wrenching subsided.

More wounded men were being carried into the tent on litters, put down in rows near the entrance. There were six surgical tables working; the steady grind of the trephining saw filled Philip's throat with bile again.

Cowper's lids fluttered closed as the rum began to take effect. The surgeon shoved the musket ball between Cowper's teeth:

"Bite."

Cowper didn't respond. Using both hands, the surgeon pressed his jaws together:

"Bite, son, *bite*—that's it." He dashed sweat from his eyes. "Give me the saw."

An orderly passed him the instrument. It still showed stains from the last amputation. The surgeon walked around to the left side of the table, stumbling once. Another orderly caught him, held him until he was able to stand on his own.

The surgeon scrutinized the exposed shoulder joint

for a moment, then put the center of the notched blade on the spot he'd selected. With quick back and forth motions, he began to saw.

Blood ran. Muscle parted. Bone rasped. Cowper turned white, started to writhe. An orderly clamped hands on Cowper's mouth so he wouldn't cry out and swallow the ball. *Grate* and *grate,* the saw cut deeper——

Philip expended every remaining ounce of his strength to hold the farmer's shoulders. At last, the awful rasping noise ceased. The severed limb thumped into the dirt beside the table.

The surgeon passed the saw to an orderly, wiped his forehead again, looked around, turned almost as red as his apron:

"Where the hell is the tar?"

"Had to heat up a new batch, sir. Here it comes—"

Two more orderlies struggled to bring up a small cauldron of bubbling pitch that had been heated on the fires burning in the hospital yard.

"Watch your eyes," the surgeon warned those around the table. An orderly took a stick and tilted up one side of the cauldron. Hot tar cascaded onto the bleeding stump just below Cowper's shoulder, cauterizing, sterilizing—

Cowper woke again, screamed and fainted.

The pitch slopped and hissed on the board table, clotted sticky-black on the end of the stump. The blood-flow stopped.

Cowper's chest barely moved, so thin was his breathing. Philip thought he couldn't stand there an instant longer—

"Appreciate your assistance, soldier," the surgeon told him. The man rubbed a red hand across his lips and gestured to Cowper's still form. "Clear him away and bring the next one."

His eyes returned to Philip.

"There's hot water outside. You can wash up. You look like you took a bath in somebody's blood. I hope it was one of the British."

iv

Outside, the near-scalding water dipped from a kettle hanging over burning logs restored Philip to some semblance of sanity. But that was almost worse than the semi-delirium of his twenty or thirty minutes in the hospital tent.

Drying his face on a rag from the ground, he tried to shut out the almost continual din of shouting and screaming from the other side of the canvas walls. It was impossible—just as winning this accursed war was impossible—

A face, bright red hair, caught his attention from the other side of the fire. The Marquis de Lafayette's fine uniform was stained and torn in several places.

"Philip! I thought I glimpsed you when I rode in. Thank God you've survived the day—"

Gil hobbled around the fire. Only then did Philip see the bandage tied tightly around the trouser leg. A ball had torn the outside of Gil's left thigh a few inches below the groin.

Gil gestured to the hospital tent:

"Were you wounded in the action? I notice no evidence of it—"

Too tired to speak immediately, Philip shook his head. Then:

"Man from my unit lost an arm. I brought him here."

There was a strange despair in Gil's eyes. He tried to conceal it with a shrug and a weak smile:

"Well, as you can see, *messieurs les anglais* favored me with a gun-shot. It's trifling. I shall wait until the doctors finish with the urgent cases."

"Where were you when you were hit?"

"I do not know, exactly. General Sullivan's men were

311

all around me. I was endeavoring to urge them to turn and stand when the ball knocked me from the saddle—"

His eyes shifted toward the bedlam of the tent; a man was baying like an animal. His face wrenched:

"I have never seen such chaos! Or such cowardice! A formal retreat is one thing—the enemy carried the day decisively. But these men run like hares. To control them—to command them—it can't be done!"

Philip sighed. "I guess that's why we keep losing battles."

"The laxity I saw when I first rode into the encampment will be our undoing!" Gil fumed. "Undisciplined children running helter-skelter, disobeying orders at their whim, cannot defeat the British. Only an *army* can defeat them."

Philip's face, still marked with dried blood at the hairline and around the ears, looked utterly weary and despondent:

"I know, Gil. And that's the one thing we still don't have."

Gil's silence represented total agreement.

v

The Brandywine position was lost on the eleventh of September. For two more weeks the rival armies feinted and skirmished through the countryside around Philadelphia. Then the beaten Americans withdrew to erect a temporary camp at Pennybacker's Mill, on a creek that flowed down to join the Schuylkill. The first hint of autumn nipped the air as Philip and the men in his mess—now down to three with Pettibone and Adams dead and Cowper off in a recovery area—wearily raised their tent.

Philip had visited Lucas Cowper once. Although conscious, the farmer refused to speak or even acknowledge Philip's presence. A stained bandage was pinned over the stub of Cowper's arm. He lay staring at the roof of the recovery tent, never blinking. After asking a score of quiet questions and receiving no answers, Philip crept away, totally depressed.

He tried to remember that if every man in the army allowed himself to fall prey to an erosion of the spirit such as he was again suffering, the struggle was already over for good. But it was hard to keep going; hard to be at all encouraged in the face of a shambles like the Brandywine. And its equally humiliating aftermath:

"It's 'ficial," Breen announced, late in the afternoon of the twenty-seventh. He'd just come from the sutler's.

"What's official?" Royal Rothman asked in a listless voice.

"Every man-jack in the Congress skedaddled out to Lancaster a week ago. And yesterday, ol' Cornwallis marched the grenadiers into Philadelphia."

"So the city's fallen?"

" 'Pears so, Royal. All the damned Tories should be mighty happy."

"What the devil happens to us?"

"Oh, we just go on drawin' our liquor ration an' doin' what they tell us. Be winter soon. Doubt there'll be much more fightin'."

Having listened in gloomy silence, Philip burst out, "Why don't we try to re-take Philadelphia, for God's sake?"

Breen shrugged in a laconic way. "Have to ask General George about that. But I wouldn't, even if I had the chance. I understand he's in mighty mean spirits. Maybe your Frenchy friend could tell you. I sure God can't."

Breen scratched his belly, hiccoughed, took a couple of wobbly steps toward the tent, pivoted back:

"Oh—and 'fore you ask, no, they ain't payin' us. Again."

"We haven't seen a penny in three months!" Royal protested.

Breen shrugged. "What's the difference? You can't hardly spend them bills they printed up for the paymaster. Only place they'll take 'em 'thout a bitch is the sutler's. I heard half the colonies—"

"States," Royal corrected primly. Breen ignored him:

"—is makin' jokes about the money. 'Not worth a Continental' is what they call somethin' absolutely not worth a damn."

Breen lifted the tent flap, acting unusually sober all at once.

"Sure's funny 'thout old Pettibone hangin' around. S'pose they'll send us some green replacements, Philip?"

"Eventually."

"An' Cowper—what the devil's that poor feller gonna do? He told me once his daddy couldn't work no more. Too old. So there wasn't nobody except Lucas to tend the farm."

"I don't know what he'll do. I don't want to think about it."

"You was there when they sawed—"

"Yes, I was there. Shut up about it!"

A moment of silence. Breen looked contrite:

"Sorry."

"Yes—me too."

Breen rolled his tongue in his cheek. "You're an all-right sort, Philip. I don't 'pologize to no other kind, y'know. That's why I can admit I don't miss Mayo Adams one whit. Wonder what become of him?"

Philip studied the sky. "Took a British or Hessian ball, probably."

"Yeh, probably."

Breen pulled up his hunting shirt to scratch his stomach again. Philip noticed a wrinkled sheet of paper stuck in the older man's hide belt.

"Breen, what's that?"

Fuzzily, Breen peered down. "My bellybutton."

"No, dammit, *that*—" He pointed.

"Well, damme if it didn't clean slip my mind. Fer you—"

As he pulled the paper loose, Philip practically leaped for it:

"A letter?"

"Yessir, mail finally come through. Picked it up 'fore I bought my ration. Clean forgot I had it. Maybe it'll perk your spirits up some. Royal, when the hell you gonna start our cook fire? I'm hungry as a grizzly cub in April—" Blinking, he ambled on into the tent.

Philip almost whooped for joy as he examined the badly wrinkled letter. The handwriting was Anne's.

He tore the letter open, read the date—late July—swiftly skipped down the lines for the essential details, his spirits soaring:

His wife was well.

Abraham was growing, talking and in good health.

Captain Caleb's two new privateers were nearing completion on the ways at Sawyer's.

The final paragraphs riveted his gaze and turned him cold.

I do not wish to put additional worry on you when your task is difficult enough, my dearest. But at the moment, there is no one else with whom I can share a problem that is proving troublesome.

I have received two notes from Will Caleb's hired captain, Mr. Rackham, whom I am certain you recall. In each, he has invited me to Sawyer's to view the vessels under construction—which struck me as an altogether suspect invitation, considering his behavior that day last winter. Neither missive received an answer, of course. However, my silence did not end his improper interest. Indeed, it produced two visits from the obnoxious man, on our very doorstep here in Cambridge.

Both were likewise of the briefest nature. I let him

315

know I did not welcome his attentions. He seemed to treat the reply as a joke. I am honestly fearful the fellow is a reckless libertine, no doubt encouraged by the thoughtless talk of some women whose husbands are away serving; such women proclaim their loneliness to any available male who is not in his dotage. So upsetting were Rackham's smiles and hints, I have decided to ask our neighbor Mrs. Brumple to share the house with me. She craves company, and I believe her presence would help deter any further forwardness on Rackham's part.

At first I hesitated to mention the matter to you, dear husband. Yet here I am pouring out my concerns in an unseemly way. With you so distant, a great portion of that strength of which I have sometimes foolishly boasted now seems altogether lacking—proof, if it were needed, that man and wife become a new whole, far different from what each might have been as an individual. What I am attempting to do, I suppose, is to reassure both myself and you that nothing is amiss—and that with Mrs. Brumple occupying the spare room, no further difficulty could arise.

I can also promise you that at the first opportunity, I shall speak to Captain Caleb about his associate's unwelcome overtures. However, the captain is presently put out into the ocean with Eclipse for a week or two, during which time her guns and procedures for operating same are to be brought into perfect trim. I will contact him the moment he returns to Boston Harbor.

God protect you, my beloved, and may your son and your eternally affectionate wife soon be blessed with your presence, or, until that joyous day, further word that you are safe and well.

Ever yours,
Anne.

The cool September breeze fluttered the page. Philip stared at the amber clouds and a flight of wild geese streaming toward the southern horizon. But he saw only the insolent face of Captain Malachi Rackham.

That night he actually thought about desertion; about damning this futile war and hurrying home.

Tempting though the idea was, he put it out of mind because he knew that it was wrong for him, no matter how anyone else chose to act. It was also wrong because it would be the most foolish kind of weakness to give in to fears that were, for the moment, of small substance. Anne was taking steps to deal with the problem of Rackham. Those steps would probably prove effective.

The mere thought of desertion made him ashamed for other reasons, too. If he did what many had already done—simply went home the moment he felt like it—he would be one of those whom Tom Paine scathingly denounced as summer soldiers; sunshine patriots. More important, if mass desertions continued, there would soon not even be a semblance of an army left. And the larger purpose, of which the army was the sole instrument of fulfillment, would be lost. He believed in what the army was fighting for, even though up till now most of the fighting had been poorly done.

He had come to his belief over a long period of years, with much doubt along the way. But he did have an unashamed conviction that the cause was just. To leave would betray both the cause and the conviction.

And, finally, it would betray Anne.

A deserter who appeared suddenly in Cambridge would not be the man she'd taken as a husband. He'd wait for the next letter. It would contain less disheartening news. Confirmation that Caleb had brought his captain to heel. Surely it would—

With struggle, he almost convinced himself of that.

CHAPTER V

"I Mean to March to Hostile Ground"

JUDSON FLETCHER rode like a man pursued.

Lather streaked the flanks of his horse. He knew he'd already pushed the animal much too hard, covering the sixty-mile distance with only very brief stops. He'd been in the saddle most of the night, his stained coat not nearly warm enough to protect him from the bite of the late October air.

From the east, first light gilded the shocked corn standing in the fields. A yawning farmer loading fat pumpkins into a wagon gave him a startled stare as he hammered along the dirt road, plumes of breath streaming from the horse's muzzle.

What if I'm too late? What if he's gone?

It was Donald, day before yesterday, who had dropped the casual remark that sent Judson speeding south. Donald had come by the Shaw cabin with another purse; the dole was delivered more grudgingly with every visit.

Judson's appearance had worsened over the summer. He'd lost more weight. He was lethargic; sullen; constantly unshaven.

Still, as always, Donald dutifully tried to spark some reaction from his brother with reports on various aspects of the war, starting with the loss of Philadelphia to General Howe's army in September. That had caused sharp criticism of General Washington even among his fellow Virginians, Donald said.

One bright circumstance offset the fall of America's

largest city: the surrender of Gentleman Johnny Burgoyne's expeditionary force at Saratoga just a couple of weeks ago.

Expecting reinforcements in the form of troops under General Howe, Burgoyne had instead been virtually abandoned in the York State, while Howe pursued his conquest of Philadelphia—then settled in, presumably, to enjoy the favors of his mistress. Outnumbered three to one by the Americans under General Gates, Burgoyne asked for terms. It was the sole piece of encouraging news in an otherwise bleak cavalcade of disasters and defeats:

"Unless you wish to count the end of the verbal war over the Articles of Confederation," Donald told his brother. "I understand a draft is just about ready."

For over a year Congress had been debating the wording of a document that would organize the thirteen states into some kind of working relationship; stipulate areas of authority; divide financial responsibility for the war fairly—

"They finally worked out a plan where expenses of the central government will be apportioned according to each state's surveyed land, which I suppose is fair. We won't properly be a country until every one of the thirteen ratifies the draft Articles, though. Considering how long it's taken to get the material written and agreed upon, that may not happen till the next century! Even if the Articles are accepted, they leave much to be desired."

Judson's vague murmur was enough to prompt Donald to continue:

"Every state retains its sovereignty, and the Congress is granted jurisdiction only in certain limited areas. It can declare war—but can't wage it unless each state approves. There's a proviso saying Congress may borrow money, but not a single word about how the central government may *raise* money to repay the loans. In

319

short, if the Congressional fiddler wants to play a tune, the states collectively pretty well tell him yea or nay."

"I'd hardly compare that kind of document to a military victory," Judson observed sourly.

"True. But what other accomplishments can we brag about?"

"Why not save your breath altogether?"

"I probably should. The Articles are a patchwork. Too many basic questions dodged while everyone's diverted by lofty sentiments about 'perpetual union.' The best you can say is that it's a start. It seems to me that a more clearly and thoughtfully drawn statement will be required before very long. Some sort of formal constitution—"

Judson's apathetic stare showed he'd completely lost interest. Donald smiled sadly:

"I'm not precisely enthralling you with all this, am I?"

Judson shrugged, as if to ask what else his brother expected. Donald sighed. Then:

"Well, perhaps something more personal will pique your interest. Your friend George has been at Williamsburg for a fortnight now—*by the Lord!* A response at last!"

It was true. Judson's blue eyes finally showed something other than contempt or indifference:

"What's he doing there?"

"Damme if I can tell you. Something big's afoot, though. He's been attending secret meetings with a special committee appointed by Governor Henry—Mr. Jefferson, Mr. Wythe and several other Burgesses. The meetings last for hours at a time. They must be debating something besides another request for powder to defend the Kentucky forts."

"Have you seen George personally?"

"Yes, I talked to him at the Raleigh Tavern before I rode home."

"How does he look?"

"Very fit. But worried. Conditions in the west are growing worse. All the tribes rising against the settlers—my guess is that George came east to raise some additional militia units. He wouldn't tell me specifically." A pause, as Donald eyed his disheveled brother. "He asked about you."

"What did you tell him?"

"Exactly what I tell Father. As little as possible. I imagine Tom Jefferson and some of the others talk more freely—"

Judson glanced away.

"George sent you his regards. Also his regrets that he couldn't stop by for a visit. I got the impression he'll be bound back for Kentucky soon after the secret meetings are concluded."

At that exact moment, Judson felt as if a door had opened; perhaps the last one remaining for him.

It was a desperate, perhaps foredoomed hope. But confinement on the tiny piece of cabin property had grown intolerable. Too often, he found his thoughts turning to the means for suicide.

He said nothing to his brother about the sudden idea that fired his mind and restored his energy all at once. But shortly after Donald had gone back to Sermon Hill, Judson was mounted and riding south.

Now, in the October dawn sparkling with hoarfrost, he pounded into Williamsburg. Flashed by the lovely rose-brick residences of the merchants and the gentry. Thundered through the farmer's market where a flock of geese honked and waddled to escape the flying hoofs. He rode straight to the yard of the Raleigh Tavern, its leaded windows reflecting the autumn dawn in diamond-shaped patterns of yellow fire.

Looking more like a scarecrow than a man, Judson dismounted and turned the exhausted horse over to a groom for feeding and stabling. As he walked toward the tavern entrance, he was acutely aware of the hammering of his heart.

In the dark-beamed foyer, he found a sleepy boy swishing a straw broom over the pegged floor. Judson's eyes showed huge gray circles of fatigue. His fair beard, scraped off in preparation for the trip, had already sprouted again, unevenly. The sweep knew in a glance that Judson wasn't the sort of gentleman who belonged at the Raleigh.

"Son, you've a guest here—"

"Got eight or nine," the sweep replied, leaning on his broom. "Most are still in bed. And the landlord don't take kindly to loud talk at this hour."

Checking a burst of anger, Judson lowered his voice:

"The guest I'm referring to is named Clark. He hasn't left, has he?"

The boy took his time answering:

"Would you be meaning Major Clark, the militia commander from Kentucky?"

"Yes, dammit! Is he still here?"

"I tell you the landlord'll tan me if you keep on swearing and yelling—"

Judson glared. "Then stop being cheeky and answer me straight!"

The sweep took a step backwards, poked his broom toward the arch leading to the public room:

"Major Clark come down about twenty minutes ago to eat breakfast. Hops up way before daylight every morning. Guess that's the style out west. You'll find him around the corner by the fireplace, I reckon."

"Thank you very much!"

Boots hammering, Judson spun away. He'd made it in time. *In time!*

Suddenly he halted, catching a whiff of the wood fire burning somewhere on the other side of the wall. The aroma wasn't nearly as strong as his own sweaty stench. He must look a sight.

He stepped to the wall where an ornamental silver plate hung on display. He bent, examined his blurred reflection, tried to smooth his tangled hair. He'd lost the tie-ribbon on the frantic ride. God, he was totally unpresentable—

But there was nothing to be done. In the public room, a chair had scraped. Boots squeaked the plank floor as someone approached the arch. Judson straightened up with a jerk, aware of the trembling of his hands as he confronted the tall figure of George Clark, red hair neatly tied at the nape of his neck.

"Judson—?"

"Hello, George."

"Good Lord, I couldn't believe it when I thought I heard your voice. You're the last person in creation I expected to see this morning! What brings you to Williamsburg?"

Judson's mouth went dry. His friend looked lean, clear-eyed, deeply tanned—and dismayed as he took in Judson's stained apparel and unhealthy pallor. All Judson could say was:

"George, it—it's fine to see you—"

He shot out an unsteady hand. George Clark clasped it in a hard, callused grip. Now that he'd ridden all this distance, Judson's courage failed him. He couldn't bring himself to tell his friend the reason for the trip.

He was afraid George would laugh in his face.

ii

Even the sweep leaning on his broom was sensitive to something awkward in the confrontation between the fine-featured young gentleman who looked as if he'd just crawled out of some hole in the earth, and the younger but somehow more poised frontiersman wearing a thigh-length fringed hunting shirt and leggings of deerhide. Apparently both were at a loss for words.

All at once Judson blurted, "Donald told me you

were here. I rode most of the night—"

"By God that's a mark of friendship! My end of it's been sadly neglected, I'm afraid."

"I know you have pressing responsibilities, George. No time—"

"And too few men. And too little powder. And every tribe putting on the bloodroot—but come on, come to the table. Join me in something to eat—"

A bit reassured when his friend laid his arm over his shoulder, Judson accompanied George into the public room. As they approached a table near the fireplace, Judson said:

"I'm afraid you've lost me already. What was that word—? Bloodroot?"

"The braves use it to paint their faces for battle."

George pulled out a chair for Judson, signaled a yawning servant girl, slipped into his own chair in front of the immense breakfast he'd been eating. Half a loaf of cornbread and most of a crock of country butter had been put away, plus part of an eight- or nine-inch stack of griddlecakes dripping with clear colorless syrup.

"All the tribes are going to war against Kentucky," George explained. "The Mingos, the Shawnee, the Piankashaws, Delaware, Wyandots—the year of the three sevens hasn't been good to my part of the country. The year of the bloody sevens, Kentuckians are calling it."

The serving girl's shadow touched the table where George's browned hand closed around his coffee mug. George glanced up.

"My friend's hungry, my girl."

Younger than I am, Judson thought with despair. *Younger, and he acts twice my age. Twice as composed and sure of himself—*

"May I bring you something, sir?" the girl asked Judson.

"Only something to drink—" he began. When

George's eyes widened in surprise, he added quickly, "What my friends having. Coffee. Put milk in mine, please."

The girl shuffled away, yawning again.

"I was pleased to have the chance to talk with Donald when he was here," George said. "If he'd shed some of that weight, his gout might bother him less."

"Well, there's precious little pleasure for him at Sermon Hill besides eating and drinking."

"He's helping your father operate the plantation, then?"

"When he's not meeting here with the Burgesses."

George hesitated. "You're not at Sermon Hill—?"

"No." Judson's mouth twisted. "Father and I had one of our famous disagreements—this one a little more permanent than the others."

"How permanent?"

"I don't intend to go back to the place, ever. Furthermore, I'm not allowed."

"I'm sorry to hear that."

Judson waved, as if it didn't matter. "I rode off to Philadelphia to replace Donald in the Congress for a time—"

George nodded. "Tom Jefferson told me, during one of our meetings."

"What else did he tell you? That I botched my duties, the way I've botched everything in the last—?"

The serving girl's return stopped Judson in midsentence. Embarrassed by the outburst, George glanced toward the fire. Judson wiped his damp forehead, accepted the mug of steaming coffee, drank a third of it in a series of gulps. The coffee was nearly scalding and took some of the chill out of him.

It didn't lessen his tension, though. He was more and more convinced George Clark would reject his proposal out of hand.

"I always suspected I didn't fit in around here," Jud-

325

son said finally. "Now, I know it." The words had a lame, whipped sound.

There was no reproof in his friend's eyes, only sympathy:

"Donald said your views on the slave question helped bring on the trouble with your father."

"It's much more than that. As I told you, I disgraced myself in Philadelphia. I shot a fat Tory to death when he challenged me to a duel—even though Jefferson and the president of the Congress warned me to steer clear of that sort of affair. There was also a scandal over a woman—" *And some things since that I'm too ashamed to speak about even to you.* "I'm not proud of any of it. Ever since I came back, I've done nothing but live day to day. No purpose, no ambition—"

He stared at his friend. It was impossible to conceal his hope any longer:

"I've thought a good deal about what you used to write in your letters. About the open country in the west—"

"It's very different than it was just a few years ago, Judson."

"The war, you mean."

"Aye. We're down to three settlements in Kentucky. Harrodsburg, Boonesborough and Fort Logan. All this past spring and summer, our people have lived like prisoners inside the stockades. When work parties go out to plant corn, other armed men go with them to stand guard. It's not safe to hunt or farm your own piece of ground. Everyone's taken refuge at the forts—"

George's mouth set, almost ugly. "There's a governor at Fort Detroit, Henry Hamilton, who's paying British silver for every scalp cut from an American corpse."

"I've heard of him."

"They call him the Hair-Buyer. He understands how easily the whole Northwest Territory can be taken if the tribes are properly incited. He also understands the value of the land. Which is more than can be said for some of our elegant Burgesses sitting here in Williamsburg pinching snuff from their silver boxes. I came back to try to remedy the situation."

Judson came closer to the issue: "Donald thought you might be raising a new levy of men——"

George Clark didn't answer immediately. He scanned the room as if searching for possible eavesdroppers. But there was no one else present besides the two of them and the girl dozing on her stool by the fire.

George clacked his fork back on his trencher, used a finger to dab a smear of syrup from the corner of his mouth. He leaned forward in his chair:

"Donald guessed correctly. After a great deal of argument and some table-pounding, I persuaded the committee of the Burgesses to authorize the recruiting of three hundred and fifty Virginians for the defense of Kentucky. They're giving me six thousand Continental dollars to buy ammunition and supplies."

"Where are you going to find the men?"

"Anywhere I can. Here. Pittsburgh——"

"I'd like to be one of them."

The sudden silence was strained. Judson thought, *He's going to turn me down——*

George Clark picked up his fork, dropped it again. In the kitchen, a man and woman argued over who had broken half a crate of eggs. A wagon creaked in the street; a cow lowed, its bell clanking. The rhythmic slow swish of the sweep's broom going over and over the same square of floor sounded beyond the arch.

George frowned. "When you said you'd ridden all night, I thought there was probably some reason other than a wish to see an old friend."

"I want to go to Kentucky, George. I want to start again."

"I don't think you quite know what you're asking."

The words, gently said, almost broke Judson's heart.

An instant later, they angered him. He slammed the coffee mug on the table:

"So I'm judged and found guilty before the fact?"

George still looked troubled. "I'm not sure I understand."

"You've listened to Tom Jefferson. And to Donald. You've heard how I failed at everything before and you've decided I'll fail again."

"Judson, for God's sake! That's a totally unwarranted accusation—!"

"Is it?"

"Yes!"

"Forgive me, George, but I think you're lying. Maybe out of kindness, but lying all the same—"

If so, George concealed it. "You simply don't realize—Kentucky is *not* the tidewater." His supple hand spread eloquently over the griddlecakes, the syrup pitcher, the cornbread loaf. "There's little or no food like this. Just a swallow of water from a canteen and a handful of dried corn from your haversack. On the trail, you live like that for days—maybe weeks."

"I can do it. I know I can."

Silence again. Finally George resumed:

"Judson, it's difficult to say this—"

"A turn-down. All right, do it and be done!"

"God, they weren't exaggerating. You're angry at everything."

Judson flushed. "I'm sorry."

"Then hear me out. You're my friend, Judson. The closest friend I knew when I was growing up. That can't be changed by anything that happens. But because you *are* my friend, I won't deceive or flatter you—despite your notions to the contrary. There is no peace in Kentucky! No freedom to roam, explore, settle where you wish. The tribes are raiding regularly from north of the Ohio. Killing and butchering any man they find alone. Or women and babies, for that matter. I hate to

328

put it so bluntly, but I need soldiers, not gentlemen-adventurers."

"Do you think you can locate three hundred and fifty who meet your high standards?" Judson blazed.

George stiffened, but he controlled his temper, and his voice:

"If I'm lucky."

"And if you're not, you'll have to take somewhat less perfect specimens——"

"Judson, I can hardly stand to listen to this."

"To what?"

"Your bitterness. What in the name of heaven has happened to you?"

"What's happened, George, is that I'm dying."

He said it swiftly; softly. But George rocked back in his chair, hammered by the ferocity and pain of the statement.

"I mean it, George. I'm dying by days and by hours and by minutes——"

"So are we all."

"Not the same way. I'm dying from failing. Dying because I hold what seem to be the wrong beliefs. I'm dying from hating my father and being hated——"

"And dying from not being strong enough to overcome all that—and learn from it?" George asked quietly, with just the barest hint of condemnation.

Bleak-faced, Judson agreed:

"Yes. That too. But I have learned this much. I think I have just about one more chance left. One chance somewhere to pick up the litter of my life and prove I can be successful at something, however small or insignificant——"

George cooled visibly. "The defense of Virginia's western counties is neither small nor insignificant."

"George, I didn't mean——"

"What happens out there in the next year will determine how much land America holds when this war is

329

settled. It will determine whether we'll be pushed back east of the mountains, forced forever to huddle here on the coast—"

"Believe me, I didn't mean to suggest—"

Abruptly, George relaxed again. "I know." A weary smile; a nod. "The fault's mine. I haven't been in the best of spirits lately—"

He picked up his coffee mug, drank. "However—that doesn't change the situation I'm facing. I need steady hands. Sharp eyes." He looked directly at Judson. "God forbid that I should sound like a Bible-thumper inveighing against the sin of drunkenness. But this much is the truth. In the forest, liquor will only get a man lost, or slain."

The quiet statements told Judson more about what Jefferson or Donald had said to George; and much more about the immensity of the change in his friend. This George Clark wasn't the young man who'd roamed the Virginia woodlands for sheer pleasure. He spoke like what he was a military commander.

Judson gave George the answer he hoped his friend wanted to hear:

"Then I'll swear off if that's what it takes. Never another drop—"

"It takes even more than that."

"What, then? *Goddamn it, I'm pleading for my life!*"

Judson had tears in his eyes. He only realized it after he shouted. The outcry roused the serving girl on her stool, brought a gray feminine head peeping out of the kitchen, stopped the swish of the broom from beyond the arch. Judson drowned in a red wave of shame, his cheeks burning—

He kicked against the table's trestle, shoved his chair back, frantic to leave. His red-haired friend was staring at him with a mixture of alarm and sorrow.

As Judson whirled toward the arch, George's fingers clamped on his arm.

330

"Sit down."

The sneer was unconscious: "What the hell for? I'm not the sort you want. Clear-eyed. Pure-hearted—"

"Sit down," George Clark said. "And if you really want to discuss it, stop that self-pitying whine."

Judson felt as if he'd tumbled into an icy brook:

"Discuss it—? Do you?"

"Yes. I think I've made it clear that it won't be easy to gather the men I need. So I have—motives for possibly accepting your offer."

Jubilant, Judson pulled his chair up again, planted his elbows on the table, pleaded with open hands:

"I'll be sober as a damn saint, George! You always said I should see the western lands—well, maybe this isn't the wrong time but exactly the right one. If you think there'll be any problem about me taking orders because we're friends—"

"I think that could be a very definite problem."

"No, no, it won't be, I give you my word."

"The word's easy. The deed's hard. I want you to realize what you're asking. Consider the effort just to reach Pittsburgh. It's hundreds of miles—"

"I'm strong—you saw how I got here. I rode all night—"

"And walked in white and trembly as poplar leaves in a windstorm. I'm not trying to be difficult, Judson, or hard on you—I could never do that easily because of all the fine times we shared. But the truth of what my men will be facing can't be dodged. Can you sleep in the open when there are ten inches of snow covering the ground?"

"Yes."

"Walk till there's no feeling left in your legs—then keep on walking?"

"I can, yes."

"Do you think you could kill a man without making a sound?"

331

Judson tried to smile. "The first part is no problem. I'll practice the second."

George didn't smile back. "The pay is negligible. Most of my funds will go for supplies."

"I don't care. Nothing can be any worse than the trap I've gotten myself into here."

"Can you fire a rifle?"

"One of the long Kentucky models? I've never tried but I'm positive I can learn. I'm fair with pistols. Always have been—"

Suddenly George Clark unfolded his lanky frame, tossed coins on the table:

"Come on."

"Where?"

"I'll saddle my horse and we'll ride out in the country and find out how expert a marksman you are."

"With a rifle?"

"Yes."

George Clark had a peculiar, almost secretive expression on his face. Judson noticed it but failed to understand its meaning.

Once more the tall woodsman surveyed the public room. Satisfied, he led Judson toward the side entrance. In twenty minutes, they were cantering along under arching limbs that streamed down yellow and scarlet leaves in the brisk morning wind. The road was alternately dark and dazzling with sunlight.

He had a chance. One chance. He dared not let it slip out of his hands—

The hands that were white from gripping his rein hard, so George wouldn't see how he was trembling.

iii

George Clark shucked his leather hunting bag off his shoulder, dropped his powder horn on top, then laid his gleaming Kentucky rifle on the pile. From a sheath sewn into the side of the bag, he drew a bone-handled knife. He set to work stripping a square of bark from the trunk of one of the trees in the isolated clearing where they'd stopped. Judson marveled at the swift, sure movements of George's fingers—and silently cursed the continuing tremor of his own.

Kneeling in the thick layer of fallen leaves, George carefully inscribed a small circle on the moist inner surface of the peeled bark. He tucked his knife back in his boot, dug under the leaves, scratched up some dirt. He rubbed the dirt all around the circular cut, then blew off the excess. When he held up the square, the dirt still clung in the cut outlining a round target.

"Ought to be able to see that," George said.

"Yes, I can see it fine." Judson couldn't remember when he'd been so jittery. Perhaps that was because the stakes had never been quite so high.

George carried the target across the clearing. He pinned it to a trunk with one stab of his knife. He left the knife humming faintly, ambled back through the rustling leaves. Off in the trees that ringed the clearing, their horses blew and stamped.

George waved Judson to his side. Both men hunkered down as George supported the long-barreled rifle on his palms:

"I'll show you how to load one of these beauties. It's slower than loading a musket, but your aim's far more accurate."

"So I've heard."

Judson eyed the blade-pinned scrap of bark across the clearing. The bark moved a little in the brisk wind. Damn, he'd never hit it. *Never*—

Yes he would. He'd hit it if he never did another thing.

Patiently, George took him through the routine. First he filled the rifle pan with powder from his smaller priming horn. Then he picked up the second, larger

333

horn, scraped down at the end so the cut-off tip fit like a cap. He pulled off the cap section, held it up:

"One of these is an exact measure of powder."

He poured the coarse black grains into the barrel, then unlatched a perfectly polished, rust-free plate in the side of the stock.

"Greased patches in here. You lay one over the muzzle opening—"

He did so, then fished in the bag for a ball. He inserted the ball over the patch. He loosened the ramrod clipped to the rifle and handed the rod to Judson:

"You seat both the patch and the ball with a good solid stroke."

Judson nearly dropped the ramrod. George smiled in a tolerant way. Judson got the ramrod positioned, shoved it down the barrel.

"More, Judson. More. Seat it all the way, good and firm. All right, that's got it—"

He placed the rifle in Judson's hand.

"Now cock and fire—and remember to use your sight. Keep reminding yourself that it's not a musket. You don't just shut your eyes and let 'er blow—"

He pointed to a spot on the perimeter of the clearing opposite the target.

"Try it from there."

Feeling as if he were walking to an execution, Judson headed for the indicated place. When he got the rifle to his shoulder, it felt immense. Despite the fall air, he was sweating. The inside of his mouth tasted like brass.

Off to his left, George leaned on the ramrod. The wind fluttered the fringe on the hem and sleeves of his hunting shirt. Judson squinted down the blue barrel. *Dammit, why couldn't he keep his hands from shaking—?*

The target seemed to be flapping a lot. Jerkily, he corrected his aim—

"Wait till the wind dies," George said. "One hit is

334

worth half a dozen hasty misses if you're aiming for a Delaware who's been stoking himself on drum talk and Hamilton's rum."

When the target finally settled in place, Judson began to apply pressure to the trigger.

More pressure.

More—

He tried not to think of the importance of this one shot. It was impossible. His chance to pull himself out of the morass he'd made was staked on one lead ball—

Steady.

Steady—

He fired.

The recoil almost knocked him off his feet. A thunderous echo went rolling through the glade toward the fields of shocked corn. Birds screeched and beat their wings, rising from the treetops. Smoke blurred Judson's vision. He hadn't heard the ball chunk into the trunk. It was a miss. A complete miss—

Dismally, he lowered the rifle to his side. In a moment George Clark came trotting back across the clearing with the scrap of bark:

"Well, you were wide of the bull."

Failure. Again.

Then, disbelieving, he saw the smile on George's face. George wiggled the tip of his little finger in the semi-circle knocked out of the lower edge of the bark square:

"But at least you hit the target itself. Not many accomplish that on the first try."

"I never heard the ball land—"

"Did you expect to, with all the echoes?"

"George, that's not good enough. Put the target up again."

George flung the square away.

"Not necessary. With practice, I think you can handle a rifle well enough. I really brought you out here for another reason entirely. A much more important one."

335

Thunderstruck, Judson felt a burst of anger over the deception. He opened his mouth—

And shut it, thinking:

That's one thing you'll have to stop, boiling every time something doesn't please you—

George Clark walked toward another tree, his hunting knife back in his hand. Judson saw that peculiar, secretive expression again.

"Before we strike any sort of bargain," George said, "I want you to know the full extent of what you'll be facing if you come west."

"I don't understand. You already explained—"

"I'm not talking about the hardships. I mean the real purpose for which I'm recruiting men."

A white-tailed hare hopped halfway across the clearing, discovered them and went bounding away. Judson felt an ominous little tickle along his backbone. His friend looked positively grim.

"You said you're raising a levy for the defense of Kentucky. To protect the settlements against the Indian attacks—"

"I have one set of vaguely worded orders to that effect, yes," George replied. "Those orders are meant to be public knowledge. But I have a second set as well. Very much more explicit And secret. Thus far those orders have been seen only by Governor Henry and the special committee of the Burgesses he appointed. Eventually all the men I recruit will know the contents of the second set of orders. But I think you should know them now, while you've still time to back out."

George started to cut a small chip from the tree to which he'd walked. "You see, I came home specifically to present a plan I've been hatching for months. Governor Henry set up the special committee because he didn't want to make the decision by himself. The plan was approved—enthusiastically by the governor, somewhat less enthusiastically by the committee—just a few days ago. I declined to bring up the subject at the Raleigh—or anywhere in Williamsburg, for that matter. No man who serves with me will hear anything about the scheme unless we're in a place where no Tories could be listening. And every man who *does* hear is pledged to absolute secrecy. Clear?"

Judson nodded.

Below the first mark he'd cut on the tree, and to the left, George cut another. Still further left, he cut one more. He drove the tip of the knife into the highest of the three cuts:

"That's Detroit—the Hair-Buyer's headquarters. From there, trade goods—hatchets, scalp knives, rum—travel south to the two British-controlled posts in the Territory—"

He stabbed the second spot.

"Fort Vincennes on the Wabash River—"

Chunk, the knife bit the third place.

"And further west, on the prairies that form the approaches to the Big River, Fort Kaskaskia. The three sources of British strength in the northwest. The three points from which they intend to *take* the northwest—"

George shoved the knife back in his boot, walked slowly toward the center of the clearing.

"A strategy of cowering inside stockades, awaiting attack, is a strategy of loss, Judson—a strategy of futility. I proposed to Governor Henry that we actively fight for control of the northwest. Destroy British power in the three forts one by one."

"Attack them?" Judson asked.

"Capture them," George corrected.

"Can it be done?"

"That's what I sent two of my best men to find out during the summer."

"Two of your own men went into British towns?"

"It wasn't all that hard. The towns are largely French-populated. The British only control the forts. Linn and

337

Moore pretended to be neutral fur traders. They weren't molested once. But I guarantee you they brought back accurate drawings of the British fortifications at both Kaskaskia and Vincennes—down to the very number of portholes for the swivel cannon. The French don't care for King George's soldiers very much, you see. They remember that the *fleur-de-lis* flew over that part of the country prior to the settlement at the end of the French and Indian War. Consequently, the French at both posts talk freely. They confirmed that war parties being sent into Kentucky are directed from Detroit and equipped from the other two forts. Vincennes and Kaskaskia supply the tomahawks—and the promises of silver for every scalp taken. I plan to put a stop to that. Then, once those stations are secure, I'm going after our friend Governor Hamilton at Detroit. With the three forts fallen, there'll be no further threat of any consequence west of Pittsburgh. And no doubt about who possesses the land, once the inevitable haggling starts."

"You mean haggling during peace negotiations?"

"Exactly. The war will end sometime. So concerning the northwest, the negotiations can have either a conclusion that's favorable to us, or one that isn't. I want to make sure it's the former. You know the saying about possession being nine points of the law. That's why I proposed my plan, and why I fought for it when some members of Henry's committee called it too risky or too expensive. Every man who goes with me must understand my aim, Judson—"

George stared in a hard, challenging way:

"Despite the peculiar technicalities of our situation—for instance, I'm informed King George still hasn't declared war officially—"

"For fear it would mean we're recognized as a country," Judson said.

"Be that as it may, I know who the enemy is, and where. You would be signing on for much more than defensive duty. I mean to march straight to hostile ground, and put it under our new flag."

"So you've answered my question. You believe the forts can be taken."

"I wouldn't have argued with the committee for days, and staked my future on the outcome of the plan, if I thought otherwise. I wanted five hundred men. I got three hundred and fifty. If they're the right kind, I can bring it off."

Judson said, "I'd be proud to be one of them."

"I confess good judgment still leaves some doubt about whether I should take you on—"

"I swear to God I'll obey every order—keep myself straight—"

Because this is the last chance left for me.

George pondered only a moment:

"All right."

Judson let out a yell of pleasure, cut short by George's raised hand:

"If you don't honor that promise, I'll do what I would with any man who fails me. Send him home if it's possible. If it's not, leave him behind."

"Understood."

"Are you sure? I'll abandon the laggards in the middle of enemy country if necessary."

At that moment, Judson was stricken with doubt. *Could* he do it? Did he have the strength and will to endure—to perform as expected?

He knew how his father would answer the question. Angus Fletcher would totally reject the idea that his younger son could overcome his own nature. Even now, the old man's words whispered in his mind, unsettling him—

Devil's blood.

That was a convenient, if vicious, catchphrase for some terrible flaw in his character; but Judson no longer doubted the existence of the flaw itself. It was a foe waiting to destroy him. A foe as dangerous as any of those tribal warriors George described. An inescapable foe; one he must confront and defeat forever.

Was it possible?

He had grave and terrible doubt. But he had no doubt about the finality of the opportunity. That tipped the balance. He committed himself with a fervency that barely suggested a fraction of the fear and hope seething inside.

"Agreed. Every bit of it—agreed."

George Clark smiled then; a cordial smile. But still not the same sort of smile Judson remembered from their boyhood. It was the controlled smile of a military commander who could never again enjoy the same equal relationship with an old friend. And Judson knew full well that the responsibility for fulfilling the bargain was his, not George's. The prospect was both joyful and terrifying.

"Then let's be leaving," George said. "You'd best clean up your affairs at home—"

"I will, immediately."

"When you've done so, meet me back in Williamsburg no later than three weeks from today." Again Judson heard that warning note in his friend's voice. "Three weeks at the outside. If you're not here, I won't wait."

"I'll be here, you can count on it. Will we be heading across the mountains then?"

"In slow stages," George replied as they collected the rifle and gear. "I plan to visit quite a few settlements between here and the forks of the Ohio. Recruit my men as I go, and have them ready to leave Pittsburgh no later than next April or May. The tribes settle in for the winter pretty much the way the armies do, thank God. But we'll still have a fair piece of ground to cover before spring—"

He tapped the rifle. "While you're home, buy one of

these. Oh, and perhaps a good compass. Do some practicing with the rifle."

"George, I'll learn how to knock out a redbird's eye at a hundred yards," Judson promised.

"Two hundred," George said, perfectly serious. "And you'll do better if you imagine it's the eye of a redcoat on the parapet at Vincennes."

But George's severe manner couldn't destroy Judson's feeling that perhaps, at last, he was negotiating a way out of his troubles. He knew one fact for certain. He wouldn't give George cause to regret his trust.

He'd die first.

iv

Judson stayed the night in Williamsburg. But he had no further opportunity to talk with George Clark. His friend returned to Governor Henry's office in the late morning and remained until well after dark. By that time Judson had already fallen into exhausted sleep in his rented room at the Raleigh. Next morning at dawn, he set out for home.

The golden radiance of the October sunrise filled him with a mystical feeling close to that which he'd experienced in June over a year ago, when Richard Henry Lee rose to introduce the resolution for independency. A long-forgotten passage of scripture popped into his head. With it came memories of how he'd learned his Bible—and then, later, consciously put it out of mind.

Verses had stayed stored in his mental baggage against his will. Because of his perpetual fear of displeasing Angus, no doubt. He remembered those dim Sundays of boyhood when he and Donald were dragged to the country church. He remembered how his father always sat perfectly rigid, and cast disapproving looks at Judson's slightest squirm.

But now, he didn't at all object to having a passage

341

of scripture in his thoughts. The story from St. John fitted him in an oblique sort of way—

Lazarus, come forth.

And he that was dead came forth, bound hand and foot with graveclothes—

He couldn't recall the next part exactly. Some line or other about a face covered with a napkin. It had probably once made sense to the Hebrews, but he'd giggled when he first heard it. Earning a sharp thwack on the ear from Angus, right in the pew.

The rest came back easily, making his backbone ripple in an eerie way.

Jesus saith unto them, Loose him, and let him go.

Risen from the dead?

Well, not quite. But stirring. Stirring.

How ironic, Judson thought as he jogged along. A Bible verse he hadn't thought of in years—a verse forced into his head by the discipline of the man who hated and disowned him—brought him cheer and comfort in an unexpected place and time. Even mental pictures of his father's face couldn't dampen his happiness.

As he rode, he savored the sight of grouse in the fields, fleecy clouds in the sky. He hailed a small girl in a cottage yard. Proudly, she held up her calico kitten as he went by. He smiled as if the scruffy little animal was the most elegant of house cats. Perhaps the black tomb of his existence *was* freeing him at last, and he was going forth, alive, onto firm ground—

Not ground free of risk, certainly. George Clark's plan was perilous, and so was the territory involved. On the other hand, one of those Indians George talked about could surely die in exactly the same way as a Philadelphia Tory. The only problem was to deliver the shot straight and true.

He wished that he could tell Peggy McLean where he was going, and with whom. It might make her think a little better of him—if that were possible after the debased, drunken act he'd committed. However, even if Peggy would be willing to speak to him again—which he very much doubted—the idea was academic. According to Donald, Peggy hadn't been at home for the past four weeks.

Donald didn't believe she was visiting her parents. He'd remarked on how curious it was that no one at the McLean place, not even the house blacks, knew where the mistress had gone. If Williams knew, he wasn't saying. Perhaps her absence had something to do with the business affairs of the plantation.

Whatever the explanation, Judson hoped the absence didn't signify more of the same emotional strain that had tormented Peggy after the uprising; a need to flee a place where terrible memories lived—

But then everyone had such memories, didn't they? And, ultimately, the need to flee from them somehow? He did. A combination of luck, friendship and providential timing had at last combined to offer him a way out. Had there not been such a way—

Well, he didn't relish thinking about that alternative.

Actually, he was ambivalent about Peggy. On one hand he hoped he'd never again have to face her. Another part of him still wished she could somehow learn that he had earned George Clark's confidence. She didn't need to know how hesitantly, and with what reservations, George had finally extended that confidence—

Perhaps Donald would tell Peggy about it when she returned. That would be easiest for all concerned.

He turned his attention to less somber subjects. After he'd ridden some five miles more, a remarkable thought crossed his mind, making him smile broadly.

He'd been concentrating on how to approach Donald for a loan to finance a trip to Richmond—and purchase of the very best Kentucky rifle available from the local gunsmiths. Not once had he thought about, or felt a desire for, something to drink.

Still, a rum might refresh him. Perhaps there was an inn—

No. That was done. Let his palms crawl and his tongue taste of ashes and the craving bring all the horrors of hell. It was *done*. He d promised

He knew the name of the worst enemy he faced— *Judson Fletcher*—and he meant to conquer him. By God he did!

As the October day turned radiant, he forced thoughts of drinking from his mind and let his soaring imagination fashion the sleek, deadly silhouette of the rifle he'd carry across the Blue Wall into the west.

v

Ahead, the familiar curve of the road signaled that he had barely a quarter of a mile to ride.

He was grimy, exhausted, butt-sore and hungry after the long trip, but still in an ebullient mood. He looked forward to easing out of the saddle, washing up, enjoying a solid night's rest and a little food from the cabin's meager stores. In the morning he'd begin to implement his plans. Contact Donald about the loan. Perhaps, if all went well, he'd be on the road to Richmond before the week was out.

He inhaled the fragrant, nippy air of the October twilight, a bemused smile on his face He let the horse find its own way to the dooryard—

Where he pulled up short, jolted out of his reverie. A sorry-looking gray nag whose hock joints showed signs of bog spavin was tethered to the dead apple tree.

The gray swung its head, whinnied. Judson's palms prickled. A lantern glowed inside the cabin. He heard a woman's voice—

Lottie.

Damn, this was an unexpected complication A quick alteration of his plans was in order. He'd have to ride downriver a ways, locate an inn where they'd accept his promise of payment until he had an opportunity to speak with Donald—

At the moment, though, his challenge was to avoid any sort of argument with Tom Shaw's widow.

Judson dismounted, caught the sound of footsteps inside the cabin. Lottie's voice had gone silent all at once. The door remained closed.

Why was she back? Had she found business poor in Richmond? Well, he'd commiserate. Even go so far as to ask that she forgive him for his outrageous act of throwing her off her own property, if that would satisfy her. Hell, he'd treat her like a princess if necessary.

The thoughts chased through his mind in the moments he stood beside the horse, patting its lathered neck. He took a deep breath, preparing to walk to the cabin—

The door opened.

"Lottie—" he began, and scowled.

He saw her, right enough. Dirty and disheveled as ever. But she was standing behind someone else. A man.

The man blocked the cabin door, worn boots planted wide apart as if to bar Judson's entrance. The fellow was somewhere in his thirties. Not bad looking, but going paunchy. He wore dirty white breeches, a ruffled shirt, a once elegant fawn waistcoat. He had a puffy, dissolute face that wasn't helped by a three- or four-day growth of beard.

Lottie clutched the man's arm, her face all nasty pleasure as she exclaimed, "Well, look who's back!"

"Evening, Lottie." Judson spoke calmly, determined to avoid an altercation. "I've been in Williamsburg a few days—"

"Then I guess we came home at exactly the right time, didn't we, Mr. Carter?"

Mr. Carter acted slightly tipsy. He gurgled something Judson didn't catch. Lottie went on:

"Mr. Carter an' me, *we're* livin' here now. You better not make any fuss about it."

"Don't intend to, Lottie." He'd guessed the laconic Carter's profession, if that was the proper word. The man continued to regard him with a peculiar stare that might have been animosity, or awe, or some of both. "I'll be leaving Caroline County soon. Just came to collect a few belongings. My other shirt, my—"

Carter interrupted: "Afraid we disposed of those right after we returned." The man affected polite speech, but handled it awkwardly. Judson had seen men of Carter's stamp in Richmond before. Why he and his whore had left there, Judson still couldn't imagine.

"We burned them," Lottie added, still baiting him.

Judson forced a shrug. "In that case I'll ride on."

Yet it required effort for him to check a mounting annoyance. He kept reminding himself that Lottie and her new-found companion weren't worth his trouble. He turned to amble back toward his horse.

"You ain't gettin' away from here that easy, Mr. Fine Judson Fletcher. Not after the way you pushed me off my own land."

"Yes, we've actually been waiting for you," Carter said. Judson didn't like the sound of it. "Lottie thinks you're due a comeuppance."

He tried to keep his smile easy, alert to the undertone of ugliness in the conversation. "I admit I treated you in pretty shabby fashion, Lottie. For that, I tender my apologies. But there's no point in starting an argument now. There's nothing to argue about—the cabin's yours. I'm bound away from this part of the country, so let's just say good evening and—"

"The hell!" Lottie fairly screamed, dashing past her slovenly friend and snatching at the bridle of Judson's horse.

Judson was faster. Bridle in hand, he retreated two steps. The horse nipped at Lottie's hand but missed. She

346

jerked back, glaring.

"I don't blame you for being angry," Judson said. "But believe me, I don't have the slightest desire to cause you further distress—"

"Doesn't make any damn difference what *you* got a desire for, I told you I wouldn't forget what you did."

Suddenly Judson stopped smiling. He had to impress on them that although he wanted no trouble, he wouldn't bear harassment:

"Lottie, keep quiet. I'm going to mount up and leave, and you and your—ah—business associate can put the cabin to any use you see fit."

"I don't care for your tone," Carter said, taking a wobbly step forward "What were you implying when you said business associate?"

God! Trifling with trash like these two tried his patience to the limit. He stood in the left stirrup, hoisted his right leg over and met Carter's stare straight on:

"I didn't see any point in using the word pimp, Mr. Carter."

Carter wilted under Judson's gaze; looked at the ground.

Judson yanked the horse's head toward the road, ignoring Lottie's burst of obscenities. At the sound of scuffling he reined in, swung around in the saddle just as Lottie pushed Carter aside and darted into the cabin. Carter's eyes flicked between Judson and the girl, out of sight in the dim interior. When Carter spoke, it was to her:

"He's agreed to ride on, Lottie. I don't think we need press—"

"Scares you, does he?" Lottie jeered, still unseen. "Well, you can turn yellow, but he's got somethin' coming for the way he treated me—"

Suddenly she was back in the door, again shoving the confused Carter out of the way. And Judson saw just how badly he'd miscalculated the extent of her wrath.

He tried to rear the horse back out of the line of fire. Both of Lottie's hands were clamped on a horse pistol that evidently belonged to Carter, who tried to grab it:

"Listen, we had enough trouble with the Richmond authorities, we don't want to be responsible for murd—"

The hammer fell, the powder ignited, the muzzle bloomed smoke and fire.

Judson ducked, but not quickly enough. The ball slammed his left side, knocked him from the saddle. All he could think of in that chaotic instant was George Clark's warning—

Three weeks at the outside. If you're not here, I won't wait.

He floundered in the dirt, hurting. The ball had hit just under his left armpit. Already he felt warm blood soaking his clothes. Coughing hard, he tried to crawl on hands and knees. Carter's voice had a frightened quality:

"Christ amighty, Lottie, you said he has friends and kinfolk in this county. They won't stand for—"

"Who's going to know who shot him when they find him lying dead by Plum Creek, like we talked about?"

Judson's hands weakened. He could barely support himself. He wanted to curse her. Wanted to curse himself for not getting away sooner. *Christ, it was intolerable, Lottie doing this to him when things had finally changed for the better—!*

In his mind, a vicious voice mocked his despair:

Why blame Lottie? Who caused it if not you?

Coughing harder, he spoke George Clark's first name aloud. He was stupefyingly dizzy. He heard his horse clatter away down the road, spooked by the shot. The dirt of the dooryard rushed up toward his blurring eyes and struck him, bringing the ruinous dark.

CHAPTER VI

The Drillmaster

ANOTHER HORSE lay on the shoulder of the road, the sleet spattering from its still flanks and huge, distended eyeballs. Philip had already counted three others, starved and abandoned along the line of march. He averted his eyes and passed by the dead animal as quickly as his split, rag-wrapped shoes would carry him.

The sleet was starting to turn to rain. Ahead and behind, ghostly double columns of men plodded in the December murk. Royal Rothman, his face half concealed by a strip torn from the bottom of his coat, bumped against Philip to attract his attention.

Philip turned his head. Even that small effort was painful. He walked and breathed in pain. The worst was in his feet.

Sometimes they felt totally numb. Then, abruptly, sensation would return. Dozens of tiny knives seemed to be slicing his flesh. A while ago, he'd glanced down and seen blood staining the rags on his left foot.

Philip hunched his shoulders against the sleet, tried to catch Royal's words, had trouble because the chandler's clerk had almost lost his voice.

"They lied to us," Royal said. "They damn well lied."

Too weak and weary to argue, Philip answered, "It's possible. They said thirteen miles. Thirteen miles from Whitemarsh to the campsite."

"Thirteen hundred, more like," Breen said just behind them. "Fuckin' liars. Fuckin' incompetents, every one."

"I can't keep walking," Royal croaked.

"Here, put your arm around my neck," Philip said. "Lean on me a while."

A little extra weight made no difference. He had long passed beyond the point of caring about anything except taking the next agonizing step; then the next; and the next. Royal Rothman's body slumping against his was just one more minor hardship among all the rest: no food; no water; no decent clothing; no conviction that anyone really knew where they were supposed to be going—

The world consisted of this long, seemingly endless road where the edges of the mud ruts had frozen sharp as axe-blades, and were only now beginning to soften a little. But the frozen ruts had already done adequate damage during the week's march. Men sprawled at the roadside in the gray of the winter morning, their feet bleeding so badly they couldn't go on.

It did seem impossible that it could only be thirteen miles from their last permanent camp at Whitemarsh to the new one, somewhere on the bank of the Schuylkill River about twenty miles west and slightly north of Philadelphia. There, presumably, they would winter. Rest. Draw rations.

But a *week* to reach the place? God, that was incomprehensible—!

Or was it? Everything seemed incomprehensible of late.

In October, at Germantown, the army had come close to revenging the humiliation of the Brandywine. General Washington had implemented an attack plan against Howe's troops. But confusion about battle orders—and a sudden heavy fog descending—turned the near-victory into another rout. Philip had even heard that American units lost in the fog had fired on one another.

For an hour at Germantown, the possibility of success had been within their grasp. Officers said the troops had fought well. Then came the fog—and disaster. Seven hundred lost, they said, More than four hundred captured—

Supporting Royal, Philip staggered on between skeletal trees rising in the mist. They passed more men who had simply stopped; given up. Then an overturned baggage wagon with two of its wheels still revolving slowly. Someone had tried to move the wagon with only one horse. The spent beast lay thrashing and whinnying in the traces. Philip saw the spectral figure of an officer approach, lift a pistol to the animal's head. The shot boomed through the rain. Royal Rothman started to cry.

Up ahead, the ground appeared to rise. Philip picked up the sound of men splashing through water, then a few weak cheers. Word came back along the line from soldier to filthy soldier:

"It's Valley Creek."

"We've reached it."

"We'll be camping tonight—pass it to the rear—"

Wearily, Philip tried. While he was shouting at Breen, Royal slipped and sprawled face down in the mud. Philip motioned Breen forward. Together the two lifted the younger soldier and carried him through the icy water of Valley Creek.

The rags on Philip's feet fell away, drifted off in the current. He refused to stop. All he wanted was the haven of the campsite that apparently waited at the top of the rise where thick tree trunks clustered in the murk.

A plateau, then. They were climbing to a plateau where there was wood for fires. There should be food, too. The prospect helped him drive his tired, hurting body the last few hundred yards. Perhaps their agony was coming to an end—

By nightfall, Philip knew the hope had been cruelly false.

A savage December wind swept across the rolling,

351

two-mile plateau in the angle between the Schuylkill River flowing from west to east and the creek that came up from the south to join it. There were pines and oaks in plenty. But they offered scant protection from the wind.

And there were no supply wagons waiting.

When Philip, Breen and Royal tried to hammer pegs for their tent into the half-frozen ground, the pegs kept popping out. Exhausted, the three finally gave up, spread the rain-sodden canvas on the ground and crawled under it.

Philip listened to the pines moaning in the darkness. He had a dizzying vision of Anne and little Abraham sitting by a cheery fire in Cambridge. At least they were safe and warm. At least they would survive—

Even that assumption, though, was not without a certain hollow ring. Philip had received no further letters from his wife since the last one in the summertime.

Thinking about that for very long was too much on top of everything else: the army's failure; his bleeding foot; his ferocious, unremitting hunger—

Dinner for the night had consisted of the one, green-tinged chunk of bread remaining in his haversack.

He shifted position under the soaked canvas, trying to get comfortable. The wind roared across the plateau, carrying the sound of officers shouting orders, horses and wagons crisscrossing the high ground. Units of the Continental army were still arriving.

Next to Philip, Royal began to cry again. Without even thinking about it, Philip reached over with one stiffened hand and patted the younger man's shoulder, trying to comfort him.

On Philip's left, Breen suddenly let out an assortment of curses. Then:

"Cap'n Webb said the general picked this place 'cause we could escape easy if we got attacked. Shit, you think

Billy Howe's gonna come out in this weather to bother with us? He's gonna let us die in the goddamned place."

"Shut up, Breen," Philip said. "Try to sleep."

"And wake up froze to death? Not me!"

Breen hauled himself out from beneath the canvas, tramped away:

"I'm gonna squat under one of them pines."

Philip might have done the same, but Royal Rothman seemed to be suffering an attack of the chills. His body convulsed for perhaps ten minutes. Philip held him with both arms, trying to transfer what warmth he could from his own body.

Finally the convulsions stopped. Royal drifted to sleep. Philip dozed a little himself. All at once, Royal started up:

"Where are we? I dreamed it was Boston—"

"Lie down," Philip said. "I wish it was Boston too."

Awake and miserable, Royal asked, "Does this place have any name at all?"

"Captain Webb said it's called Valley Forge."

Royal collapsed against him like a child, burrowing against Philip's filthy coat and starting to sob again:

"I'm sorry, I—I shouldn't cry, it's—not manly, but —I can't help it—"

"Go ahead, Royal. There's nothing to be ashamed of. Christ, I'd cry too if I had any strength left."

Philip pulled the soaked tent canvas up over his head as the rain started falling again.

ii

By January, axemen felled enough timber for construction to start on a hut city on the plateau that took its name from a Quaker-owned iron works beside Valley Creek. The works had formerly supplied Washington's army; the British had stopped in September to burn it out.

The commanding general, who had finally moved into a fieldstone house near the junction of the creek and the river, ordered regulation army huts built by each unit. Philip and the men of his company spent their days laboriously putting up theirs according to the approved design: fourteen by sixteen feet, with a rise of six and a half feet to the steep timbered roof. They had a chimney chinked with cat and clay, but no windows.

And no meat, other than an infrequent issue of salt pork.

And no yellow soap to bathe their filthy, infected, foul-smelling feet.

And no drinking water save what they could carry from the partially frozen creek.

And no hope. Worst of all, no hope.

iii

A knock at the hut door brought Breen's head up where he lay dozing. Just as quickly, he lay down again and snored. Breen had spent three pence for a gill of peach brandy at the sutler's. Philip had purchased a quart of vinegar instead.

One of the camp physicians had told him vinegar would keep his gums from bleeding; prevent his skin from bursting open with countless sores. Philip hated drinking the vile stuff. But the doctor had apparently been right. Breen wouldn't waste his money on vinegar, and his already malodorous person had fallen prey to the scurvy. So had a good percentage of the eleven thousand men settled in for the winter in the hut city.

The knock came again, more insistently. With a disgusted sigh, Philip turned over the last of three fire-cakes heating on the stones next to the fireplace logs. That was their evening meal: peach brandy—or vinegar in Philip's case—and flour mixed with water, then cooked till it hardened. Wind whined in the chimney, blowing smoke back in Philip's face as he said:

"Will you see who's there, Royal?"

The younger man nodded apathetically, shuffled to the door on rag-covered feet. He opened the door to admit a gust of snow—and Captain Webb, who hardly resembled an officer any longer.

Webb was hatless, white crystals powdering his hair. He wore an old padded blue dressing gown he'd adopted for warmth on night duty. In the distance, above the wind's wail, Philip heard men bawling a contemptuous song around some campfire, to the tune of the marching air *Yankee Doodle:*

> *"First we'll take a pinch of snuff,*
> *"And then a drink of water—"*

Raising his head again, Breen focused his eyes until he identified their visitor. Then he passed wind, loudly.

Webb said, "I appreciate your gesture of respect."

"Think nothin' of it. You finally bringin' us some replacements? Food would be too much to ask—"

"I'm hunting for cards and dice," Webb snapped. "The general's making an inspection tour this evening."

"Likes to keep track of our luxurious livin' conditions, does he?"

"For God's sake, Breen, that doesn't help anything."

"Captain Webb's right," Philip put in. Breen shrugged, uncaring.

"You know how set against gaming the general is," Webb said, too tired—as they all were—to worry about breaches of discipline and courtesy. "Some bunch of nabobs called a Committee of Conference rolled in from York this afternoon."

"The Congress is sitting at York now, isn't it?" Royal asked.

"Correct. The committee's purpose is to inspect and improve on conditions here, if possible."

355

Another oath from Breen indicated what he thought of the whole idea. The singers in the distance were repeating their chorus with an even nastier intonation to the final lines:

> *"And then we'll say, How do you do?*
> *"And that's a Yankee supper!"*

"That won't be hard," Philip said. "I swear to God, Captain, if we don't get some decent food, there'll be a riot like nobody's ever seen before."

"And clothing," Royal added, pointing at his bandaged feet. The brown of dried blood shaded into the green of pus.

Philip hadn't spoken idly. For days now, as the bitter January sleet and snow continued without letup, certain sections of the hut city had taken to chanting *"No meat! No meat!"* for half an hour every evening. The poison of incipient rebellion was spreading through the entire encampment.

"There's nothing I can do about that tonight," Webb told them. "I just want you to look reasonably sharp if the dignitaries come this way."

"You know where you can put them dignitaries," Breen said, farting again. "Will you shut the fuckin' door before we freeze to death?"

Looking defeated, Captain Webb withdrew into the snowy darkness. Philip closed the door.

He almost said something to Breen about his discourtesy to the officer. But such talk wasn't uncommon, and was seldom punished. Besides, Philip identified it for what it was: not a disease, but the symptom of a disease. The problem Henry Knox had predicted still plagued them. They were amateurs at war, and except for a few isolated victories now forgotten, they had performed badly. Untrained as soldiers, they could hardly be expected to behave like soldiers.

Philip had no answer for the problem. But he knew it

could only grow worse unless something drastic happened.

Saying little to each other, Breen, Royal and Philip ate their hard, blackened fire-cakes. Moments later, Philip experienced one of his frequent attacks of nausea because of the hut's almost insufferable stench. Their unwashed bodies, Royal's diseased feet —and Breen's stubborn refusal to expose himself to the winter air to urinate—created a stew of smells Philip could bear only so long. He drank another half cup of vinegar, put on his tattered coat and hurried out to the company street.

Head down, eyes slitted against the wind-whipped snow that had come at nightfall, he trudged aimlessly between the uniformly built log huts facing one another on both sides of the dirt avenue. The rows of huts were perhaps the only detail in all of Valley Forge that gave the encampment a semblance of order.

In the distance he saw an immense bonfire blazing near the artillery park where Henry Knox kept his cannon. He thought briefly of going to see his friend. But just as he did, he heard strident voices off to his left.

He peered between two huts, glimpsed lanterns a-bob in the next street. He thought he recognized the tall, angular figure of Washington, cloak flapping like wings at his shoulders. A party of officers and civilians had halted around the general. An argument was in progress.

Philip dodged between the huts, huddled against the logs, numb hands in his bottomless pockets. He heard one of the civilians say:

"—distressing and unbelievable filth, General. Corrective measures must be taken, and swiftly."

Suddenly Washington snatched off his tricorn and slammed it against his right leg:

"Corrective measures, sir? Why don't you gentlemen in Congress take corrective measures? Hire honest teamsters, instead of cheats who drain the brine from

357

the salt pork barrels to lighten the load, then deliver us spoiled meat? Why don't you hire men who can draw accurate maps? Half the supplies we're sent never arrive because the drivers get lost for want of proper directions, and finally dump their grain sacks in empty fields to rot!"

Another member of the committee spoke up:

"Yes, those criticisms are fully merited. The Congress is aware—"

"I don't give a damn whether they're *aware*, I want to know what's being done to change things!"

"We intend to return with a full report."

"On the miserable state of affairs you've discovered?"

"Certainly we shall have to detail that, but—"

Another disgusted oath from Washington. "So instead of help for these brave men, I'll receive remonstrances and more remonstrances. Well, let me assure you and all the gentlemen of the Congress—" Even above the singsong of the wind, his furious voice could be heard a good distance. "—it's a much easier and less distressing thing to draw remonstrances in a comfortable room by a good fire than to occupy a cold, bleak hill and sleep under frost and snow. Some of my troops are not yet hutted—you tell *them* that the immediate result of your visit will be a report instead of food and blankets!"

Yanking his cloak across his chest to protect his blue and buff coat from the pelt of the snow, Washington glared at his critics:

"And where is that German officer you promised for my staff?"

Another of the Congressmen said, "Baron von Steuben is having his credentials examined by one of our committees."

"To perdition with your committees! I've heard his credentials and they're more than satisfactory. Get him into this camp with a suitable rank and ready to assist

358

me. I need someone who can teach these men proper military drill! At least they can learn something while they're starving to death!"

"We shall do everything possible to expedite—"

The rest was blurred as the big general stamped past the front of the hut and out of sight, followed by the Congressmen and his officers with the lanterns.

Shivering by the hut wall, Philip thought about the reference to a German. Another of those volunteers?

Some, like Gil, had proved themselves brave and able; effective additions to the army. Others were held in contempt. But it was interesting to hear Washington tell a Congressional committee that he and his own staff lacked the ability to shape the Continental and militia units into a cohesive, well-trained force capable of fighting in the best European style.

Many at Valley Forge still called Washington a poor leader in combat. Yet Philip had heard few openly declare that they would refuse to continue to serve under him. Specific complaints were always directed at Washington's senior officers, or the Congress. The general himself somehow escaped most of the direct criticism.

But Philip could understand that. The man was an aristocrat; yet he cared about the welfare of the ordinary soldier. He had a rare forthrightness when it came to admitting and correcting his own mistakes, and the lowest private was aware of it. Perhaps that was why Washington was admired even when his battlefield ability was questioned. Perhaps that was why, despite almost intolerable conditions, Valley Forge hadn't yet succumbed to insurrection and mass desertion—

Returning to the hut, Philip settled down to sleep. As he was drifting off, he speculated about the German officer. A baron, they'd said. The Germans were generally considered excellent in the field. The hired Hessians were respected, even if they were openly cursed and

359

universally hated. Now Washington was getting his own German. It remained to be seen whether the man could accomplish anything.

The last flames flickered out on the hearth. Philip listened to Breen's snores and Royal's wheezy breathing. The wind had picked up. It howled around the chimney and blew fireplace ash back into the cramped, fetid room. Thoughts about the German were replaced by thoughts of Anne—and the familiar worry:

Why hadn't she written? Was she safe in Cambridge? Did the silence spell illness? Or something worse—?

Under a violent gusting of the wind, the hut door flew open. Shivering, Philip leaped up to close it. He stared a moment into the snowy dark.

Annie, for God's sake write me. Else I can't go on here. I just can't go on.

iv

Baron Friedrich Wilhelm Ludolf Gerhard Augustin von Steuben set the Valley Forge camp to buzzing when he arrived in February. He was accompanied by a trio of aides and a lean Italian greyhound called Azor. The dog trotted after the new inspector-general of the army wherever he went.

Philip first saw von Steuben two days after he reached the plateau. He didn't quite know what to make of the officer.

The man rode well, looking huge and formidable in the saddle despite his middle age and a bandy-legged body. Some who had seen von Steuben hurrying through the camp on foot guffawed and said he waddled. They also said he could speak no English except the word "goddamn," which he apparently used quite often. He and his suite had reached the New Hampshire coast the preceding December, presenting themselves to the Congress as available for service to General Washington.

Encountering Gil one February twilight near the

sutler's. Philip discovered that the Marquis de Lafayette was not impressed:

"That red uniform with the blue facings he sports? I have it on excellent authority that he designed it himself. And that medal—faugh!"

Gil's mouth pursed to emphasize his contempt. Studying his friend, Philip thought he detected more than a trace of jealousy.

"Have you seen it?" Gil asked.

"Yes. It is fairly large—"

"*Large?* It's gigantic! A sunburst big as a soup dish—disgraceful ostentation, disgraceful! The Star of the Order of Fidelity of Baden-Durlach, he calls it. Well, my good friend, I am not certain he ever fought for Baden-Durlach—let alone under Frederick the Great whom he's claiming as his 'close associate.' I am convinced his estate in Swabia is a fiction, just like the 'von' in his name—he probably added that himself, to enhance his credentials. He keeps prattling in that wretched French of his about having surrendered various 'places and posts of honor in Germany' in order to come here. But one can't pin him down as to precisely what places or posts! If he was ever more than a subaltern, I am King Louis! And yesterday—*yesterday* he had the effrontery to tell *mon ami* General Washington that the officers in camp have too many servants! That the soldiers must not be kept so busy shining boots and laying fires in our huts, but must learn soldiering instead! Can you conceive of such advice coming from him? A rascal, a pretender, a windbag equally as mercenary as Howe's Hessians? I understand his salary is incredible—*another* swindle of the Congress! Learn soldiering from a man like that? The very idea is an insult to the rest of us who have volunteered!"

"Well," Philip said when the tirade sputtered to its end, "I heard one of his suggestions, and it seemed to make sense."

361

"Pooh, that clock business?"

"Yes. I wonder why it never occurred to anyone else?"

Gil waved. "Because it's unimportant."

Von Steuben had reportedly made a scene when he discovered that not a single timepiece in all of Valley Forge was coordinated with any other. He had insisted that all clocks be synchronized with the one at Washington's headquarters. In Philip's view, Gil's too-curt dismissal of the idea was evidence that he wished he'd thought of it.

"I repeat—you'll learn nothing from a man who is patently an adventurer and a fraud," was Gil's final opinion before he and his friend parted. Philip hid his amusement at Gil's professional hostility, deciding he'd wait and see.

The wait wasn't long:

"Rothman, Kent, Breen," Captain Webb said when he showed up at the hut a few evenings later. "Turn out on the parade field tomorrow at six. With muskets."

Breen scratched his genitals. "Six in the evening?"

"Six in the morning."

"Jesus Christ, what for?"

"The baron is organizing a special company. One hundred men from all units, to whom he's going to teach musket drill and marching. The men will then teach other groups of a hundred. That damn Dutchman is trying to turn this army inside out! He rises at three in the morning to write a drill text—and I understand he's also developing a manual of procedures for officers." Webb clearly didn't care for that.

"Well, I sure ain't wakin' up at six—" Breen began.

"You'll wake up at five thirty," Webb cut in.

"—to take lessons from some fat-ass German," Breen finished, emphatically.

"Like it or not, I'm afraid you will. The order to form the company of a hundred is direct from the commander-in-chief. So you'll be there or you'll be flogged."

"Son of a bitch." Breen shook his head. "I guess I'll be there."

Royal Rothman actually looked pleased at the news. He reached up to the small black cap pinned to his hair, plucked out something, crushed it between his fingers, threw it away, then said:

"It might actually be worthwhile, don't you think, Philip?"

"It's bound to be more diverting than hunting lice or watching your feet bleed."

"Jesus Christ and the Holy Sepulchre," Breen grumbled as Webb bent to go out into the bitter February wind. "Six o'clock in the fucking morning."

V

Philip shivered in the dawn wind, gritty-eyed and yawning. The Baron von Steuben, his dinner-plate medal bouncing against his red-uniformed stomach, struggled to control his prancing horse. The greyhound Azor nipped at the horse's legs, causing the brown-haired, round-faced inspector-general to lash downward with his crop:

"Azor, goddamn—*nein!*"

The dog temporarily at bay, von Steuben pointed his crop at the blushing captain from New York, Benjamin Walker, who was serving as his interpreter. The baron blistered a stream of French orders at Walker. The captain nodded feverishly every second or so until the harangue concluded. The French was mingled with German phrases, and Philip could follow it only with great difficulty.

Next to Philip, Breen used a few highly obscene words to characterize the peculiar man on horseback. Walker overheard but chose to overlook it. Von Steuben didn't. If he failed to comprehend the specific words, he caught their general meaning. He fixed Breen with a glare that started the latter blinking rapidly.

Walker cleared his throat.

"Men, the general has instructed me to say that he is personally going to undertake your training. That he, ah—"

Walker licked his lips, hesitated, almost winced as von Steuben stared him down.

"He, ah, finds conditions in this camp—ah—appalling. He is equally shocked to discover there is, ah, no standardized set of procedures for marching and handling weapons."

Walker glanced at the general for further instruction. Von Steuben let fly with more French.

"He says he has noticed a difference between American troops and those of Europe, in that European soldiers will follow orders without question but —ah—Americans seem to want to know *why* first. So he will try to explain the reason for each maneuver as we go along."

Several surprised exclamations and even some applause greeted the announcement. Whatever his pretensions, Philip thought, the German had assessed the temperament of the soldiers correctly. Some of Philip's reservations began to fade. He rather liked the hard, capable look of the middle-aged officer—ostentatious Order of Fidelity and all.

"Now the first thing the general wants to see you do is the drill for loading and firing your muskets. On the count of one—"

In haphazard fashion, Philip and the others went through the drill's twenty steps, Captain Walker counting each one. By the time the young New Yorker had called *"Fifteen!"* von Steuben was scarlet. The conclusion of the drill, muskets at the shoulder in position to shoot, produced another torrent of French.

"The general wishes me to inform you that in his opinion, that is—ah—the most slovenly and time-consuming drill he has ever seen——"

Still more French.

"——in any part of the globe——"

And more.

"——in his entire life."

Von Steuben uttered a few guttural barks just to make sure the point got across.

"The general is going to introduce you to a new drill for the same procedure. A drill which will shortly be available in written form for you to study. The general's drill requires only ten counts——"

Suddenly there wasn't a whisper in the ranks. Walker had caught their full attention at last.

"——the idea being to save time so more shots may be discharged at the enemy in the same interval."

Walker bent down to pick up the musket lying at his feet.

"I will now demonstrate the drill, following the general's instructions."

Walker's face showed that he disliked the assignment intensely. Actually handling weapons during training was considered beneath the dignity of any officer.

Von Steuben noticed Walker's expression. He swore, cropped his horse to a standstill, leaped to the ground and waddled to his translator. He snatched the musket from the astonished captain's hands.

Then von Steuben jerked at the strap of the cartridge box Walker had picked up, slung the strap over his own shoulder, settled the box on his hip and stalked out in front of the hundred men.

He presented the musket for viewing by the soldiers, shouted, *"Ein!"* and immediately brought the firelock to half cock.

Philip saw jaws drop and eyes go wide. The demonstration was absolutely unbelievable. A high-ranking officer *off* his horse? Handling a musket *personally*——?

"Zwei!"

With thick but somehow swift fingers, von Steuben took out a cartridge, bit off the end of the paper and covered the opening with his thumb.

"Drei!"

He primed the pan.

When the entire ten counts were finished, von Steuben had armed the musket and brought it to his shoulder in half the time the normal drill required.

The stocky man stumped forward, eyes darting in search of a pupil. Bad luck brought Breen to his attention. Von Steuben literally jerked Breen out in front of the others, slammed the musket into his hands, flung the cartridge box strap over the confused victim's head and bawled:

"Ein!"

Breen managed to remember the first step—half-cocking the piece—but when von Steuben shouted the count of two, he grew fuddled. Turning red again, the German thrust his face up near Breen's and screamed, *"Zwei,* goddamn, *zwei!"*

Breen lost his grip on the musket. It fell to the ground. Apoplectic, von Steuben shoved Breen back into line and pulled out another man, a Marylander. He managed to get to five before von Steuben dismissed him with an even more torrential outpouring of French and German profanities. Some of the former —anatomically colorful—Philip could translate, with considerable amusement.

The baron proceeded to go through the entire drill three more times before dragging another man forward. Fortunately, the Virginian completed the count with a minimum of error. The German beamed—and so did most of his trainees, letting the smiles drain away the built-up tension.

While the February wind grew stronger, bringing a few snowflakes down, the hundred soldiers repeated the drill together ten times. Then ten more. And ten more after that. Von Steuben waddled briskly up and down the ranks, correcting the slant of a muzzle here, the grip of a ramrod there, occasionally slapping a student on the back but more often cursing.

Finally, around ten o'clock, the baron remounted his horse. Walker ordered the hundred to prepare to repeat the drill one last time, while von Steuben called the count.

By then Philip had fairly well gotten the hang of it. He was amazed at how the drill did pare the time required for the vital operation. But the unison drill was still uncoordinated. By the time Walker had reached six, von Steuben was screaming and pointing at poor performers:

"Nein, nein!" Another storm of profanity, concluding with a thunderous, *"Viens, Valkair, mon ami! Sacre!* Goddamn *die gaucheries* of dese *imbeciles! Je ne puis plus!"* Growing almost incoherent, he shrieked, "You curse dem, Valkair—*you!"*

He wheeled his horse and went pounding away across the parade field, Azor streaking behind him through the slanting snow. Captain Walker once more cleared his throat.

"Ah—you men realize—I have orders—"

"Ah, go ahead and get it over with!" someone yelled. There was laughter at the captain's expense.

Flushing, Walker cursed and condemned the soldiers in a monotonous voice for the better part of two minutes.

Relieved when it was over, he said, "All right, let's resume the drill. *One—!"*

Philip observed von Steuben resting his horse at the far edge of the field. Before long the baron was lured back by his own interest in the proceedings. By noon, alternately swearing and complimenting in his strange pidgin mixture of French. German and very occasional English, he had the entire hundred going through the drill with reasonable precision.

Philip noticed something else as they ran through the final counts—*shoulder firelock; poise and cock firelock; take aim and fire*. The weariness and despair on the faces in the snow-covered ranks seemed to have been replaced by something else. Something he too was experiencing. It gave him the first glimmer of hope for this conglomeration of unruly men nominally called an army.

He saw shoulders a little straighter. Fatigued, reddened eyes a little more alert. Hands blue-tinged with cold moving with a little more speed and deftness—

There in the February snow he saw—and felt—the stirring of pride.

vi

On their way back to their hut after the remarkable morning, the trio of Massachusetts men discussed the bizarre drillmaster.

"I think maybe the man has a touch of genius," Philip said.

"Fucking maniac," was Breen's contribution.

Royal Rothman said, "I think he's both. I like him."

vii

So did the rank and file of the army, as it turned out. Except with those officers such as Gil, who considered the baron's methods both unorthodox and degrading, von Steuben was soon the most popular commander in the camp after Washington.

The German ignored the jealous jibes and rumors circulated about him, and kept working. As the winter wore on, leavened at last by a growing trickle of supply wagons that brought in foodstuffs and clothing, the baron's original hundred taught new contingents of a hundred. Those hundreds taught hundreds more. By early March, Philip and even Breen had become busy and proficient instructors of all of von Steuben's lessons:

The new musket drill.

The new cadences that smoothed the execution of flanking and counter-marching by masses of troops on the move.

The new marching formation—four abreast, instead of the traditional single or double file. This, the baron had explained, would allow the regiments to enter or retreat from a battle zone in an orderly way, as well as faster. Another obvious innovation, yet quite astonishing when it was suddenly introduced into an army that had never thought of it before.

The German also insisted that bayonet drill be taught —and demanded every soldier have one. Philip could imagine how that order alone increased business at George Lumden's forge back in Connecticut.

Uniforms began to look a little sharper. Although few had been completely replaced, the men took to maintaining them more carefully, sewing and patching them instead of letting them simply fall to pieces. When wagonloads of soap became available, the men washed their clothes as well as themselves. It struck Philip that had von Steuben not arrived when he did, the next engagement of the army might have brought total anarchy—wholesale refusal to fight. Now there was actually talk of wanting to face Howe's soldiers; of wanting to discover how well the new techniques worked in battle.

Henry Knox expressed it when Philip encountered him one day in March:

"I thought no one could create a military force out of this rabble. But I do believe that strutting, egotistical German's done it."

The long, dark night of the winter seemed to be ending. The calendar ran on toward spring. Only one grave concern still infected Philip's waking thoughts and haunted his sleep.

He still hadn't received a single reply to his letters to Anne.

At a special evening muster in the company street, Captain Webb read the message sent to all the troops from the gray fieldstone house near the Schuylkill:

"Headquarters, Valley Forge. The commander-in-chief takes this occasion to return his warmest thanks to the virtuous officers and soldiers of this army for that persevering fidelity and zeal which they have uniformly manifested in all their conduct. Their fortitude not only under their common hardships incident to a military life, but also under the additional sufferings to which the peculiar situation of these states has exposed them, clearly proves them men worthy of the enviable privilege of contending for the rights of human nature and the freedom and independence of their country—"

Philip noticed Breen wearing a smug smile. And the older man joined with all the others in a round of cheers when Webb concluded.

Tramping along to the sutler's after the formation broke up, Philip said to his messmates:

"I don't think it makes a damn bit of difference what they say about his losses in the field. If we win the war and the general had ambition to be king of this country, he could ask and it would be done."

No one disagreed.

ix

Attendance at divine worship every Sunday was, supposedly, mandatory. But skimpy crowds in the log chapel usually testified to the lax enforcement of the commanding general's order. The last Sunday in March was an exception. The eleven o'clock service was to be held on the parade field because a bigger than usual crowd was expected—without duress.

The predictions proved correct, solely because of the

identity of the preacher. Even Breen went along to listen.

The morning, although gray, wasn't excessively chilly. Philip and Breen found places in the huge crowd of seated men—two or three thousand at least, Philip guessed. In front of the gathering, regimental drummers had stacked their drums into a three-tier platform, on top of which boards had been laid.

The regular chaplains presided over the hymns and prayers. But the men were clearly waiting for the sermon, to be presented by one of Washington's most loyal and hard-driving officers, General Peter Muhlenberg, the Pennsylvania-born commander of the Virginia line.

When Muhlenberg mounted the drum platform with a Bible in one hand, a wave of surprised comment raced through the crowd. The general wasn't wearing his uniform today. Instead, he wore the somber black robes of his former calling.

There was hardly a man at Valley Forge who didn't know a bit of Muhlenberg's story: his training at a theological school in Europe—which he found too dull; his military service with the dragoons in one of the German provinces; and—this part was told most often—the Sunday morning in January of '76.

Ordained at last and tending to a small parish flock in the Blue Ridge, Muhlenberg had mounted his pulpit while his congregation thundered *Ein Feste Burg*. As the hymn faded away, he flung off his black robes to reveal a colonel's uniform. Then he launched into a blistering sermon directed principally at one sinner—King George III. That was his last official message to his congregation before leading the Eighth Virginia off to war.

A powerful, commanding figure against the gray sky, General Muhlenberg leafed through the front of his Bible. The tactic had its effect; the last talk quieted—though Breen still whispered questions:

"What kind o' preacher did you say he is, Philip?"

371

"Lutheran. It's a German denomination, mostly."

"Well, I hope he's good, 'cause I don't usually hang around this sort o' function—why, look yonder! What's he doin' here? His church don't meet on Sunday."

Philip peered past the men seated nearby, saw Royal Rothman lingering at the very back of the crowd, darting glances every which way, as though anticipating some kind of trouble. Philip smiled, shrugged:

"I suppose he wants to hear the general as much as we do. No law says he can't."

The sermon of the preacher-turned-soldier was very much worth hearing. Philip soon realized Muhlenberg had chosen his text with care. It came from the twenty-third chapter of Exodus, and was perfectly fitted to the mood of the troops—especially their growing sense of becoming an army worthy of the name.

Muhlenberg first read his text:

"Behold, I send an angel before thee, to keep thee in the way, and to bring thee into the place which I have prepared. Beware of him, and obey his voice, provoke him not. For he will not pardon your transgressions, for my name is in him—"

Then, skillfully, Muhlenberg began to weave military propaganda into his theology. He likened the Lord's angel to an army commander whose every order must be executed without question. Discipline and obedience—whether he who followed was a lowly private or one of the Children of Israel—would surely bring the desired rewards. Muhlenberg saved the biblical version of those rewards for the end, rolling them out from the drum pulpit to his rapt, wide-eyed audience:

"But if thou shalt indeed obey his voice, and do all that I speak, then I will be an enemy unto thine enemies, and an adversary unto thine adversaries. For mine angel shall go before thee, and bring thee in unto the Amorites, and the Hittites, and the Perizzites, and the Canaanites, the Hivites, and the Jebusites—

"And I will cut them off!"

It required only a moment's mental translation for the men to understand the real names of the enemy: the light infantry; the grenadiers; the Hessians. The sermon's conclusion brought the soldiers jumping to their feet to applaud, embarrassing Muhlenberg and provoking the other chaplains to what amounted to glares of envy. No one ever applauded *their* sermons.

Breen admitted to being "a mite excited" by the message, and confessed he'd never quite considered obeying a superior to be as vital as Muhlenberg claimed.

But the sermon had still left him thirsty. Even though it was Sunday, he annouced with a wink, there were ways—

Losing track of the older man in the crowd, Philip made a point to catch up with Royal Rothman:

"Didn't expect to see you, Royal. How did you like the general?"

"He's every bit as fine a preacher as I've heard. Though I must say, Philip, I was startled by the concept that General Washington—or Captain Webb—could be considered as important in the scheme of things as an angel."

"Still, it was pretty stirring stuff."

Royal nodded with a shy smile. "By the way—I've been meaning to say something to you. About an idea I've had for several weeks now. This printing house we've talked about—where you're going to publish a deluxe edition of Mr. Paine's *Crisis* papers—" He hesitated. "You haven't forgotten—?"

"No, Royal. Seeing my family again is the first thing I want when this war's over. My own business is the second."

"Good! Where do you plan to set it up?"

"In Boston."

"I mean where in Boston?"

The extremely serious tone of the question checked

Philip's impulse to chuckle. "Why, I don't know, Royal. I hadn't thought that far. At the start, I'll have to rent space—"

"That's my idea. Rothman's is the second largest chandler's in the whole town. My father always has extra loft room. I'm sure you could strike a good bargain for renting some of it. My father's conscious of the value of a penny, but he's fair, and—" Royal almost blushed. "—I've even taken the liberty of writing him about you and your plans. I think he'd do anything for you, after—"

"After what?"

"I must confess I described how you and Lucas helped out when Adams was baiting me."

A vivid memory of Mayo Adams dying in the ditch after Brandywine stained Philip's thoughts a moment, destroying the high excitement and good feeling the sermon had produced. He forced the ugly recollections away, said:

"Royal, it wasn't necessary to say anything to your father. Or to extend special thanks of any kind."

The young man's brown eyes were round and intense. "I felt it was."

"Well, then, I think your idea's a capital one."

"Do you? Honestly?"

"I do. I'll need a good place to operate my press—but I won't be able to pay much. Loft space sounds first rate. I'll tuck the thought away and take it out again at the right time—"

The recurrent streak of pessimism that plagued him produced a final thought:

"—if we all survive this business."

"We will," Royal Rothman declared as they reached the edge of the parade field.

"If we follow that angel, eh?"

Royal appeared embarrassed. "My father is a very religious man, Philip. He'd scold me ferociously for saying this. But if it's a choice between trusting an angel or General Washington, I'll favor the latter."

Philip laughed. "You don't have to make the choice. I'd say at the present time they're one and the same person."

X

"The shad are out! The shad are running upriver!"

The cry in the company street one April morning brought Philip and his messmates tumbling outside. Excited soldiers were racing through the camp with the news:

"Thousands of shad—"

"Running right now!"

Under a chilly sky of pale blue, Philip, Breen and Royal located whatever implements they could—a pitchfork, a shovel, a broken tree branch—and joined the hundreds of men streaming toward the Schuylkill River. Some carried barrels, baskets or the all-important salt. The human tide poured down to the Schuylkill's banks, where an incredible sight stunned Philip:

The river was dark, almost black with the bodies of thousands of fish swimming toward its headwaters like a second, living surface underneath the first. The whole river seemed to churn. The passage of the immense schools filled the air with a strange, whispery hum.

All along the bank, men rushed into the shallows, clubbing and stabbing and grabbing with their bare hands while they yelped and swore like profane children. Fresh fish to be cooked or salted away was a miracle whose importance was almost beyond reckoning.

Philip peeled off the new shoes supplied him only a week earlier, darted into the water, felt the eerie movement of the shad around his ankles. He slashed downward with the pitchfork, brought up two fish on the tines. He raised the fork to show Royal, but the young man was flailing at the water with his tree branch, oblivious to anyone's delight but his own.

A major of dragoons galloped by on the bank, headed upstream to plant his horsemen in the river to turn back the fleeing fish. The strategy worked. The Schuylkill shallows soon boiled white with frantic shad trying to swim back downstream against thousands of others still heading the opposite way—

The starvation of the Valley Forge winter ended in the largest fish banquet Philip had ever seen.

That night the Pennsylvania air reeked of broiled shad and rang with singing, a sound unheard for months, except in protest. As the smoke of cook fires climbed to the sky, Captain Webb purchased an extra gill of rum for each of his men, and reported an item of camp gossip about Martha Washington.

Mrs. Washington had joined her husband at the Potts house in February. Since then she'd been a regular visitor to the camp hospitals—when she wasn't busy taking instruction from a neighborhood farm woman on how to darn the general's stockings. Tonight, Webb declared with tipsy pride, he knew for a fact that the lady too had served shad.

"Picked up some other tasty tidings," Webb went on. "Still talk, mostly. But it's coming from the Congress in York. May be a big announcement in the wind—"

Relishing his control of a secret, he crooked a finger so Philip would lean closer. Then he whispered:

"Something about the French coming into the war. Sending us ships. Soldiers, even. Don't breathe a word. Nothing official—"

He tottered away toward the next hut to tell another confidante the same secret.

All at once, Webb about-faced. Fumbling in his uniform pocket, he returned to hand Philip a wrinkled letter:

"This finally came down the line from headquarters. Got sent by mistake to an officer named Philemon Kent in Moore's Fourth Rhode Island."

Abruptly, Philip forgot how stuffed he felt from the excellent fish. He forgot the exciting hint of a French alliance. He forgot everything except the letter.

Quills had scratched and re-scratched the names of different units across the face. The original address had been smeared by water; rain, perhaps. But the name *Kent* in Anne's hand was unmistakable.

He tore the letter open, held it near the cook fire to read. The date was the preceding November, 1777.

In the midst of pleasantries, endearments and news of their son, Anne reported that Captain Malachi Rackham had written her *another distressingly impertinent letter, which Mrs. Brumple, who is now moved in, considered alarming in its tone of familiarity.*

Philip went white at that; read on:

But I do not, and neither should you, my darling. I did find the occasion to speak with W. Caleb concerning his captain's behavior, and Caleb assured me he would take corrective steps. He stated that while Rackham was a most able sailor, he was known to be of erratic temperament, and had only been engaged out of necessity, and with considerable reservation on Caleb's part. Evidently Mr. Rackham's chief problem is a conviction that he is irresistible to females—which only strikes me as proof that inwardly, he fears exactly the opposite is true, and must constantly disprove the suspicion. Since I discussed Rackham prior to the arrival of the aforementioned letter, it is evident that any efforts Captain Caleb may have made to curb R. have not availed. However, Mrs. Brumple's presence surely will, in the event the unpleasant gentleman should dare present himself here again.

"Henry, I'm going home."

Overflowing the seat of the crude wooden chair provided for his officer's hut, Henry Knox stared at his visitor in puzzlement.

Philip had arrived at four in the morning, after a sleepless night. Knox had come to the door wearing a shabby robe and carrying a lantern. Now the lantern flickered on the mantel of Knox's fireplace; the officers' quarters were duplicates of those of the enlisted men, except that they were somewhat larger.

The fat artillery colonel tented his fingers. "Philip, I can plainly see that you're overwrought. But I believe I misunderstood what you said."

"You didn't. I'm leaving for Cambridge. Now, before daylight—" He stabbed a hand through his dark hair. "I had to tell someone who'd understand. The two men in my mess wouldn't. They don't know Anne. Besides, I need—"

"Wait, Philip," Knox interrupted, sounding much less sleepy. "You are telling me that you've desertion in mind?"

"Much more than in mind. I'm going. Here, I received this last night. You can see it was written in November, then sent by mistake to another man in a different unit."

Knox scanned the letter, his normally placid face still showing some confusion.

"That I see very clearly. What I do not see is what there is on this page to bring you to such a state."

Quickly then, Philip poured out the story: the investment in Caleb's privateers; the first encounter with Malachi Rackham; Anne's subsequent references to him in her letters:

"I know her, Henry. Each time, she tried to reassure me that she wasn't worried. But she'd never have brought it up if—well, let's just say I can read what's behind the words, too. She's terrified of him. One look at him and you'd understand. He's handsome. Fancies himself a prize for the ladies. But there's a nastiness about him—"

The words trailed off. Philip had the dismal feeling that he wasn't getting through.

Knox confirmed it: "You still haven't explained why you feel you must commit a very rash and dangerous act."

"Because I'm afraid something's happened to Anne! It's April and that was posted in November. I've had no other letter from her—"

"Like everything else, the mails are plagued slow—"

"Not that slow." Philip paced, feeling trapped. "Not that damned slow."

Knox frowned again, lifting the letter. "Isn't there another person sharing your house? I noticed a reference to a Mrs.—"

"Brumple. An old lady next door. She moved in with Anne last year because Annie was already afraid of Rackham then."

"And so you've decided to return to Cambridge to look into it? Just like that?"

"I have to, Henry. I'm convinced—"

"You do *not* have to," Knox cut in. "In fact, it's not permitted."

The words hit Philip like physical blows. He could barely speak:

"For Christ's sake, I know it's not permitted! I'm telling you because—"

"Because you want me to sanction what you're going to do? I can't. I am an officer in this army."

"Don't talk like someone making a speech at a parade review—!"

"Then kindly do not shout!"

Silence. Finally Philip let out a long sigh.

"All right. I'm sorry. I need traveling money, Henry. Just a little, but I didn't know who else to ask—"

"The answer is no."

"Dammit, Henry, you've got to—!"

"Philip!" This time it was Knox who shouted. "It's not pleasant for me to employ the differences in our ranks—but you forget yourself. I agree with what you say to this extent. You may have cause for concern. *May.* There is no evidence to support any stronger word. But do you think you're the only man at Valley Forge with worries at home? Some have wives and children facing outright starvation because no one can operate a family farm—a family business! Others have lost loved ones and learned of it only months later, in letters that went astray just like this one. With the spring campaign ahead, no leaves are being granted for any reason."

"I don't give a damn what you say, I'm leaving," Philip exclaimed, wheeling for the door.

Knox lunged after him, spun him around, flung him against the mantel so hard the lantern nearly toppled off:

"You will get control of yourself!"

"Goddamn it, let go! I won't listen—"

"You will! Either go back to your unit or I will have you arrested and flogged."

Aghast, Philip stared at him.

"You're my friend. You're *Anne's* friend—"

"That makes no difference. You're being driven to this by fear and fear alone. If you desert, I'll have you hunted down at once—and brought back." Abruptly, Knox's tone changed. "You have a duty here. We all do. After the winter we've endured—the deaths— the near-rebellions—my God, and the work you've put in with von Steuben—learning, teaching others— To quit now for any reason save being brought down by an enemy ball is nothing short of treason."

"Treas—?"

Philip couldn't even get the whole word out. The accusation from his long-time friend seared him like an iron—

And crumbled the facade of the almost hysterical rationalization he'd constructed in his mind to justify what he planned to do.

"Friend or not," Knox went on, "if you go, I promise you I'll report it—and see you punished."

Numb, Philip picked up the letter that had fallen to the dirt floor. He felt drained—and dismally aware that everything Henry Knox had said was right. He stumbled toward the door:

"I'm sorry I came here—"

"So am I."

Philip spun to glare.

"Because we are friends, Philip. Ordering your arrest wouldn't be easy for me. But I will do it."

Philip started out. At the sound of his name repeated, he turned again.

Knox asked, "Where are you going?"

"To—" Philip swallowed. "Back to the hut."

"Is that the truth?"

"Yes."

Knox let out a long, relieved sigh:

"Good."

Philip closed the door behind him, avoided the suspicious stare of a guard posted at the head of the officers' street, walked with slumping shoulders through the spring dawn, repelled all at once by what he'd wanted to do until Knox's rough treatment jarred him out of it.

At the same time, he felt trapped. Trapped and frightened.

He glanced up at the paling stars.

Annie, he thought. *Annie, are you all right?*

CHAPTER VII

Rackham

UNCONTROLLABLE annoyance edged Anne Kent's voice:

"Abraham, for the third time—eat your porridge."

"Don't want to," declared the stocky, dark-eyed boy teetering on three worn books piled on his chair. He dipped his wood spoon into the bowl. With a wrench of his small wrist, he sent a gob of porridge flying across the kitchen.

Anne jumped up from the table. "Oh, Abraham, you're such a trial sometimes—!" Her hands slapped against her skirt, bringing an alarmed look to the boy's face.

At once, Anne regretted the shrill reprimand. She believed in discipline that was firm yet loving. Whenever her son misbehaved, she tried not to raise her voice, even as a prologue to one or two quick whacks of his behind. But in recent weeks she'd been losing her temper more and more frequently.

She started around the table to make amends; substitute cajolery for insistence. But Abraham had already made up his mind about what he wanted—and didn't:

"Don't want to eat. Want Papa."

"Papa can't come home. Papa's in Pennsylvania at a place called Valley Forge. I've showed you his letters. The word that spells his name and yours. Kent—"

She bent to caress the boy's dark hair. But Abraham was still upset from her sharp outcry of a few moments earlier. He pulled away:

"I want Papa. No more porge. Papa!"

The tension and weariness plaguing Anne these cold winter days of early 1778 came out again unbidden:

"Stop it, Abraham! You can't see Papa because he's not here! Now eat your breakfast or I'll give you a spanking."

She showed him her hand to illustrate. It was precisely the wrong thing to do.

Abraham Kent, going on two and a half years old, hurled his spoon to the floor. With one stubby-fingered hand, he pushed the bowl off the edge of the table. The crockery shattered, splattering the gooey paste of oats and water all over the hem of Anne's dress. She slapped his hand:

"You're a wicked little boy!"

Abraham puckered up his eyebrows, turned beet color and bawled.

"My heavens, catch the child before he falls!" exclaimed a new voice. Mrs. Eulalie Brumple, tiny and frail, darted from the doorway through beams of watery sunlight and snatched Abraham to her shoulder an instant before he tumbled to the floor.

Ashamed and upset, Anne covered her eyes, turned away.

"I don't know who's in worse temper this morning, Mrs. Brumple, Abraham or me."

She felt the start of tears, fought them with all her will as the neighbor woman rocked Abraham back and forth, ignoring his sharp pulls of her mobcap and his repeated shrieks:

"Want to see Papa. *Want to see Papa!*"

"Here, here, that's no way for a young gentleman to behave," Mrs. Brumple said as Abraham yanked the cap down over her right eye. "Let's find that drum your father bought you, shall we?"

Abraham was diverted from his sobbing, and sniffled instead:

"Drum?"

"Drum," Mrs. Brumple repeated. "You can relieve your frustration by banging away to your heart's content." She glanced at Anne. "Not here, however. In the parlor."

Anne stared in dismay as Mrs. Brumple marched Abraham to the front of the house. In a few moments the toy drum began to rattle and thump.

The erratic rhythm grated on Anne's nerves. *But what doesn't these days?* she thought as she hung the tea kettle up to boil.

The kitchen in Cambridge was chilly this February morning. Anne had risen early, unable to sleep—again. She'd started another letter to Philip, determined to keep the contents cheerful, free of any indication of the growing strain she felt in his absence.

She'd written exactly one paragraph, describing how Cambridge's population had increased now that a huge number of Gentleman Johnny Burgoyne's redcoats and Hessians had been marched east after Saratoga. The enemy troops were locked up in compounds, pledged not to fight during the remainder of the war because Burgoyne had agreed to that as part of the terms of his surrender. Anne had broken off the letter in the middle of a sentence speculating about whether English transports would ever arrive to take the soldiers away, and then she'd simply sat staring into space, her body aching with an all-too-familiar tension.

As Abraham's drumming continued, Mrs. Eulalie Brumple marched back into the kitchen. The small-boned sixty-year-old lady with the hawk's eye and the firmly set mouth never walked anywhere, only marched.

But her presence in the spare bedroom was a comfort to Anne. Prickly as the widow Brumple might be, once she had moved a few belongings from her home next door, Anne had felt much less alarmed about the occasional, all-too-obvious overtures from Captain

Rackham. Happily, she hadn't been bothered by the man since the autumn. She assumed it was because Rackham had finally put to sea in search of prizes.

Anne busied herself pouring tea for the two of them. She recognized the expression on the older woman's face and braced for another lecture.

"Mrs. Kent?"

"Yes, Mrs. Brumple?" Neither woman had yet breached the formality of using last names.

"I certainly hope you won't take offense if I mention another condition which I believe needs rectifying." Mrs. Brumple always preceded one of her declarations with some such empty apology.

"Won't you have some tea before it gets cold?" Anne asked, hoping to forestall the impending remarks on— what this time? Child guidance, she guessed. She was correct:

"In a moment. First I must speak my mind."

Dark circles showed beneath Anne's eyes. She sighed, sank down in a chair.

"Go ahead."

"I'm not criticizing, I'm only trying to be helpful—"

"Yes, yes, I know. Go on." Anne had heard the preamble dozens of times.

"In my opinion it's a shame you can't in some wise show that dear young child his father's likeness."

"I don't have any pictures of my husband!" Anne exclaimed, almost to the point of tears. "We're not the sort of family that can afford to commission painters of miniatures!"

Mrs. Brumple considered that, then observed primly, "Perhaps it would have served you better to hire a third-rate artist—keeping him at the proper distance, of course; artists are all immoral rascals; I was once unwholesomely propositioned by such a person—than to have put so much money in two pirate ships which have yet to pay you a penny."

"They're not pirates, they're authorized priva-teersmen."

"Makes no difference, they've repaid not one cent of your investment."

Anne said nothing. Mrs. Brumple's statement was correct. Caleb's small fleet of prize-hunters, all of them reportedly in southern waters, had captured not a single enemy vessel. She was beginning to regret her decision to invest two hundred pounds in the construction of *Gull* and *Fidelity*. And not just because of the character of Captain Caleb's associate, who had relinquished command of *Nancy* and become the skipper of *Gull*. Caleb himself was sailing the other new privateer.

Mrs. Brumple went on, "A child does need to become familiar with his own father's face. What a pity your husband is not as vain as Brumple—"

The little widow always referred to her late spouse by his last name only. Brumple had evidently been a tailor who had achieved only modest success. Anne knew far more about his faults than his virtues, which were apparently almost non-existent.

"—Brumple was always presenting me with this or that little charcoal sketch of his likeness. He fancied himself handsome. The more fool he! May I have some more tea, dear?"

Anne poured the smuggled Dutch brew, not knowing whether to laugh at the little woman's pretensions or burst out sobbing in hopeless frustration.

"Naturally I would have welcomed all those portraits of Brumple if we'd had babies," the widow said. "But after the first several years of our marriage—years in which I reluctantly permitted Brumple to indulge in his constant pecking at my cheek and pawing at my small-clothes—that sort of thing always led to the inevitable conclusion which I only suffered as part of my female duty—where was I? Oh yes. I was speaking of how it became evident that Brumple and I were not going to leave heirs in this world. Believe me, after that I saw to it that he left my smallclothes alone! However—" She sipped tea. "My original contention remains valid. Little pictures of a faraway loved one can be valuable in helping a child remember the loved one."

Mrs. Brumple fixed Anne with a direct stare. "Is it possible you could sketch such a likeness of Mr. Kent?"

Anne shook her head. "I'm hard put to draw a straight line."

"Pity." Mrs. Brumple finished her tea.

A crash from the parlor brought Anne half out of her chair. The widow too:

"Oh dear, the boy's upset something. No, you let me see to it, you're much too tired to deal with him properly." She marched from the kitchen at quick step.

Anne felt resentful. But the reaction passed quickly. In her peculiar, flinty way, Mrs. Eulalie Brumple liked her neighbor—and loved Abraham. Anne, too, was basically fond of the old busybody. She knew that the widow's last charge was not maliciously spoken—and was entirely correct. She *was* worn out—

Worn out from coping with Abraham without the help of a father's masculine hand and voice. Worn out from lying alone too many nights, shivering despite the footwarmer she religiously took under the covers. Worn out worrying about whether the two hundred pounds loaned to Caleb were gone forever. Worn out fretting about Rackham, whose name kept slipping into the letters she wrote Philip, despite her best intentions that it shouldn't. Worn out with the war that seemed to bring nothing but minor victories and major defeats for the American armies. Worn out with thoughts of Philip meeting his death on the point of a British bayonet.

Worn out imagining how she would survive if he never came home, never held her again, never kissed her and made love to her—

Worn out. Beyond her capacity to endure it any longer—

She wasn't even aware that she'd pressed her palms to her eyes and started crying there in the pale February sunlight. She sat bolt upright at the touch of a hand:

"Mrs. Kent—let me tuck you in for a rest."

As it could on occasion, Mrs. Eulalie Brumple's face had softened. Her fundamental kindness was showing through the hard Congregationalist facade.

"Did you sleep at all last night?" she asked softly.

"Very little."

"Then come along."

"I'm sorry my tongue's been so sharp, Mrs. Brumple. I don't mean to be so curt with the boy, or you—"

"Now, now, let's have no apologies. I'll bundle Abraham up and we'll walk to the market. Come, my dear, stand up—"

Anne did. She was soon in bed, listening to the stillness of the house. A patch of melting snow slid off the roof shakes, a loud scraping. She was literally aching with exhaustion and the hunger for Philip's presence.

But no matter how she tried, she still couldn't sleep.

ii

It seemed an eternity since Anne had found anything the least amusing about the war. But here it was at last, reported at some length in a month-old copy of Ben Edes' *Gazette*.

The wet, gusty April night seemed momentarily remote. Curled up in a chair by the cozy fire, Anne laughed out loud, causing Mrs. Brumple to glance up from the scarf she was knitting for Abraham.

"Mrs. Kent, I certainly hesitate to criticize, but I

believe Abraham is finally asleep—"

Giggling, Anne covered her mouth a moment. "I was being too noisy, wasn't I? But this is just delightful. Some chap from Connecticut—let's see—" She checked the paper. "David Bushnell's his name. In February he launched a whole flotilla of what they call infernals."

"What is an infernal, pray? Another name for a husband?"

"No, Mrs. Brumple! A keg of powder with a contact fuse. Bushnell set them afloat in the Delaware River above Philadelphia. His idea was to blow up the British ships anchored in mid-river. But because of floating ice, all the frigates were moored close to shore. The paper says the British were absolutely terrified of the kegs, though. The soldiers peppered away at them with muskets, trying to explode them."

Mrs. Brumple rested her knitting in her lap, her expression saying clearly that she thus far failed to find anything hilarious in the story. Anne went on:

"The part that amused me is the song composed by a Mr. Hopkinson from the Congress. It's called *The Battle of the Kegs*. Here, listen—"

"Brumple was always fond of light verse. It did little to improve his already frivolous mind."

But Anne couldn't be deterred:

"Sir William Howe and that doxy of his are sleeping when some of the kegs start exploding, you see. Hopkinson says—

> *"Sir William, he, snug as a flea,*
> *"Lay all this while a-snoring.*
> *"Nor dreamed of harm as he lay warm*
> *"In bed with—"*

Anne's finger ticked against the page, her wan face merry:

"Ben Edes left two blanks right there, but I can imagine our soldiers hooting out the missing words. 'Mrs. Loring.' Here's the rest—

> "*Now in a fright, he starts upright,*
> "*Awaked by such a clatter.*
> "*He rubs his eyes, and boldly cries*
> " *For God's sake, what's the mat—?*" "

A knocking in the hallway interrupted Anne, and diverted Mrs. Brumple from whatever remark of disapproval she was about to make.

Being closest to the front door, Mrs. Brumple went to answer. Anne returned to the verse, laughing as she hadn't in weeks. The doggerel truly wasn't all that excellent, but she'd gone too long without finding anything to lighten her spirits. She barely heard Mrs. Brumple speaking sharply, and a man's voice replying. The exchange lasted less than a minute. Then the front door slammed.

Mrs. Brumple marched back to the fringe of the firelight:

"Well, I certainly didn't like that person's looks."

Anne glanced up. "Who was it?"

"Some sort of seaman. Terribly scruffy. He was inquiring for the Russell house."

"There's no family named Russell living in this neighborhood."

"I'm well aware of that. I think it was a subterfuge. I didn't care for the man's cut one bit, I tell you. Shifty eyes. Just like Brumple's."

Even though she realized Mrs. Brumple's concern was probably unfounded, Anne was troubled. She laid the paper aside, her earlier mood gone. For no reason she could adequately explain, the word *seaman* brought Malachi Rackham instantly to mind.

390

Before she went to bed she scanned the rainy street for a sign of anyone suspicious. She saw no one. But she made doubly certain that the front and rear doors were bolted and all the windows latched before looking in on Abraham to see that he was adequately covered.

iii

Two evenings later, with the late April rain still pelting Cambridge, Mrs. Brumple collected her cloak, gloves and parasol to pit her Christian courage against the elements:

"You're certain you don't mind me leaving you this evening, Mrs. Kent?"

Anne smiled. "You're the one who's going to get soaked, not I."

"In the Lord's work—and General Washington's. Our prayer circle has reorganized. Not only to read scripture but to sew hunting shirts at the same time. We shall be convening every Wednesday evening from now on. I should certainly be home in an hour or two—"

"I'll be up, don't worry."

"I attend religious functions with a clearer conscience than I did when I was married," the little lady said as she tugged on her gloves. "Brumple sat in the pew with me every Sunday because he felt it was good for trade. Underneath, I always suspected him of being a free-thinker. Good evening," she concluded, marching out the front door.

Despite the coming of spring, the house still felt a trifle cold. Anne kindled a small fire in the parlor, then sat down to her mending. She worked for nearly an hour, until her concentration was broken by sounds from Abraham's bedroom.

She put the mending aside, hurried to the back of the house. The boy was breathing loudly. As she watched at the bedside, he shifted position several times.

She felt his forehead. No fever. Perhaps he'd been thrashing because of bad dreams—

A loud, hollow clatter startled her. It echoed from the front of the house. She frowned. Who could be calling at this hour—?

Apprehensive, she hurried to the parlor, then to the bay of windows. She lifted a curtain. Outside, barely visible in the rain, a closed carriage sat at the curb. The horse was tied to the hitch post. She saw no sign of a driver.

Anne's palms turned cold. The logs on the hearth cast slow-changing shadows over the walls. She felt a peculiar, nervous fluttering inside her breast. Perhaps whoever it was would go—

More knocking. Louder.

"I say, Mrs. Kent, are you at home?"

"Oh my God," she breathed, recognizing the voice.

Terrified, she dashed for the front hallway. *She hadn't latched the door after Mrs. Brumple left—*

Three steps from the door, she stopped—too late. The door opened inward, spattering her with rain.

Like some hobgoblin, the tall man slipped inside. His tightly curled dark hair glistened. The hem of his cloak dripped. His right eye, so strangely drawn into a slit by the small scar, caught firelight from the parlor and glowed like a coal.

"Pardon me for just walking in, but I thought it possible you didn't hear the knock," said Captain Malachi Rackham.

iv

Anne went numb as Rackham stared at her, that nasty, cocksure smile seemingly fixed in place. He swayed a little. She smelled rum on him—

A dreadful suspicion leaped into her mind. The man the other evening—the seaman—had he been sent to see whether she was alone? *Had Rackham been keeping watch—?*

No, no, that was too fanciful by half—

Or was it?

She tried to compose her features. But the fluttering sensation persisted. In a second, she became certain that her initial guess was correct. Rackham had waited to call until his man reported Mrs. Brumple's departure.

"See here, I didn't mean to shock you to total silence!" Rackham declared, pulling a face. "I stopped off because I thought you might welcome a report concerning your investment in *Gull*."

He glanced beyond her to the empty parlor. "Are you at liberty to discuss it?"

"I—" God, why was her throat so dry? "I've been working in the kitchen. I've a cauldron of soap cooking—"

Rackham wrinkled his nose. "Odd. I don't smell it."

"I was about to put it on the fire when you arrived."

"Then you are at liberty for a few moments—"

He accidentally brushed her elbow as he slipped past into the parlor.

Rackham unfastened his cloak and dropped it over a chair. He swung to face her, one knee bent and his boot planted out in front of him. The pose of a man aping his betters. His clothing reinforced the impression. He wore dove gray breeches, an ostentatious coat of yellow velour, too much lace at collar and cuffs—

He flexed his hands behind him, warming them near the fire. "Come, come, Mrs. Kent! You can at least be hospitable to a man of whom you've spoken ill."

"Captain Rackham—" Anne struggled to keep her voice level. "—it should be evident many times over that you're not welcome here."

393

He shrugged, surveying the closed curtains at the bay of front windows. "That may be. But you'll have to put up with me for a bit, my girl, because you owe me a kindness."

"What do you mean, a kindness? I owe you nothing!"

Under the drooping right lid, the pupil of Rackham's eye seemed to burn. "But you do. I did not appreciate your speaking to Will Caleb about my letters and my visits."

"Oh? I'm so sorry. Be assured I'll speak to him a-gain, Captain." She started for the hall. "You will please leave."

"In due course."

Still smiling, Rackham sat down and crossed his legs.

More frightened than ever, Anne stood in the hall, not knowing what to do. She realized Abraham had been wakened by the voices. His faint cry sounded from the darkness at the back of the house:

"Mama?"

"Go to sleep, Abraham," she called. "It's all right, I'm here."

There was a fretful murmur from his bedroom, then silence.

Slowly Anne looked back at the man lounging near the hearth. Rackham was studying her figure that her dress showed to advantage despite its shabbiness. He made no attempt to conceal his interest.

She glanced at the French sword hanging above the mantel. Could she pull it down fast enough, if necessary? The Kentucky rifle beneath the sword was empty; useless, except perhaps as a club—

Determined not to let her fear get the best of her, Anne folded her arms across her breasts, addressed Rackham sharply:

"Was it you who sent someone to the door two nights ago? A man pretending to be hunting a family named Russell?"

"Aye, I used a lad from *Gull* for that duty. Same one who watched the place tonight, then drove me out here in the coach."

"So you have been spying—!"

"Call it what you wish. We have private matters to discuss. I didn't want anyone else's company but yours, my dear."

Once more he showed his teeth in what he presumed was a charming smile. To Anne it resembled the grimace of a fanged animal. Rackham went on:

"*Gull* anchored in Boston harbor last Sunday morning. We took a mighty handsome prize off the Carolinas. As I remarked when I came in, I thought you'd be interested in that." He feigned readiness to rise and leave. "However, if you insist you're not—"

Despite her fear, Anne said, "A British prize?"

"Correct. With some sharp sailing and gun work on our part, she hauled down her colors mighty fast. The total proceeds of the auction come—ah, came to about half a million sterling pounds." He paused. "Care to hear more?"

The sum stunned her; left her confused and uncertain about how to proceed.

She had an overpowering urge to dash from the house; Malachi Rackham would never have spied on her, nor come all the way to Cambridge in the rain, out of sheer concern for the Kent investment. That was doubly obvious from the way he continued to glance at her breasts, the line of her hip, like a man anticipating a sumptuous dinner—

Yet if he wasn't lying to her—if *Gull* had indeed captured a merchantman—the prospects were dizzying, and she ought to know the whole story.

Rackham tried to resolve her quandry:

"Fetch me a port—or a rum if you have it—and I'll be happy to share the details."

"I'm sorry, I've nothing to give you."

"Ah, Mrs. Kent, that's where you are quite wrong." His smile left no doubt about his meaning.

"Get out," Anne said, livid. "At once."

"Belay that, if you please," Rackham chuckled. "I'm not your husband, after all. In fact I assume your husband is still far away—? Serving his country honorably while his wife remains unconsolable because her bed's empty—?"

"Get *out!*" Anne exploded, raising a clenched fist.

Rackham's veneer of sham politeness crumbled. He reached her in two swift strides, jerked her upraised hand down, leaned close until she nearly choked from the stench of rum:

"You listen here, Mrs. Kent. That very first day we met, I tabbed you for what you are—a lass who fancies herself stronger than any man she'll ever meet. And shows it. Well, permit me to tell you something. Captain Rackham is a fellow who doesn't hold with being put down in such fashion. I don't like being put down with haughty looks or nasty no-thank-you's at the doorstep. Still—I'll admit that's part of your charm—the fact you think I'm a nobody and don't bother to hide it. I expect that's the reason I made up my mind that morning on Hancock's Wharf that I'd take you—with your agreement or without."

"*Take—?*"

"Here, here, no silly prudery." The cocksure smile somehow acquired a malevolent twist. "I've been sporting a good twenty years with the gentle sex. Never had one of 'em turn me down. Till you."

"You drunken popinjay liar—!"

He grabbed her wrist again. "You watch your language, woman—"

Anne raked his face with her free hand, her nails leaving bleeding scratches. Rackham struck her.

She staggered, crying out. Her mind held one dreadful word—

Madman.

She didn't know what warped memories or conceits made him what he was. But she knew that every rebuff she'd given him must have festered weeks, months in the mazes of his head. She knew he was drunk, and dangerous—

"Mama?"

Abraham was calling again, frightened by her outcry. Anne struggled to her feet. But somehow, she couldn't avoid Rackham's hands. Big hands; hair-matted; sliding under her arms—

Rackham's thumbs pressed the fabric over her breasts. "Even in a temper, you're a soft, dear sight, Mrs. Kent. I can't properly explain it, but I've never fancied a woman as much as I fancy you. Perhaps it's because I'm not supposed to, eh?"

"Damn your eyes—*let me go!*"

That only provoked more laughter:

"Ah, stop, Mrs. Kent. You must want a man so bad you hurt from it. That little fellow you're wed to—he can't be much in the cock department, now admit—"

Writhing away from him, she spat in his face.

Again Rackham struck her. She tumbled at his feet, stunned. Abraham started to cry loudly. Rackham leaned down, his shadow distorting across the wall as he jerked her head up by a fist in her hair:

"I want to tell you about your property, Mrs. Kent. Your investment—a man who wants to do that should be treated right, eh? *Eh?*"

He yanked her hair. She uttered another hoarse yelp. Rackham laughed:

"Yes indeed, I want to invite you aboard *Gull* for a pleasant and diverting evening. As I say—you owe me. You got me roasted by that sanctimonious old bastard Caleb. But I'll forgive you—if you'll visit the ship and be nice and agreeable when we get there—"

Anne screamed deliberately, hoping to attract

someone's attention outside. Abraham's terrified cries sounded as stridently as her own.

"Be quiet!" Rackham shouted, letting go of her hair and smashing the side of her head with his fist.

She lurched sideways, reaching clumsily toward the mantel; toward Philip's gleaming sword—

Rackham hit her harder. She fell, struck her temple on the floor, moaned, opened and closed one stretched-out hand, then lay still.

v

Anne awoke briefly to the sensation of motion.

She heard carriage wheels and springs creaking. The clop and splash of hoofs along a rutted road. Rain pattering overhead—

Through a slot window she glimpsed a distant farm-stead, a yellow smear of lamplight in the rain. She realized she was leaning against the curve of a man's left shoulder.

She struggled away, only to have a sweaty-smelling hand clamp over her mouth.

The places where Rackham had hit her and the other place where she'd struck her head all hurt terribly. Rackham inclined his head to slobber a kiss on her face. She tried to wrench the other way.

That made him burst out with his damnable laugh—and hold her more tightly.

His left hand still covered her mouth. She bit at the fingers. He jerked them away, freeing his arm so he could squeeze her throat in the vee of his elbow, cutting off her wind:

"Screaming's useless, my girl. I told you it's one of my lads up on the box of this hired rig. Even at the dock in Boston, the sight of Malachi Rackham knocking some wench about to get her into a dinghy and out to his ship ain't—isn't likely to cause any commotion. The

398

tavern trulls, they sometimes say yes, then start a squall on the pier, wanting a higher price. I've often been seen roughing 'em up a wee bit. So you won't get any help by yelling or—*bitch!*" he howled as she bit hard into the fleshy back of his hand.

He flung her to the floor of the rocking carriage, kicked her twice in the ribs, bashed her eye with his knuckles, bringing new, nauseous darkness swirling over her.

vi

A pinpoint of light; dull orange.

And motion again. But of a different order this time. Gentler—

She recognized sounds. The lap of water against hull planks. The creak of a ship's upper and lower capstans being turned in tandem. Chain being pulled up by the messenger cables—

Anchor chain?

Anne Kent opened her eyes; saw her skirt and petticoat hiked around her knees. She was lying in a ship's bunk.

She shifted her throbbing head to the left, saw Malachi Rackham—and a cabin where a single glass-paneled lantern swayed overhead on a beam hook. The two large oval stern windows showed a spatter of lamp-gilded raindrops.

Rackham lounged in a chair beside an oak table. Both chair and table were bolted to the decking. Rackham lolled a drinking cup back and forth in one hand as he watched Anne with an amused expression. His showy coat and breeches hung on a peg near his wall-mounted drop-front desk. He wore drawers of soiled gray linen, nothing else.

"Hallo, Mrs. Kent," he said, scratching the curled

hair on his chest. It was as dark as that on his head. "Wondered how long it'd take you to liven up. Been an hour since I brought you aboard."

He held out the cup. "Little rum?"

"The—" She was so dazed, she could barely speak. "The ship's under way—"

"Oh, not quite as yet. But getting there, getting there. My pilot'll take us through the island channels as soon as the tide's fair. We may meet some foul weather, but I decided to risk it. I thought it'd be advisable not to tell Captain Caleb how we disposed of the prize we took with *Gull.* Caleb and me—I—we're only temporary bedfellows. As he'll find out shortly after he sails *Fidelity* back to Boston. The British prize I mentioned did bring a handsome sum at the sell-off. But not in American waters, I'm sorry to say."

Rackham feigned sorrow. "We encountered unfavorable winds, don't you see. Had to beat south to Saint Eustatius in the Leewards. Only safe harbor available—"

He was amused at his own reporting of the lie. He clucked his tongue:

"Yes, truly unfortunate. But the Dutchmen were accommodating, damned accommodating. We had the trial—the auction—the only problem being, as Caleb explained, that under the terms of our Articles, a prize disposed of in a foreign port means all the proceeds go to captain and crew. The owners, God pity 'em, miss out. We've already divided the share belonging to you and your husband. Understand now why I've such a loyal bunch of lads? They'll help me abduct a lady anytime."

Grinning, Rackham slopped down more rum.

Anne had to struggle to form a coherent sentence:

"You—you cheated Caleb—"

"Oh, no, Mrs. Kent! We couldn't help what happened. Unfavorable winds!"

"Liar. You—you planned something like that—all along—"

Rackham shrugged. "Well—it's possible. But it's done. Now there's an even more profitable prospect ahead. We'll be setting a coasting course for New York."

"The—British—the British hold—"

"New York? Indeed they do. Why do you think I'm heading there? The privateersmen are taking a lot of prizes, you see. I'm sure I can find a buyer for a spanking new beauty like *Gull*. A little work and she'll serve nicely as a transport to replace one of the captured ones. I wager plenty of Tory merchants in New York'll be glad to bid on her."

"The ship isn't yours to sell!" Anne cried hoarsely.

"Why, who's here to dispute my right—except you? And we've other matters to attend to, yes we do—"

Still grinning, he ran a hand down between his thighs and squeezed his crotch.

Anne felt gagging sourness in her mouth; felt an urge to scream and keep screaming and overcame it only with maximum effort.

"Right here—" Rackham was still fingering his groin. "—right here I've the machinery to keep your thoughts diverted to subjects more pleasant than ships and who owns 'em. Soon as I strike a good bargain for *Gull*, we'll have a grand holiday together in New York town. Live elegantly, I'll guarantee it."

"You—you'd sell out Caleb when he hired and trusted you—?"

Rackham's face wrenched. "Caleb's a fool who thinks as ill of me as you do. We only did business with each other out of necessity. Captains—good captains—they're mighty scarce. I was down on my luck, so I took the first arrangement offered. But every time that

401

bastard looked down his nose at me, I remembered. Every time he ordered me this way or every which, I remembered—"

Slowly, like a muscular animal rousing from its den, Rackham laid the drinking cup aside. He stood up, unfastened the tie-knot of his drawers and let them fall.

"Just like I remembered every time you gave me the cool stare or the turn-down. Aye—"

Rackham started for the bunk, his immense engorged maleness swaying on a level with Anne's eyes.

"—we'll have a fine and lively time in New York. We will provided you learn one lesson. I mean who is giving orders and who is taking 'em—"

"Traitor."

"You be quiet, you bitch."

"A traitor to the country that—"

Rackham chuckled, terrifying her to silence.

"Ah, you're a delicious one, Mrs. Kent. And why should I be at all angry with you? You've already called me more names than I can remember. Sure you have! It'll take me a month to punish you for each—"

He moved a step closer.

"A dollop of punishment, a dollop of pleasure—all at the same time, what d'you say—?"

He reached down, crooked his hand around his own reddened flesh. From beside the bunk, he crooned to her:

"Come on, now. Come on. Be good. *Give us a kiss*—"

This time Anne Kent screamed the wild wail of hysteria. But Rackham only laughed as he climbed on top of her.

vii

She awoke in the fouled bunk sometime near dawn.

She had never hurt so terribly in all her life. Not even at the height of her labor when she bore Abraham. She felt almost destroyed by the repeated punishings Rackham had inflicted on her all night long, beating her and forcing her legs apart each time, tearing and plunging in her until the pain became so intense that it turned to a perverted blessing; a sort of drug to deaden some of the anguish.

Disconnected thoughts flickered through Anne's mind as she tried to climb from the bunk, fell when *Gull* rolled sharply. She groped for the captain's table. It took her almost two minutes to pull herself to her feet.

Through the oval stern windows she saw the steep-sided hills and valleys of the ocean.

And no land anywhere.

She brushed hair from one eye, leaned on the table, stared down at the blood that had dried along the inside of her left thigh. On her breasts three vivid blue-yellow bruises showed.

She grew aware of intermittent sounds. The rush of water against the hull; the stamp of sailors' feet overhead; a muffled yell—

In a weak voice she repeated her husband's name. Her child's. Her husband's again, as if the litany would somehow rescue her; waken her from this unbelievable nightmare of captivity and pain—

She hammered on the door. Tugged. Wrenched—

Bolted. On the outside.

She opened one of the oval windows, smelled the salt tang and watched the wake foaming white. *Gull* was running through a moderately heavy sea.

After staring at the water for a moment or so in a forlorn way, she latched the window, slipping and falling once more as she negotiated her way back to the table. She sank into the bolted-down chair, on the brink of another fit of uncontrollable weeping. She hurt; she hurt so terribly—

Then, out of her pain emerged a different sort of emotion.

Rage.

Rage at the vile way in which she'd been used.

Rage—and a determination not to surrender to despair while one breath was left.

All right, she said to herself. Think, now. Hard as it is, if you want to see Philip again—see Abraham, again, ever—*think!*—

Rackham would return to the cabin eventually. But how could she get *out* of the cabin?

Only by eluding him. Disabling him, even.

If she managed to gain the deck, she might—*might* be able to convince a few of the crew to side with her; possibly put back to Boston. Rackham's boasts about the loyalty of his men might not apply to every single one—

A slim, almost impossible chance.

But what else was there?

She began to turn her head slowly, searching for a weapon; any weapon to hold Rackham at bay—

All at once she realized that she'd failed to see the one serious flaw in the scheme. Rackham would never allow her on deck more than a moment if he could follow her. *If he*—

Hair hanging down into her eyes, Anne Kent shivered. She wiped her mouth. She literally forced the completion of the thought:

If he were alive.

Remembering something, she raised her head. She stared at the lantern swaying from the beam hook. The lantern was paned with pebbled glass.

Rackham would notice a broken stern window instantly. But he might not notice a broken lantern pane—

Whimpering a little because the effort hurt so much, she knelt on the table. Groped upward—

The pitch of *Gull* nearly toppled her off. She managed to seize the lantern, twist it slightly. She bit down on her lower lip and struck her knuckles against the pebbled pane on the side away from the door.

She inhaled sharply. Someone was coming along the companionway!

She started to scramble off the table. The footsteps came closer—

Then passed by, and faded.

Panting, she waited a few moments. Then she hit the pane again.

And once more, harder—

Soon after, she lay in the bunk, her naked back to the door, her body curled not only to feign sleep but to hide her left hand that held the shard of glass. Her right hand bled steadily onto the stained bedclothing.

She lay as still as possible, thinking of Philip's face, and Abraham's. She tried not to dwell on how much she hurt. Or on how the pain might slow her; ruin her sole chance—

She lay with her eyes closed and her heart beating in a fast, irregular way and her ears straining for a sound of Rackham returning.

viii

The bolt rattled. Anne tensed.

Her right hand hurt horribly. She'd gashed it breaking the glass and carrying the shards to Rackham's desk, closing its drop front to conceal all but the piece she gripped in her left hand.

She heard hard breathing as the door opened. Heard Rackham's heavy tread.

"Having a spot of rest, my girl?"

Philip, she thought, *pray for me. I've just one chance at him—*

"Come along, wake up, let's see how you came

405

through the evening—"

Rackham's hand closed on her left shoulder, pulling her over. He groped past her forearm to pluck at a nipple—

And went white as Anne shot out her left hand with all her remaining strength, tearing the sharp edge of the glass across his face once, twice—

"Goddamn you for a deceiving whore!" he screamed, knees buckling. He slapped hands over his face. The glass had pierced his left eyeball.

Pink fluid leaked between Rackham's fingers. His slitted right eye began to quiver in involuntary spasm.

Anne started to crawl from the bunk. Rackham was teetering back and forth, cursing and pushing at his ruined eyesocket as if he could somehow stop the leak and bleeding. She ducked as he flailed at her with one arm. She dodged by him, ran—

She almost made it to the unbolted door. The deck tilted sharply. She lurched backwards against Rackham.

The lower half of his face was drenched red. His lips spewed unintelligible words. He grappled her around the waist, his spittle and blood running down her arm, her breasts, her belly—

Making wheezy sounds, Rackham hauled her around the table. Shreds of tissue hung from the hole in the left side of his face. His pulled-down right eye glared with beast's pain as he lifted Anne bodily, started to hurl her away from him toward the stern—

She dug fingers into his face, felt one slip into the pulpy socket. *Gull's* bow rose, coming out of the trough of a wave. Rackham's thrust carried him along, stumbling, screaming as Anne kept her clawing hold on his face.

Too late, Rackham tried to release her. They fell together, against the glass of an oval window that burst outward at the impact.

She let go then, both of them plunging toward the
406

boiling white of the wake. She heard Rackham's dreadful shriek of fear but she had no time for fear; no time for anything save a last strident cry of the soul:

Philip, I love—

The water smashed her and took her down.

Book Three

Death and Resurrection

CHAPTER I

The Wolves

A CLOCK TICKED in his mind. Ticked ceaselessly, hurrying him another mile, then another.

The clock drove him on when his exhausted body almost refused. It woke him early every day, false dawn or sooner, the time when the spring air was piercingly cool and cardinals were just beginning to swoop through the waving meadowgrass. A mouthful of dried corn from the haversack—a twist or two of jerked beef bitten off and washed down with canteen water taken from a bubbling creek—then he was off again, mounted on the big bay he'd purchased at the Will's Creek trading station.

He'd chosen the horse for stamina rather than speed. But as the days warmed, speed became his paramount concern. He began to push the horse harder than he should.

In small valleys between the ranges of mountains, he'd sometimes stop of an evening with settlers—one family, or several living in close-clustered cabins. He'd luxuriate in the comfort of a slab-wood chair beside a smoky hearth constructed of mud-plastered sticks.

And always, he'd ask the people a variation of the same question:

"Do you know the day of the month? I reckon it to be about the fourteenth, but I had a fever for three days after I crossed Savage Mountain and may have lost track somewhat—"

"It's the sixteenth."

And the clock ticked louder, a tormenting rhythm reminding him that it might already be too late. He'd be up and gone from the settlement before sunrise, ignoring the healed wound in his left side that still ached when the air was cold.

The first week or two, traveling across the Blue Ridge that turned all smoky indigo in the twilight hours, then up through the meadows along the meandering Shenandoah, he'd wondered if the prophecies put to him before his departure had not been wholly correct. Maybe he *was* a madman to set out alone.

True, he was well enough equipped. And he faced little risk of Indian attack this far south. Most of the fury of the British-incited Six Nations was focused miles to the north, across the tier of tribal towns from the valley of the Genesee to the valley of the Mohawk in York State.

Yet there were many other ways for a lone man to perish in the wilderness.

And he was inexperienced; possessed no forest skills as such, only his rifle and a compass and a couple of sparsely detailed maps.

But he had an almost demonic will to succeed. To follow and find the man who had warily put trust in him; the man who now surely felt that trust betrayed. He kept going when rainstorms drenched him; stopped only when the fever and flux made his head spin and his bowels run until he was so weak he felt he could never stand up again.

But somehow he did, listening to the great clock buried in his mind; the clock ticking and ticking the hours and days like whip-strokes being laid on.

He followed the trails that wound up the dark, forested grade of Little Allegheny Mountain, then

Savage Mountain where the fever felled him a second time and he lost another three days, too feeble to do more than lift corn kernels to his mouth.

At last he reached Allegheny Mountain, in the highest range. The wooded peaks looked almost black against the April sky. Bobolinks wheeled over him and hares jumped in the brush as he climbed the slope on horseback, sitting quite tall on the bay, the Kentucky rifle held one-handed across his thighs. He was never more than a foot or two from the rifle, even in the pleasant green valleys of cabins and small tilled fields.

As the clock beat, something burned out of him. An older self became a stranger.

After weeks on the trail, his deerhide trousers and shirt felt not stiff but supple; a second skin. His flesh took on a darker tone, changing from the dead white of the winter sickbed through the burned red of the first days of exposure to the sun and wind and beating rains. When April came to an end, his cheeks had a mahogany shine. Not a single extra ounce of flesh remained on his body. Strangely, the new gauntness didn't give him an unhealthy appearance, but the opposite.

On the downslope of Chestnut Ridge, beyond the Great Meadows where General Washington had once built a fort to withstand a siege by the French, the bay horse broke its leg stepping in a burrow. He shot the animal and left it in a grove of shimmering mountain laurel and went ahead on foot, along a trail that should bring him to the junction of the two rivers—the Monongahela flowing up from the south, the Allegheny rushing down from the north—

If his compass and maps were correct.

But it had to be May already. The breathtaking beauty of the mountains and the intervening green valleys no longer exhilarated him. The clock in his mind beat louder—

George Clark had said he would depart from the

forks in mid-April or early May.

He was proud of having come this far alone. Proud of surviving on sheer persistence, with not one drink of liquor since he'd left the tidewater. Those times when he'd sickened and lay shivering in the night woods astir with unfamiliar, unseen creatures, he'd wanted a taste of alcohol so badly his throat burned.

But he had gotten through without it. He'd summoned up resources in himself long unused. There was deep satisfaction in finding them still present, ready to lend him the stamina and stubbornness he needed for the trek.

Yet even that pride was fading as he plodded on foot, fearing—knowing—he'd be too late.

The weather changed from spring sunshine to cool, windy gray as he followed gullies where black coal-veins showed along the eroded walls. He slept less and less every night, tossing by the small fire he always built with his chip of flint and his little steel bar and the supply of tinder shavings kept carefully dry in his haversack along with his powder and ball. Dozing, knowing he must rest but wishing he didn't need to, he'd hear a howling off in the trees, and occasionally see a glittering animal eye reflect the firelight. The wolves smelled him. They came to prowl close by. But the blaze kept them at a distance.

As he came out of the woods one gray morning, a farmer's wife guiding a plow on a poor, cleared patch of land reached for her musket lying a few feet away. She watched him warily as he approached.

He touched the floppy brim of his old loaf-crowned hat—a gift from a family for whom he'd chopped some wood in return for dinner at the start of his trail in Maryland. He tried to smile in a cordial way:

"Morning, ma'am. My name is Fletcher. I'm headed for the fort at the forks. Can you tell me how far that is?"

The lean, weary-looking woman, thirty or so but already minus most of her teeth, leaned on the plow handles while the dray horse clopped a hoof impatiently. He saw one of the woman's palms, ugly and moist with old and new blisters.

"At least thirty miles, give or take a few," she said. "Where you from?"

"Virginia."

"You bound to the forks alone?"

"That's right. I'd hoped to arrive by the first of May."

"You're two weeks late."

He touched his hat brim again. "Then I'd best not delay. Thank you—"

"You—"

He turned around at the sound of her voice.

"—you wouldn't want to stay a while? I could use help with the planting."

"I'm sorry. I can't."

"All right."

He started on along the fresh-turned furrows, hearing a faint rumble in the gray sky to the west. The woman wiped her forehead with her forearm, pointed toward the ramshackle cabin surrounded by stumps at the edge of the field:

"There's a spring out behind if you want to fill that canteen."

"Thanks very much, I will."

He said it quickly, his tone matching the impatience he felt. The clock in his head beat its warning. *He'll be gone—*

HE'LL BE GONE

As he bent to hold the mouth of his canteen under the stream spilling from the rock ledge behind the cabin, he wished suddenly that the earth could pour forth more than water. The old craving hit him, thickening his tongue.

415

Near the spring, an upright slab of wood bore a man's name carved out with the point of a knife. Evidently the father of the two small girls he heard chattering and giggling in the cabin. Perhaps he should stop; help the woman in return for a few meals and a few nights of rest. Then turn around and go back east. He felt too incredibly tired to travel one more mile if, at the end, he failed to find his friend—

Now listen, he reprimanded himself. *You'll find him. You'll find him if you have to go all the way to the shore of the Kentucky country alone—*

But he had scant confidence.

His throat burned as he capped the canteen, walked around the cabin, waved to the woman at the slow-moving plow and set off through the forest while the May sky rumbled.

ii

Judson assumed that what had spared his life was the clean passage of Lottie Shaw's pistol ball in and out through the flesh of his left side. That and the cowardice of Carter, the man who was living off her diminished earning power following their flight from Richmond.

He had no way of knowing whether Carter had deterred Lottie from putting another ball into him and seeing him surely dead. In fact he had no recollection of anything in the hours immediately after the shooting.

Lottie and Carter had evidently left him where they planned: in the damp autumn leaves along Plum Creek. Somehow he'd stumbled up and away from there, guided by an instinctive sense of direction, until he reached the road that wound to the Rappahannock near Sermon Hill. He learned later that a field black spied him staggering along the road and summoned help.

He was borne to Sermon Hill in a wagon. There, according to Donald's subsequent report, he was looked at by Angus Fletcher.

The old man recognized that his son might be bleeding to death. He sent for a physician—and told Donald that Judson would be permitted to remain at the plantation until he recovered or died.

But Angus insisted Judson be put in one of the slave cabins. His principles would only bend so far.

iii

Judson did remember waking in the cabin, thrashing and yelling and feeling thick bandages wrapping his chest under an itchy nightshirt.

Flushed of face, Donald perched on a stool beside Judson's pallet. Gently, he tried to push his brother down:

"You'll kill yourself for certain if you flop around that way."

"I promised to meet George Clark in Williamsburg!" were Judson's first words.

"You *what?*"

Breathing hard, Judson explained in labored sentences. At the end Donald shook his head:

"You've been lying here the best part of two weeks. There is no way you can make that rendezvous."

"Send a message, then. You've got to!"

Donald agreed, and arranged it. But the black messenger returned in three days with the news that George Clark had already departed.

"Then—" Speech and even breathing still cost Judson considerable pain. "As soon as I'm up—a week or so—I'll follow him—"

Donald rubbed his gouty leg, shook his head a second time:

"It'll be more like a month before you're well enough to hobble. The wound was clean but quite deep." An ironic smile touched Donald's lips. "Father said you were to be given the best possible care. Do you know he

417

summoned a second doctor all the way from Richmond because he felt the local sawbones didn't know enough? I've never seen him so shamefaced as when he told me he'd done it."

Judson was too astonished to say anything immediately. He gazed at the cabin's dirt floor, listened to the voices of blacks moving in the street outside, experienced alternate pangs of bitter mirth and exultation. Finally, he spoke:

"I can't conceive that I'd even be allowed at Sermon Hill. I'm surprised Father didn't order me floated in the river immediately, to save possible funeral expenses."

"Stop that," Donald said, angered. "He's a narrow-minded, vile-tempered old devil, and no one knows it better than I. But he's not a monster, just a man. And you *are* his son. So let's have no more vituperation. There's been enough hate on both sides too damned long."

Judson lay back, hurting. "Yes," he murmured. "Yes, I guess that's right—"

A moment later, he re-opened his eyes:

"When I am able to leave, I still intend to follow George."

"By yourself? That's insanity."

"Maybe, but I'm going. I'll settle with that Shaw bitch first, though."

Donald waved. "You'll be spared. She's disappeared, along with the flash gentleman who arrived with her while you were in Williamsburg. They either left you for dead or feared to finish what they'd started because they could guess the consequences. Father sent drivers searching for them. With pistols and muskets."

"*Nigra* drivers?"

"Three of his most trusted. He armed them personally."

"You can't be serious."

"I am."

"I'll be goddamned."

"Why should you be so surprised? Blood outlasts everything. Overcomes everything—including hatred. Blood and time are the world's two great healers."

Judson repeated it, bemused: "Blood—" He shook his head slowly. "Odd you should light on that word."

"It's common enough."

"But the old man thinks I've a bad strain running in me. Devil's blood, he calls it."

"He has the same kind." Again that ironic smile. "Don't tell me you've never noticed. Of course, I don't doubt he softened somewhat because you were shot. That made you vulnerable, you see. It's easier to forgive a wounded creature than one who's raring up to snap at you. I wouldn't question it too much, I'd just be thankful. The hate's ruined both of you for years."

Sleepy, Judson sighed. "I feel too stinking rotten to hate anyone but myself. Yes, I—I'm grateful he relented. Would you tell him?"

"Of course. I doubt he'll have any reaction."

"I'm not looking for a reaction, just tell him."

"I will."

"Also tell him I'm going to follow George. It's the only way I can turn my life around. Even if I don't catch him, or—if something should happen to me on the way, I have to start over. Do you understand?"

Donald answered quietly, "I do. And that's a great virtue of this country. One of the things which makes a disheartening, tiresome war worth fighting."

"What are you talking about?"

"We've much to win besides all those lofty principles declared in Philadelphia, Judson. I've heard Tom Jefferson speak of it time and again—the country in the west. The chance it offers for people to begin again. Lord—" A brief sigh. "I sometimes wish I could go."

His eyes sought his younger brother's. "But I hope

you haven't conceived this venture only to prove something to Father."

"No. As I told George, I tangled my affairs so badly in this part of the world, I have to leave or I'll die here."

Donald tried to joke, pointing at Judson's left side: "I agree—it damned near happened, didn't it?"

iv

On a bright morning in late March, Donald walked down to the river road with his younger brother.

Though still pale, Judson looked fit. He carried a haversack and the Kentucky rifle Donald had sent to Richmond to procure. Misty March afternoons when he could manage to keep his powder dry, he'd practiced loading and firing in a remote field. His target was a chunk of log set on top of a tree stump. Before too many days had gone by, he could hit the section of log, six inches high and four across, nearly every time.

Donald looked ponderously heavy and tired as he leaned on his cane at the point where the main road intersected the one leading from the great house. At sunrise, Judson had packed his haversack, tucked away the pocket money Donald had loaned him, dressed for his departure and left the cabin. Not once during his recuperation had he entered the main building at Sermon Hill, nor seen his father, except to catch glimpses of him riding the fields.

"I still think you are absolutely lunatic," Donald said. "But I also have come to the conclusion that with a spot of luck, you might find what you're seeking."

"I don't know what that is, Donald."

"Yes, but when you find it, perhaps you'll recognize it."

"You're more confident than I am."

"Brotherly intuition," Donald smiled. "You're not the same person I used to know—"

"Of necessity," Judson said. "I guess we drive out our

420

demons the best way we can, just to survive. I don't really know where I'm going, but I know I can't stay here. That's a splendid declaration of purpose, isn't it?"

And he gave Donald a wry smile that hid a very real ache. The melancholy had overwhelmed him without warning on the slow walk down to the river.

"It's an honest one," Donald said. "By the way—I'll take care of your request that Peggy McLean be told."

Judson's head lifted sharply. "Is she back home?"

"Why, yes. In all the bustle of perparation these past couple of days, I must have forgotten to mention it. I ran into Williams. He told me. He said she returned about a week ago. She's been staying inside because her health is poor again, evidently."

Concern stabbed Judson. "What's wrong?"

"Williams professes not to know. It's very odd—you realize she's been away since last fall—? Williams said she let slip a remark about sailing home on a coasting vessel."

"A *coasting* vessel? Why in God's name would she risk a sea trip, north or south, when the British are everywhere?"

"So are the American privateersmen. But I agree, in wartime, a pleasure cruise anywhere is deuced peculiar—and a holiday the length of hers downright astonishing. Where could she go? Neither Philadelphia nor New York in the north, only Boston. Possibly Charleston or Savannah south of here—"

"I'm sure Peggy has no relatives in Charleston or Savannah," Judson said, trying to puzzle it out. "It seems to me she told me years ago that her mother had kin somewhere up in New England. Maybe my memory's faulty, though—"

"The sad truth is, the uprising is probably still affecting her. To the degree that wild jaunts offer the only release she can find. Williams said nothing about—" Donald sought the term he wanted. "—mental difficulties. But he's intensely loyal, so he wouldn't."

I doubt the cause is solely the uprising, Judson thought somberly. *I expect it's also a certain event that happened afterward—*

For a moment he entertained the notion of stopping at McLean's on his way out of Caroline County. But he rejected the idea. Nothing he could do now would ever make amends for the despicable act committed in the summerhouse.

His thoughts lingered a moment on an image of Peggy's face. Not without effort, he blanked the image from his mind as part of the past he had to shut out forever.

"Well—" He couldn't bear to protract the parting much longer. "—if you do have the opportunity, tell her where I've gone, and why."

"Be assured I'll do so. I know it wlll be months if not a year or more before we hear from you—"

"I promise I'll write when I can."

"Yes, but with the tribes rising, I doubt the post operates on any sort of regular schedule between here and Kentucky!"

And not at all from the British-controlled territory beyond, Judson added silently.

"I don't want to sermonize, Judson, but I do believe you've made the proper choice. I'm thankful that despite all the turmoil in the west, there's open land to which a man can go if need be—"

Tears glistened in the corners of his eyes. He wiped them away quickly. "God keep you, brother."

"And you," Judson answered, starting up the road.

"Oh, wait—damme! I'm forgetting everything—!"

Judson wheeled around, startled to see his brother pull a small black-bound book from his coat pocket.

"I saw Father while you were putting your things together. This is a present—"

Judson's jaw dropped. "Not for me—?"

"Don't be too overwhelmed until you examine it. It's what you'd expect of him, I think."

"I didn't expect anything."

"No, I mean the nature of the gift." Donald's thumb bent around to the gold stamping on the binding. Judson smiled that old, brilliant smile that could light his face:

"A New Testament. I see what you meant."

"Go on, open the flyleaf."

Judson took the book. Something caught in his throat when he saw the familiar handwriting, a little shakier with age than he remembered, but still recognizably his father's. The inscription read:

> *To my son Judson.*
> *Angus Fletcher*
> *March 29, 1778*

Judson's smile faded. His face grew almost stark as he stared at the words. Donald chuckled with false heartiness:

"Of course Father thinks you're even madder than I do. Yet all the while he's inveighing against your waywardness, I get the feeling that in some queer, perverse way he approves of what you've chosen to do."

Judson's eyes widened in fury. "I told you I chose it for myself, not to please him."

"Somehow I believe he appreciates that. I think it's the very reason he does approve. Maybe he recognizes that you've become a man."

"I wasn't aware I was anything else."

"Oh yes," Donald said quietly. "Until a few months ago, you didn't deserve the name. Ah—!" A hand was quickly raised. "None of your temper, now. It's the truth. Most of us come to it in our own time and in our own way, and some never come to it at all. But you have. And while you didn't exactly turn out as Father wished—" A shrug. "Well, life is endless compromise. You wanted Peggy and couldn't have her.

I loved my wife and lost her. Father wanted a dutiful pair of boys, appropriately Tory in sentiment—he still abominates the rebellion, you realize—and instead, he got one gouty old lump who barely manages to help him run the place and is on the wrong side politically to boot. He also got an atheistic rogue who has decided, God save us, to be one of those rude frontiersmen—"

Donald smiled. "Every father desires a lot from a son, I suppose. If he can't have everything, he settles for what good things do come about."

"I don't think Father really cares about m—"

"Dammit, now, no more! He does! He told me he is convinced you'll probably die of the ague after your first week of sleeping in the woods. But I swear he sounded just a mite proud when he remarked on it."

Judson started to speak, found he couldn't. He tightened his hand around the testament, tucked it carefully down into the haversack. Something in him fought to bring forth words; the hardest words, perhaps, that he'd ever uttered—

Something else resisted. For a moment his fine features showed the tormenting struggle.

Then, almost blurting it:

"Tell him I thank him very much for the gift."

"Certainly."

"And—"

My God, there were tears in his eyes!

"—and tell him I said—"

The tide burst through—older than all the terrible resentments built between them, timeless in its force and power:

"Tell him I said I love him."

"That, he will welcome most of all."

Judson grinned. "But he won't believe it, the old bastard."

They laughed together, clasped hands, and Judson turned west in the morning sunshine.

Late in the afternoon of the day he met the woman plowing in the field, Judson felt the first drops of rain. Before long, with thunder rumbling intermittently, the drizzle changed to a downpour. He was quickly soaked to the skin.

The woods grew darker, the faint trail increasingly difficult to follow. Squinting through the rain, he saw the way ahead blocked by an immense, lightning-felled tree.

He decided to bear to the left, go around. He was thankful for the deerhide trousers; brambles grew among the ferns.

The forest smelled of rich earth that steamed as the rain slacked off. But for several minutes, the fall had been torrential. Footing was hazardous.

He reached the rim of a gully perhaps ten feet deep. He started to work his way along it, keeping an eye on the position of the fallen tree on his right. When he was well past it, he'd cut back to the trail and—

Weakened by the rain, the gully's edge gave way under his left boot.

Judson flailed, toppling over with a yell that went echoing through the dense trees.

He struck the gully bottom, left leg bent back under his right knee. At the moment of impact, the leg was lanced with an excruciating pain.

He lay gasping for a minute or so. He searched the crumbled side of the gully until he located his rifle and haversack, both dropped during the fall. He braced his hands in the mud beneath him, straightened his left leg—

The fierce pain exploded again.

Damn! He'd twisted something, badly.

He floundered onto his chest, tried to push up that way. But the moment he gained his feet, he grimaced

425

and clenched his teeth. He'd never get a quarter of a mile on that leg. Not till he rested it. Overnight, at least.

He attempted a few abortive steps, only to give up in exquisite agony. He was conscious of the clock ticking in his mind, every wasted moment spelling ever more certain failure to find George Clark at Pittsburgh. Christ, he'd *crawl* on—!

But good sense prevailed. The scant amount of time he'd gain if he kept going would be better spent letting the injury repair itself a little. Better to make his camp and start at daylight. By then, he might be able to move faster.

Trying to control his anger over the sorry turn of affairs, he clawed his way up the mud and rock of the gully side, retrieving his rifle and tossing it up to the rim, then the haversack. After what seemed an endless climb, he reached the top. He pulled himself over, resting his cheek on a fern while he gulped air. Thunder rocked the forest. Rain began to patter the back of his neck.

No damn possibility of finding dry wood now, he thought. The best he could do was drag himself to the nearest large tree—and hope that the lightning he saw flickering in the west would not strike the particular tree he selected. Actually, he couldn't very well avoid trees, they grew so closely here. One was no more or less dangerous than another.

Lugging rifle and haversack, he reached the big maple he'd chosen, settled himself so his spine rested against the trunk. The new leaves overhead would protect him from all but the heaviest rain.

The injured leg throbbed. What a blasted, damned piece of bad luck! He was so *close!* Less than thirty miles to the forks—

Still, there was nothing to be done except rest and wait for morning. He let his mind drift, trying to free it of frustration and fury. The patter of the rain and the murmur of the receding thunder had a soporific effect.

His eyelids grew heavy. Leaning the back of his head against the maple bark, he yawned—

And popped his eyes open, disoriented, alarmed—

Blind—

No, no—he'd only slept. Till dark.

All around him, the woods were still. The silence was accentuated by the occasional, barely audible scurry of some nocturnal animal, or the drip of water from a branch. The air was cool, moist. He rubbed a hand across his mouth, reached down to the aching leg, squeezed it and winced.

Thirsty, he groped for his canteen. He had it tilted, ready to take a swallow, when he heard the sound—

A yipping bark that slid higher, into a howl.

Wolves. Somewhere out in the darkness.

He understood instantly how vulnerable he was. The howl multiplied, two, three, perhaps four predators blending into a weird chorus that set his teeth chattering. He couldn't run away from them. He had to stay here and defend himself here—

At least he had the rifle, and the hunting knife in his boot.

Thunder again, booming. He fumbled for the haversack, face and chest covered with a sudden sweat. Laboriously, he loaded the rifle, readied it in his lap while the howling grew louder.

As a new thunderclap died away, he heard another sound. The drip from the trees was quickening. The rain was starting again. Heavy enough to reach his protected position and soak him—

A streak of lightning zigzagged through the sky, showing him three black-nosed snouts not four yards from where he lay. Fangs shone white and animal eyes glowed until the lightning flickered out.

He swallowed, heard a wolf's guttural snarling; heard clawed feet moving across the wet earth—

He flung the rifle to his shoulder, aimed it blind in the

dark, triggered it—

The damp powder in the pan didn't ignite.

Swearing, he fought to his feet. He almost yelled aloud at the agony in his leg. But he had to stand up. They were coming. Three at least. The Lord alone knew how many more might be gathering further out in the impenetrable black of the woods.

He hunched his right shoulder, snaked his hunting knife out of his boot sheath, closed his teeth on the blade's dull edge and gripped the rifle muzzle with both hands. He concentrated all his attention on the sounds of the wolves closing, cruelly aware of the one central fact of his situation:

He would kill them, or he would be killed by them and never reach the forks of the Ohio.

The rain beat down harder, making detection of noises more difficult.

Well, he thought, *if this is the end of it, at least I needn't be ashamed of how it happened.*

He tried to buoy his confidence with a silent assertion that he would not *permit* himself to be killed.

Well and good. That didn't alter reality. He could very well die in the next few minutes even if he made a thousand resolves. The most disheartening part was realizing that if he did perish, George Clark would never know how he'd tried to catch up to him and honor his pledge to serve—

Strangely, though, when he accepted the possibility of dying, a deadly sort of calm swept over him. It helped him take a firmer grip on the rifle muzzle, and almost completely forget the terrible pain in his leg.

A snarling, clawing thing of fur and fangs hurled against him. Judson wrenched his head aside. The twisted leg gave way.

He lurched against the tree, slid, landed on his side, gashed the corner of his mouth on the knife clenched in his teeth. Fangs tore through his deerhide trousers. He brought the rifle whipping over and down. The wolf's jaws loosened as bone cracked.

Judson kicked at the flopping, clawing animal. Beat at it with the rifle stock, smashing, *smashing*——

The wolf let out a weak yelp and fell away from him—

Just as the other two converged, snapping, slavering—

He clubbed at them, kicked them while the rain fell steadily. He switched his rifle to his left hand, took the knife out of his mouth with his right, stabbing and clubbing simultaneously, hardly a man any longer; he was an animal almost as savage as his attackers.

His knife opened the throat of one of the wolves. The other clamped its jaws on his left arm, shredding flesh, starting blood running.

Crazed with pain, Judson dropped the rifle from his left hand, lashed his right hand over and buried the knife in the wolf's belly. In its death-throes, the animal bit him to the bone.

Judson screamed, jerked back against the tree, knocking his head hard. The gut-stabbed wolf twitched at his feet and lay still.

He panted, tried to close his left hand into a fist, could not. He felt warm blood trickling down over his knuckles.

But they were dead. All three, dead. He was safe from—

Lightning lit the forest. He let out a single short sob of despair.

The glow in the heavens showed him two more, jaws dripping. Thunder pealed as they crouched to spring.

CHAPTER II

The Guns of Summer

TO PHILIP THERE was a peculiar and frightening familiarity about this moment. The heat reminded him of Breed's Hill. So did the dull glare of bayonets; the scarlet coats—

The British foot soldiers were advancing from the east, through steam rising after the most recent downpour. The sunlit vapor fumed up between the trees like some outpouring of infernal ovens, lending a spectral quality to the figures of the enemy.

He was awash with sweat. It ran down to the tip of his nose, rivered over his chest and along his legs, soaking clothing already wet from the June rain. He guessed their position to be somewhere to the west of the little Jersey hamlet of Monmouth Court House. While the ghost-soldiers marched toward them through the mist, the Americans waited in a north-south line on the east side of McGellaird's Brook, a ravine whose bottom resembled a swamp more than a creek.

The army of thirteen thousand had marched north from Valley Forge a week ago. Philip guessed that perhaps half that number of men were strung out in advanced positions to which they'd moved starting around seven that morning. Thus far, Philip's contingent had met only light resistance.

The temperature in the woods had to be close to a

hundred. Up and down the line men lay fallen, fainted away. A few others struggled to revive them, without much luck.

Philip's musket felt slippery in his hands as he squinted through the steaming air. Each breath he took was labored. He heard the British infantry drummers hammering the cadence somewhere behind the dim figures advancing in the steam between the thickly clustered trees.

Sword pulled and ready, General Anthony Wayne slipped along the rear of the American line. His sweat-sheened face showed an emotion that might have been frustration—or rage. From the brush where he crouched near Breen and Royal Rothman, Philip heard Wayne repeat the same command over and over:

"Hold fire. Hold fire until your officer signals."

The handsome, flamboyant young general—as dirty, stinking, sand-covered and fly-bitten as the rest of them today—passed within a yard of Philip. Wayne broke step, stopped a moment as recognition registered.

Philip was too weary to return Wayne's brief, comradely smile. But he did ask a question:

"Are we to hold, General? Our own drum signals don't make much sense."

Wayne's mouth wrenched. "As long as I have charge here, we'll not only hold, we'll attack. As for the signals—I'll be damned if any officer in this sector can make sense of 'em—or knows what our esteemed commander's up to. Order, counter-order, disorder—that seems to be the rule for the morning. Charlie Lee didn't want this action in the first place. So we'll just forget him, eh?"

Wayne smiled again, the kind of bravado grin that had given the young Pennsylvanian a reputation as a commander impatient with hesitation and virtually unconcerned about his personal safety. Philip watched the general move off through the sodden weeds, working his way south along the ragged line awaiting the red-coats.

They were much closer now. Philip could distinctly see facial features through the confused interplay of sunlight and steam. Far away, thunder rumbled. Another storm.

Or could it be cannon-fire?

In Breen's eyes—in Royal's—in the eyes of all the stubbled, sweating men watching the advancing enemy, Philip saw the same concern that kept a triphammer rhythm of fear going in his own chest.

The army had not formally engaged the British since leaving Valley Forge on the twenty-third of June.

And now the British had a new commander.

Unfortunately so did all the Americans holding advanced outposts in the field this morning. To a man, they distrusted the general who was supposed to be giving the orders. As Wayne had said, Charles Lee had argued against this pursuit. Despite all von Steuben's training, the Americans, Lee was convinced, were still no match for British regiments—

Very shortly they would resolve the issue. Resolve it in this patch of Jersey marshland where the tree trunks were surrounded by pools of water left from the huge storms that had alternated with intense heat and humidity for days on end. Philip watched the British closing in the ordered ranks he remembered so well from Breed's Hill—

Then suddenly, from behind the marching redcoats, he picked up a terrifying new sound.

"Oh Jesus," Breen exclaimed. "They're throwin' cavalry at us!"

Philip peered through the sweat blurring his eyes. The British infantrymen were flanking right and left. Into the openings burst the hard-riding vans of mounted units; men in green-faced blue coats and hussar busbies, their drawn sabers flashing—

"Queen's Rangers!" someone cried in fright.

The American officers up and down the line called the count for cocking and poising firelocks. Philip heard Walter Webb yell:

"Hold for the signal—!"

Looking inhumanly tall in their saddles, the Tory Queen's Rangers thundered between the trees, riding down on the Americans, sabers raised.

Philip watched one jouncing cavalryman's busby tilt askew so that it touched his right eyebrow.

Sixty yards away now.

Fifty—

Coming at the gallop, dozens of them, hundreds, a surging wave of blue coats and steel—

A man to Philip's left shrieked in panic, threw down his musket and began to run back toward the ravine. Webb shouted at him but let him go, whirling to concentrate on the cavalrymen. In the distance Philip thought he heard an American drum signal for a retreat.

Or was that thunder again?

Where was General Washington? Why had they been thrust forward like this under the over-all command of a man everyone considered a braggart, a fool, even a coward?

The Ranger horse came on.

Forty yards.

Thirty—

The great chargers rolled their eyes and bared their huge yellowed teeth against their bits. In patches of sunlight, the sabers glared like a spiked wall rolling forward—

Finally—much too late, Philip feared—he heard the command bawled from company to company:

"Fire!"

ii

A wild but all too brief elation had greeted the news

of the French alliance.

The agreement between the American commissioners in Paris and the government of King Louis XVI had actually been reached in early January. A treaty stipulated that France would come to the aid of the new country with men and materiel if and when war broke out between Britain and her traditional enemy.

Very few doubted that such a war was inevitable. According to the rumors reaching Valley Forge in the late spring, France actually seemed to be encouraging incidents that would provoke open conflict. A French armada commanded by Admiral Count d'Estaing had already sailed from Toulon with four thousand soldiers aboard. The soldiers were prepared to land on American soil if, by chance, their country and England were at war by the time the ships made a landfall.

Alarmed, the king's ministers in London had replaced the sluggish, luxury-loving Howe with a new commander in America, Sir Henry Clinton. Upon hearing the news of the French armada, Clinton promptly abandoned the prize of Philadelphia and began its evacuation in mid-June. Washington ordered the march from Valley Forge a few days later, moving the American army into New Jersey, an inferno of summer humidity and sandy roads and sudden storms.

Somewhere ahead of them Clinton zigzagged toward New York with his troops and his precious train of fifteen hundred wagons loaded with supplies and equipment. According to the scouts, Clinton was at present heading northeast, to reach the safety of New York via Sandy Hook. Only General Charles Lee and a few other senior officers were in favor of letting him go unmolested.

But thus far the pursuit had been a fiasco.

Washington pushed on without directly contacting the retreating enemy, listening meantime to the counsels of his various generals, and weighing each opinion. Everyone knew Anthony Wayne's terse advice:

"Fight, sir."

Von Steuben had theoretically brought the army to a new, higher pitch of readiness. Yet Washington had finally decided on a compromise. They would engage Clinton's rear guard only. If that action proved successful, the entire American force could sweep forward.

Regrettably, the general who demanded personal command of the exploratory action was thin, ugly, egotistical Charles Lee, nominally the highest-ranking officer after Washington.

Lee had seen service in Europe. He considered himself much more of a military expert than his superior. There was even talk that he had penned not-so-secret notes to the Congress denouncing Washington as "damnably deficient." Lee stubbornly maintained that the army to which he'd pledged his service could never win a major engagement against crack British and Hessian units.

Conscious of his rank and its perquisites, he still demanded command of the probing action aimed at Clinton's retreating troops. Washington reluctantly agreed—

And Lee began not a vigorous chase but a slow, aimless dallying. The men in the field this steaming twenty-eighth of June, 1778, were already aware that while Lee vacillated, Clinton had started his precious baggage train moving again. During the darkest hours of the preceding night, the quarry had begun to widen its margin of distance from the Americans.

Now, along an irregular front near tiny Monmouth Court House, the forward American units braced for what appeared to be a protective counter-stroke from Clinton's rear. And, as General Wayne had disgustedly noted, no clear-cut instructions had yet been issued by

General Lee.

"Order, counter-order, disorder." Every man, it seemed to Philip, was left to fight as circumstances dictated.

Or flee.

Or die.

iii

The first of the Tory Queen's Rangers had nearly reached the American line. Philip's musket bucked against his shoulder, cracking out flame and smoke.

His ball struck an officer's huge roan in the neck. The animal bellowed as it went down. A fountain of horse blood sopped the officer's breeches.

Three and four deep, the cavalry charged the line of erupting muskets. Some blue-coated men dropped. Others broke through to hack and chop with their sabers. The area immediately in front of Philip quickly became a melee of downed horses and mountless men, with other Rangers from the rear charging through as best they could.

And now came the frantic business of re-loading—

The officer Philip had unseated dashed to his right, grabbing at the reins of a horse whose rider had been shot. Philip saw this while he fumbled with powder and ball and tried to remember von Steuben's ten-count. All around him he heard screams, shots, curses, the sickening *chunk* of sabers striking exposed flesh.

The bloodstained officer gained the saddle, spurred the new mount forward. Sections of the American line began to break, the men scrambling toward the ravine. Philip and Royal Rothman held their places in a clump of shrubbery that afforded them only minimal cover. The smoke, the steam, the uproar of hoofbeats and shrieks and explosions constricted Philip's world to little more than a few yards of ground—

Just as Philip finished loading, the officer with the

blood-reddened trousers tensed in the saddle, ready to leap his new horse straight over their heads in pursuit of the men fleeing to the ravine.

Royal Rothman jumped to his feet, took two short steps to the side, rammed his bayonet into the horse's belly as it went over. A hoof struck Philip's ear, drawing blood—

The big cavalry horse wrenched in midair. The Ranger cried out, his blade arcing crazily as horse and man tumbled. Breen was back-stepping and re-loading at the same time. He slipped in a muddy place. The falling officer's saber, coming down at a chance angle, cut Breen's neck from the right side.

Breen's head seemed to loll toward his left shoulder. Blood cascaded over his chest. The officer's bayoneted horse was down, thrashing, loosing its stinking bowels in its death-agony.

The officer pulled himself from under the fallen horse, staggered to his feet. Philip aimed his musket at the blue-coated back, decided instantly not to waste a shot, leaped over the dying animal with bayonet thrust out ahead.

The officer heard him coming, spun. A bar of steaming June sun lit young, frightened blue eyes. The saber flashed up defensively. Philip dodged under, stabbed his bayonet home and yanked it out.

The Queen's Ranger spilled forward into the mud. American muskets were crackling and flaming again.

"Have at 'em with bayonets!"

Off to his right Philip recognized Wayne's voice, very nearly a maniacal shriek. A riderless British horse went by, almost knocking Royal over. The horse tried to check at the edge of the ravine. Philip watched it tumble over—just as he heard other hoofbeats behind him—

More of the Rangers on the attack. He shot shoulder to shoulder with Royal. Their two balls killed one cavalryman, wounded a second. They jumped apart to let the horses race past. The dead Ranger hung head down, his boot caught in his stirrup.

Again Wayne ordered the bayonet charge. This time sections of the American line began to move.

Philip and Royal bent low, stumbling toward the trees. Philip gulped air. God, he was dizzy. The heat was enough to make anyone pass out—

Quickly he glanced up and down the line. What he saw restored his spirits and re-sharpened his senses. The American musket-fire had blunted, then broken the Ranger charge. A few last horsemen were wheeling to head back the way they'd come, retreating wraiths in the forest steam.

A ball whizzed past Philip's head. He ducked automatically, realized that the infantrymen who had stopped to permit the Ranger companies to charge through had now started a defensive fire.

But the Rangers—superb soldiers—had been *beaten!*

Philip and Royal converged on a kneeling infantryman who desperately tried to decide which of them to shoot. His face plastered with sweat and sand, Royal took advantage of the hesitation and dispatched the luckless redcoat with one stroke of the bayonet.

When the man fell, Philip glanced at his friend. There was something strange and terrible and old in Royal's eyes. As he smiled, the sand cracked from his cheeks and dribbled onto his filthy shirt. His teeth had the white look of a skull's.

Ahead, they heard Wayne's bellow. Out in front of all the rest, he was leading the bayonet attack. Philip and Royal staggered toward the voice, hunting for redcoats.

But in the steamy, uncertain light they were hard to spot. And now they too were pulling back.

Philip stumbled and sprawled in a pool of water. By the time Royal had helped him to his feet, they both heard a new, readily identifiable sound in the woods:

American drummers beating a familiar cadence.

Anthony Wayne came storming back toward them, shaking a bloodied spontoon:

"Form up in column of fours! *Column of fours!*"

"General, why are they beating retreat?" Philip shouted. "We've got 'em running—"

Wayne stopped long enough to mop his forehead with his sleeve. He was shaking:

"You go tell that to General Lee—you can probably find him having breakfast behind the lines! It appears we nipped Clinton's tail a little too smartly. A scout came through before we started the charge. He said Clinton's turning the main body of the army back against us. He's afraid of losing his wagons. We're *that close*—"

Wayne's index finger and thumb illustrated. His face was still white with fury.

"—consequently, Charlie Lee's called a retreat!"

He stalked on toward the ravine, screaming:

"Column of fours, goddamn you! *Retreat formation!*"

Wearily, Philip and Royal began to trot after the retreating general.

Philip's temples hurt. So did his chest. Sand and tiny insects tormented his exposed skin. He cursed long and loud, finally exclaimed:

"That damn yellow Lee still thinks we can't hold against the British!"

Astonished, he heard Royal echo his anger with one foul word after another. The boy, it seemed, was no longer a boy—

They loped back past the horse Royal had killed, to rally around two drummers signaling from the other side of McGellaird's Brook.

iv

They marched while the sun blistered them. They marched on a road half mud, half sand, in a direction

439

Philip presumed to be westward. Back toward English-town; back toward the main body of the army.

They mached along in a column of fours, cursing but keeping step. Every man in the ranks knew how close they'd come to blunting the British counter-thrust and breaking through.

It seemed to Philip that the horror of Breed's Hill had been repeated with an eerie, subtle variation. This time the American bayonets could have won the day. At least in his limited sector—

Then, once again, the retreat signal. Not to keep them from defeat, but to prevent a victory. *Damn!*

They tramped along the sandy, hell-hot road, complaining bitterly.

The pullback had been orderly, and without casualties. Von Steuben had taught them that. He had also taught them a great deal they were unable to use, Philip thought in disgust.

Next to him, Royal said, "Do you suppose anyone will go back for Breen's body?"

Philip grimaced. "How can they? Looks like we're going to be driven back miles from where we started."

"Will Captain Webb write Breen's family?"

Philip shrugged. "Breen never told us his real name. It would take a visit to Andover to find out who he really was."

"For all his coarseness, he wasn't a bad sort."

"No—" Philip ached at the memory of the older man dying from the chance cut of the saber. "No, he really wasn't, he—"

"Look sharp!" Royal exclaimed. "Horsemen coming!"

A man behind suddenly groaned and pitched sideways, overcome by the heat. Royal jumped to grab him and support him as Philip caught a clatter of hoofs in the shimmering air down the road to the west.

At the head of their company, Captain Webb called

for a left-face to the roadside. With fair precision the men executed the movement as von Steuben had taught them, holding their lines in the damp weeds at the shoulder. Royal lowered the fainted man to the ground and fanned him with both hands.

"Bet we got to fight here," someone said. "Bet the fucking British swungaround the flank and cut off the road—"

For a moment there was more cursing, and consternation until Captain Webb cried:

"Shut up and listen! Hear that cheering? That's not for the enemy—"

Men craned insect-bitten necks, jostling to see. And suddenly, out of the west, Philip heard it: a massed roar of voices.

The outcry grew louder and louder under the sweltering sky. A wave of sound, it rolled toward them along with a cloud of boiling dust in the center of the road.

A rider emerged from the leading edge of the cloud. Hatless, wearing blue and buff, he galloped his huge white horse in the direction opposite that of the retreat. *Toward* Monmouth Court House—

Behind Washington an entourage of officers rode full speed. The cheering was unbelievably loud.

The commander-in-chief glanced neither right nor left to acknowledge the bellow that rolled across the countryside as he passed. He paid no attention to the muskets thrust up in the air in rhythm with the huzzahs. Philip had only a momentary glimpse of the tall general's face before he disappeared beyond the dust streaming out behind the horses. But that glimpse was enough to give Philip pause.

Washington's profile had looked savagely scarlet. If not with sunburn, then with anger.

Almost stupefied, Royal and Philip gaped at one another. They heard yet another new sound, this time from the east. A different pattern of flams and ruffs—

Tootling fifes joined the drums. And from man to bedraggled man, cries ran along the roadside:

"Counter-march!"

"They say he caught Charlie Lee and blistered him with curses!"

"Called him a damned poltroon—a coward—"

"Lee's relieved. Washington's in personal command—"

"No more retreat!"

"All right, form up!" Captain Webb shouted, vainly trying to shove his men back onto the road as the uproar all but drowned him out:

"We're going back!"

"We're going back!"

"WE'RE GOING BACK!"

v

Mid-afternoon.

They were in an orchard, behind a hedge that rimmed its eastern perimeter. As far as Philip could tell, they were holding the orchard somewhere near the center of the American lines. They were south of the Englishtown road, still west of Monmouth Court House—and firing through the shrubbery as the British grenadiers advanced in those splendid, never-wavering formations.

Philip's hands were beginning to blister from the combined heat of the weather and the musket-metal. Royal was still alongside. Wayne was in over-all command of the orchard position; Philip could see him peering through the barely breathable powder-smoke that drifted from muskets and the cannon booming on their flanks. The entire afternoon had been mind-numbing. Endless shifts of position; charge and counter-charge.

Philip wearily pointed the musket through the hedge and picked off a fur-capped, perspiring grenadier coming toward him in rote step. The grenadier toppled forward, his bayonet stabbing into the ground. The soldier knew he was dying, but he clung to the butt of the Brown Bess to keep himself from falling, as if that in itself could undo the effect of Philip's shot.

Slowly, the grenadier's slippery hands gave out. He slumped to his knees, fingers sliding inexorably down the muzzle. Philip blinked twice. When his vision cleared, the grenadier had let go of his musket and lay on his back, unmoving. The upside-down weapon stood beside him in the earth like some obscene parody of a churchyard marker. Other grenadiers with bayonets at the ready marched past the corpse, never glancing down.

Philip wondered how much longer he could survive without water. Just to his rear, an older man flopped in the grass, felled not by a wound but by prostration that purpled his cheeks. The man's tongue protruded like a frog's as he compressed his hands against his belly and made retching sounds—

Philip had no energy for thinking of the danger of their situation. No energy to speculate about strategies, or the over-all success or failure of the engagement of the entire American army. Clinton had struck swiftly, throwing unit after unit against them across a broad front. But for Philip, the world had again constricted to a small patch of ground where he crouched behind the hedge, concentrating on the steps of von Steuben's ten-count drill.

Philip's flayed hands almost worked independently of his exhausted mind. He loaded, fired, dodged instinctively whenever he heard a ball hiss through the leaves—

The American fire broke the grenadier charge thirty yards from the hedge. In the smoke, Philip saw redcoat after redcoat falling. Suddenly someone stumbled against his legs.

Philip wrenched his head up. Saw Webb, a sooty
443

ghoul who grinned and pointed a bleeding hand through a break in the foliage:

"We've hit Colonel Monckton, their commander."

Up and down the line, men picked it up:

"Monckton's killed—someone shot Monckton!"

As the grenadiers began to pull back, re-form for another charge, Webb's hand closed hard on Philip's shoulder.

"He's one of their kingbirds. Can you two bring him back to our colors?"

Gulping for air, Philip said, "Can try. Come on, Royal. Leave the musket. Stay low—"

The two of them crawled forward on their bellies, out past the hedge into tall grass. Occasional musket fire still crackled over their heads. All at once, Philip stopped.

He burrowed his elbows into the soft ground. His ears rang. He let his head hang like an exhausted dog's. Waves of nausea left him helpless.

"Royal, I can't," he gasped. "The damned heat—"

"It's only a little further," Royal panted, grabbing the back of Philip's hunting shirt and giving him a tug. "They want Monckton's body at the colors. You can make it—"

The perimeter of the orchard was a miasma of smoke and dimly seen sky. He was tired beyond the limits of comprehension. He rolled his head sideways, saw Royal watching him with almost wild-eyed intensity. The boy had lost his little black wool cap during the day, Philip realized.

"Come *on!*" Royal said.

Philip dug his elbows into the grass, pulled his numbed body forward a few inches. And a few more—

Royal Rothman speared out one hand, closed it clawlike on the powder-blacked uniform of the grenadier commander who lay with eyes and mouth open. Out of sight in the tall grass, the British drummers changed cadence to start the next advance.

"Help me pull him!" Royal pleaded. "If you don't, the grenadiers will catch up to us——"

Philip's right arm felt dead. He forced it to move by will alone, reaching down across Colonel Monckton's nose and open mouth to dig his fingers into sweat-drenched wool. Then he began to crawl backwards, feeling as if he were dragging the weight of the world.

His head buzzed. Buzzed and rang. Distantly, as though in a windstorm, he heard Royal's voice, now louder, now fainter:

"A little more. Only a little more, Philip. *Don't let go of him——!*"

"*I can't stand to look at him that way!*" Philip screamed, shifting his hand to the dead officer's face. One by one he pushed down Monckton's eyelids.

Just after he touched the corpse, something started his hand shuddering; then his whole arm. It was all so damned senseless. The heat; the slaughter——

He just wanted to give up. Stop. Rest. Close his eyes——

"Keep pulling, Philip! The grenadiers have spotted us. But we're close. *Pull!*"

He tried. God, he tried. He had no strength left. His arm shook uncontrollably——

What sort of man had this Monckton been? Surely he'd loved someone. A wife. Children. Surely he believed he was just as right as those on Philip's side. It was a waste. A wretched, damnable *waste*——

All that kept him tugging the corpse was a memory of Anne and Abraham on which he forced himself to concentrate.

He knew there was a purpose to the struggle beyond the immediate one. He knew because Anne had revealed it to him, little by little, in their first months of courting.

He'd believed in it when he married her. Did he now——?

445

Yes, he supposed so. But he was spent; so spent, the nature of the purpose was beyond his power to recall. What he clung to—what kept him floundering and flopping on his knees and elbows to drag the body were two faces. All else was stripped away; dross.

A woman. A child—*that* was why he was here. Why he had to fire his musket. Obey orders. Stay alive, so he could return to—

"Up, Philip! Drag him through! Quickly—I can see grenadiers aiming at us—"

A foot from the hedge, Philip struggled with the incredibly heavy body. He seemed incapable of raising it properly. Warning shouts rose from the American side of the hedge. He wondered about the reason, the instant before musket fire exploded behind him.

Royal shouted and flattened out, letting their burden drop. Dazed, Philip was a fraction slow. On hands and knees, he presented a clear target. He seemed to see Royal's sweat-shiny face across some great abyss of smoke and noise. Royal's mouth opened to utter a cry of warning. Something buzzed near Philip's ear. Leaves rustled, a dream-like sound—

The buzz was a grenadier ball. Royal's yell dinned suddenly:

"For God's sake get down—"

Another musket-blast obliterated the rest. Philip felt something thump his right calf. There was searing pain.

A moment later his dazed mind finally recognized that something had pierced the top of his right boot. He flopped on his buttocks, propped up by one hand on Monckton's shoulders. Incredulous, he stared at the hole in the boot's thin, worn leather.

Something large and hurtful was lodged in the flesh inside that boot. All at once, another peculiar sensation made him grimace. His lower leg not only hurt like fury, it felt as if it had just been plunged into a pot of boiling honey—

Idiotic, he thought, blinking back a haze that wouldn't go away. It was in his mind. *Honey's never warm, never—*

He saw the redness pouring through the place where the ball had penetrated the leather. *My God, I'm hit*, he thought with a curious, light-headed detachment.

Royal shouted urgent warnings he couldn't understand. The drums of the advancing grenadiers hammered. Trying to focus his eyes on the glistening blood, he sagged over against Monckton's corpse.

Blearily, he came back to consciousness a few minutes later. Royal was slapping his cheek. His whole lower leg and foot burned fiercely. When he rolled his head sideways to squint down the side of his body, he saw his trousers soaked with blood where the fabric was stuffed into his boot-top.

"Get up, Philip. If you stay here you'll be caught or killed. We've got to get you to the surgeons."

"I—" Cracked lips formed thoughtless words. "I'm hit."

"I know you're hit! That's why we have to get out of here."

"Not sure—I can walk."

"Try."

"Tired. So damn tired, Royal—"

"Listen to the drums!"

"The grenadiers?"

"No, ours. We're pulling back."

"Don't think—don't think I—"

"You *have* to! I didn't drag you through the hedge to see you left for the enemy."

"Good of you," Philip mumbled, afraid he wasn't making much sense. "Good of you, Royal. But I'd rather rest. You go on—"

"You don't know what you're saying!" Royal panted, his face a barely recognizable blur. He pressed his hands against Philip's cheeks. "Listen to me! I'll help you walk."

"No, I—"

"Yes! You must walk! *Listen—!*" So desperate that he was close to tears, Royal wrenched Philip's head from side to side, trying to rouse him from his wound-induced lethargy. "Do you want to spend the rest of the war on one of their prison ships in New York harbor?"

"No."

"What kind of medical help do you think they'll give you? None! They won't see to your wound. They'll probably let the gangrene take over—rot your leg—do you want that?"

"No, but—"

"Then stop fighting me and *get up!*"

Savagely, Royal dug his arms beneath Philip's back. Philip saw Royal's musket lying on the ground. It seemed to bend and quiver like a snake even as he watched.

Royal almost dropped him. Philip thoughtlessly put weight on his right foot, cried out. But somehow, he got upright, Royal beside him.

Philip hooked his right arm around Royal's neck, bent his right leg at the knee. Something Royal had said drove him to the effort. *Gangrene—*

Mustn't think of that. Just hang onto Royal.

The younger man was panting now, his retrieved musket dragging from his right hand. They hobbled away from the hedge on Philip's one good leg and Royal's two, moving through the orchard.

After a few minutes, it was a little easier. Philip's head cleared slightly.

But why couldn't he feel anything in his right foot?

Sweat streamed down his neck. Mosquitoes and sand flies stung him. "Must be—hundred and ten—" he mumbled.

"At least. Come on, we're making it—"

448

The drumming pulsed in Philip's ears. He felt ashamed of his lack of strength. Biting his upper teeth into his lower lip, he stung himself out of the dulled weariness that made him want to lie down again. In the nightmare of smoke and noise, of thudding drums and steadily reddening afternoon light, they crossed the orchard, the last stragglers in a column retreating to the next holding position. The two kept up as best they could.

Soon Philip completely lost track of his surroundings. He heard a clatter of hoofs, a creak of wheels—then Royal's jubilant exclamation:

"Here's a medical wagon! We'll have you aboard in no time." Royal raised his voice: "Driver, hold up! Wounded man—"

Royal's supporting arm inadvertently relaxed. Philip sagged forward onto his knees, then slammed face first into the dust, never feeling the impact.

vi

He woke in the inferno of a medical tent, wishing he hadn't. It was like living Brandywine all over again, except that this time, the man writhing on the gory planks wasn't Lucas Cowper.

He tasted rum in his mouth. Bit the ball when he was ordered. Shifted and moaned softly as unseen pincers dug into the flesh of his calf just a few inches above his ankle.

Then he saw two spheres floating near; one huge, white and moist, the other smaller, red and wet—

"Got her out nice and clean."

The white sphere was the surgeon's perspiring face, the red one the flattened lead ball held in dirty pincers. The surgeon discarded the ball and the instrument, gripped Philip's shoulders.

"Hold steady, now. We're going to cauterize it with an iron."

Before Philip could move his lips, the heated metal touched his skin. He started to scream. From behind, a hand jammed his jaws together so he wouldn't swallow the ball held between his teeth.

A foul odor of burning flesh rose into his nostrils, starting uncontrollable gagging. At once, the ball was jerked from his teeth.

Rough hands seized the injured leg, held it. His calf and foot, numbed again by the searing iron, felt curiously thick. The surgeon's sticky face peered down. A lantern hanging above him lit droplets of sweat in his unpowdered hair.

"They're wrapping it with clean rags, and we've a crutch for you," he said. "One of your messmates is outside. He'll help you walk. We can't let you lie in here, we need the room for more serious cases. You understand—"

The man's exhausted voice indicated that he didn't care whether Philip did or not.

The surgeon barked over his shoulder, "Let's have his crutch! And one of the chits, so he can draw all the rum he needs to kill the pain."

"Is—will I walk all right?" Philip gasped out.

The surgeon wiped his hands on a filthy scarlet apron. "You saw the ball. It came out clean. I can't say whether or not there's muscle damage."

And that was the end of his attention, because another patient on the next table was shrieking as the bone-saw rasped back and forth. Philip's doctor ran to answer a cry for assistance.

Like some animal being shunted out of a pen, Philip was propped up on one foot, dizzy as he was. The crutch-pad was jammed under his right armpit. Then he was helped to the tent entrance, where Royal waited anxiously, his face indistinct in the glow of the lanterns flaring in the twilight.

Philip breathed hard. Moving was difficult. But he

wasn't excessively uncomfortable. The rum, the cauterizing iron and the rag bandages had reduced his lower leg and foot to little more than a lump of meat, devoid of feeling.

"Come on," Royal said, maneuvering Philip's left arm over his back again. "I think I can locate our unit. Are—are you all right?"

"Little—out of my head," Philip answered truthfully. Something fluttered from his hand. "Royal—that paper—need it for extra rum tonight—"

Dutifully, Royal stretched and half-squatted, recovering the chit. Philip closed the fingers of his hand as if the bit of paper were a nugget of precious metal or a priceless gem.

He was too dazed to worry about the possibility of gangrene, or how his leg would feel when the mortifying effects of the hot iron wore off. He wondered if he would ever walk properly again, but he couldn't bring himself to think much about that, either. For that he was thankful.

vii

Not long after dark, they were resting in another apple orchard, among several hundred men, quite a few of whom had light wounds. Philip was grateful the day's action had been called to a halt. He couldn't have hobbled one more step if General Washington had personally ordered him to do so under threat of court-martial.

Royal lay near him, sprawled on his side. Philip sat against the trunk of a tree, his right leg stuck out straight, the bandage that wrapped him from sole to mid-calf looking gigantic and grotesque in the dim light. His crutch rested across his thighs.

Royal had brought Philip his extra ration of rum. He sipped it from his hand-carved wooden drinking mug, taking a little every time the pain became hard to bear.

With his other hand, he slowly slapped at sand flies deviling his cheek. It was all the effort he could manage.

Once twilight came on, the fighting had ended. In the steaming darkness Philip heard a dim buzz of many conversations. He wondered which portions of the field he and Royal had occupied during the frantic maneuvering of the afternoon. He supposed he'd never know—

He grew aware of Royal speaking in a tired monotone:

"—some say we whipped them. But I've heard just as many say it was a standoff. Clinton's gotten away in the dark with his baggage, and we'll never catch him now."

Philip could only utter a single wordless syllable to show he'd heard.

"They say we lost over a hundred dead from sunstroke, too."

Again Philip could do no more than murmur.

A lantern spread a widening glow off to their right. Several subalterns and a senior officer, shadow-figures, were slowly working their way among the resting men. Philip thought he recognized a voice that was asking a question for which no one had the answer.

Royal did, though:

"General Wayne?"

"Who spoke?"

"Over here, sir."

"Who is it—?"

The party of officers approached. Philip lifted his head, saw a disturbing double image of a bedraggled Anthony Wayne.

"Private Rothman, sir. I heard you ask about General Washington."

"Can't find him anywhere."

"One of the other fellows told me he'd already gone to sleep. Yonder under a tree at the far side of the orchard. He found General Lafayette lying exhausted and spread his cloak over both of them."

452

"Many thanks—"

Wayne started on, then hesitated, his eye fixing on Philip.

Wayne said, "I recognize you. Kent, am I right?"

Each word seemed to weigh a ton in his mouth:

"Yes, sir."

"You were at McGellaird's Brook."

"Yes, I was."

"Took a British ball, it appears."

"Yes, sir. Nothing—" He forced each word, hoping they were true. "—nothing too serious."

"Well, savor that rum, Kent. You and the rest of these men earned it." His handsome face broke into a prideful grin; the kind of devil's grin that had earned him his fierce reputation. "Today wasn't Brandywine, by heaven."

"No, sir," Philip said. "Thank God for that."

"We can thank the commander-in-chief while we're at it. God grant you a swift recovery."

Before Philip could offer a reply, Wayne strode off, a tall silhouette between the two resting soldiers and the subaltern leading the way with the lantern.

Philip closed his eyes, let his whole body go slack. No conscious effort was required. His right leg was throbbing again.

He brought his hand up; tilted the cup; dribbled rum over his chin before his tongue caught the rest.

Royal sighed. Then:

"Philip?"

"Uh?"

"Do you feel any better?"

"Some."

"Then I think I'll sleep a little myself."

"Good." It was barely audible.

After a moment's silence:

"Philip?"

"Mm?"

"Captain Webb told me General Washington ordered a huge celebration back in camp at Englishtown tomorrow. Said we'd behaved like a real army, and won a victory over the flower of the British troops." Royal's tone was unmistakably proud. "The flower of the British troops, those were his exact words. Captain Webb said there was very little panic, despite all the confusion at the beginning. I suppose a lot of the credit goes to that German. Maybe our luck's changing. Maybe we'll win against them yet—"

Philip's answer was a snore.

viii

Before a week passed, Philip knew something was seriously wrong with his right leg.

The wound had been re-dressed twice by army doctors. Each commented that Philip had been lucky to escape the kind of ravaging infection that produced gangrene, then amputation. But when Philip was told by the second doctor to test his weight on the wounded leg, he fell over in a child-like sprawl. The doctor avoided Philip's eyes when he was back up on his crutch. Philip demanded an explanation.

"I think the ball may have damaged internal tissues," the doctor said. "A great tendon, possibly. If it doesn't heal properly, you—you may have difficulty walking."

A cold lump clotted in Philip's throat. "For how long?"

"For life. Our knowledge of anatomy's inexact, you understand. But—"

Philip's ghastly whiteness made the doctor stop.

"You mean I'll have to get about on a crutch from now on?"

"I can't be certain. I saw a somewhat similar case after a pistol duel over cards at Valley Forge. The man was left with a permanent limp."

Tears of humiliation and rage sprang to Philip's eyes. "Jesus Christ."

"Here, here," the doctor said with false heartiness, clapping Philip's shoulder. "At least there's one benefit. You'll be mustered out very promptly now."

"To go home and live as a cripple?"

"I—I told you, soldier. I can't be positive one way or another—"

"I'm sorry, doctor, but I think you're lying."

The man said nothing, averting his gaze a second time. White-lipped, Philip hobbled out of the tent.

ix

The July twilight was cool. After picking up the mail that had finally come north through Jersey to Washington's summer encampment at Haverstraw Bay, Philip started immediately for the bluffs.

The doctor's prediction had proved partially correct. Two days ago, Philip had started getting about for short periods without the crutch. The injured right leg no longer caused him much pain; the wound was healing, and evidently no bones had been broken.

But there was permanent damage. His foot was stiffer than before, lacking natural springiness. He had looked at the foot closely the last time it was dressed, and it seemed to him that the arch of the sole had flattened somewhat.

Tonight he leaned on the crutch. Without it, his progress was awkward, and the limp noticeable—just as his bitter, brooding silences had become noticeable to Royal and Gil and Captain Webb and others who knew him.

The doctors had also confirmed that he was no longer fit for fighting. His separation orders were being prepared. Before many more days passed, he would be free

455

to return to Boston. It was ironic that the prospect filled him with so little joy, when it was all he'd wanted for so long.

But he'd never planned on returning to his wife and his son as a cripple.

Behind him, Philip heard singing around the cook fires. Even on the tiring march north from Englishtown—a march on which he'd been permitted to travel most of the way in a medical wagon—the spirits of the other men had improved dramatically.

True, the army had lost a prime chance to destroy Clinton's force. The enemy commander was now safe on the island of New York, some miles downriver. But for the first time, the Americans *had* fought like first-class troops. Even Gil said so, riding in the medical wagon and trying to cheer his friend. Washington, awaiting Clinton's next move and planning his own, expressed his pride in his men openly and frequently.

General Charles Lee, relieved of command and facing disciplinary action—perhaps even court-martial—had not been heard from on the subject.

To hearten the men even more, a courier had arrived at headquarters this morning bearing word that spread through the encampment by noon. The Count d'Estaing's frigates and ships of the line had been sighted off the Delaware capes!

Extra rations of alcohol were allowed, on Washington's order, and permission was given for another all-out celebration. Perhaps, as Royal had said that night in the orchard, the fortunes of the Americans were reversing at last—

But that was of small importance to Philip just now. He was finally able to forget his own injury, and the problems it posed for the future. Forgetfulness came with concentrating on the two much-wrinkled letters he pulled from his pocket as he reached a secluded place where the cliffs dropped away to the wide, blue-black

Hudson. The river flowed serenely, its surface pricked silver by the first summer stars.

Philip had practically snatched the letters from the postal clerk, noting only that one was in a man's hand, the other in a woman's. Clumsily, he lowered himself into the long grass and laid his crutch aside, unable to suppress a smile as he started to open Anne's letter.

All at once he noticed what he hadn't noticed before. The handwriting, though feminine, was not hers.

A moment after he tore the seal, the first thunderblow fell.

x

The letter from the neighbor woman, Mrs. Eulalie Brumple, was dated the end of April. Phrases leaped out to sear him:

—*sad duty to report distressing events*—

—*and when I returned, she was not present*—

—*within hours I had begun to fear for her safety*—

—*a seafaring gentleman of your acquaintance has called, and believes he may have some clue to the perpetrator of what now seems a most foul act of abduction*—

—*hope this will reach you with dispatch, bringing you at least the small assurance that I will care for your son Abraham devotedly until some resolution of the situation is effected*—

One word burned Philip's brain and set him trembling.

Abduction.

xi

The second letter, dated the tenth of May, was from Captain Will Caleb. It told the rest of the dreadful story.

Returning from a voyage aboard *Fidelity*—a voyage capped by seizure of a valuable British prize—Caleb had discovered that his other new vessel, *Gull*, had vanished from Boston harbor with Malachi Rackham in command. Even Caleb's somewhat stilted phrasing—an indication, perhaps, of how difficult it had been for him to write the letter—couldn't conceal his fury:

The rogue likewise captured a prize off the Carolinas. To auction it, he sailed to the Leewards rather than an American port—his express intent being to defraud the rightful owners of their share, I am certain.

Upon his arrival in Boston late in the month of April—I now fear with the foulest purpose in mind—he stayed not overlong.

Word first reached me only to the effect that he had set sail for an unknown destination. I subsequently learned, through that network of seamen's intelligence which operates despite the presence of the army of a foreign tyrant, that said destination was the port of New York, where Rackham planned to compound his fraud and multiply his illicit gains by selling Gull *to a new Tory owner—selling, in effect, what he neither owned nor had any right to sell.*

But I am ahead of myself, and will shortly explain how I come to use Rackham's name in past tense. Learning of Gull's *abrupt departure, I repaired at once to Cambridge to report the sad turn to your most esteemed wife, hoping to offset the disappointment with my own happy news—that in command of* Fidelity, *I had secured a British merchantman whose sale here has increased your investment some thousand-fold, a right handsome profit—*

Racing on through the letter, Philip could not summon the faintest stir of delight at what should have been welcome news: he was modestly rich. It made no difference because of what he already sensed lay ahead.

*In Cambridge, the good Mrs. Brumple relays to me
the horrid story of the surprising disappearance of yr.
dear wife, a most perplexing and puzzling affair, but
only that—until more news came to me from New
York—this very day.*

*The news was brought by a neutral vessel, Dutch
flag, which called at the aforementioned port last
week. Gull did indeed put in there, but under mystify-
ing circumstances.*

*Her first mate, a fellow who was privy to
Rackham's plan, was in command. The captain himself was lost at sea between Boston and Gull's
destination; lost, I regret to report, along with a
Massachusetts Bay woman of unknown identity
whom Rackham caused to be brought aboard the
night before he sailed.*

*Evidently a struggle ensued, as both fell to their
deaths from Rackham's own cabin. In the cabin was
evidence of blood, and one window was shattered.
The whole business is the talk of New York, and
was narrated in detail by the Dutchmen.*

"God," Philip said in a stricken voice. "Oh dear
God." He virtually forced himself to read the next:

*Thus a perverse pattern has shaped itself; a pat-
tern, I say, unguessed and unglimpsed till I
recollected Mrs. Brumple's odd tale—as well as certain other incidents, viz., the unsavory and reckless
interest of the d——d Rackham in Mrs. Kent.*

*I will endeavor to find out whether my suspicion as
to the identity of Rackham's companion has foundation, or, mercifully, is but grim coincidence. I debated
long over whether to inform you of matters herewith
reported. However, since Mrs. B. later told me she
was writing an urgent message concerning yr. wife's
absence, I felt I had better take the step.*

I trust Divine Providence will prove all worries ungrounded, and reveal the person who perished with Rackham to be some other—

Philip couldn't read the rest. Captain Will Caleb's hope was fruitless. He knew it with a heavy, dead feeling; knew it as certainly as he stood shivering on the solid brink of the cliff.

Finally, he looked back at one passage in the letter.

Late April, Caleb said.

After his decision not to return home.

He damned himself and his idiotic sense of duty. He damned Henry Knox and he damned Washington and he damned the war most of all.

A lightning bug winked soft gold in the wind-stirred grass high above the river. What could he do?

Nothing. *It was too late—*

"Anne!" he cried, a small dark blur on the brow of the bluff. From the silent forests on the Hudson's far shore the frantic echo pealed back.

AnneAnneAnneAnne—

A sentry came running, musket at the ready, to see who had shrieked like a madman in the July twilight.

xii

"I feel partially responsible—" Henry Knox said in a feeble voice. Philip had hobbled to Knox's quarters, a dead man who yet moved and thought. Solitude was unbearable; he needed to speak to someone. Share his grief with someone—

Or was it guilt he wanted another to share?

Realizing it, he was ashamed. Guilt was quite evident on Knox's round face.

Forcing himself, Philip shook his head.

"Henry, there's no blame. You were right in everything you said at Valley Forge. And no one forced me to stay and take a British ball. But—"

The decision was spoken an instant after he made it:

"—I'm not waiting for the mustering-out papers. I'm going home now."

"Yes. I fully understand. Is there someone to care for your son until you arrive?"

Philip balanced on his crutch, tugged out the first letter. "The lady who wrote this, Mrs. Brumple. She can give Abraham her complete attention since—" His mouth wrenched. "—since there's no one to bury."

Knox frowned sadly, silent.

Philip stared down at his right leg in the new, larger boot that permitted a bandage to be worn inside. His voice sounded faint, almost like an old man's, as he went on:

"Once I met Dr. Franklin in Philadelphia. He told me a story from his boyhood. How he bought a pennywhistle, not knowing its small value and paying far too much. He said that afterward, he always judged everything in those terms—was he paying too much for a whistle?"

Suddenly, uncontrollably, tears streamed down Philip's cheeks.

"She's dead. I know that bastard took her aboard his ship. She probably died trying to get away from him— that would be like her. I know I had to stay. I know we all had to fight for the country if we mean to keep it. But the price is too high, Henry. The whistle cost too much—oh, Christ—*Annie*—"

Not caring that it was unmanly, he covered his face and cried.

Henry Knox continued to stare in silent misery. At last he managed to say:

"I'm sure it's precious small consolation for your injury and your personal grief. But as Mr. Paine wrote in that famous pamphlet of his, anything worth-

461

while—worth having—ultimately commands a high pr—"

Philip swallowed back the tears, silencing his friend with a hateful stare:

"I don't want to hear any more, Henry."

"Philip, you mustn't lose sight of the goal! You said it yourself—if we win this war, we secure liberty for—"

"Yes, Henry. Yes, goddamn it, I know *very well* what we'll secure. But doing it, you haven't lost the woman you love."

CHAPTER III

The Shawnee Spy

THE LOW-LYING sun set fire to the great bend of the river sweeping away west of the point of land where the American flag flew above the five-sided fort. The fort was constructed of heavy logs, reinforced on the landward faces with brick and stone. East of the fort, mercantile establishments, shanties and a boatyard straggled along the shore of the Monongahela. He saw it all through a haze of June humidity as he came down from Coal Hill like some kind of walking corpse.

His deerhide shirt and trousers were stained and torn. Strips of the shirt were wrapped tightly around his upper left arm. The arm was bandaged in two other places, below the elbow and at the wrist. All three bandages, and the exposed skin above and below each, were filthy with dirt and dried blood.

The fair-haired man had a strange, almost maniacal glaze in his eyes as he limped along the street in the early dusk, dragging the stock of his Kentucky rifle in the dirt. There were men and a few women abroad, the men mostly in hunting outfits. Despite the heat, a couple of them wore fur hats with raccoon tails dangling down the back. One or two of the men were dark enough to have some black or Indian blood. Nearly everyone gave the stranger a stare. Several pointed to call a companion's attention to the shambling figure.

The man continued to move with that sleepwalker's gaze and gait. His passing stilled the voices of loungers on the shadowy porch of a two-story boardinghouse. The man seemed not to hear any of the clatter of the river settlement: the hammer and thud of mallets from the boatyard; the riffle of an evening drum from Fort Dunmore; the creak of a wagon almost overflowing with glistening black lumps of coal coming up behind him.

As the wagon went by, the man glanced up. The driver was instantly uneasy because the man's eyes burned with fever or hunger or something else. In a hoarse voice the man asked:

"Is George Clark here?"

The driver hauled on his reins, stopped his team. "George Clark of the Kentucky militia?"

"Yes."

The driver pointed between crude buildings to the boat landing on the Monongahela. "Them's his five flatboats moored yonder."

The man with the rifle swayed, as if he were having trouble standing up. But his eyes were still afire.

"I didn't ask you about Clark's flatboats, I asked about him."

Fearfully, the wagon driver swallowed. "Try Semple's Tavern."

"Where is it?"

"Right down there."

Without so much as a thank-you, the grim figure stumbled on. The driver wiped his mouth and shook his head.

Judson saw. But he didn't give a damn what anyone thought about him. His sole objective was to reach the end of the journey, and stop. It wouldn't be too long, hopefully. A few more steps—

Lord! If only he could relieve his thirst with a swig of rum. Just one drink, to ease the tension in him; to moisten his raw, parched throat—

Since the night when he'd killed five wolves between sunset and dawn, emerging from the experience half alive, he'd wanted nothing so much as a strong drink. It would have eased his pain; mitigated the agony he felt at every step. But, of necessity, he'd gone ahead without it, pushing on—dragging on—toward the forks with the ache of clumsily bandaged wounds a constant companion.

Now, stumbling toward the door of Semple's, his thoughts grew confused. Why was he here? For a drink?

No, that wasn't right—

Dizzy, he swayed back and forth again. He knuckled his eyes, planted his feet wider until the spell passed.

He licked his upper lip, all peeled and split and hard. He blinked a few times, then realized someone was watching him.

The man was a dim figure in the fast-lowering dark. He was seated against the corner of the building. He wore buckskins with long fringing, and hide moccasins. An English dragoon pistol and a hunting knife were thrust into his belt. The man's face was completely in shadow. The sinking sun was behind him; and his flop-brimmed frontier hat helped to conceal his features.

Oddly, the fellow hadn't so much as stirred when Judson showed signs of passing out in front of him.

Not that Judson Fletcher expected an outpouring of humanitarianism from the citizens of Pittsburgh. He knew he looked far too grimy and forbidding for that.

But as his mind cleared a little, he mentally remarked on the man's absolute lack of motion. Quite different from the reactions of the other inhabitants he'd encountered while walking into the settlement.

In the few seconds that he and the seated man stared at one another, Judson noticed one more peculiarity. The man had his arms crossed over his chest, and his hands tucked out of sight next to his ribs.

Judson's scrutiny made the fellow nervous. He jumped up and disappeared around the end of the building. But not before Judson saw the back of a hand that was either a white man's burned extremely brown by the weather, or was naturally dark—

Well, he'd seen a few similar types in the little town already. He supposed it was possible for half-breeds to venture into Pittsburgh so long as they proclaimed themselves loyal to the American side.

Having decided the strange spectator was indeed an Indian—and cleared his head a little more in the bargain—Judson shuffled on toward the tavern door and thrust it open.

He heard a blast of boisterous talk, saw a blur of faces in the sullen redness leaking through greasy windows. When he entered, heads turned. Some of the conversation diminished.

At the bar, in the shadow of a stag's horns hanging on the wall, a tap-boy drew foaming mugs of ale from a cask. The smell drifted to Judson clear across the room; set his tongue moving in his mouth.

Abruptly, the interior of the tavern seemed to tilt and distort. Again he fought to stay on his feet. Searched —but didn't find the face he sought.

He staggered forward between the tables, smelling the sweat of the long hunters, the teamsters and rivermen gathered over venison and fish and hominy. He was aware of foreheads scratched; comments murmured about his ghastly appearance. None of that made any difference. Two emotions gripped him as he took his faltering steps:

Disappointment that his friend wasn't here.

And anger over his own consuming awareness of the rum and ale fumes.

As through a fog that receded ahead of him, stirred and swirled back by the motion of his weary body, he saw half a dozen rough-clad men watching him with particular attention from a table beside a window. The men had been poring over a map. As it became apparent that Judson was heading in their general direction, one

466

of the men quickly folded the map and slipped it inside his greasy shirt. His eyes slid to the ravaged arm, then back to Judson's face, suspiciously.

Judson went by a table of three noisy men wearing homespun shirts. One of the three, in his cups, grabbed Judson's rifle.

"Stranger, where you come from? Looks like you tangled with—"

Judson wrenched the rifle away so violently the drunk nearly toppled out of his chair. The drunk's face and those of his companions sobered as Judson stared at them.

"Are you with Major Clark?" Judson asked, hoarse.

One member of the trio had enough courage to meet the glowing blue eyes. "You mean Colonel Clark? He's carryin' that rank now."

"I see. Are you with him or not?"

"Nah, we ain't. But them lads are." A thumb indicated the map-readers who sat silently, watching the exchange.

Judson's features lost a little of their hostility. "Obliged," he mumbled, shuffling on. The drinker who had seized the rifle swallowed as he eyed Judson's profile obliquely, then swung around and yelled for another rum, too loudly.

Near the table where the six were seated, Judson squinted into the smoke.

"Have any of you seen Colonel Clark?"

"Yes," replied the man who'd put the map away. "He's off lookin' to the supplies."

Judson concealed his resentment of the curt tone, asked:

"Will he be coming back here?"

"In a while. Do you have business with the colonel?"

"That's right."

"He expectin' you?"

"I'll discuss the details with him personally," Judson

467

said. The fellow who'd answered his questions shrugged. No one invited Judson to sit down.

He supposed he couldn't blame George's men for that. Who was to say he wasn't some Tory sent to spy on the famed frontiersman? Still, the rejection rankled; his anger nearly burst out in a flash of cursing.

Just in time, he remembered the larger objective. With effort, he shuffled away from the six unblinking pairs of eyes and reached a small, unoccupied table along the wall.

It was blessed comfort just to stretch out in the hard wooden chair. The tap boy negotiated a path through the tables, appeared beside him:

"Something, sir?"

"I'm just waiting for—"

He stopped. His pain, his fatigue, his anxiety about the sort of reception he'd get from George, and the cool suspicion of the six men by the window combined in an instant to loosen the rein he'd kept on himself during the long, agonizing miles to Pittsburgh.

The boy tried to be polite: "Waiting, sir? For a friend?"

"Exactly right." Judson fished in his trousers pocket, touching coins. Something bleak and sad seemed to fill his blue eyes as he finished, "A friend you keep in one of those kegs. Bring me a rum."

As the boy started away, Judson added, "But just one!"

The boy glanced back, puzzled by the remark. Judson saw the six at the window whispering to one another behind the cover of lifted mugs.

Hell, they're drinking, he thought. *I'm certainly entitled to one.*

He needed that rum. It would relax him. Put him more at ease when it came time to explain to George why he was so late catching up to him. The boy returned shortly, Judson paid, then clamped both hands around the battered pewter mug, raised it and gulped.

Yes—better. His teeth chattered less after the very first swallow. Much less after the second.

The last daylight was leaching from the sky outside the window where the six still talked softly, their map spread again. One of the men was pointing to the map with the tip of a pelt knife that caught lamplight and flashed—

To his astonishment, Judson discovered that the contents of the mug had disappeared without him even being aware of it.

And no George yet.

Ah, but it was marvelous to stretch his legs. Feel the rum soothe the lingering pain, and his apprehension. The taproom seemed to grow noisier and more smoky. Extra lamps were lit now that full dark had fallen. Judson put away a second rum that tasted even better than the one before.

His spirits improved with remarkable speed. He had just about convinced himself that he should approach George's suspicious friends, identify himself and state his business. It certainly wasn't to his advantage that they'd backed him down at first. Hell, he was as valuable to George as any of them!

Yes, he'd speak to them a second time; he made up his mind to it. And if they grew insolent, he'd give them cause to regret it—

"Boy!"

The lad came scampering in response to the yell. "Yes, sir?"

"One more rum—and buy a round for that glum crew at the window."

Consternation among the six. Surprised, eyeing one another, they didn't know what to make of Judson's bold assault on their privacy. Leaning back in his chair, vastly amused and feeling like a new man, he allowed himself a loud chuckle.

When the boy brought a tray of mugs, Judson boomed a thanks, flung coins onto the tray and tipped an extra penny. Then, holding his full mug, he shoved the tap boy lightly with it:

"Go on, now. Serve Colonel Clark's lieutenants. But they needn't reciprocate. They don't look the sort to understand good Virginia manners anyhow."

He saw a deep scowl at the window table. He responded to it by lifting his mug in a mock toast. Another of the frontiersmen rose from his seat, flushed. Two others pulled him back down because Judson was grinning. A tipsy, insolent grin, but a grin all the same.

His behavior was beginning to cause puzzled comment among others close by. Just as he raised his mug still higher, prolonging the pantomimed toast, he heard a voice at the window table. Belonging to which man, he couldn't say; the tap boy blocked his view. But the words were clear:

"—some common drunk, that's all. Not worth a quarrel—"

Judson's fingers whitened on the mug handle. His cheeks turned livid as he slammed the mug on the table, started to jump up. At that instant, he was aware of heads turning near the door. Through the smoke he saw flame-red hair.

The first expression on George Clark's face was surprise. Then came brief bewilderment; next, disappointment. And finally, disgust.

George saw Judson half risen from his chair, the rum mug in one hand. George's eyes grew sadly accusing. His cheeks were white.

Judson let go of the mug, paying no attention to the location of the edge of the table. The mug tipped, clanked on the floor, splattering the rum in a huge pool.

Judson tried to untangle himself from between table and chair. The drinks had addled him more than he'd realized. He slipped on the wet floor, sprawled on hands and knees, his rifle crashing beside him as he called his friend's name. The name came out as a slurred yelp.

Laughter, then. Scornful laughter, and loud.

Judson's temples hammered as fast as his pulse. His face felt hot. He fumbled for the rifle, staggered up, ready to call out those who'd laughed—

There were too many. Gaping, guffawing mouths ringed him. In stunned confusion, he saw the terrible consequences of his behavior—

The doorway of Semple's Tavern was empty. George Clark had seen him drinking and walked out.

ii

A full moon haloed George's head as he stalked away from the tavern. Judson reached the doorway a good half minute after his friend left, and he would have lost him in the darkness save for that silvery light. George was moving rapidly in the direction of the boat landing.

As Judson lunged across the tavern yard, he heard voices raised behind him, and chairs overturned. But he gave little thought to George's friends who might consider him a threat to their commander. All that concerned him was the contempt on George's face the moment before he turned and stalked from Semple's.

Knuckling his eyes and fighting off the rum-fumed dizziness, he kept the dwindling figure in sight only a moment longer. Then George disappeared into the shadows under the log wall of a mercantile establishment.

Desperate, Judson began to run.

He dashed past the front of the darkened store and down along the same wall where he'd lost sight of his friend. Panting, he pulled up at the building's rear corner, conscious of a violin squeaking somewhere ahead.

He glanced back, saw George's half-dozen friends clustered in the spill of light at Semple's doorway. He held his position in the shadows until five of them went back inside following a brief, noisy discussion. The alarmists in the group evidently lost the argument. But a sixth man set off toward the fort on the point.

Judson's breathing had a fast, panicky quality as he crept around to the back of the store. He lost his balance, nearly fell when he stepped into a deep wagon-rut. Cursing, he jammed the butt of his rifle into the rut while he searched the riverfront for a sign of his friend.

With a gasp of relief, he saw him—silhouetted against the mellow glow of lanterns shining inside the moored flatboats.

Five of the river craft were tied to the landing, three along one side, two on the other. Each boat was roughly sixty feet long, twenty wide, and squared off at the ends Above the timbers of hulls that rose a good three or four feet higher than the moon-dappled water, walls and roofs enclosed most of the deck space. A great wooden steering sweep swung to and fro at the stern of each flatboat.

Windows and roof trapdoors on four of the vessels were thrown open, letting the lamplight show. Only one boat—the one farthest out in the row of three—was totally dark. From the others came an assortment of sounds: that scraping violin; voices; the bleating of sheep; the low of a cow. In one unenclosed section of deck, the horns of a massive bull caught moonlight.

But it was George Clark on whom Judson centered his attention. Near the head of the landing, George was walking back and forth with quick strides, pausing now and again to lift his head toward the moon. Judson was reluctant to abandon the protection of the shadows from which he watched. George's posture, and his pacing, were conclusive evidence of how angrily his friend had reacted to the sight of him drinking.

With the back of his free hand, Judson wiped sweat off his forehead. He had only two courses: either slink away and hide until his friend departed down the Ohio, or confront him and try to explain the circumstances that had caused him to break his vow. When Judson thought of all the distance he'd come—thought of the terrible fight with the wolves, and the brutalizing trek to Pittsburgh afterward—he really had no choice at all.

"George?"

George's trained reactions brought him whirling around in a defensive crouch. One hand dropped toward the long knife tucked in his boot. Judson called the name again, and stepped into the moonlight so the red-haired frontiersman could identify him.

George Clark's supple hands fell to his sides. On the flatboat where the violin sawed away, playing a reel, Judson was astonished to hear female voices, then children's laughter. His heart hammering, he walked toward the head of the landing where George waited, a slim, almost blade-like figure in the moonlight.

Never had such a short distance seemed so long. Judson's hands itched and shook. And he was bitterly conscious of the telltale reek of rum. But shock and despair had already sobered his mind.

George turned his head slightly as Judson approached. The moonlight fell across the red-haired Virginian's lean face. Judson trembled at the chill aloofness of his friend's features, and found himself wishing for one more drink.

He walked to within three feet of his friend, catching the pungent aroma of pigs drifting from one of the flatboats. Aboard another, a child bawled suddenly. A woman's gentle voice murmured comfort. Those on a third boat blew out their lamps and pulled the roof trap shut from inside with a loud thump.

Judson started to speak, couldn't. A night bird sailed low over the Monongahela, moon-silver on its wings. For a brief moment the bird shone as a glowing dot against the woods on the far shore. Then darkness hid its flight.

473

George said coldly, "I never expected to see you, Judson. When you failed to arrive in Williamsburg—"

"I couldn't help that." God, how thick his voice sounded. "I was shot. A light wound, but I couldn't leave till I recovered. I—I came overland—"

"Alone?"

"Yes. I had a little trouble, but I made it all right. I traveled as fast as I could because I thought you might be gone from here already."

"Should have been. We were delayed at Redstone, up the river. To my surprise, I picked up twenty families who want to make the trip to Kentucky, danger or no." He gestured toward the boats. "Getting their belongings stowed took time."

"You can carry twenty families on those five craft?"

"Yes, and all my men. The boats are exceedingly roomy. And I recruited only a hundred and fifty. I even had trouble finding those. That's another reason for the delay."

"I saw some of your men at the tavern," Judson told him, then added a word that went straight to the issue: "Drinking."

George Clark uttered a long, almost sad sigh.

"Judson, if that remark is supposed to excuse what I witnessed in Semple's, I must tell you it won't. Those men can be trusted with their liquor."

"Meaning I can't be?"

"Meaning you gave your pledge. That was the only condition under which I accepted you."

"My God, I came miles and miles—!" Judson began.

"And look a good deal the worse for it." George pointed at the filthy bandages.

"Shouldn't I be entitled to one mug of rum, then?"

"You answer that," George shot back. "You're the one who gave the pledge. I'm afraid you traveled to Pittsburgh for nothing, Judson."

"For nothing—?"

474

Stunned, disbelieving, Judson was speechless for a moment after that. Then his anger burst out:

"You pious, arrogant son of a bitch! You're short of men, yet you'd turn me away for downing one drink!"

George's pale eyes flared in the moonlight. "How many?"

"Well—not one. But not many more. George—"

The other cut in sharply, "I told you in Virginia, we have serious military business down the Ohio. Where we're going, each man depends on all the others for his safety. I'm responsible for everyone in my party—I must have men I can trust not to weaken when the going's difficult. You knew that before you started west. You knew that when you ordered up liquor at Semple's. I am not being puritanical, only practical. Believe me, I didn't accept every recruit who presented himself these past months, and—"

Suddenly there was unhappiness on George's face. He pivoted away to keep from displaying it as he finished:

"And much as I might want to, I won't accept you."

At first Judson didn't know whether to guffaw in astonishment or drop to his knees and beg. Then, slowly, he understood that the rejection was final. He understood just how wide the gulf separating him from his boyhood friend had become. And he felt completely stripped of every hope he'd cherished since that day he and George had ridden into the country outside Williamsburg, and he had shot the Kentucky rifle with trembling hands, and given his pledge—

For a moment he almost seemed to see wispy, leather-skinned Angus Fletcher in George's place. Angus shaking his head. *The devil's blood will tell—*

He started to pull the little black-bound testament from the breast pocket of his hunting shirt, ready to fling the book at that tormenting image. But the mind-phantom disappeared. Only George remained, condemning him with austere silence.

The violin fell quiet. Sheep bleated. The river lapped the flatboat hulls with a tranquil rhythm.

"What the hell am I supposed to do, George?" Judson asked finally. "I've left everything behind. Everything!"

"I don't know," George admitted, weary-sounding now. "Perhaps you can find work here in the settlement."

"*Work!* Christ, I don't know how to do any work! But I can fight—"

"Not in the forest. Not on the Illinois prairie. Not craving spirits so terribly that it hampers your judgment, ruins your stamina, makes you worthless—" Abruptly, George bit off the loud reply. He went on more moderately, "If I could make the decision as your friend, I would. But it's not possible any longer. All I can do is invite you aboard my boat—" He indicated the dark vessel at the outer end of the three. "—pour you one more rum—"

"Now that the damage is done, eh?"

George winced at the bitterness. Softly:

"No, just—just for old times' sake. I'll loan you a little money if you need it, but—that's the end. Come on, let's not quarrel any more. The decision's made. I'd feel much better if you'd enjoy the hospitality of the boat for a bit—"

Ears ringing, eyes blurred, Judson still caught the guilt in George's voice.

He tried to hate his friend. Tried to summon wrathful words again, but he was unable. *He* was the guilty one. *He* was the betrayer. Of everyone including himself.

A dreadful weight seemed to push down on his shoulders. Something George had said a moment ago rang through his mind, almost like a bell tolling for his own life:

But that's the end.

Lazarus, reborn for a few hours, had lacked the fortitude to survive. Angus Fletcher was right after all. Judson betrayed and destroyed at every turn. Never quite strong enough; never quite knowing why—

Well, at least there was the promise of a drink.

"All right, I'll accept the offer," Judson said with a wan smile. He and his tall friend started along the landing.

George moved with his customary silent grace. The bull bellowed and tossed its horns as they passed. Judson gazed at the swift-flowing river, thinking of the ruinous tide that coursed through him. That tide had swept him to a final chance—then, just as quickly, swept the chance from his grasp.

Uncomfortable in the awkward situation, George tried to make conversation:

"These are interesting craft, you'll find. They're one-way boats. Designed to be torn apart again, and the lumber used for shelters once we reach the falls of the Oh—"

Judson barely heard his friend hesitate. He was ready to turn and flee, his guilt deepening moment by moment. He decided to tell George he'd changed his mind; intended to make his way back into the settlement at once. Just as he was about to speak, he grew aware of a peculiar tension in his friend's stance.

George had stopped talking—and walking—just where the square stern of his flatboat bumped gently against the landing pilings. The moon burned in the pupils of George's narrowing eyes as he raised a finger to keep Judson silent.

Wrenched from the morass of his own misery, Judson followed George's pointing hand. Up the plank sidewalls, past a latched wooden window to the slightly arched roof. Judson sucked in a breath. The trap lay back; open.

And, running to it from the far edge of the roof, was a track of small, glistening puddles of water.

George bent close to Judson's ear:

"Someone's inside. Crawled up from the other rail—from the river—"

"Who would it be?"

"No idea. But I keep my public orders aboard, locked in a strong box. I've wondered if some Tory sympathizer might try to steal them. The other set's here—" He touched the belly of his hunting shirt. Then he tapped Judson's rifle:

"Is that primed?"

"Yes."

"All right, look sharp—"

George sidled near the rail of the moored boat, one hand darting down to his boot. The blade of his long knife flashed as he raised it waist high.

"I don't care to jump through the trap and surprise our visitors in the dark," he whispered. "But maybe we can flush them out into the light—"

As Judson lifted his rifle with sweaty hands, George leaned forward and started hammering a fist on the sidewall of the flatboat.

iii

The moment George stopped thumping, he heard sounds inside. Quick, light footsteps; then an oath, as something banged the deck planks.

"After my strong box, all right—" George began.

Hands shot from the black square of the open trap. A tall-crowned hat with a flop brim seemed to levitate swiftly into the moonlight. By the time the lithe intruder hauled himself onto the roof, Judson recognized him.

It was the lounger from outside Semple's Tavern. The man who had concealed his hands. Judson thought he understood why—

The intruder's hat blew off as he scrambled for the river side of the flatboat. Judson had a swift impression of a knife blade glittering in one brown fist, and metal-work shining on the pistol in the man's belt. George Clark leaped up onto the rail, then to the roof.

Judson jammed his rifle to his shoulder. He had a clear shot at the moon-silhouetted stranger. He steadied his grip, triggered the weapon.

An explosion—a dull glare of orange—

Then the aftermath of silence, signaling a flash in the pan. *Damn!* Either he'd lost most of his priming, or it had gotten damp—

"Stop!" George yelled, starting across the flatboat roof. He was between Judson and the intruder now, so that even with another weapon ready, no further shots would have been possible. Judson put a knee on the flat-boat rail, stretched out his bandaged arm, clenched his teeth, dragged himself up to the roof as George lunged across it, knife in one hand, the other shooting out to catch the fringe of the intruder's hunting shirt.

The man let out a wild, terrified cry that instantly raised voices of alarm from the other boats. By sheer strength, George held onto the spy's shirt while Judson painfully hauled himself up to the roof. As he did, he saw the chiseled starkness of the intruder's face; saw black, moon-washed eyes blinking with rage and terror; saw dark, grease-dressed hair hanging straight to the man's buckskin collar—

The Indian fought as George tried to drag him back to the center of the roof. Judson gained his feet at the roof's edge, unsteady because the struggle had set the flatboat bobbing. All at once he saw something else stuck in the Indian's belt:

Folded papers. The orders from the strong box.

With a guttural yell, the Indian yanked his knife from his belt, swiped at George's throat with a bright arc of steel. Judson shouted a warning but George was even quicker. Releasing his hold on the captive, he jumped backwards.

His left boot landed in the trail of water left when the Indian stole aboard. George skidded and sprawled, hitting the roof with a loud clump. By then Judson was moving, peripherally conscious of clamoring voices, of boots pounding the landing as people poured from the other flatboats—

But all he saw was the Indian's throwing hand jerking back, then streaking forward.

The knife was poorly aimed. George wrenched his right shoulder up. The blade struck the roof where he'd been lying, skittered away.

The Indian's other hand closed on the butt of his English dragoon pistol. Crouching, he transferred the weapon to his right hand with startling speed, drew back the cock—

George Clark was a target too large and too close to miss. The Indian's teeth shone, clenched in a kind of death's-head grin as he extended his pistol arm full length. Frantically, George started to roll aside. But he was too late; too late—

Judson launched himself hard and fast. He had a dream-like sensation of almost flying across the roof. The Indian swung instinctively. The pistol discharged at close range. Judson doubled as the ball struck him in the gut.

Smoke drifted. Judson felt flowing warmth in his middle. Then pain.

He dropped to his knees, holding back a hurt cry. He heard the shouts of men clambering up the flatboat's side behind him, several bringing lanterns whose light flooded the roof. George Clark had regained his feet and caught the Indian. He wrenched one arm around the spy's windpipe. With his other hand he pressed his knife to the writhing captive's throat.

Judson watched with a dreamy sense of unreality, even though ferocious pain was eating through his midsection, and blood was washing down under his trousers

480

into his crotch. He knew very well why he had endangered himself deliberately. It was more than friendship. It was the terrible need for absolution.

Curiously, despite the pain, there was tranquility in him. Paying the high price of expunging some of his guilt brought a light-headed feeling of release; freedom. For a moment a strange parody of his old, shining smile wrenched his mouth.

Harsh voices sounded as the flatboat men rushed by him across the roof:

"You all right, George?"

"Who'd you catch? Who fired?"

"Damn half-breed, looks like—"

Clear and strong above the clamor, Judson heard George's voice:

"See to Fletcher there. He took the Indian's ball."

George flung the captive into the hands of others as the lanterns tossed grotesque shadows back and forth across the swaying roof. In the pen area of a nearby boat, frightened sheep bleated louder than ever, quickly joined by squealing pigs, then a wailing infant.

George rushed to the men gathering around Judson, pushed them aside as Judson lowered himself clumsily to the roof. Breathing seemed difficult. The initial violent pain in his middle had subsided, replaced by a steady ache. From the waist downward he was bloodsoaked. He could feel the drenching along his thighs.

George knelt beside him, face pale in the starlight. Several of the other men seized the Indian, pressed pistols and knives against his body, struck him in the face, barked questions:

"You speak English?"

"What's your name, you red bastard?"

"Where'd you come from?"

"Say something or we'll shoot your damn head off."

In a rasping voice, the Indian snarled a word:

"Nen-nemki."

About to speak to Judson, George Clark glanced back over his shoulder.

" 'The thunder.' I've heard of him. Part English, part Shawnee—and one of Hamilton's roving agents. He was after the orders in the strong box."

"Got 'em, too. Almost," a man said, jerking the folded papers from the spy's belt.

Judson coughed. That worsened the ache in his belly. He rested his head against the flatboat roof, seeing George outlined against the moon. His friend's hair glowed like silver fire, and his voice had an odd, strained quality:

"You took that shot deliberately, Judson."

"You—" Speech required immense effort. "—you—would have gotten it—otherwise. And—"

More coughing, this time with a phlegmy sound.

"—it's more important—you get—where you're going than—that I go with you—"

"Let's have none of that kind of talk. We'll carry you to the surgeon at the fort—"

"What—whatever you say. Doubt—if it's worth the trouble, though—"

Over the muted conversation, rougher voices were continuing the interrogation of the half-breed. He fought in the grip of the men holding him, tried in vain to avoid the kicks to his groin, the yanks of his hair, the knife-points raked along his exposed skin. George kept staring at Judson, stricken to silence.

Nen-nemki started to scream at his tormentors, an outburst of badly pronounced English:

"*Goddamn long knives! Come just for pelts, there is land enough for all. But now, goddamn Kaintucks, you want the land too! Come with your women, come with your plows, come with your houses of log and steal our hunting fields, our deer forests, so we fight you for Great Father George! You can kill Nen-nemki—*"

"You bet your damn greased-up hide we will," someone growled.

The Shawnee paid no attention, his shrieks silencing the clamor of the growing crowd on the landing:

"—*but others will run the trails with guns from the Hair-Buyer, powder from the Hair-Buyer. You steal the land, we throw down the red war belt until we die or you die—!*"

Listening to the shriek over a steadily rising roar in his inner ear, Judson somehow felt sorry for the captive. Beneath the fury of the Shawnee's ranting was an almost pathetic undertone of misery and loss. Judson grieved for the savages in that strange moment, because he understood why the Shawnee cried his outrage. As the tidewater planters had gradually taken the freedom of the blacks, the frontiersmen too were taking what was not theirs: the lush woods and meadows Judson had seen only through the descriptions in George's letters; but on those lands, Nen-nemki's forefathers had roamed for generations—

Now George Clark and his boatloads of riflemen and pigs and children would ride the river westward. And if George's great plan succeeded, the tribes would have even less land than they'd had before.

Perhaps it had to be. But, oddly, there was little hate for the Shawnee in Judson, even though he knew the half-breed had mortally wounded him.

Judson couldn't hear the rest of Nen-nemki's harangue. The roaring in his ears had grown too loud. He felt an overpowering desire to rest.

Fingers touched his cheek. George's—

"We'll fetch you to the surgeon now, Judson."

"Still think—it's useless—" One hand struggled up to clasp his friend's, because he was all at once cold and afraid. "I'm—only sorry—I'll never—see Kentucky with you—"

Sudden darkness descended.

483

He woke on a straw pallet in a log-walled room at Fort Dunmore. George was there, and the post doctor as well.

The doctor hesitated a long time and cleared his throat twice before saying softly that the pistol ball couldn't be removed; that Judson was evidently bleeding internally; that an opium tincture had been forced down his throat to ease his pain; and that saving his life was next to impossible.

Judson listened in a detached way, light-headed. When the doctor finished, Judson whispered that his wound didn't hurt all that much, thanks to the tincture. He endured a fit of coughing, then asked George when he intended to head the flatboats down the Ohio. George said they would push off shortly after sunrise next day.

"I—" Judson swallowed, then smiled, his sweat-slicked face shiny in the flickering light of the room's one lantern of pierced tin. "—I'll live—long enough to see that, anyway."

George and the doctor glanced at one another. Despite Judson's feeble voice, he sounded certain.

How remarkable, Judson thought. He *did* feel peaceful. As if a struggle had reached an end, and he could rest in good conscience.

Before drifting off again, he mumbled a question about the Indian spy. George told him that Nen-nemki had confessed. The Shawnee had indeed been dispatched by Hamilton at Detroit. His mission was to watch for signs of any substantial military force being assembled at Pittsburgh.

"I suppose Hamilton chose him because he's half white, and therefore less suspect. Nen-nemki did make one most revealing statement, though I doubt he himself understood its significance." George paused a moment. "Hamilton wants to know how many men might be coming to fortify and defend the Kentucky settlements."

"The Kentucky—? That—that means the British still haven't guessed—"

Judson stopped, realizing the doctor was still in the room. He started to mutter an apology, but George's icy smile said it wasn't necessary:

"Our true purpose? No, evidently not."

Judson breathed one more word—all he could manage:

"Good."

He remembered George staying with him a long time, hunched on an up-ended section of log with his hands locked around his ankles while his pale eyes watched with a mixture of guilt and regret. Judson woke occasionally, attempted to speak to the tall young man. He wanted to tell George to have neither regret nor guilt because he, Judson, had been the one with the tally of guilt that required erasing. That was one reason he'd lunged between George and the Shawnee with the pistol. One reason, but only one—

He couldn't muster enough strength to say what needed saying, though, and that saddened him. He floated in a foggy limbo where the pain was constant and, at times, close to unbearable. He made no outcry.

In one of Judson's wakeful intervals, one of George's men—a member of the six from Semple's Tavern—appeared to say that Nen-nemki had been hanged.

v

Barely awake, and having consciously willed himself to live the night, he asked to be carried to the shore in the morning sunshine.

He sensed a sizable crowd around the litter on which he lay; he could hear their excited voices. Though he couldn't feel it in his chilly hands, he knew he must be holding the small New Testament because he recalled asking for it.

Gradually, he separated other sounds from the hubbub: an almost continual thud of boots on the landing; the sharp commands of George's men making the flatboats ready for departure.

Judson saw next to none of the actual activity. His eyes were slitted against the bright daylight. He felt the sun on his cheeks but it was curiously heatless. From his chest downward, his body seemed thick. He knew he was bandaged and doped with the surgeon's tincture.

Time dragged. At last, a woman near him exclaimed, "Oh, they're going—!"

A round of huzzahs split the early summer air. Judson cried feebly, "Lift me up! Please, someone lift me up—!"

At last, he was heard. Hands grasped the end of the litter where his head lay, elevated it slowly. He was disappointed. He could see little more than a glare of sunlit water.

He blinked and kept blinking until, finally, in a welter of confusing shapes and colors, he discerned a glowing patch of red.

Red hair—

George Clark.

Where was he standing? On the roof of one of the flatboats? It must be so. The tall figure of his friend burned bright as an angel's in the sunshine. And it was receding ever so slowly.

"Man the sweep when we pick up the current!" a voice boomed in the distance.

Suddenly Judson was more afraid than he had ever been in his life.

His hands had turned to ice. He had to exert tremendous effort just to feel the grainy surface of the testament cover between his fingers.

Shining and fierce and powerful, the figure of George Clark floated off in the sunshine. The cheering started again. *Gone away,* Judson thought. *Gone away into the west I never saw. Gone away to—what were the names?*

Kaskaskia was one. He couldn't recall the other.

But he did remember that George had an important secret mission in the Northwest Territory. By paying the price of his guilt—a price that had needed paying for so many years—he had helped make George's journey possible. It was a good thing to think about. One good thing to balance against all the bad—

Faces drifted through his mind. A wrathful Angus. A disappointed Donald. Butchered Seth, and Alice, drowned. Vengeful Lottie. Sorrowing but stern Tom Jefferson—

Peggy. Lovely Peggy.

The memories disturbed his sleepy comfort. He'd brought others so much sorrow; done so much that was despicable. He had so few good memories. The best, perhaps, was having seen the nation born—

And there was George. There, he could be proud. He'd helped one of Virginia's finest captains set out to extend the boundaries of the new nation. That could be written down in the meager column opposite the much longer, blotted one.

He concentrated on the distant red-haired figure that now seemed to be floating in a gathering mist. With a shiver, he realized the mist was not external; it was within himself. He clutched the testament tightly, whispered the word, *"Father—"* while the cheering thundered.

The first of George Clark's flatboats swung into the bend at the forks and, with sweeps churning back and forth, caught the current that would bear the little army down the Ohio, into the west.

But Judson never saw. Slowly, he closed his eyes. His head lolled to one side, a faint smile fading away.

One of the men holding the litter said, "I think we can put it down now."

CHAPTER IV

The Price of Heaven

ON A SPRING afternoon some eleven months later, two men climbed Breed's Hill overlooking the Charles and the Mystic and Boston harbor.

The older of the two, Philip Kent, walked with a slight limp that contrasted with the frolicsome skips and jumps of the small boy clutching his hand. The boy was dark-haired, handsome. His brown eyes sparkled as he surveyed the orchards and stone fences and wind-blown pastures of the peninsula.

The boy tugged his father's hand. "Papa, couldn't we have a race?"

"You know I can't run a footrace," Philip said in a sharp voice.

"But we run together sometimes."

"Only because you insist, Abraham. And only at home."

The boy frowned. "All right, But can't we go over to that other hill? I want to see the ships better—"

"You'll stay here. We won't be all that long."

"Papa, please—"

"I said *no!*"

The Marquis de Lafayette adjusted his tricorn against the slant of the sun. On one of the hat's upturned sides, Gil sported the white-centered cockade that symbolized the French alliance.

"My good friend," he said, "would it hurt to let your son roam? I shall be a little while examining the redoubt."

Philip shrugged wearily. "All right. You can run by yourself, Abraham. But no farther than the top of Morton's—" He pointed. "And stay in sight!"

Abraham gave a quick nod, a half-fearful look in his dark eyes as he watched his father's severe face a moment longer. Then he turned away.

Freedom quickly restored his spirits. He was soon racing through the grass on his way to the summit of Morton's Hill.

"A splendid lad," Gil remarked as he watched the diminishing figure. "Four years old, isn't he?"

"Not quite. In September. But he's bright for his age. Mrs. Brumple has already taught him to read a little."

The young Frenchman turned to gaze at the rooftops of Boston across the Charles. "Tell me. Are you and he—shall we say—on good terms?"

"I don't know what you mean by that. I'm his father."

"Do you spend time together?"

"I see Abraham whenever I can. And twice a week—Wednesdays and Sundays—very early in the morning, we both go out to Watertown."

Gil asked lightly, "What's the attraction there, pray?"

"My wife's memorial."

"Ah, certainly. My deepest apologies—I forgot—"

Recovering from his embarrassment, Gil pondered Philip's blunt statements silently. Philip was thankful, because he'd heard quite enough on the subject of Abraham from Mrs. Brumple. Only the other morning, she had launched into one of those well-intentioned but infuriating lectures that would have caused Philip to order her out of the house if he hadn't needed her to care for his son. Even now, he could recall the conversation—

"Mr. Kent, sir, you'll forgive me if I interject a comment—"

"Of course!" Philip retorted, displaying the bad temper that had afflicted him of late. "I forgive you for it

489

constantly, don't I?"

A forced, belated smile didn't mitigate Mrs. Brumple's irritation. "I certainly never intend to be critical, Mr. Kent—"

"Yes you do, my good woman, so go right ahead."

"Really, sir, this is intolerable—!"

Philip sighed. "I apologize. Please do continue."

"Well—all right. I've been meaning to speak to you about these continual trips to the place where your dear wife's memorial is."

"You sound as if you don't approve. I see nothing wrong in paying respects to Anne."

"But must Abraham go with you each time? Twice weekly?"

"Why shouldn't he?"

"Well, sir, this is a personal opinion—and you may find it odd coming from one who constantly deplored her husband's lack of piety. But I feel that your insistence upon Abraham visiting Mrs. Kent's memorial so often is harmful to him."

"Harmful?" Philip arched his brows. "In God's name, woman, how?"

"Sir, please accept this in the spirit in which it is offered. The Lord's name should never be taken—"

"Yes, yes, I realize! I'm sorry. Now please get to the point."

Mrs. Brumple clamped her lips together and nodded. Unhappily, Philip realized he'd roused her combative spirit:

"The point is this. A small boy should associate his father with cheerful events and surroundings, not exclusively with graveyards—no matter how revered the departed."

Philip replied quietly, earnestly, speaking the deep hurt that was always with him—and was especially painful during long, wakeful nights in his solitary bed:

490

"Mrs. Brumple, I loved Anne above all other people in this world. I repeat—her memory deserves to be honored."

"I wouldn't have it otherwise, sir! You miss my meaning entirely. Your visits have become a fixation! The boy barely remembers the dear lady, and he only thinks of you in connection with situations of sadness —bereavement. I cannot help but believe it will warp his nature if it continues indefinitely."

Curtly, Philip said, "Thank you for the advice. I will give it serious consideration."

Ye gods, how the old goose annoyed him sometimes! He certainly *didn't* intend to give her words even a moment's serious consideration—

But now, standing with Gil and watching Abraham's whirls and turns in the long grass, the discussion slipped back into his mind, and he felt a twinge of guilt.

He'd seen the fear in his son's eyes when he spoke harshly to him a few moments ago. Perhaps he *was* giving excessive attention to mourning—and, more important, forcing the boy into the same pattern.

But dear Lord, he did miss Anne! Was it so wrong to pay homage to that undying affection?

Gil continued to study him with thoughtful hazel eyes. Somehow the glance prodded Philip to expand his defense of himself and his relationship with his son:

"I don't deliberately leave Abraham to his own devices, you understand. But I've all I can handle running the presses and watching those damned apprentices. Also, as you're well aware, I've sunk a great deal of money into the preparation of my first book."

Gil nodded, tugging the slim volume from the roomy pocket of his coat. The book was bound in lustrous brown leather over boards. Philip had invested in the paper and other materials necessary to produce the sort of book Royal Rothman had suggested—a deluxe edition of Tom Paine's *American Crisis* essays.

More essays were still coming from Paine's quill, of course. But Philip had collected all those previously issued as individual paper-bound pamphlets, re-set them in a highly legible typeface, run off the sheets and sent them to a bindery. He was gambling on being able to eventually sell two thousand copies to private collectors and circulating libraries.

He had received the books from the bindery three weeks ago, and thus far had disposed of perhaps two hundred copies, on consignment to Boston book shops. Less than fifty had been sold. He had expected to do much better.

"If business doesn't improve," Philip said at length, "I may go out of the trade altogether."

"What?" Gil exclaimed. "You've only just started!"

Philip stared over the sunny hillsides shadowed by a passing cloud.

"Yes, but Anne's death changed a great many things, Gil." He swung to face his friend. "I didn't tell you everything when I showed you the shop this morning. Selwyn Rothman, whom you met, is pressing me for a long-term commitment. A lease on the space I rent by the month. I've put him off because I frankly don't know whether I want to continue. A few months after I opened the shop, I ordered a signboard to be hung outside the entrance to Rothman's loft. Although the sign's completed, I've never called for it. The sign painter's apprentice devils me about it practically every other day—"

Gil looked genuinely concerned as he returned the book to his pocket. "If you abandon your enterprise, what will you do?"

Philip shrugged. "I might have a stab at a different trade. In another city."

"Printing is all you know!"

"That's true. But without Anne, I've damned little heart for it."

"My friend, it saddens me to see you grieving so deeply," Gil said. "It makes you sound like an old man at twenty-five."

"Twenty-six. That's about half an average lifetime, don't forget."

"Still, you talk like a veritable ancient. I've been only a week in Boston, but I've noticed it almost constantly. A change since we last saw each other—a distinct and unhappy change."

"I'll remind you that any new business is taxing. Especially when you wonder if you should continue with it. I wasn't aware of sounding ancient, however."

Sensitive to Philip's sarcasm, Gil veered the subject slightly:

"I was quite impressed by your shop, I might say."

"Over and above the gamble on the book, I have to fight like the devil to get orders. Old Rothman's a fine gentleman, though. He's used all of his contacts to help me. But other people would pay him much more than I do for the loft space. So he's pressing me about a lease. Gently, but pressing nevertheless."

"The chandler is the father of the young man from your mess, am I not correct?"

"Yes. Royal's still with the army—"

Philip sat down on a stone fence, folding his hands around his knee. It seemed to him that he heard drumming in the sunshine; distant drumming. Voices crying *"Push on—!"*

He shivered. But the illusions refused to depart. He heard Anne's laughter—

He searched for the spot where he'd rowed to their very first picnic. Centuries ago, it seemed. Melancholy, his eyes lingered on the strip of beach.

"Philip, you mustn't think of giving up so quickly," Gil said suddenly. "I venture Kent's will prosper if you only give it time."

"I'm fearful no one can really prosper till we have

peace again. And the war goes on."

"Ah, but in our favor! Such a change since a year ago! The splendid Colonel Clark's victories—both British posts in the northwest taken, and that perfidious Hamilton forced to surrender at Vincennes! Captain Paul Jones sailing his *Ranger* into Whitehaven in England and spiking the very guns of their fort! Now the rumors of conciliation attempts being undertaken by Lord North—let us hope the Paris commissioners stand fast. Nothing short of independence. Full independence!"

Philip rubbed his right leg absently. "They'd better not settle for anything less. Thank God for the French, anyway. Without your country, we wouldn't have a fraction of the negotiating power that we do now."

It was true; especially since the preceding December, when King Louis XVI's council had elected to recognize the United States as a fully independent nation.

"So it is a bright picture!" Gil said with false cheer. "And I hope to brighten it more by taking this leave and returning to Paris. I am going personally to the king, to request a larger fleet, additional troops—believe me, Philip, it is only a matter of time before the war is decided in America's favor. Of course, until it happens, there will continue to be pulling and hauling on both sides—"

"They *have* captured Savannah. And they seem to be mounting a campaign down south."

"Yes, but Clinton's strategy is most interesting. More important, I believe it is significant."

"I honestly haven't paid that much attention—"

"Since Monmouth Court House, the British have not committed an entire army to the field anywhere. I think they scent stalemate or defeat in the wind—just as I scent victory. If not this year, then within twenty-four months. Thirty-six at most. I'd wager on it."

"I hope you're right."

"France's entrance into the war has turned this to a global struggle. The sort of struggle England can least afford. We are harassing her from the Indies to the Indian Ocean. She can no longer give full attention to you rebellious Americans—"

Gil's jab at his friend's shoulder, lightly delivered, produced no response. Nor did another forced smile. Philip continued to stare moodily at the sunlit hills, the ships at anchor, the raw buildings of the new Charlestown rising where the old one had burned.

Gil perched on the stone fence alongside Philip, frowning now:

"I begged General Washington's permission to sail from Boston in part because I wanted to see you, my friend. I'm afraid I almost regret doing so."

"Well, I'm sorry. I wouldn't pretend I've been in the best spirits since I came home last summer."

"One cannot mourn forever, Philip."

Philip didn't answer.

Gil sighed, tried to start the one-sided conversation on yet another tack:

"I would like to see the remains of the redoubt where you fought."

Philip raised a listless hand. "There."

"You won't come with me?"

"I'd rather not."

"Damme, you are a gloomy one!" Gil indicated the small figure scuttling across the sunny landscape. "If you have no thought for yourself, have a thought for that child. You'll pardon me for saying so—" Philip glanced around sharply, hearing the echo of Mrs. Brumple. "—but sometimes you treat him as if he were some Hessian's brat instead of your own son."

"I told you, Gil, I have a lot to do these days. For one thing, I'm rushing to finish a circular to promote the Paine book in other cities."

"Yet at the same time, you are uncertain whether it's worth the effort!"

Philip said nothing.

"No wonder the boy suffers," Gil murmured.

Philip jerked his head up, defensive again:

"Mrs. Brumple is a very adequate housekeeper. She feeds Abraham—sees to his clothing, his naps—he doesn't want for anything. Our—" The unconsidered word seemed to bring a shadow across Philip's eyes. "—our investment in the privateers paid off handsomely. Of course much of it's tied up in equipment and loft rental and the new book. But I'll always make sure there's enough left for Abraham's needs."

"His material needs. A woman you have hired as your housekeeper is no substitute for a father's attentions and affections."

Philip rose quickly.

"Did you come here to see the redoubt or to lecture me, Gil?"

Gil flushed. "The former. Again I beg you to excuse my impertinence."

Philip sighed. "If you'll excuse my temper. It must be obvious that I'm having trouble with it lately."

Gil asked softly, "With the boy?"

"With everyone."

The admission was a hard one, but truthful. The months since he'd come home from the camp at Haverstraw Bay had been confused, hectic—and miserable. Everything he had confessed to the young marquis he felt twice as deeply inside:

Once, he had looked forward to every step involved in establishing his business. The purchasing of two second-hand presses—the hiring of two devils—the long hours spent meeting delivery deadlines on his first hard-won orders for handbills and broadsides all seemed devoid of the joy he'd anticipated from the days when he first caught the excitement of the printing trade at the

Sholto shop in London.

Reality, somehow, hadn't matched his expectations. Without Anne to share it, his life was nothing more than a succession of tiresome days and fretful nights. It was an emotional strain to make his frequent visits to the cemetery in Watertown, though he felt he had no choice.

He'd erected a headstone in Watertown, alongside the one marking the resting place of Anne's father. He'd erected it even though no mortal remains would ever fill the grave—

Gil had been eyeing his friend speculatively for several moments. Now, finally, he jumped to his feet.

"Philip, I regret to say I must renege on one arrangement we made."

Philip's dark eyes narrowed. "What arrangement?"

"My promise to take your letter to your father the duke, and see to its smuggling across the Channel to England."

That, at last, got a strong reaction:

"You promised to do it! I haven't written him in a couple of years—"

"Yes, I realize that. However—" Gil pursed his lips, shrugged. "—you are not precisely being a cordial companion. I frankly resent being treated in such boorish fashion."

For a moment Philip believed his friend was wholly serious. Then he saw the faintly mocking gleam in Gil's hazel eyes. He didn't immediately comprehend the reason for it, though.

"Here I am," Gil continued, "faced with my final night in America—my ship due to sail shortly after sunrise—and I will go to this very fine late supper which has been arranged in my honor, but the whole evening will be spoiled by memories of my friend's glum spirits."

"If this is some elaborate joke, Gil, I fail to understand it. I'm not trying to ruin your damn supper party!"

"Never mind—just take my word, you have. I cannot

497

do a service for someone who treats me so shabbily. However—" He arched his brows, studying the slow-sailing clouds. "—if, for example, you were to show your sincere interest in my well-being—"

"How?"

"By accompanying me tonight."

"What?"

"I said I would like you to accompany me to the supper party."

"Out of the question."

"You're engaged?"

"There's a cracked leg on one of my presses. I planned to go back to the loft yet this afternoon and start on the repair. I imagine it'll take me a good part of the evening—"

"Ah, pouf! Tomorrow will be soon enough."

"I've got to finish that blasted circular!"

"You are inventing excuses," Gill declared with an airy wave.

"That's not so, I—"

"Why bother with repairs and circulars if you intend to give up your trade?"

"I haven't definitely decided to do that—"

"But you're thinking about it. So neither repairs nor advertisements are that urgent. Besides," Gil hurried on as Philip started to protest again, "there's a practical reason for my desiring your company. The kind family issuing the invitation to me has also included another guest. A young woman who is the niece of my host's wife. Since I am a married man, the host and hostess have arranged for my partner for the evening to be a grand dame quite advanced in years. Some antique relative of Mr. Hancock's, I believe. But the other lady I mentioned—a young widow—is thus far without a suitable compan—wait, wait, hear me out!"

Philip had limped off along the stone fence to stare at the cloud-dappled sky.

Gil rushed after him, still speaking in that light, half-mocking tone:

"You needn't curdle up so! You might enjoy an evening of feminine companionship."

Gazing obliquely at Philip to see if he'd piqued his curiosity, Gil waited. Philip merely scowled. Gil went on in spite of it:

"The young woman is from Virginia. Her name is McLean. According to my host, she is pretty and quite intelligent. To have dinner with her, while possibly a pleasant diversion, should not be construed as an attempt at matchmaking, if that's what's troubling you."

It was, in part, but Philip didn't admit it, saying instead:

"Hauling a stranger along, Gil—that's ridiculous."

"Let me decide that, please. Will you go?"

"No, of course I won't go. I doubt the lady would care to have someone like me for a partner. I mean—" He spread his fingers downward to indicate his right leg. His mouth twisted in an ugly way. "—I'd hardly cut a fine figure dancing."

"There is to be no dancing. But your concern is revealing. I've suspected you were overly anxious about your injury. You probably pay it more heed than anyone else would."

"I *am* a cripple."

Gil shrugged again. "You are if you think you are. It is that simple, I believe."

"To you."

"So you definitely will not go?"

"I've already answered that."

"In other words, you reject your friend and his interest in you?"

Philip uttered a long sigh. "If you insist on putting it that way, yes."

"Very well. I shall have my secretary return your letter to the duke."

"Damme, you promised—"

"Ah, but I have my price."

"Lectures, supper invitations—*what the hell is this all about*?"

Suddenly the Marquis de Lafayette grew completely sober-faced. He looked much older than his years as he laid a compassionate hand on Philip's arm.

"It is about you, my friend. It is about your life, which must go on even though your beloved wife's has ended."

Gil spun and thrust one hand toward Abraham scampering on the sunlit hilltop in the distance.

"Will you consign him to misery the remainder of his days just so you can revel in it too? I think that is decidedly short-sighted. And selfish. Earlier, I tried to suggest that every grief must have an end. You paid no attention—"

"My wife *died* because I was away when I should have been *here!*"

"*Why* should you have been here? Explain to me exactly—why? You professed belief in the army's purpose, did you not? You pledged yourself to that purpose, did you not? You committed yourself to helping deliver this new nation into freedom—freedom for each man to choose his own path without consulting kings or ministers. I am a foreigner, but I have the distinct impresssion that what has happened in this country in the last few years now means more to me than it does to you!"

"That's a damned lie. I believe it was worthwhile to—"

"Faugh, you do not believe it was worthwhile at all. Otherwise you would not throw it all away."

"Throw *what* away, for Christ's sake?"

"The future that has been and is being so dearly and preciously won! You make a mockery of the struggle. You no longer care about the future! Oh, you run about

500

pretending to be busy—you substitute frantic motion for authentic purpose—but you've admitted you've lost hope—abandoned yourself to wallowing in grief—even reached the brink of throwing away the career you once hoped to create for yourself in this country! If all of that weren't so, you'd clearly see, for example, that your behavior is creating an irreparable gulf between yourself and that boy. No, don't deny it—I saw how he looked at you a few minutes ago! In twenty years you'll have no son worthy of inheriting what you've begun, because what you've begun is already disappearing in apathy and bitterness. Your son's love will have disappeared too—and no doubt your son himself, when he's old enough to flee the moody creature who's a father in name only! I repeat, do not argue—I am not finished!" Gil cried, cheeks scarlet now.

"I know I should not speak this way. It is none of my affair if you wish to entomb yourself, give up and rot in despair all your days. But a week in Boston has been quite long enough for me to see the pattern evolving. You are driving that boy from you, and just as surely, you are counting as nothing all that's been spent to give him a future—a country to grow up in that is unlike any other this world has ever seen. Once, you faced death for that. Now you dismiss it! You dismiss out of hand all the decent men who have surrendered their lives for this new nation. You very conveniently forget they died not only for themselves but for you. More important, for that boy! You forget, and you spit on their sacrifice!"

Gil was trembling. He averted his head, as if ashamed. Philip tried to blunt the stinging accusations with sarcasm:

"Those are fine sentiments. But over-optimistic, don't you think? You're talking as if we've won."

"*We have!* I am willing to take my oath on it! America will surely triumph now that its own army has

501

shown fighting teeth, and allies are on your side—"

"Allies? We've only France."

"I suspect there will be another soon. Perhaps not formally tied to America but declaring war on Britain nevertheless. I refer to Spain. However, you're dodging the issue."

"Gil, I can't help how I feel!"

"But certainly you can. You are a man. Grieve inwardly if you must. Of course you will never forget your wife. But the world goes on. So must you."

"I'd rather have lost the war than Anne!"

Hazel eyes pinned him. "You see? My indictment was entirely correct."

"I—" Philip hesitated. "Well, dammit, not entirely, but—"

"What you mean is, you want both the war won and your wife alive, and it has not worked out that way because things of value carry a high cost. One which must be paid despite our bitter reluctance. Mr. Jefferson named the price explicitly. 'Our lives. Our fortunes. Our sacred honor.' If you were not willing to pay it, you should have said so at the beginning—and stuck with the damned, cowardly Tories! It is a measure of what a weak, pathetic creature you are allowing yourself to become that you put those same sentiments into type—"

Gil snatched the slim book from his pocket and shook it at Philip.

"—you print them in hope of a profit, yet you're blind to the very words on the page! Mr. Paine knows Heaven sets the proper price on its goods. In your miserable self-pity, you have forgotten!"

He hurled the book at Philip's feet and stalked off.

ii

Stunned, Philip reached down for the volume that represented so much of his stake in the future—a future which, in his darkest moments, he was indeed ready to

502

abandon.

As he straightened up, he saw Gil glaring at him. The young Frenchman turned his back.

Philip swallowed, remembering almost word for word the passage Royal had first shown him; the passage he'd set so carefully as he began work on the Paine edition.

What we obtain too cheap, we esteem too lightly; it is dearness only that gives everything its value . . . .

Heaven knows how to put a proper price upon its goods . . . .

It would be strange indeed if so celestial an article as freedom should not be highly rated . . . .

But it was dearness and struggle that had given Anne her importance in his life, too. Now she was gone. Irretrievably gone. That was the loss, the price, that had reduced him to confusion and depression and uncertainty about what he wanted for himself in the years ahead—if indeed he wanted anything at all.

His temper in control again, Gil walked slowly back to his friend. With a polite half-bow, he said:

"Once more I was grossly intemperate. But this time I offer no apology. The words needed speaking."

"Gil, I—perhaps you just can't understand. Believe me when I say I feel *responsible* for Anne's death."

"Then you have fallen into dire error."

Philip shook his head, resigned: "It certainly wouldn't be the first time—"

"I do remind you of this. If you cannot or will not lift yourself out of your despondency, then you *will* be responsible for that young boy dying—even though he lives physically to be a hundred years."

"Gil, this—"

Philip stared into his friend's face, still shocked and hurt by the assault, even as he began to understand Gil's motives.

"—this is pretty damned thick stuff for you to spout just because I don't want to have supper with some damned widow from Virginia."

"The dinner is incidental. Your willingness is not."
Gil touched his arm, adding softly, "Come—will you
deny your old comrade in arms?"

A lengthy pause. Philip's face hardened a little.

"Let's get back to the basic issue. If I go, will you
carry the letter?"

"Yes."

"Otherwise you won't?"

"No. You will have to see to it yourself. I will consider our friendship at an end."

"You're not serious."

"Perfectly."

Philip remained silent even longer. The sound of the
wind seemed to intensify, then fade. Shaken, he began:

"What time—?"

He couldn't get out the rest, because Gil exclaimed:

"My coach will call at seven sharp!"

Feeling exhausted by the argument, and more than
slightly traitorous to Anne's memory, Philip let out a
long, defeated sigh:

"All right. Seven o'clock."

"Splendid! *Splendid!* You don't even have to enjoy it.
Just go. Now—"

Gil whirled him around by the shoulders, drawing
Philip's attention to what he'd perceived only dimly a
moment before:

"—your son is calling you. Evidently he's found some
object of interest." Another of the billowy, slow-moving
clouds darkened Gil's face. "Why don't you go to him?
Speak to him? This time, out of more than necessity?"

Philip stared at the summit of Morton's Hill as Gil
added, "I shall stroll by what's left of the redoubt and
rejoin you shortly."

All elegance, lace and gold trim that gleamed in the
sun, the Marquis de Lafayette walked off through the
high grass.

CHAPTER V

The Woman From Virginia

PHILIP CLIMBED awkwardly over the stone fence and started down the slope toward the base of Morton's Hill. He was continually conscious of his limp now, and certain that the other guests at the supper party would be also. What a blasted fool he was, to allow a moment's weakness to overcome his initial refusal!

Or was it weakness? Could Gil be right about the necessity for abandoning his excessive preoccupation with Anne's death?

The blatant bribery concerning the letter to James Amberly had been relatively incidental to Philip's change of mind. He could have found other, though less certain, means of posting the letter to England. He could not have endured the dissolution of his friendship with the marquis quite so easily.

The more he thought about it, the more convinced he was that Gil's threats were deliberate devices for breaking through to the heart of his personal crisis and jolting him, if possible, from the despair that had held him in its grip for months.

Still, the idea of dining beside some strange woman was unnerving. But he had said he would, so now he must suffer through. The evening was certain to be a disaster—

He was glad to be momentarily distracted from contemplating it. The distraction was provided by Abraham, waving and calling from the summit of Morton's Hill.

As Philip reached the depression between the hills, the boy pointed to something in the grass. Philip blinked against the sun, thinking he saw Anne standing on the hilltop, lovely as he remembered her from that first picnic in the pastures of farmers Breed and Bunker—

So long ago.

He heard the distant drums again. The distant voices—

Push on! Push on!

How that cry had terrified them, just before the redcoats stormed the redoubt where Gil was wandering, trying to mark its outline in the overgrown grass.

Philip started up the hill toward Abraham, still upset about the prospect of an evening in the company of some Virginia charmer. About all he'd learn from such a person might be a few details of the widening war in the southern states. He might not even learn that if she were a vapid creature who paid no attention to affairs of the country.

He thought about the long conversation just concluded. Realistically, Gil was correct in one of his comments. There *was* confidence abroad now. Philip heard it in every lane and coffee-house in Boston.

It was a boisterous, be-damned-to-you confidence risen phoenix-like from the humiliation of the early days of the war. It was a confidence forged in the bitter struggle to bring military discipline out of disorder. It was a confidence instilled by steady, courageous, honorable men like Washington, and bizarre professionals like Baron von Steuben. It was a confidence heightened by France's open and growing support of her ally, even though that support was birthed in expediency as the result of centuries-old hatred.

Whatever the motivation for the act, France had tipped the balance. The bastard nation had at last been legitimized; recognized by another country. Surely others would follow suit—

Laboring up Morton's Hill, Philip hesitated at the halfway point, jerked back to the immediacy of his surroundings. There were too many ghosts stirring here; ghosts whose presence threatened to overwhelm him with grief—

Sweating suddenly, he stood with one hand at his brow to blot out the sun. He failed to notice Abraham's wigwagging arms fall to his sides, indicative of his disappointment as he saw his father come to a stop in the rippling pasture grass.

Philip was pale. The eerie drumming became a thunder that conjured up too many faces he wanted to forget.

Black-skinned Salem Prince and handsome Dr. Warren facing bayonets in the redoubt, and going down to death—

Eph Tait, begging for a rifle to end his own life in the winter-clutched mountains—

Lucas Cowper, screaming as pitch on the stump of his arm seared his whole future out of existence—

A schoolmaster with a fly crawling in the moist, dead cavern of his mouth; never again for him the pleasure of shiny faces over hornbooks, or the companionship of a girl called Patsy—

There were more, thousands more, whose names and histories he would never know. Gil said they had died for him. He would have died for them if that had been his lot and luck. And collectively, they would have perished for a piece of paper drawn up in Philadelphia and flung at the world in magnificent defiance of tyranny; magnificent affirmation of everything in which a lovely, tender, strong-minded Boston girl had believed—

Everything *he* had believed.

Once.

A new thought struck him. Anne, too, had given herself. She was a casualty of war just as surely as the others were. He was certain that, to the end, she had kept her faith in the worth of the difficult struggle—

What we obtain too cheap, we esteem too lightly.

Heaven knows how to put a proper price upon its goods—

All those he remembered, including Anne, had known the value of the goal for which the nation fought. And had paid the price. Not by choice. But they had paid.

He stared down at his right leg and thought, *And so did I.*

Would he have had it otherwise? Seen freedom lost in return for personal safety and security? That was the fundamental question Gil asked. In conscience, Philip had to admit his answer was no. But in that answer, there was heartbreak—

"Papa? Come see—I've found a bird. I think it's a waxwing!"

Once more Philip shielded his eyes, shifted position for a glimpse of his son's face. He was disconcerted to see that the boy looked apprehensive. No doubt he expected an absent stare; or a scowl and a reprimand—

"I'm coming, Abraham."

He resumed his slow ascent of the hillside, the phantom drumming a crescendo; the sound seemed to throb all around him.

Then, as he concentrated on the boy's tense, expectant face, it began to fade—

As did the horrible massed cry of those long-ago voices:

Push on! Push on!

Suddenly, there was no grimness at all in the voices dying away in the sunny wind. There was only a challenge. His mouth framed the words softly:

"Push on—"

It was what he must do. Put pain and grief behind as best he could, and live the rest of his life in the now, not the yesterday or the tomorrow that should have been.

God, it would be hard. But the spur was there.

In the boy.

A good thing, he thought wearily. A good thing, or I never would do it—

He went as fast as he could to the top of Morton's Hill. When he reached Abraham's side, the boy pointed down:

"See, Papa, isn't that a waxwing?"

"Yes, I think so."

"Mrs. Brumple showed one to me last week. She said they come and they go and nobody knows when or why—"

Studying the brown, crested bird pathetically flopping in the grass, Philip nodded in an absent way.

"He's hurt, isn't he, Papa?"

"Yes," Philip said, kneeling and starting to touch the bird. He pulled his hand back for fear of injuring the already mangled wing.

"Do you think we could make him well if we took him home?"

"Abraham, I don't know anything about caring for birds—"

He saw disappointment stain Abraham's round brown eyes again, added quickly:

"—but I'll venture Mrs. Brumple knows. If she doesn't, she'll pound every door in Cambridge till she finds someone who does."

"Yes, she knows just about everything," Abraham said, his jutting lower lip testifying to his bittersweet relationship with the elderly housekeeper. "She said cedar waxwings eat mulberries and cherries, I remember."

Philip stroked his son's hair, saw Anne's face shimmering like a double image over the boy's. So close he could almost touch her.

"I'll tell you one thing I'll bet she doesn't know, Abraham, and that's how to build a wood bird cage. It's the sort of thing fathers are supposed to do. Let's pick the bird up. You'll have to do it because your hands are smaller and softer. And we'll need something to carry him—I'll borrow Gil's hat. By the way, I've promised Gil I'd go to a supper with him tonight—"

His stomach knotted at the mere thought of it.

"—but I needn't repair that broken leg on the press until tomorrow, so we'll go along to Rothman's right now and ask Mr. Rothman for a packing crate we can chop apart. I'll build a slat cage for the bird and we'll take him home to Mrs. Brumple and let her ply her skills. If it's possible for that wing to heal, at least the fellow will have a place to recuperate comfortably. Are you agreed, Abraham?"

"Oh, yes, Papa, yes, let's go at once! May we call Gil?"

"Yes, we—"

Philip paused as he started to stand up. Still kneeling, he took his son's small hand in his larger one.

"Abraham."

The old uncertainty blurred Abraham's smile:

"What, Papa?"

"Abraham, you're a good son and I always want you to know I love you. I haven't been in very good temper these past months, but I promise you that's going to change. I want to show you I love you, not just say the words."

The boy flung himself at his father and wrapped his arms around his neck and held him tightly.

Philip pulled Abraham close, holding him around the waist, feeling the beat of life and warmth in the small, strong body. Presently he drew back, looked into his son's eyes, seeing for a moment the other flesh that had given the boy life: the remarkable chestnut-haired girl who had taught him to love liberty as much as he loved her.

"One more thing, Abraham—"

"Yes, sir?"

"From now on, I don't believe we'll be traveling to Watertown quite so often."

"To Mama's place?"

"Yes. I will go occasionally myself, but you need not. After all, you must have extra time to tend the waxwing. And you and I should do other things together—"

"I wish you would let me go to the shop with you, Papa."

"You like it?"

"Yes, the ink smell, and all the noise, and the boys who work for you—I wish you could find something for me to do there."

"Perhaps I can, Abraham. I'll try."

"I know I am not very old—"

"Big enough to carry an ink ball, I should imagine." He patted Abraham's cheek. "At any rate, let me make what visits to Mama's place are called for, eh?"

"Of course, Papa."

Philip was ashamed of the relief he saw in his son's face.

But he was gratified by the merriment that quickly replaced it.

ii

At dusk, Gil's hired coach wound through the dimly lit Boston streets. The elegant young officer lounged on the forward-facing seat. Philip sat uncomfortably on the other.

He hadn't been so finely dressed in months. But putting together an outfit for the supper had required Mrs. Brumple to postpone care of the waxwing for an hour, and to make a quick trip to a haberdasher's. From there she rushed to a neighbor's, to borrow a decent pale blue shirt of the proper size, and a cravat of the same shade.

Philip's coat and velvet breeches of dark blue did not precisely match. But his white waistcoat and hose looked new-bought, which they were. Eulalie Brumple had fussed over him as if he were her child instead of her employer—"You'll forgive me for saying so, Mr. Kent, but your hair ribbon is not neatly tied. It looks every bit as sloppy as Brumple's always did. Come here!"—and despite his nervousness, Gil's arrival had come as a genuine relief.

But his anxiety was back full force now, heightened by a continued sense of betraying Anne's memory. Gil watched Philip drum his fingers on his right knee, then reached over to grasp his friend's wrist:

"Stop that! You're fidgeting worse than a green recruit going into battle."

"That is exactly how I feel."

Gil laughed. Philip glanced out the coach window for the first time in several minutes and exclaimed, "Where the devil is this party? Either your host and hostess are in financial straits—"

"I assure you they are not."

"Then your coachman's lost."

"Not that either. We are going to call for the young woman whom I mentioned to you this afternoon."

Philip jerked his gaze back from the row of houses rolling past outside. Quite without his being aware of it, the coach had proceeded to a North End street which was distinctly run down.

Scowling, he said, "When I agreed to come, I wasn't aware the bargain included calling for the widow in person."

"It didn't—then," Gil grinned. "I took care of that after we parted."

Irked and not a little confused, Philip gestured to the shabby houses. "This widow—she's staying in this part of town?"

"No, she is staying at our ultimate destination. The home of our host and hostess. The latter is Madame McLean's aunt on her mother's side."

"Gil, you aren't making sense! What the hell are we

doing in the North End?"

"Well, there's a snippet of gossip attached to the answer to that. We are calling for Mrs. McLean where she boards her child."

"Her *child!*" Philip shouted. "You *have* got me into some old woman's match-making session!"

"Philip—"

"You've paired me off with some panting bitch who's lost one husband and is desperate to trap another to support her brat! I've a mind to climb out right now."

Amused, Gil restrained Philip with a hand on his arm:

"My friend, I am assured that Madame McLean has neither the desire nor the intention to go shopping for a mate among cold-blooded New Englanders."

"Then what's she doing boarding a child in Boston? Was her husband from here?"

The hazel eyes grew more somber as Gil answered, "He was not. Philip, please treat what I'm going to tell you in confidence. It is my understanding that the young woman's daughter was born well *after* her husband died. Born out of wedlock, I suspect."

"Then I've more in common with the baby than the mother," Philip grumped.

"I believe the child was brought into the world here in Boston, however."

"Not Virginia?"

"No. The child's mother comes of good stock. No doubt she wished to avoid scandal at home. I do know for a fact that she has made two difficult voyages from Virginia in order to see to the child's welfare."

Philip shook his head. "I still don't understand—" He pointed outside to the less than elegant dwellings with ramshackle stoops and grimy front windows. "Why is the child lodged in this area, instead of with prosperous relatives?"

"Why, simply because the widow's aunt and her uncle by marriage are too advanced in years to handle a bumptious infant. You'll see when you meet them. A private home would therefore be preferable over an orphan's asylum, I imagine—and no financial hardship for Madame McLean. She is reputedly quite well off. So don't flatter yourself into thinking you'll be examined up and down for husbandly earning power! I promise you, Philip, it's a social occasion only—"

Scowling again, Philip said nothing.

"See here! Are you so ungallant that you can't help escort Madame McLean to the party in style?"

Philip's face turned bleak. He pointed to the new white hose showing at his calf.

"I hardly cut a figure that could be called stylish."

"Will you stop that confounded self-pity?" Gil barked, his smile humorless all of a sudden.

Regretting his irritation, he started to add something else. Just then the coach rocked to a halt, in front of an unprepossessing house on another shabby street.

"We have arrived. Philip—" The hazel eyes caught lamplight from the windows of the residence. "—if I have erred, forgive me. I only arranged to call for Madame McLean because I thought you might be more comfortable making her acquaintance before we descend into the somewhat stiffer atmosphere of the party."

"Well, I'm decidedly *un*comfortable. You fetch her out by yourself."

"No, I will not," Gil said, gently nudging his friend toward the door one of the coachmen had handed open. "The snail must emerge from his shell sometime!"

Climbing down, Philip swore a blistering oath which Gil pretended not to hear.

iii

As they ascended the steps, Philip tried to keep his shoulders squared. It was impossible. His right one sagged a little each time he put weight on that foot.

To make matters worse, he and the celebrated marquis were being peered at from numerous windows on both sides of the street. Within the house itself, Philip heard a high-pitched squalling.

"Plague on it!" Gil muttered. "Sounds like her child's fretful. She'll not be ready—" He let the knocker fall.

"How old is this offspring of hers?" Philip wanted to know.

"Let's see, I was told—" He thought. "A year? Something on that order—"

The door opened to reveal an obese man in his middle thirties. The man was either a member of the merchant class, or had attempted to dress like one when he learned who was to call at his front step. From the quality of the neighborhood, Philip suspected it was the latter.

Wig slightly askew, the poor fellow dry-washed his hands and hopped from one foot to the other as his distinguished visitor introduced himself and his friend. From somewhere upstairs, the devilish squalling continued as the obese man said:

"Come in, sirs, please do! I am Chadbourne Harris. My good wife and I board little Elizabeth—" A piercing shriek made him gulp.

Harris had a comfortable enough home, Philip decided, glancing into the parlor that opened off the front hallway. But the air was tanged with an odor of cooked cabbage, which he detested. Opposite the parlor entrance, double doors to a dining room stood slightly ajar. Philip spied a gleaming eye on the other side.

Goodwife Harris, perhaps? Embarrassed to confront her distinguished guest in person?

Gil, however, was all civility and kindness as he passed small talk with the nervous master of the house. Harris kept fidgeting with his wig and getting powder on his fingers while the screaming continued upstairs. Philip noted a woman's hooded cloak of fine velvet lying

515

on a hall stand. Of the woman herself, there was still no sign—

She appeared all at once in the lamplight of the upper landing, startling Harris, Gil and Philip because, over her shoulder, she carried the howling infant.

The young woman was elegantly gowned, with dark hair and fair skin. Her quite pretty features showed her distress. But she wasn't the least hesitant about coming downstairs. The little girl wearing a nightgown squealed and struggled on the widow McLean's shoulder.

"Mr. Harris," the young woman said, "is your wife nearby? I can do absolutely nothing with Elizabeth—"

"My wife? Ah—somewhere—I'll see—"

He bolted for the parlor, remembered something, hurtled the other way and jerked the double doors open to reveal a flustered woman whose girth nearly matched his.

"Mrs. Harris, Mrs. McLean requires you!"

Goggling at Gil—it was obvious which one of the visitors was the French officer—Mrs. Harris crossed to the younger woman and took the wailing infant. Philip got a brief look at the child's face: angelically beautiful, with fair hair and pale blue eyes. But the beauty was marred by the infant's rage and continual thrashing.

"Madame McLean," Gil said, "may I bid you good evening? I am your humble servant, the Marquis de Lafayette."

She curtsied prettily, though her pink cheeks showed her embarrassment at the child's behavior, and she had to raise her voice to be heard:

"It's indeed a privilege to meet a soldier and patriot of your distinction, sir."

The widow McLean's speech was softer, more rhythmic than that of New England. It had a pleasing sound; but Philip was more impressed at the way the young woman managed to maintain composure while her daughter was yelling.

He had to admit the lady from Virginia had a handsome figure, too. What drew his sympathy, however, was a certain quality in her eyes. A sad quality that didn't match her smile—

Gil was just about to present Philip when the child gave another cry and hit Mrs. Harris on the head.

"Elizabeth!"

Mrs. McLean ran to the older woman, seized the little girl's wrist and slapped it smartly. The child cried all the louder, while Mr. Harris gestured and grimaced, urging his wife to remove the source of the noise.

This Mrs. Harris did. The wail slowly diminished. The young woman brushed at a lock of dark hair that had loosened over her forehead. In her eyes Philip saw the sadness intensify for a moment.

Then she overcame it, and smiled again as she turned to her escorts:

"My deepest apologies to both of you gentlemen. Sometimes Elizabeth is so uncontrollable, I'd swear the child is an imp tutored by Satan himself." Her smile was dazzling now. But Philip sensed a grimmer undertone in the remark.

As Gil assisted Mrs. McLean with her cloak, he said:

"Permit me to present my dear friend, Mr. Philip Kent of Boston."

Fastening the ties of her cloak, Peggy McLean met Philip's eyes with cordiality, nothing more. He stepped forward to acknowledge the introduction—and realized too late that he had automatically put his weight on his right foot, revealing his limp. The young woman's glance dropped for an instant; she had seen—

Philip reddened, found it impossible to speak. Gil filled the strained silence:

"Mr. Kent is lately returned from the Continental army, where he served with distinction. He was injured in the battle of Monmouth Court House, in New Jersey."

"An injury in a noble cause, Mr. Kent," Peggy

517

McLean said. "I have read that the army fought splendidly there. But for the lack of a few more officers with the courage of Virginia's General Washington and Pennsylvania's General Wayne, the enemy would have been destroyed."

Gil beamed. "Quite so. Philip and I have known each other many, many years, by the way. We fought together at Monmouth, and in other actions as well. Happily, my dear comrade survived to lend his considerable talents to that admirable enterprise for the promulgation of knowledge, the printing craft."

Even as Gil finished the embarrassingly flowery pronouncement, he swept the front door open and stepped aside to permit Peggy McLean to go through. Philip caught his friend's prompting glance. He raised his hand and let the young woman rest hers on top.

"Thank you, Mr. Kent," she said.

They descended the stairs together. Philip was conscious that he was shorter than his companion, and that, too, was unsettling. He recalled feeling the same way in his first days of courting Anne—

As he assisted the widow into the coach, it occurred to him that Gil had deliberately raised the subject of his limp in order to minimize it; keep it from being an additional source of tension during the rest of the evening. Climbing into the coach himself, he realized with relief that Peggy McLean didn't appear to be the least repelled by his disability. In fact, as the coach set off, the driver hallooing to warn a crowd of urchins out of the way, she put Philip further at ease by saying:

"This printing business which the Marquis mentioned—I assume it's located here in the city, Mr. Kent?"

"Yes, that's right. My firm's a modest one so far. Broadsides, advertising notices—"

"But I agree with the marquis—printing *is* a craft of great worth to society in general. Especially in these times, when all the states depend on the printed word for encouraging news."

"It is the owner of the firm who is modest," Gil broke in. "Philip has just published a very handsome library edition of Mr. Paine's *Crisis* papers."

"Indeed! I've read several of them. I admire the content as much as the prose. Is your edition doing well, Mr. Kent?"

"Not as well as I'd like. I'm preparing a circular to promote its sale by post to booksellers in other cities—"

"Perhaps I could take a quantity back to Virginia with me. I have friends in both Richmond and Williamsburg, and I'm sure I could prevail on them to place the circulars in the proper hands."

Despite himself, Philip smiled. "Why, that's very kind. I understand you do travel between your state and ours occasionally."

"Yes, when the weather's favorable and the seas reasonably safe. Tell me, what's the name of your firm? Is it a family firm?"

"Well, I have a young son, named Abraham after my late wife's father. Of course I entertain some hope that he might continue in the business. For that reason I christened the establishment Kent and Son."

"I wish both Kents much success and prosperity," Peggy McLean said, returning his smile with warmth.

Philip felt a peculiar sensation then. With a touch of surprise, he realized what it was. He was enjoying this young woman's amiable and literate conversation as he'd enjoyed nothing else in months. He even caught himself eyeing the swell of her figure beneath her cloak.

That produced another severe twinge of guilt. It was embarrassing to find himself responding to widow McLean's presence with even a flicker of physical pleasure—

Perhaps the evening wouldn't be so disastrous as he'd

imagined.

Gil tapped Philip's shoulder, interrupting his reverie:

"By the by, my friend. That signboard for your doorway—have you made plans yet to put it up?"

"No, I—"

He cut the sentence off abruptly, realizing how skillfully he had been maneuvered into a trap. But Philip couldn't be angry. Behind Gil's smile and apparently innocent question lay genuine concern.

"I have been too busy to think much about it," he resumed. A moment later, the decision was made:

"I expect to call for the sign and have it erected within a week, though."

"First-rate! I'm sorry I shan't be here to watch."

Peggy McLean said, "Most business signboards here in Boston seem to have distinctive designs, Mr. Kent. Is that true of yours?"

"It has a design. Whether it's distinctive, I can't say. Just the name, Kent and Son, lettered in gold, Kent at the top, the other two words at the bottom. In between, there's a green bottle painted black for about a third of the way up. The black represents tea. I was present at Griffin's Wharf when—"

"When Mr. Adams held his famous tea party," Peggy nodded. Her stock rose immediately with Philip, for whatever else she might be, she was no empty-headed beauty languishing disconnected from the world.

Sitting forward on the coach seat, aware that he was looking at her with perhaps too great a degree of interest—and sinfully enjoying it!—he went on:

"Yes, exactly right. During the cutting and dumping of the tea chests, my shoes got filled with the stuff. I put some in a green bottle to save it. I have it as a souvenir at home. I like the bottle's symmetry, but more important, I like what it stands for. So I chose the bottle for the signboard instead of something more typical such as a press or a book—"

He realized the coach had stopped. A large, impressive house loomed outside. All the downstairs windows were aglow with candles, and the rooms themselves shed brilliant lamplight into the street. Liveried servants sprang to the coach door. Glancing out the other side, Philip saw they had returned to the vicinity of the Common.

One of the servants handed Peggy McLean out. Philip followed, alighting with only a slight awkwardness. He was feeling less self-conscious by the moment.

Moving to Philip, Peggy McLean said, "I will need to pick up those circulars before I sail home, Mr. Kent."

"I can have them brought around to you."

"But I've never seen a printing shop. I should like an invitation to visit yours."

"You may have it, of course."

"I hope you don't think me too forward. Since my husband was killed some years ago, it's been necessary for me to involve myself in many areas not normally considered proper for a woman. With my overseer's assistance, I manage my own plantation, for example. I've found I have an interest in commerce—even a certain small aptitude for it. I like to broaden my knowledge of all areas of business—"

"Then you'll surely be welcome at Kent and Son, Mrs. McLean."

"Wonderful! We can work out the details over supper. And on my next trip to Boston, I'll give you a report on my success with the circulars."

"You'll be coming back reasonably soon?"

"Yes, Mr. Kent, most assuredly."

Standing perhaps a foot from him in the glare of a torch held aloft by one of the host's footmen, Peggy McLean looked at Philip a moment longer. Color rushed to her cheeks. She glanced away, adding:

"I wonder if I might have your hand to climb the steps—?"

Philip smiled. "Certainly."

When he lifted his arm and she touched him, there was a peculiar prickling all along his spine. And, within him, only a vestige of guilt.

Philip couldn't see the Marquis de Lafayette smiling broadly as he followed the couple up the stairs in the shifting light of the windblown torches.

Epilogue

The World Turned Upside Down

ON THE NINETEENTH of October, 1781, some eight thousand British and German troops laid down their arms outside the tiny tobacco port of Yorktown in the state of Virginia, in token of the surrender of their commanding officer, General Charles Cornwallis, Earl of Cornwallis, to the combined American and French forces under General Washington and his ally, Count Donatien de Rochambeau.

The Hessians who had been besieged in Yorktown, trapped between the American army and the French fleet of Admiral de Grasse, stacked their arms with phlegmatic resignation. The British were a shade less gallant; embittered redcoats were seen to crack the butts of their muskets on the ground, and regimental musicians staved in the heads of their drums. Lord Cornwallis himself pleaded indisposition, sending a deputy to the ceremony.

General Washington refused to treat with the deputy.

He insisted that Cornwallis' alternate speak with *his* alternate, an American general of lesser rank, Benjamin Lincoln.

During the unti-by-unit abandonment of arms and musical instruments, the British bands played a peculiar assortment of music. Few were marches; some were airs with a distinctly melancholy strain. One, a popular nursery tune entitled *The World Turned Upside Down*, seemed ironically appropriate to the failure of the last thrust of the army of His Majesty. The army had swept up along the southern coast of the United States, hoping to win the victory that had eluded the British in the north.

At Sermon Hill, Caroline County, Donald Fletcher heard the story of the siege and surrender not many days later, from relieved residents of the district. There had been an ominous period of several months in which all the farmers and planters along the Rappahannock had feared they would be fighting redcoats from their own fields and verandas.

News of the surrender brought jubilation. And word of the playing of that particular children's melody tickled Donald's fancy as very little did any more.

Donald felt his age. His gouty leg kept him in constant pain. He did leave Sermon Hill occasionally, but not without enormous effort.

Donald's stomach had swollen to immense proportions from his continuing refusal to cease his excessive eating and drinking. The task of operating the plantation after his father's death from a paralytic seizure in mid-1780 had become a burdensome routine without real purpose; only massive meals and massive quantities of port and claret could relieve the lonely sameness of his days.

So he enjoyed hearing every detail of the humiliation of Cornwallis, a humiliation most interpreted as the end of hostilities, even though peace was by no means official as yet.

Before the year was out, the gentry along the Rappahannock found their own world turned topsy-turvy by other unexpected happenings. Hints of the first one circulated about Thanksgiving time, and Donald, through his house blacks, soon managed to confirm that the rumors had a factual basis.

Williams, the overseer who had helped Seth McLean's widow keep her plantation operating as efficiently as was possible during the war, had been authorized to place the property on the market.

The actual owner, Peggy Ashford McLean, was away on one of her frequent trips to the city of Boston when the estate went up for sale. She returned to Caroline County in early December—and to the astonishment of Donald and everyone else in the district, she brought with her a new husband, plus two children.

One was her bridegroom's son by his first wife. The second was a little girl a few years younger, who was supposedly related to Peggy's distant kin in New England.

There were no fetes, no gala balls to welcome the new couple, because they had expressed their desire for privacy, keeping to their great house except for Sunday worship at the little Presbyterian church six miles from Sermon Hill. The children were not present on those occasions.

Like most other persons of substance along the river, Donald at first harbored private reservations about the fellow Peggy McLean had married. A mere tradesman, it was said; a printing-house owner! Neighbors who came to visit Donald stated unequivocally that the Bostonian had to be a fortune-hunter. The opinion was widely held until Williams gradually let slip certain details to disprove the charge.

According to the overseer, Mr. Philip Kent had some wealth of his own, due to successful investment in a privateering enterprise. His printing business was, if not yet overwhelmingly prosperous, at least successful.

And he had important personal connections.

He was a good friend of a wealthy Jewish merchant of Boston—there were several thousand Jews in America at the time, many quite affluent—and Kent's friend, Selwyn Rothman by name, was said to have been one of those who had quite literally helped stave off the total collapse of America's finances during the war. He and others had advanced the government huge sums from their personal treasuries. Rothman, it was reported, had given nearly as much as the Polish-born Haym Solomon and, like Solomon, had not demanded any definite terms for repayment.

Further, Donald learned that Rothman had helped Peggy McLean's new husband through his first difficult days of establishing the firm called Kent and Son. But what gave final approval to Kent's credentials was his widely discussed friendship with the Marquis de Lafayette. The Frenchman was a heroic figure in the eyes of Virginians, both because General Washington thought so highly of him, and because of his presence during the fighting at Yorktown.

Curious about the new liaison that was to result in Peggy Ashford McLean Kent's removal to a new home in the North, Donald made a difficult trip to worship services one drizzly Sunday morning. He noted that Peggy looked radiantly happy as she entered the tiny church on the arm of her new husband—who, Donald saw with some astonishment, was a good half a head shorter than his wife. Also, he limped noticeably.

Yet the Bostonian had a rather cocky bearing, and a certain pugnacious set to his dark features. To Donald he appeared a man of determination and quiet vigor.

In the churchyard afterward, Donald had a chance to greet the New Englander. He found Kent to be well educated, at least superficially. What continued to impress Donald the most, however, was Kent's steady, almost bold stare—as if he would cheerfully thrash any person who dared to question his right to marry a woman of such impeccable background as Peggy.

All smile and blushes—looking healthier, in fact, than he'd seen her in many a year—Peggy invited Donald to call at the McLean house that afternoon. He accepted.

In the carriage on the way back to Sermon Hill—Donald could no longer exert the effort or withstand the pain of riding horseback—he lingered on some far-from-godly thoughts which had teased his mind throughout the tedious sermon.

Peggy certainly seemed pleased with her new spouse. But Donald wondered about the more intimate details of the marriage. Having endured the nightmare of the uprising of '75—been raped, was the long and short of it—would she be capable of fulfilling what were euphemistically known as wifely duties?

And had the groom known the quality—or should one say "limitations?"—of the goods he had acquired?

Donald realized he'd never know the answers, and supposed they were none of his business. But he wondered all the same.

At the McLean house, he visited for an hour while the drizzle continued to fall from the December sky. He found himself enjoying conversation with this Kent chap, who had served with the American army for several years, and been mustered out after Monmouth Court House, where he had received the wound that crippled him. At one point, their talk was interrupted by the sudden arrival of the two children.

One was a rather stocky, dark-haired boy of about six. The other was a bad-tempered but lovely little girl of about three.

Philip Kent presented his son Abraham, but Peggy had scant chance to do the same with the girl, whose name was Elizabeth. The child seemed preoccupied with turning over small tables, pulling books from shelves and howling like a fiend when Peggy tried to discipline her—gently at first, then crossly.

Fortunately, the little girl caused so much commotion in the couple of minutes before Peggy seized her and carried her out bodily, both Peggy and her new husband failed to notice the absolutely thunderstruck expression on Donald Fletcher's face.

When Peggy returned, out of breath and murmuring apologies, Donald had concealed his surprise behind a bland expression. But he did ask a question or two about the little girl. She would of course become part of the new household along with the boy Abraham, Kent said.

Peggy supplied the information that the girl was an orphaned relation of the northern branch of Peggy's mother's family. Elizabeth had been raised in a private home in Boston. It was the child, Peggy explained, whom she had gone to visit by ship, twice annually at first, then more often. Donald concluded that the shortened intervals were probably prompted by a ripening romance with Kent.

During the discussion of the vile-tempered little girl, Peggy seemed to be staring at Donald in an odd, apprehensive way. Still privately agog, he struggled to keep his features bland, and to give her no cause to think he suspected much of her story was a lie. Soon she lost her air of tension. The visit ended on an equable basis—though Donald could still hear the little girl yelling her head off somewhere upstairs as he bundled into his coat and muffler. Just before he stepped off the veranda to the open door of his carriage, he shook Kent's hand, then Peggy's. On her wrist he saw a pattern of red marks; she had been bitten.

Riding back to Sermon Hill for the second time that day, he asked himself if his senses had deceived him. But he was certain they hadn't. He didn't know whether to feel horribly sorry for the new Kent household, or to laugh at the unexpected twists and turns fate could take.

The rain fell more heavily throughout the rest of the afternoon. That evening, in Sermon Hill's huge and lonely dining room, he found he had no appetite for food. After the blacks had left him, he sat with a decanter and glass, his bandaged left leg propped on a stool and his eyes resting on one of the more recent and unprecedented additions to the furnishings of the house.

On the inner wall, its canvas glowing in the candlelight, hung an oil portrait of Angus Fletcher.

The portrait was of immense size. It showed the old man dressed in elegant gentleman's apparel—a suit and accessories which, in fact, he had never owned, but which were added by the artist at Angus' insistence.

Throughout his entire life, the elder Fletcher had shown no concern whatever for his personal appearance. Indeed, he'd shown few traces of vanity at all, except for the vast and unspoken one of operating Sermon Hill exactly as he wished, and at a profit. Then, unexpectedly, he had commissioned the painting—one month after receiving the news that Judson had been shot to death in Pittsburgh.

George Clark was another hero to the Virginians along the river. After his victory at Kaskaskia, then the more incredible one at Fort Vincennes which his little army had approached in the dead of winter, across flooded prairies others would have considered impassable, George Clark had sent Angus a letter. Donald had read the letter several times; it was still stored among his father's few personal effects in the office.

In the letter, the Virginia frontiersman paid glowing tribute to Judson's heroism. He made it quite clear that, except for Judson's sacrifice, the great enterprise in the west would very likely never have come about.

It was after the receipt of the letter that Angus Fletcher began making inquiries about qualified portrait painters—insisting on references and answers by mail to a series of questions. He finally selected an artist from Baltimore.

The artist boarded at Sermon Hill six weeks while completing the canvas. Angus sat willingly, though he put forward certain demands which the artist protested. Sermon Hill must be glimpsed in the background of the painting. In the middle distance, one or two figures must appear in a field, standing passively. Black figures; slaves.

The artist said all those stipulations would limit his thinking; hamper his artistic expression. But Angus' hectoring ways, and the high price he was paying, won out. So there Donald's father hung, resplendent in a white lace cravat such as he never owned in later life. And there were the docile blacks behind him, and Sermon Hill a whitish rectangle in the upper right.

The artist from Baltimore had professed to be an admirer of the well-known Boston miniaturist and portrait painter, John Copley, who had gone off to Italy before the war and was now settled in England—colonial migration in reverse! The artist told Donald that Copley had painted a number of the Boston radicals responsible for precipitating the conflict—Samuel Adams and the express rider Revere were two—and that in their portraits, Copley had striven both for verisimilitude and for composition that captured the essence of the subject's character. Thus Angus Fletcher had been posed with one fisted hand on his hip. And he was shown full face, so that the tough, lined countenance assaulted the viewer head on. Whether by accident or intent, the artist had brushed tiny highlights into Angus' pupils, lending them a suggestion of temper about to be unleashed.

At first, Donald had charged the whole business off to senility, plus Angus' abrupt if belated realization that he, like all men, would go to the earth in the end. Only gradually did it dawn on Donald that Judson's behavior at Pittsburgh had given Angus something of which to be genuinely proud; something which therefore made the old man worthy of memorialization in a family portrait. It was as if, for all his days, Angus Fletcher had harbored doubts about his principles, his style of life, his very worth—doubts which he had successfully concealed. Donald came to the conclusion that he never wholly understood his father until the portrait was completed.

Now, with the winter rain ticking the glass of the dining room windows and the candles burning down in their graceful chimneys, Donald refilled his glass and regarded the portrait with a sardonic smile.

In the hours before Angus Fletcher had closed his eyes for the last time, he had rambled a good deal to his older son who sat by the bedside. Angus confessed his joy in Judson having partially redeemed himself by the way he died. But Angus again stated that he thanked the God he would soon confront that Judson had fathered no children. In spite of his manner of dying, Angus said with regret, Judson had been driven by the devil. Pride and grief wove together in that, Angus' final verdict on his second son.

It was a blessing that Angus Fletcher wasn't alive today, Donald thought, to have seen what he had seen at

McLean's.

He understood at last Peggy McLean's long absence in New England before Judson's departure to the west. She had been bearing the child.

When had it been conceived? So far as he knew, Judson had visited Peggy only that one time after Seth's burial. Perhaps there had been additional meetings of which Donald was unaware.

Obviously others in the neighborhood would now suspect an illegitimate birth as one possible reason for Peggy's mysterious behavior. Donald thought that only the most perspicacious would identify the father, however.

He understood Peggy's apprehension during the afternoon visit, too. He was thankful he had done nothing to show he recognized the little girl's resemblance to his younger brother.

But there could be no mistake. Elizabeth had Judson Fletcher's bright hair and Judson Fletcher's bright eyes, and she bore a certain facial resemblance to Judson as well.

She had also inherited Judson's violent tendencies, it seemed.

And that fellow Kent was taking the child into his household! Donald wished him the strength and luck to survive the ordeal.

God, it was funny how the world revolved.

A collection of contentious, stubborn-minded colonials of all degrees of literacy, wealth and dedication had somehow defeated the military might of the globe's greatest empire. In the process, a new country had come into being.

And Judson, who had squandered most of his life in uncontrollable excesses, had redeemed himself in his father's eyes by dying a hero of sorts—

And leaving no heirs.

And now an angel-faced little harridan was carrying the Fletcher blood straight to the table of a Boston family. *Thank heaven I won't be around in fifty years to see what havoc that's wrought!*

Laughing aloud, Donald poured more wine while the rain beat harder on the house and the Fletcher eyes glared from the wall in the guttering candlelight.

From the Indian uprisings
in the Northwest Territory
to the opening of
the Rocky Mountain fur trade,
two generations of Kents
struggle to find their places
in the new nation
in

The Seekers

Volume III

of

The Kent Family Chronicles

Afterword

Authors sometimes think (misguidedly) that once *The End* is written, all the important work has been done.

The truth, of course, is far different. The publication process is never completed—a real link is never created—until a book reaches the hands of a reader.

And a great many people collectively perform the indispensable job of seeing any new book out into the world where that happens. But those same people are usually overlooked in the author's haste to thank everyone from his postman to his dog.

So recognition and appreciation are due to the ladies and gentlemen of the Jove Publications sales and marketing staff—and also to Mr. Sy Brownstein and all his associates at International Circulation Distributors —for their dedicated and enthusiastic effort on behalf of this series, and this writer.

JOHN JAKES

About the Author

JOHN JAKES was born in Chicago. He is a graduate of DePauw University, and took his M.A. in literature at Ohio State. He sold his first short story during his second year of college, and his first book twelve months later. Since then he has published more than 200 short stories and over 50 books—chiefly suspense, nonfiction for young people and, most recently, science fiction. With the publication of *The Furies,* volume four of the Kent Family Chronicles, he became the first author in history to land three novels on the best-seller lists within a single year. The author is married, the father of four children, and lists among his organizations the Authors Guild, the Dramatists Guild, and Science Fiction Writers of America. In both 1976 and 1977 he was awarded honorary doctorates for his contribution to the Bicentennial observance. He says the most satisfying aspect of the phenomenal success of the Kent family novels is "the mail which reports that a reader has been motivated to seek out some good nonfiction in order to read about American history in greater detail. That kind of direct response is what writing is all about—and it makes all the hard work worthwhile."

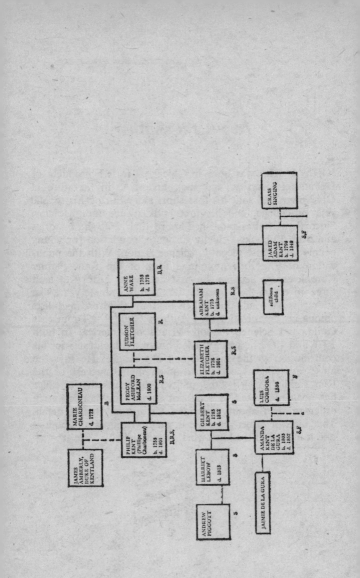

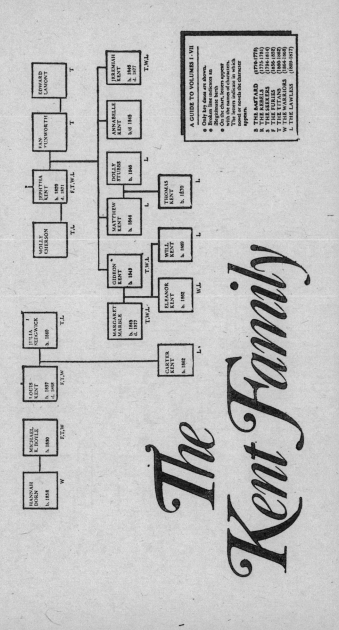

The Kent Family

A GUIDE TO VOLUMES I-VII

- Only key dates are shown.
- Broken line indicates an illegitimate birth.
- On the chart, letters appear with the names of characters. The letters indicate in which novel or novels the character appears.

B	THE BASTARD (1770–1775)
R	THE REBELS (1775–1781)
S	THE SEEKERS (1794–1814)
F	THE FURIES (1836–1852)
T	THE TITANS (1860–1862)
W	THE WARRIORS (1864–1868)
L	THE LAWLESS (1869–1877)

HANNAH DORN b. 1858 — W

MICHAEL K. BOYLE b. 1850 — F,T,W

LOUIS KENT b. 1837 d. 1868 — F,T,W

JULIA SEDGWICK b. 1840 — T,L

JEPHTHA KENT b. 1820 d. 1871 — F,T,W,L

MOLLY EMERSON — T,L

FAN FUNWORTH — T

EDWARD LAMONT — T

CARTER KENT b. 1862 — L

MARGARET MARBLE b. 1840 d. 1877 — T,W,L

GIDEON KENT b. 1843 — T,W,L

MATTHEW KENT b. 1844 — L

DOLLY STUBBS b. 1846 — L

ANNABELLE KENT b/d 1845 — T,W,L

JEREMIAH KENT b. 1846 — T,W,L

ELEANOR KENT b. 1862 — W,L

WILL KENT b. 1869 — L

THOMAS KENT b. 1870 — L

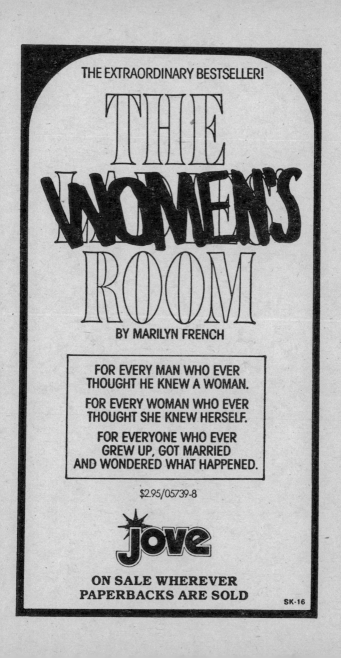